D0720692

Steps and Exes

Steps and Exes

a novel of family

LAURA KALPAKIAN

Perennial

An Imprint of HarperCollins*Publishers*

A hardcover edition of this book was published by Bard, an imprint of Avon Books, in 1999.

First Perennial edition published 2000.

Designed by Kellan Peck

The Library of Congress has catalogued the hardcover edition as follows:
Kalpakian, Laura.
   Steps and exes : a novel / Laura Kalpakian.—1st ed.
   p. cm.
   I. Title.
PS3561.A4168S74 1999   99-21621
813'.54—dc21   CIP

ISBN 0-380-80659-2 (pbk.)

00 01 02 03 04 RRD 10 9 8 7 6 5 4 3 2

This book is for
BEAR AND BRENDAN
and all those island days

ACKNOWLEDGMENTS

The author wishes to express her gratitude
to the following individuals:

Juliet Burton
Deborah Schneider
Jennifer Hershey
Tia Maggini
Nick Sayers
Fiona Stewart
Connie and Bob Eggers
Gen Galloway
Jay McCreary
Meredith Cary
William J. Johnson
and
Peggy K. Johnson
for her tireless artistry at the keyboard

Steps and Exes

PART I

Men Spit, Women Swallow

Sometimes I think about Eve. Not the Eve of the Garden, supple, young, seduceable, innocent perhaps, ignorant certainly, beautiful above all, not Botticelli's Eve, but the other one. The one on the other side of Eden. Predawn, lying here in bed, I think about Eve and all the women like her, like me, who rouse early to work, day after day, rain pelting the still-dark windows, the house yet cold, the dream unfinished, the man beside me asleep, his breathing even.

The alarm will buzz, inescapably, and I will sonar my way downstairs, the daily route predestined, certain as death or taxes: turn on the kitchen lights, turn up the heat, grind up the coffee, boot up the computer, turn on the burner under the stockpot, read the faxes, feed the dogs, flip on the marine radio to hear the singsong weather voices rattle marine poetry—the wind in knots, the sea in ripples, the ridges and fronts bearing down, the eternal

1

chance of showers here in the Puget Sound, the San Juan Islands, these last terrestrial apostrophes thrown off by the continent millions and millions of years ago.

But I have time now. Stretch, groan, curl up, but sleep won't come, nor come back. Insomnia's worse when Russell's here. He snuffles down into his comfy dream while I lie awake and wade through whatever the night tide's brought up, whatever old thought-flotsam bobs before dawn, sloshes to the top of my bilgewater brain, the day ahead, the days behind, my Lot in Life. The Lot I share with Eve. I always thought of Eve as a real person with her own life and woes. Especially woes. Woe is reserved for women, Mom used to say, women shared Eve's Lot in Life, as though that lot could be surveyed, divvied up and parceled out amongst all of us.

What happened to Eve, Sister Broadbent? The Bible doesn't say. Sister Broadbent taught Sunday school to us, the children of the New Disciples. Since she had raised eight kids of her own, no budding post-puber could ruffle her composure. A battleship of a woman, Sister Broadbent, iron-plated breasts and a high turret of a chignon atop her head with two chopsticks sticking out on either side like radar antennae, alert for any commotion which might smack of sex or heresy, which were identical in her mind. *Why didn't God tell us anything about what happened to Eve, Sister Broadbent? He didn't even tell us how she took the news about her sons, Cain and Abel.* Sister Broadbent's chopsticks twitch and bristle and she zaps me with her anthracite eyes, but she announces (with Almighty authority), *Celia, it is not your place to question God's word or His judgment. Good Christian girls don't ask those kinds of questions.* Oh, I know what good Christian girls do. I had four older sisters, didn't I? Each one had a slobbering babe at the breast before she was eighteen. Good Christian girls applied themselves to the begets and begats. Literally. They went forth and multiplied. They were fruitful. They left fruitless speculation to the Elders. Men got Elder, women got older. From the time I started Sunday school where we chanted the books of the Old Testament, my childish voice ringing with the others, I'd mutter under my breath, *Not me not me not me. This is not me, not my life.*

But that Old Testament stuff, it's like tattooing your lover's name on your butt along with a heart and a wreath of roses. After the affair is finished, *Bye Bye Love,* there's his name still emblazoned for your next man to ask after. So even though I'd left Idaho and came eventually—circuitously—here, to this island, this house in which I've lived my whole adult life, raised my kids (my own and those who came with the men I loved, children born into one union, and brought up in another), I brought those Old Testament voices with me, a booming patriarchal bass. God's opera has no sopranos.

Eve, she came too. It was like she lived here, my Lot in Life near hers, companionably close by, her daughters and mine, stepdaughters, stepsons and the fathers of all these children, families constantly fluxing. I have cooked, I figure, a million breakfasts, packed two million lunches, made dinners, yea without number, and caused, for over a quarter century, that holy and mysterious ascension of the laundry: the white dove who falleth soiled to the service porch, *This is my laundry in whom I am well pleased,* washed in the blood of the Tide, transformed and soaring up unto the bedrooms. Women and children first? That's a laugh, isn't it? A sop to some imagined gallantry. A theory, a song or story perhaps, perpetrated by men. But in practice? Ever since Adam, it's always been men first. Ask any woman. Ask Eve— you can see her over the back fence of your Lot in Life.

Back in the seventies when we all got our consciousness raised, all the women on this island, every woman under eighty and a few over, we enclaved and conclaved and mavened. We guru-ed ourselves silly with serious reading and discussion groups, sessions spent over books like *The Goddess Within* and *Man Proposes, Woman Disposes,* tomes thick with information, gray with facts and wonders, explaining to us how it was capitalism that had done all this to women. Back before capitalism, there was an antique time, a golden moment when men and women were equal, some remembered Eden. These books said back when people were living in mud huts and scratching the ground with sticks, clubbing their kill, communicating with a palette of expressive grunts, men and women were equal because they contributed equally to the tribe's food supply and well-being. Men were the hunters, women the gatherers.

Me, I flung this book across the room. That author doesn't have the brains she was born with. Imagine: the hunt is over and everyone's back at the hut and the fire's roaring and the kill is crackling away on the spit. Now, I ask you—where are the men in this picture? They are sitting on their haunches in front of the warm fire trading bullshit stories about whose mighty stick felled the beast. And where are the women? They're stuffing the animal entrails for sausage, tanning the hides for leather, boiling the hooves and antlers for soup or soap (or both together). Imagine their hands. Tough as the hooves they boiled.

My hands are like that. Can't see them in this darkness, these undistinguished hands. Blunt. Strong. Nails cut short. Ringless fingers. How many tears have they wiped from childish cheeks, snot from childish noses, shit from baby bottoms? How many meals prepared, spills mopped, clothes wrung, dishes washed, pots scrubbed, toilets plunged, how many, how much, how often, all of that work? Lost work, unremunerated, unremembered, unsung work, all of it mulched into mere process with no product to show. Men keep the products. Women get the process, and their work all vanishes, as Eve vanished from the Bible. The woman who was once coaxed into Cosmic defiance, charmed by a snake (and what woman hasn't been charmed, at least once, by a snake?), who was fig-leafed and finally driven out by a pissed-off God, Eve was sent not merely out of the Garden, but into Oblivion. Vanished from the story, from the Bible, Eve was, except as a birth canal, a pair of open legs, all bloody, pulsating, pushing, grunting, bringing forth in sorrow boys who would inflict on her more sorrow, the worst sorrow a mother could endure: fratricide.

And even then the Bible's omnipotent narrator *(God? Was it really, Sister Broadbent, God Himself who wrote this down?)* didn't see fit to stick around while Eve got the baleful news that Cain killeth

Abel. One son dead, one son exiled, both sons lost. The Bible's remarkably silent on this, isn't it? But you can guess, reading on, you can guess what happened, what this fratricide did to the marriage of Adam and Eve. Another hundred years or so passed before Adam again made love to Eve. Adam was 135 when he begat Seth on Eve. That's what it says, isn't it? *(Yes, Celia, Genesis is God's Own Word.)* Did Eve mind the long abstinence? A hundred-plus years of celibacy—and you have to guess she was celibate. Who else was there to sleep with but Adam? Then she brought forth Seth and then she vanished from the story. Adam didn't. Adam lived some nine hundred years and begat sons and daughters. On Eve, you have to suppose. Eve probably had hundreds of kids. And even after they'd all grown up and left home, she'd still be carping and coping and carrying on with Adam. She probably shuffled around the hut in a goatskin housecoat, her feet splayed in leather thongs, skinny haunches, her hands sinewy, rugged as bark, her knees knobby, her breasts all hangydown from suckling those thankless boys and ingrate girls, her teeth gone, bones brittle, hair thin, nerves shot. And still, she had to wait on Adam and fuck him whenever he felt like it. *Thy desire shall be to thy husband,* declareth God, *and he shall rule over thee.*

Bullshit, said Eve, but not too loud. No, after that little debacle in the Garden, she would have kept her voice low, her head down, her eyes fixed on the pot she was stirring.

I like to think Eve got a break now and then. Just up and told Adam: *Hold down the fort, dearie, I'm off for a long weekend.* Pack up a thermos and some sandwiches and she'd join a caravan of goats and camels, complete with tour guide to the land of Nod, her companions a gaggle of other thick-handed matrons and their balding, paunchy husbands. Eve would have been alone. Adam would never have consented to such an outing. (Adam wanted to put the whole thing behind him. Adam was the world's first whiner. *She made me do it, Lord, she made me . . .*) So Eve would have been a woman alone on this jaunt, obediently following the guide East of Eden where she could peer past the flaming cherubim picketing the Garden gate, denied entrance, but able to gawk, like holidaymakers peering through the gates at Buckingham Palace. Unlike the other tourists, Eve remembered a world before the snake, remembered the lion beside the lamb, the tree as yet unplucked. Perhaps, if she could just see past those cherubim and their flaming swords, perhaps she could see that tree. Maybe old Eve thought, *Well, perhaps it wasn't foreordained after all, and maybe other endings might have ensued*. You'd have to be old to think that. Older, anyway. Mature, as they say.

Like Eve, my whole life—or the life I ended up with anyway—dangled, hung from one central transgression. An unoriginal sort of sin, mine: six joints and a few sugary tads of LSD that day on the 28-foot sailboat, *Deo Volente*. God willing. God willing? Thy will be done? What the hell kind of joke was that, *Deo Volente?* That afternoon all those years ago, sailing all around Useless Point. Both of us naked as Adam and Eve, and I went to sleep, but when I woke I was alone. My Adam gone. Irrevocably gone as though God Himself just reached down and plucked Henry Westervelt from that sailboat, picked him up by the nape of his beautiful neck, held his broad, tanned shoulders and snatched Henry unto Him. *Deo Volente* itself pitched and a couple of boat fenders tumbled along the deck, hit me and I lurched awake, falling in what I thought was a dream: the boom crazily, cruelly squealing above me, pulleys rattling, the sail helplessly flapping overhead. I roll out of the boom's path, the boat heeling to one side, and I scream for Henry. I scream and scream and finally some holiday boaters hear me, hear my cries for help and for Henry. Help came, but not Henry. The boaters right the boom, right the boat, fig-leaf me. The Coast Guard comes and I'm still crying out for Henry. But Henry was never found. His body, anyway, never even washed up. Full fathoms five lies Henry Westervelt, my husband, my ever and only husband, full fathoms five, or however deep is the Puget Sound, a feast for fishes. Henry.

Or maybe it wasn't Henry's death. Maybe it was the marriage from which my life dangled, the single salient fact. Without this actual legal marriage, my attorney, Mr. Ellerman, told me I would have found myself in a very different kettle of fish—fish heads, tails and guts more to the point—*Deo Volente* or not. Old Man Westervelt had as much Will as God ever had—and more money. The Westervelts thought I killed Henry, sailing stoned that day, and the old man tried to get me charged with murder. Murder won't work? OK, how about manslaughter? No? Criminal negligence then, let's try criminal negligence. But all this king's horses and all this king's men couldn't manufacture enough evidence to get me criminally zapped, not for Henry's death anyway. There was, though, that little matter of felony possession, marijuana and LSD. Mr. Ellerman managed to get me off with probation, pleading to the court that I was only twenty-three *(Widowed at twenty-three, your honor)* and I had no previous record and I had suffered enough.

Ellerman didn't know the half of it.

Mad with suffering, crazed with grief and loss, smashed, flattened, empty of everything except suffering, alternately inconsolable and raging at the Westervelts who wanted to keep Henry all to themselves, as though in death they could have him back forever. They hoarded his memory. Big memorial service. Six hundred people filled the pews at St. Mark's Episcopal Cathedral in Seattle and I was not amongst them. Not invited. Not even informed. I was not there when into that Valley of Death streamed the six hundred, sucking up to the Westervelts. *How sad, too bad, your youngest son has drowned.* That's all there was to say. There was nothing to bury. Full fathoms five lay Henry Westervelt, my lover whom I last saw as I drifted off to August sleep, naked in the sunshine on the *Deo Volente,* Henry naked at the tiller, his skin pinking in the sunlight, laughing when cold spray would hit him, splash across his back and belly like dew. I, smiling, slept, dreaming how I would lick the salt water off his skin, the boat rocking me to sleep, water-whispering, while I, loose-limbed, wide-legged with anticipation, eager because when I woke, Henry . . .

But when I woke, I was alone. *Deo Volente,* how could that happen?

Your husband, Ellerman said when he came back over to the island, just showed up one afternoon, maybe six weeks later. He didn't call because we didn't have a phone, didn't want one, Henry and me, and now it was just me, and I was mad with grief and didn't want to talk to anyone. So Ellerman showed up and said *your husband,* and I had to think, Who in hell is he talking about? I said to Ellerman, *It was a wedding, not a marriage.* We didn't care about marriage. We were lovers and the wedding was just a golden groovy thing to do, a lovely way to ennoble a summer afternoon on Sophia's Beach with our friends and a handful of the old Isadorans hanging around for Dearly Beloved. Even the minister, Launch, was a friend, very spiritual and into Indian mysticism, but he'd sent in his twenty bucks for a certificate as a minister of the Universal Life Church and he wanted to marry someone just to prove he could legally do it. Henry and I said, OK, fine, let's get married. We stood there on Sophia's Beach, ribbons tied to the trees, sweet-weed incense blowing in the wind, and repeated a bunch of poetry we'd written and promised to love each other always. The wedding took a really long time because weed always makes time slow, slower, then still. Still-unto-stagnant time becomes, and you can see it for the truly gelatinous thing it is. We were standing close to the water and the tide was rising, and now and then the icy water would pluck at my sandals and nibble my bare toes and I knew we should have stood further back, closer to the woods where the water couldn't get Henry and me, where the tide couldn't rise and get us.

Mr. Ellerman listened to all this, sighing sort of, eyeing his watch. (You never forget time when you live on an island and have to ride ferries back and forth; time perks along, all staccato, not gelatinous at all.) And since Mr. Ellerman couldn't leave before the ferry did, he listened till I finished talking and then he said again, *Your husband, Celia, wrote a will. He came to my office to start proceedings for changing his name to Henry West.* Yes, yes, I knew that. What has that to do with me? *And at the same time he drew up a will.*

I didn't believe it. No one who knew Henry would have believed it. Henry Westervelt would never do anything so conventional, so—well, so ordinary and tomorrow-oriented, so law-abiding. So dull. *A will?* I said to Ellerman. *A will? Deo Volente, that kind of will?* But Mr. Ellerman said a will outlining the dispensation of his property in the event of his death. *Sorry,* I said, *but Henry Westervelt invented the Unfettered life. Single-handedly. Unfettered people don't think about property and securities and inheritances and all that trash.*

It wasn't all trash. There was some money, not a lot, and some securities and stock in Westervelt Corporation which I sold (stupidly) and this island property: Sophia's great school, all gone to ruin and decay, I inherited that, as well as this upright narrow two-story house behind the school where I've lived ever since. I inherited all that, and the apple orchard in between and all the land sloping down to the Sound, Useless Point, all mine. Everything Sophia had left to her great-nephew when she died in 1964—it all belonged to me. I never knew Sophia, never knew any of them except for Henry. I never even saw them except in court.

They contested the validity of Henry's will in civil court and Mr. Ellerman defended my right to inherit. Amongst other things, the Westervelts said how could it possibly be a binding document when I was constantly referred to as *my lovely girl? My lovely girl, Celia,* that's what Henry had written about me over and over in the will. Mr. Ellerman informed the court that Henry could have called me a horny salamander and it wouldn't have mattered: as long as I was indeed his legal spouse and had a marriage certificate filed in the State of Washington to prove it, the will stood, and the property that Sophia Westervelt had bequeathed her great-nephew, it was mine.

Sitting there in court I could feel myself mutating like a character in science fiction: *Bye bye, lovely girl* and Hello! to the woman I would become. Became. In that woman there is something gritty, decidedly unlovely. Much as I detested those New Disciples, from whose girded loins I had sprung, I was like them. They were mean and tough and ugly, dried up, hard-handed and hollow-hearted, but by God, they would lie down for no man. Fight or spit, it was all the same to them. For generations my people had this unlovely raw stamina, and when they failed at sugar beet farming, they prayed, packed up and moved on. They failed at wheat, prayed, packed up and moved on. They failed at sheep farming, shopkeeping and well digging, prayed, packed up, moved on. They failed at mining too, prayed, but stayed put in Colby, Idaho. They finally ran out of energy. The mines died, closed down, the town wizened up, but by that time my people were too spent to move. We didn't have a pot to pee in. A rented house with running water and a woodstove, sheds and pens for animals. Old Man Westervelt knew all this about my family. (Though he didn't know when Henry and I had said our vows on Sophia's Beach because we didn't invite him. We didn't invite either family. Henry wanted shut of his as much as I wanted shut of mine.) But when Henry died and left a will, oh, then the Westervelts knew we'd gotten married. And after that, it didn't take Old Man Westervelt long to find out that my father worked in the boiler room at the prison and faith-healed animals on the side in Colby, Idaho. They accused me of marrying Henry for his money, their money, Westervelt money. I went on the witness stand and said when I met Henry he told me his name was Henry West and his father owned a lumberyard. How was I to know his father's lumberyard was the entire Northwest?

I won the case, and I inherited, even though I wasn't a lovely girl anymore. But the old man, he never gave up trying to make my life a misery, pursuing me, full of spite and vinegar, making everything as hard as he could. He tried to buy back Sophia's school and all the land sloping down to Useless Point, offering a big, fat price for it, and even though I didn't give a rat's ass about it, not in the beginning, I still wouldn't sell, not to him or anyone who offered after him because I knew they were all working for the Westervelts. The old man set the county inspectors on me and the county surveyors. There were fees and back taxes that hadn't been paid and faulty sewer lines and improper title transfers and wiring not up to code and levies that hadn't been assessed, or assessment that hadn't been levied. I didn't understand any of this. But I had to. Finally, Nona York—she had loved Sophia and she had loved Henry and she loved this island, and she hated old Westervelt—she said to me: Celia, take all this confusion to Lester Tubbs, Isadora Island's only accountant. Lester will cost you, but he knows all about this sort of rubbish and he'll straighten it out for you and keep it straight. It was true. Thank you, Nona. Lester's still my accountant and my friend. But it was terrible for years, Old Testament terrible, to be pursued by Old Man Westervelt. Like being stalked by Yahweh.

So Eve and I have that much in common, pissing off the powers that be, and our lives suspended from a single error in judgment. But *what if* . . . Predawn, *what if* tiptoes barefoot across the bare boards of my mind, *what if*? What if Henry had not died? Would he be the man sleeping beside me in this bed? Would we—would I—be in this bed at all? Would Henry be paunchy and balding? Gray? Would he finally, and against his every conscious wish, have inherited that sour stain that taints the Westervelts? (Every August, till he finally died, Old Man Westervelt hired someone to sail the *Deo Volente* round and round Useless Point on fine summer days, betraying, as Henry once remarked, a zest for cruelty rather than a thirst for revenge.) Would Henry and I have endured, our love endured? Or split at the seams like everyone else? One thing I'm certain of: our marriage would never have degenerated into one of those functional unions, pious, empty, regulated as a gasoline pump, fish on Friday night, sex on Saturday morning. For Henry and me, it was—it would have been—love or nothing. That's just the kind of people we are. Were. Love or nothing. Our love would have endured everything other loves could not, the strains and drains of daily life. Would we have had boys beautiful as he was? Girls? My girls, my beautiful daughters, Bethie and Victoria, were begot and begat by other men, other lovers. I've had other children too (not mine, not exactly, but not not-mine either), children who came with the territory, stepsons and stepdaughters, children begat and begotten by my lovers in other unions with other women who once loved the men I loved, men who—like old Russell here—occupied what I always think of as the passenger side of the bed.

Russell wants to change all that. He wants us to get married. He says he's been divorced long enough (four years) and we've been together long enough (three years) and marriage is the mature thing to do at our time of life (pushing fifty, pushing, pushing, like some kind of athletic event). It's time to ratify all this, says Russell. All what? I don't believe in medicinal marriage, in getting married because it's somehow good for you, like Vitamin C. I don't believe in marriage at all. No marriage for me (except for Henry), but oh, I have had some great weddings, Bobby, Andrew, Phil: food and flowers and musicians and handwritten vows, lovely dresses, Dearly Beloved gathered on Sophia's Beach, but thank you, no license, no legal records, no pastors or preachers or judges. Just a hell of a good party. But that's not what Russell wants. He wants a Mrs. Russell Lewis. Another one.

It'll never happen, Russell. Marriage doth not true lovers yoke; marriage chains spouses. Marriage makes of love not the union of hearts and minds, but an Institution. And then you get swept into the Institution and with it the crusts of custom, the old carapace of civil codes, and your love hardens into law. Later, at the end (death or divorce, whichever comes first), lawyers shuffle through your human misery like ragpickers at the dump of love.

I won't live like that. It won't happen to me. *Not me, not me.* But Russell says my expectations are unrealistic and my wish (insistence, I tell him, insistence) on being happy is overwrought. He says to expect happiness at our age (pushing fifty, pushing) is immature; we should wish for contentment, good health, a reliable retirement and comfort. It's perfectly natural, he says, for expectations to be softened by experience.

Bullshit. I don't want my expectations softened, mushy as if I have no teeth to tear into life, as if my brains have gone to some kind of candied-yam consistency. Don't feed me softened expectations and expect my contented *yum yum* in response. And if that's immature of me, well then, just send me to my room and I'll come down when I'm a big girl in about thirty years.

Russell says I need to plan for retirement, to look ahead. Russell says, *Celia, without planning, you'll be doing the same thing you are doing now, working just as hard in twenty years*. Well, so what? I'm used to it. I'm still working just as hard (harder, maybe) as I was when I started Henry's House, just treadwater work, lots of it, unremitting, but essential to the thing I've created: Henry's House, the most famous bed-and-breakfast in the San Juan Islands. In the whole Northwest, I like to think, but that may be stretching it. Then again, maybe not.

It's work I would not have done, except that I stumbled on that broom. That phantom broom appeared one day—and one day vanished. I'm sure it was Henry. Henry's way of reaching me, of whispering, *Wake up, Celia, don't let your life drift, don't let your days just swing like that boom that killed me. Wake up, Celia!* Because after Henry died, I see-sawed along, even after I recovered from the depths of grief and pain, I rocked along. Started at the college across the bay, but never graduated. Mostly my days were pretty shapeless, living on bits and pieces of the inheritance Henry left me. An uncomplicated life. Friends. Lovers. (A few good men, as they say. A few real disasters.) Then I had Bethie, and later, after I'd settled down with Bobby and his daughter, Sunny, we had Victoria. We lived in this house and I seldom went over to the great decayed wreck of Sophia's school, rotting further with every year that passed, the shell of Sophia Westervelt's great dream and the incarnation of her failure.

Blackberry bushes had enveloped and invaded the place, and belladonna too, twisted up all through the eaves and snaking along the floors. The fuse boxes were full of birds' nests and wiring had frayed everywhere, poking out of holes in the walls, all those electrical nerve ends, like copper ganglia, unsheathed and naked. The walls had cracks, holes, some made by vandals, some made by time and neglect (a few made by a man I broke up with who went over to Sophia's school, broke off a couple of banisters and beat hell out of the place). The building was a palace for squirrels and raccoons, mice, probably rats too. (You live by water, you always have rats to worry about.) Wind whistled through the jagged holes in the windows and inside, if you walked inside, your feet would grind over broken glass littering the floors, that and fallen plaster and the crunchy skins that snakes had slithered out of and abandoned. You can't have Eden without snakes.

The day I found that broom, I'd had a fight with Bobby (admittedly one of the most exasperating men ever to draw breath, Bobby Jerome), a colossal fight. Bobby, in his blissful way, refused to acknowledge that it was a fight. I stalked out, crossing the orchard, over to Sophia's school, punching through a French door (the brass handles long gone), and kicked everything in my path as I stormed inside, crying, cursing, having myself a merry little tantrum. Blubbering tears, smashing through the debris and fallen plaster, I could not see, nor breathe for the dust I raised, a cloud, a curtain of dust. I sneezed and sneezed. Dust suspended in the slices of sunlight streaming through broken windows, rising up and then slowly succumbing, a glittering, granular free fall. Through that dust I saw the broom. It leaned against a pillar. I'd never seen that broom. Your ordinary, garden variety broom: paint worn off, as though many hands had held it, bristles uneven, sheered and at an angle, shaped by work. But what work? Everything around me was a wreck, a mess, a disaster. Still sneezing, I walked over to the broom and stared at it, like I expected it to talk. I fit my hands to the handle and started to sweep. I coughed and choked. I raised more than dust with that broom, I roused Sophia's old dream. The more I sneezed and swept, the more I knew I could, would, do something with this place, this big, wrecked shell. I didn't know what, but if I kept on sweeping, I was certain it would come to me. Not a school, I'm no educator, but in the rustle of the broom, *swish, swish, swish,* Henry whispered to me, the old remembered conversations about the ways we wanted to use our lives, the dreams we'd hoped to fulfill. And so it became Henry's House. It had been all along.

Not just bed-and-breakfast. More than that. A place of peace, full of those disarming simple pleasures (which, of course, require a wealth of complexity), those romantic particulars which, gathered together, create universal conviction: embroidered pillows and silver creamers and ironed counterpanes, vases of flowers, ever fresh, wooden bowls with green apples, hand-painted dressers and hand-polished wood. Stability. Serenity. Security. Here the tea is always hot and served in thin cups, porcelain so fine the tea warms your hands, all the way to the heart. All the clocks are ticking clocks and the scents all fleeting, to tease the nose, to tweak memory, to imply desire, to suggest fulfillment without ever quite granting it: lavender and lemon, cinnamon and rose and something else, a whiff of what must have been—surely, from some remembered Eden. At Henry's House it's not remembered. It's created. Created, compounded, ambience distilled into assurance. Manifested physically in a place like Henry's House, the notion of family is an irresistible confection. The place all but insinuates a voice at your ear, *Yes, yes, Henry's House is what your family had, or could have had—what you deserved in any event—this sense of entitlement, of certainty, the ties of tradition, the confidence intrinsic to roots, warmth, reliable relationships.*

Of course it's all complete, compelling bullshit. That's what makes it so powerful. In truth families will tether you to their values and reward you only while—and if—you kiss your own shackles. Families in general want not to launch you, but to humble you, to fetter you with whatever weapons are at hand, money, religion, disapproval. And in my experience, oh I've seen how those long legal arteries of begat and begot get twisted, braided, woven into long, long ropes. The tie that binds all right. Enough rope to hang yourself.

My family would have been secretly joyed to see me roped, umbilically bound to Colby, Idaho, by a squirming ball of baby begot on me by some local boy, a New Disciple, natch. As it was, after I graduated from high school I got a job in the law office of Eugene Wenger, a Communist lawyer in Colby who defended prisoners' rights and (it was well known) helped draft dodgers on their way to Canada up the Idaho panhandle. Mr. Wenger was as close as Colby came to an antiwar protester. In fact he wasn't a Communist at all, but a Democrat, the only one in Colby, probably, except for the felons in the prison and they couldn't vote. My father called him an unconverted Commie Jew and forbade me to step foot in his office. If I disobeyed, my father vowed he would cast me out. Well, it wasn't exactly Eden to begin with, was it? And Mr. Wenger paid $400 a month for an eight-hour day.

I was saving to go to Paris. This obsession was an unexpected gift from my high school French teacher: three years of Mme. Johnson whose idea of teaching French was to extol the beauties, the heritage, the wonders of Paris to ignorant American yahoos. She had been a university student in 1944. Swept into the arms of a handsome Yank, she married him and off to America! No doubt Colby, Idaho, was a surprise to her and the handsome Yank less appealing in his prison guard uniform. She'd been pissed off ever since. But I loved to hear her talk.

When I mentioned to Mr. Wenger I was saving to fulfill that dream, he said that wishing to go to Paris was the noblest aspiration any young person could have. He said it was good I was living at home to save money. I told him I wasn't living at home, but in a room over the Colby drugstore (though I did not say I'd been kicked out for working for an unconverted Commie Jew). Mr. Wenger offered to let me live, rent free, in the studio apartment above his office. I climbed the stairs to the studio apartment and dropped my two suitcases on the floor. Mr. Wenger had used this studio to house (or hide) draft dodgers on their way to Canada. The place had an air of makeshift anxiety. When I moved into this room, the news spread all over Colby (and back to my parents no doubt) that I was whoring for the rent. Working during the day, whoring all night. (That's certainly the way the New Disciples would have described it.) In truth, I half-expected to hear Mr. Wenger's tread on the stairs, coming up to collect his rent off my young body. If that's what he wanted, fine, I'd do it. I'd already decided that. I put no especial value on my virtue and had gotten rid of my virginity the year before in the back of a Ford Falcon. Mr. Wenger never did come upstairs to extract anything of me, though he was demanding in the office. A sad, intense man, Mr. Wenger's personal scent was brewed somehow of cigarette smoke, Old Spice and alcohol. He drank seriously. He offered me once, after work, a drink called a Sidecar, a wonderful concoction with sugar round the rim of the glass. We talked of Paris.

When I had enough money for Paris, I gave a month's notice. Mr. Wenger drove me to the bus station, kissed me goodbye and wished me Godspeed. (My own family, when I called, told me I was going to the devil and not to come back.) It was perhaps my experience with Mr. Wenger, who was better to me, kinder than my own father, that crystallized for me, early on, the belief your blood ties could be dispensed with, never minding the shared receding hairlines or blue eyes, that family could be something you created, that really, your relatives are relative.

And yet, weirdly, I've spent my whole working life at Henry's House maintaining the illusion that family is essential, that happiness is allied to begets and begats, family trees of tradition. Henry's House is not so much a B-and-B as an Experience. In the drawers of dressers and vanities at Henry's House I keep little oddball items. Originally I'd just put them there so that people would open the drawers and see something, so the place would feel like a home and not a hotel. When these small things disappeared, at first I was surprised, annoyed. Truly, people who wouldn't dream of shoplifting a candy bar from Target will sticky-finger little objects out of Henry's House. But gradually I understood the impulse for what it was: people need some physical testament to the experience of Henry's House, something they can hold, their faux-family heirloom from the faux-family homestead. And in its way, the disappearance of these objects (easily replaced in the off-season) is a compliment to the vivacity of what I've created here.

And it is a creation, not a conviction. Personally I believe family can be replaced. It's connection that's essential. To live without connection is a sort of solitary confinement. Death by loneliness. Enforced celibacy. Not a pretty picture. Less pretty as you get older. As you become mature. Ah yes, mature. Right, Russell?

Dear old Russell. I turn to him on the pillow. Sleeping so peacefully, his face all smooth, relaxed. Breathing metronomically. Never guess how pissed off he was last night to look at him now. I loved you once, Russell. Didn't I? I remember loving you. Do I love you still? Do I? Sometimes memory of love can itself get you through the transitions with a man. The transits of Venus are always painful. Goodbye Venus, hello Mars! That's where Russell and I are. A transit of Venus. Something's moving and moving away, though we are two stationary bodies in this bed. We are slowly transiting our way through Venus toward Mars.

Russell says he wants to get married, for clarity, for definition, for commitment. His athletic insistence on commitment, definition, drives me into pissedness. *(Pisséd are the meek for they shall inherit the earth they are buried in, and not another divot of sod*. That's what Christ really said. St. Luke got it all wrong.) I am driven to a state of pissedness when Russell announces, declares his love for me, frequently and at startling moments. When I am up to my cheekbones with one minor crisis or another, Russell says, *I love you, Celia,* and the declaration itself obliges response, affirmation. Whatever else, it can't be ignored. Another woman might find this endearing. A younger woman might find it enchanting. I find it exasperating—worse, because these declarations of love become the text, the pretext, the subtext for extended discussion. Which Russell adores. And when I decline to participate—not even pissedly refuse, just obliquely decline—he sulks, or makes a scene, or goes all pouty and punitive like last night.

He says we need to spend time working on our relationship. I tell him, last night, I explained to him as best I could, speaking neutrally, calmly, *Russell, I already have enough work for three or four women, or a dozen men. Russell, I have so many other obligations and deadlines that require my ongoing tension and attention* (Bethie's getting married, Russell. Remember Bethie? My eldest daughter is having her engagement party at Henry's House day after tomorrow. Lunch for 150 people for Bethie's engagement party . . . yoo-hoo, Russell) *that I just can't spend time working on a love affair.*

People don't have love affairs anymore, Celia, says Russell. *Love affairs are for people in 1940s black-and-white movies because they had to swoon at one another rather than having actual sex. Two unmarried people who have sex over time are said to be in a relationship. In an enduring relationship—you know this, Celia—the couple needs to contribute mutuality, and share responsibility, to be alert and sensitive to each other's needs. They need quality time undistracted, lots of communication and a willingness not to be bound by gender stereotypes.*

Really? I say. *I guess that's why I still take out the garbage, is it?*

He rolled over and accused me of being on the rag. Well, that's as good an excuse as any. Better than some.

How comforting to be able to pin my every foul mood on something inevitable as biology, incontrovertible as Nature. But what will happen to me when I have to take hormones instead of blaming them? What will happen when Nature is through with me? When I cannot be on the rag, but become the rag itself? When I am flung out because I'm biologically threadbare?

Who was it, some guru, who advised women after menopause to grow herbs and tend their gardens? Is that all there is? Just a new Lot in Life where we can sniff the mint and come into the fullness of our being undistracted by biology? I like being distracted by biology. By men who appeal to me. Distracted by that glandular conviction of interest, of reciprocity, that glimmer and spark: a man who might be flint to my tinder, all that distraction you can feel racing around your bloodstream like your corpuscles are on some 911 high. Spread the alarm! Wake up! Something distracting and exciting (at the very least, entertaining) is about to happen. It's not love, this feeling. (Love is like virtue, and worthless untested.) It's not even happiness. It's a sort of discovery. Perhaps this is the only discovery you can make more than once, make over and over, and still have it be fresh and sweet, savory, compelling.

Will it ever again be fresh and sweet for us, Russell? Do I still love you? In this intimate predawn dimness, I study Russell's well-known face on the pillow. I won't marry you, Russell. Not you. Not any man. I could not weave my whole life around a man. Only reckless and romantic girls do that, girls who come to bad ends, to early widowhood and long court battles over controlled substances and undeserved inheritances. That girl died with Henry Westervelt. The woman who lived on—me—well, I am chastened if not chaste.

After Henry died, the closest I came to that kind of single-minded passion, consuming love, was my love for my children, my firstborn, especially. When they put that baby girl in my arms, oh, I have never been so moved to tenderness as at that moment. I thought: This is it, this baby, my beautiful daughter here in my arms, she is the center, the meaning of my life. But she wasn't. She is the center, the meaning of her own life. She grew out of my arms, but not out of my heart.

And now she's marrying Wade Shumley. And I'm the only one who thinks he's unworthy of her. Even people you'd expect to know better, they all just melt into little pools of superlatives when they meet Wade. They gush: *Oh, Celia, isn't it marvelous that Bethie is marrying Wade? Bethie's so flighty. He is so mature, decent, upstanding, hardworking, dependable, churchgoing, community-spirited and honest.*

What am I supposed to say? Thank you?

Should I say: Well, I think such people are fine. Such people are dandy. I don't mind people like that at a distance. I don't mind them at a party. I can be polite. But I sure as hell don't want my daughter to marry one! My free-spirited Bethie? Footloose, charming Bethie, ready to change jobs or change lovers at a whim? Bethie—who adores lost animals and Fred Astaire movies and bicycling—marrying Wade Shumley? He brings up the hair on the back of my neck. Just like the New Disciples used to do.

From the time I was old enough to go to Sunday school, I chafed at the New Disciples, strangled on their starchy diet of Old Testament injunction, their reflexive repression served up in neat little spoonfuls of thou-shalt-nots. Wade makes me feel the same way. Even though I'm a grown woman, I feel like a kid around him, antsy and pissed off and foul-mouthed. I gag.

Like a gob in the throat, I gag at Wade Shumley. Something I can't quite spit out. Not because I can't spit. I can. A real accomplishment, spitting. For a woman, anyway. For a man, it's nothing. Everything in society says to a man: Hey, you got something in your throat? Some nasty taste? Something yucky you pulled out of your sinuses? Out with it! Spit! Don't hold it in! Get rid of it! But to a woman, society says: Swallow. Swallow, honey, and smile while you're at it. And having swallowed, perform its corollary process, hold it in and work it through slowly, out over time. No instant expectoration for women. No wonder women hold things in, hold on, why they can't let go. No wonder women cling to everything, regardless. No wonder they can't release pain, however crippling, can't release hope gone putrid, or men turned bad. It's because we've been swallowing ever since Eve: take it inside you, keep it up inside of you, in all those dark and secret places till you have to puke or bleed just to get rid of it.

This is a fundamental difference. When I was a kid, my brothers could spit. They could be talking to you, and just turn, hack one off to the side, never missing a beat. I've seen my dad roll down the truck window and hurl out a lugie, middle of winter, blinding snowstorm. Then, one day—how old was I, five? six?—we're all out back by the shed watching Dad faith-heal a goat. This goat, whew, he was sick and he smelled fierce. My brother turned and spat and I did the same. Mom just reached over and smacked me. *Girls don't,* she said. Then she turned her attention back to Dad and the goat.

Girls don't. More's the pity. Because if girls don't, women can't. Literally. They cannot spit.

Except for me. I taught myself. In secret. Practicing with

21

watermelon seeds in summer, apple seeds the rest of the year, walking to school, practicing spitting. I got pretty good. In the ninth grade I was the envy of the other girls and a lot of boys. I was behind the gym one day, teaching some girls to spit when the PE teacher strolled by. You'd have thought she'd caught me crucifying baby rabbits. The girls lit right into Adam's refrain, *She made us do it, she made us . . .* and I got marched down to the Girls' Vice Principal, Mrs. Digby. Mrs. Digby was a New Disciple.

Mrs. Digby had allergies and she kept handkerchiefs stuffed down the front of her dress so they looked like an extra boob-ette in between the other two. Her eyes were always red and teary. She told me she was suspending me for three days. Immediately. Calling my parents this minute and telling them what I'd done. She reached in between her buttons, pulled out her hanky and dabbed her eyes. *Celia,* she said, weeping, tears welling up, spilling, *men spit, women swallow.*

So then I understood, didn't I? Ninth grade is old enough. You begin to see the weird things your body's doing to you and you have some inkling that if girls don't, women can't. Women have to hold, to process, develop. You begin to see that women can bring to birth a lifelong sorrow just as easily as a baby. And maybe you have to get fucked, or fucked over to do the one, same as the other.

My dad came to school to collect me in the truck. When I got in the cab, he asked who in the hell did I think I was? *Not yours,* I said. *I'm nothing of yours. Not any of you. All of you smell.* And that was the truth, literal truth. Everything around our rented place, garage, sheds, all of it smelled like sick animals. My dad claimed to have the power of healing in his hands and he would do the laying-on-of-hands for animals, just like the Elders would do for people. He ran quite a little side business with sick animals, though sometimes he'd dose them with this or that, vile stuff he cooked up on the stove. He'd never admit to the dosing. Just to the laying-on-of-hands.

He laid his hands on me. *Whap! Whap!* So what? I knew I

was free of all of them. It was only a matter of time before I left. They'd never be able to hang onto a girl who could spit.

I tried to teach my girls, Bethie, Victoria, and Sunny, how to spit. Took them down to Sophia's Beach with a watermelon when they were all little and I said, *Have at it, girls. It's important.* Sunny took to it right away. Quite the champion, Miss Sunny Jerome. Victoria refused on the grounds that spitting was gross. Bethie lost patience and interest when she didn't win the spitting contest and she wandered off to find some poor stray cat or puppy, some lost animal she could bring home.

Like Wade.

I roll over, hit the alarm so it won't buzz. Russell can sleep. I can't. *No rest for the wicked—and the righteous don't need it.* So saith Sister Broadbent. I know which camp I'm in. The bed groans as I get out and shiver, slide my feet into the Birkenstocks, my arms in the old robe. I rattle downstairs to greet the dogs, Sass and Squatch, who follow me to the bathroom like there are Milk-Bones in the toilet.

I turn on the marine radio weather, grind up the coffee, start the coffeemaker, turn on the burner, a low flame under the stock-pot, turn on the computer, hit the button for yesterday's voice mail. A far cry from the days when it was just Henry and me, no phone at all. The first message is Shirley, Russell's ex-wife. Russell lives here, but maintains the fiction of his own apartment over in Massacre. Russell only moved to Isadora to escape. Not to escape Shirley, but to escape a grad student he'd been involved with (an affair that ended with considerably less dignity than his marriage). Russell is on this island, but not of it.

Shirley always leaves long messages reminding Russell what he's left undone. She calls here because I run a business and there's no bullshit about the machine not working. I've never met Shirley, but I can picture her, just from having met her kids and from her voice. Her kids are joyless and her voice is full of want. She was a faculty wife because Russell was faculty. And after the divorce Russell was still faculty. And Shirley? What was she?

I glance at the long white tongue of paper lolling out of the fax machine, but I won't read the faxes now. I like e-mail best because it's easy to ignore. When I bought all this business equipment, Lester Tubbs was so proud of me. I even built on this addition, a sort of electronic shed just to shelter all this beeping and flashing, clicking, paper-dribbling, memory-hogging, disk-eating personal servant plastic stuff. *Welcome to the modern world, Celia,* said Lester, naturally thinking he'd soon be out of a job. Wrong. I have all this technology, but I don't trust it. I don't embrace it. I trust Lester, but I don't embrace him either. Still, I've been running this B-and-B, Henry's House, successfully all these years, doing things my own way, no MBA, no bullshit courses in hotel management, no certificate from the Cordon Bleu, just my own good instincts and Julia Child's cookbooks. I learned from Julia and I work from instinct. This house is my command post. Henry's House can be beautiful because mine isn't. Not efficient. Not pretty. I keep notes to myself all over the huge kitchen (huge because I tore out the interior wall fifteen years ago) and notes on the service porch and menus stuck to the doors of the fridges, reminders on the cupboards, yellow stickies with shopping lists taped to the door and a big, dusty chalkboard on one wall. I impale receipts on those vicious-looking little spindles, and my reservations are written out by hand in a big ledger, penciled so the pages are blurred and fogged and begrimed, a sort of graphite swamp. I like life in pencil. So it can all be changed.

Sass and Squatch want their breakfast, but they know the drill. First the morning counterpoint: weather on the marine radio, messages on the voice mail, while I stand at the kitchen window and drink my first coffee. Dawn pales over the yard, light coaxed, eked from silverside of clouds, like a picture emerging from a photographic negative. Rain ripples down the unprotected windows and my utilitarian yard is puddled and muddy. From the outbuildings, the sheds and garage and Launch's apartment, water, splashing from the gutters, rivulets its way through little gullies in the tough and rangy grass. The eaves drip. Year after year, in these eaves, the same sparrow families conduct their quarrels in public. No shame whatsoever. And in the orchard, the apple trees host generations of robins, stellar jays and nattering finches and all these birds, their wars with the worms go on in the rain. Everything goes on in the rain in Washington. Moss grows on the north side of your bones.

Is that Sunny on the voice mail? Sunny Jerome? She's on her way up here? She's left California. What did she say? The 4 p.m. ferry? I'm just about to punch the buttons so Sunny can repeat herself, but the next voice halts my hand. A woman from *Joie de Vivre!* in New York, an editor there, Diane something. She waxes on about the wonderful things her readers have told her about Henry's House and our famous reputation all over the Northwest. She and her assistant and her photographer would like to come to Henry's House and do an article, run a feature in *Joie de Vivre!* about our ambience and cuisine.

The dogs are deeply interested in cuisine. I bring their dishes to the sink, scoop up their chow and mush it for them with hot water while I tell them, "Hot tamale, Sass! *Joie de Vivre!* Squatch! Imagine that! The first national notice for Henry's House. Oh, this is great!"

Dog dishes in hand, I back the message up to listen again to her, Diane Wirth of *Joie de Vivre!* "Even here in New York we've heard that the cuisine and ambience of Henry's House are so marvelous, so satisfying, a place that embodies the essentials of warmth and affection, those family ties that reflect all our deepest needs."

I put the dishes down. Sass finishes first and tries to eat Squatch's. "Stop it, this minute, Sass! Russell's up. You hear him upstairs?" The drains in this old house gurgle and groan as Russell starts to shower. When he comes downstairs, he'll say: *Celia, I think we should talk. It's a question of protocol and appearances.* Russell is completely pissed off that I didn't place him at the family table for tomorrow's luncheon. *Especially since Bobby isn't even Bethie's real dad.*

It's not even the wedding yet, and everyone in this family (and a lot who aren't) are already bitching and griping, getting their feelings hurt. Only Bethie is oblivious to what's going on. Bethie is in love.

Oh, Bethie, Bethie, fine, be in love, but don't marry. You don't have to marry someone to love them. Look at your sister. Look at Victoria. Victoria can live with Eric Robbins and be in love, build a life without being married. Victoria and Eric didn't need to mutter a lot of mumbo jumbo in front of a preacher to know they could have a life together. Fine, Bethie, pledge yourself to Wade at some wild, free place that reeks of magic and light, but why should you, why should everyone stand closeted, claustroid in a church, Wade's pastor droning, with all that weight—civil and religious—bearing down on us?

But I can't say any of this. If I did, Bethie would just shrug and ignore me. She knows, everyone knows, I've always been against marriage. Not against long-standing unions, just legal marriage. I've always told my girls to keep their love unfettered and their unions free. Like Victoria and Eric. So if I object to Bethie's marrying Wade, it will seem merely reflexive on my part, and not worth heeding. Bethie will say, You've done weddings for lots of others who've got married at Henry's House; you did a great wedding, five hundred people, last year for that TV newscaster. Can't you do the same for me, your own daughter?

If this engagement party is a preview of Bethie's November wedding, then oh, Sister Broadbent, you were so right! There is no rest for the wicked. Everyone with any sort of claim (however tangential) on the bride, they're at it already, fighting and sniping, carping, sulking, chewing on remembered wrongs, creating new ones, digging up old wounds. Oh yes, the nuclear family. Nuclear's all wrong to describe families. Nuclear smacks of physics, doesn't it? So dry and theoretical: random particles crash into one another indifferently, bloodlessly. Nuclear is the wrong way of describing families, metaphorically incorrect, misleading. Forget physics. Families reek of biology—and not quivering-cell biology, those little liquidy units shivering under the microscope—but the great, broad-canvas biology, Darwinian biology. All those warm-blooded mammals, begetting and begatting, the grunt and thump, bloody birthing, wet suckling, the pain of dying, rot, decay—only to begin again. That's what families have done since the beginning of time. Since Eve.

And at least Eve didn't have a bunch of steps and exes to contend with. Me, I have to write to San Jose and tell Bethie's sperm donor—excuse me, her father, Gary Alsop—she was getting engaged and would be married in November. Of course he'll come. He'll bring his wife too. Oh God, I can just see the reception line at this formal wedding Bethie insists upon. Mr. and Mrs. Gary Alsop, they stand there, lined up with the rest of us: smile, shake hands, heads bobbing up and down. *We're Bethie's parents.* This is what Bethie wants? Oh yes, says Bethie, who wants the whole family to be here to share her nuptial happiness. She wants Gary Alsop there—but she doesn't want him to be father of the bride. No, that's for Bobby. Bobby Jerome was a true father to her and Bethie loves him best. So Bobby and his wife Janice, they'll be in the reception line too. *We're Bethie's parents.* And because Bethie wants Grant and Lee, her ex-stepbrothers for ushers, then that bastard Andrew Hayes must come too. He and his current wife. And they too will join me and Russell, and all the rest of us in the reception line-up. *We're Bethie's parents. We're Bethie's parents . . .*

I put a halt to this. At least for the engagement party, I told Bethie, there will be no formal reception line. My last word on the subject. But at the wedding? Bethie is adamant. I'll have to endure it, and take such comfort as I can. At least Gary Alsop called and he can't attend the engagement party. He's in the middle of a really big corporate audit and the IRS can't spare him. But on the phone he's indignant: *If I go to all the trouble and expense to come to the wedding, Celia, I ought to be able to walk my daughter down the aisle. Why should Bobby Jerome give the bride away?*

I'm her father. Well, yes, Gary, and your last known contact with the bride was a check on her eighteenth birthday.

Oh Lord, how can I face this? The wedding of the TV newscaster last year, feeding the five hundred, that was nothing. Bethie's wedding will be a nightmare. Even the engagement party is unendurable. Maybe a big asteroid will hit the earth before then. Make it tomorrow, Lord, so I won't have to deal further with Janice, who has let me know, repeatedly, that she expects her mother, Thelma, and her son, Todd, to be seated at the family table for the engagement party. I've tried to make it clear that Todd and Thelma are no relation whatever to Bethie. Tweaked off, Janice informs me that Todd and Bethie are step-siblings, and that Thelma is the only grandmother poor Bethie has ever known. Janice gave me an earful.

I'd no sooner hung up with her than Andrew calls. It's been years since he's called me, since I've heard his voice on the phone. It was his old seductive voice. But he'd called up to bitch. He thinks it's unfair we haven't asked his wife's children to come to the engagement party. I tell him, Andrew, Bethie wouldn't know your wife's children if they mugged her. Why should they come? Grant and Lee are coming, says Andrew. So then I have to remind him that Grant and Lee lived with us, with all of us: once upon a time Andrew moved in with me, and shortly thereafter his ex-wife dropped his twin boys off at the Useless post office. They had ringworm. They were brats and in perpetual trouble. The fact that they grew up to be fine young men reflects at least as much on me as on Andrew.

Sunny never did RSVP so I figured she wasn't coming, and now she's showing up. Sunny will certainly have to sit at the family table, and maybe her little girl, though she didn't say if she's bringing the little girl. I'll have to make up beds for them in the girls' old room, but she didn't say a word about the party, did she? She didn't say if—

"Celia! I think we should talk about this, about this luncheon tomorrow," Russell calls out as he opens the bathroom door. Steam rushes out and the dogs scramble upstairs to give him the canine equivalent of a standing ovation which he accepts with ducal noblesse. "I think it gives the wrong impression to everyone on this island, to the family, to Wade and Bethie and their friends if Bobby Jerome sits with you at the family table, as if you and he are still a couple. You and I are a couple, Celia. Bobby's not even Bethie's real father. If Bethie wants him to be the father of the bride, fine. But Bobby is not the husband of the bride's mother. Celia?"

He has a way of elongating my name so that it floats downstairs like a banner. I sneak into the computer room and glue my gaze to the brilliant blue of the screen. The little arrow scurries across; bleeps and rings connect me to the outside world, but the words flicker in front of me without my reading them at all. I pretend I don't hear Russell. Pretend I am immersed in e-mail, but I watch the rain instead. I don't want to hear Russell. Don't want to talk. For Russell, even the simplest conversation (like, *Goodbye!*) requires deconstructing.

Honestly, I don't care where they sit. Any of them. Russell, Andrew, Bobby and Janice, Todd and Thelma. The lot of them, their spouses and lovers, their steps and exes. I don't give a flying fuck. I feel like a general conducting a campaign in which I have no stake, no interest and no objectives. I want only to live through this awful engagement party and get on with my life.

I hear Russell calling my name and I wonder if my life will include Russell. Perhaps I ought to break it off with him. He wants to get married. So let him. Just *Not me, not me.* The longer Russell and I go on, the more we get on each other's nerves. I feel constricted. He feels ignored. Not like a love affair at all. I'll say, *You're right, Russell, it's not a love affair, and since it's not, what the hell's the good of it? It's going nowhere.* But I know I won't say this. In truth, the fact that it's going nowhere with Russell is part of its appeal, if not its pleasure, part of its comfort, if not its charm. I must be getting old. Old and ugly, PMS goodbye, farewell to the rag, I am pushing fifty, sniffing mint and wading through the weeds grown all over my Lot in Life. Give it up, I tell myself, you've long since ceased to be a lovely girl.

But I am not a wise woman. Life has larded me with experience, but shortchanged me on wisdom. Maybe for wisdom, fifty years isn't enough time. Maybe for wisdom you need a hundred years, or eight or nine hundred, like Eve, centuries spent squatting in the ashes of oblivion, ankle deep in the dust-unto-dust you created. Eve peopled the world with her progeny, but after eight hundred years, could she tell one from the other? Were they not all faceless begats, anonymous begots by then? Unmemorable, save for those two, those two indelible boys, the lost sons. Maybe wisdom is distilled from regret, a sour brew of alcoholic consolation. The aged Eve probably clutched her bottle, pressed it to her loveless breasts and drank in swift and bitter swills, hunched beside the dying fire, remembering Abel's sweet face and Cain for the reckless boy he had been, the winsome youth.

PART II

Return of the Native

All those years in Southern California had blinded Sunny to the color gray, to the shades implicit, the nuanced grays stippling and brindling, watercoloring the coves and beaches of Puget Sound. Late on this dank, raw afternoon, Sunny and her little daughter sat in a small outboard motorboat across from a man, middle-aged, leonine, leathery and tanned who kept a practiced hand on the tiller. Leaving the ferry landing at Dog Bay, they still kept close to the shore. The boat and the people in it were dwarfed by the great brooding mountain in whose shadow they passed. This mountain, its steep slopes home only to nesting seabirds, eagles and gulls, was completely inaccessible, threaded only by logging roads, but it dominated Isadora Island. From this mountain, land formations swept down and out in a northwesterly fashion, sloping into hills and farmlands, woods, meadows and finally out to a broad and lacy apron of rocky beaches and inhospitable coves. Never an altogether invitational place, despite its wild beauty, even Isadora's landmarks rang with some foreboding. Massacre, the island's one real town, was built on an afterthought of land that curved, fanning out, forming a sort of earthly question mark around Moonless Bay. That name commemorated the slaughter, two hundred years before, of an entire village of sleeping Indians, killed by another warlike tribe who crossed the bay one moonless night in their canoes. For a hundred years all civic attempts to change the name to something less grim, all these conscientious efforts had failed, and the anonymous victims of that ancient massacre would not loose their hold on the island's imagination. A ferry landing could not be built at Massacre because Moonless was too shallow, nor at Useless Point because of the low tides and rough currents, so ferry service had come late to Isadora Island, and the landing at Dog Bay was more or less midway between Massacre and Useless and inconvenient to everyone.

Sunny and her daughter had left their few other bags at the ferry landing and Sunny carried only a black canvas travel bag, beaten gray in places, and the little girl's Minnie Mouse backpack which held a blanket, crayons, paper, several much-thumbed books, a much-loved doll named Baby Herman and a silver spoon with her name engraved on it, *Brio*. None of the three in the boat spoke, though their silence seemed agreed upon, rather than enforced, and the only sound punctuating the watery quiet was the outboard motor, spluttering rhythmically. The man, universally known by the single name of Launch, did not speak by choice. Brio, at four, had sunk into one of those long bouts of infant resignation, since she was powerless to change anything and too tired for a full and proper tantrum. But Sunny had been startled into silence. Living in Los Angeles had inured her to constant change, change as certain as the tides, if not as predictable. So she was shocked to return to Isadora Island and find it unchanged: the water, the woods, the taciturn evergreens, everything exactly as she had remembered, everything as it was in some ancient age, as though the island had bought itself immunity from human time and subscribed only to geologic time, ignoring those brief chronometers of human bloom and vegetable decay.

Hugging the shore, the small boat made its way past shallow coves, in some of which pilings, vestiges of past docks, rose out of the water like rotting teeth. Trees stubbled the shoreline, the woods so dense that sunlight never reached the ground. Even those places where houses were tucked in the trees, the roofs were carpeted with moss and in the windows, lamps were lit, summer and winter. As it was March now and the afternoon sky thickly quilted with clouds, those houses with unlit windows probably belonged to summer people who would not return for months. As the boat chugged past a darkened cove swallowed up in the trees, Sunny saw a small house, its roof completely furred with moss, and she believed that was the suicide's cottage. How the island children had scared themselves spitless with tales of the undead. Sunny could all but hear her own young voice, calling all the other kids chickenshit babies, leaving them at the road while she alone plunged into the woods. She had raced breathlessly through the overgrown path, knocked on the suicide's door and returned to the road, triumphant, telling the waiting children that a clawed and disembodied hand had opened the door, just a crack, and slid a Hershey bar at her. She let the other children all smell the chocolate on her breath. Now Sunny wondered if that was where she had first learned—not to say remembered— that the fear was worse than the feat.

The suicide's cottage had been sold finally to summer people, ignorant of its pall, but it too looked unchanged. Even Launch looked virtually the same. Grayer, she noted on peering more closely, though it was hard to tell since he was wreathed with so much hair. Eccentricity was a precondition for living at Useless Point (not obliged of summer people), but Launch was visibly weird. He cut his hair and beard only four times a year. At each of the solstices and equinoxes, he would go down to Sophia's Beach at high tide and there amongst the driftwood logs, he would sit, cross-legged, facing the water, scissors in hand and cut away, without benefit of mirror. The vernal equinox, March 21, was some weeks from now and so, Launch approached his hirsute apogee. A longtime friend of Celia's, an island fixture, Launch had worked as a resident gardener and handyman for her for years and lived in one of the little outbuildings clustered in her yard. He had gone to India in about 1974 and Sunny could still remember the day he returned some two years later. He had passed around to everyone a hand-lettered note, which said he had decided to forsake speech for spiritual reasons, and after unspecified experiences in India. Would they all understand? He had not said a word since.

Following the coastline, the boat rounded a curve leading along a graceful beach which swept in an arc, perhaps a mile long, a broad beach, rocky and strewn with great driftwood logs, pale and massive as the bones of dinosaurs. Sunny pointed landward. "This is Sophia's Beach, the most magical place on the island, Brio."

"How can you get there? There's no parking lot," Brio observed.

Across from them, Launch grinned, his head happily bobbing up and down; enthusiastic assent was Launch's response to virtually any observation.

"There's a path. Can you see it, there through the trees? From the high road you come down that path," Sunny advised, waving toward some obscured, remembered path, not visible at this distance. Sophia's Beach was protected by low, thickly wooded cliffs, sheering down to a dense stand of trees, maples and madronas, their baroque branches resisting the advance of spring, though the underbrush had already succumbed, and a web of new-green tangled with autumnal rot. The threadline path had been beaten out by generations of feet and it led down the slopes to the rocky beach where the driftwood, the very stones mottled all those myriad hues of gray. As it was low tide, they could see great bony formations clawing at the water, like metacarpal tide pools.

"There is a swing hanging from one of those tall trees, Brio. Is the swing still there, Launch?" In reply, he nodded, grinning furiously. "My dad put that swing up. It was a gift to all of us girls, but everyone has used it ever since. The swing is so high and on such a long, long rope that you can go so far out over the water, especially at high tide, you feel like a bird. Like you can fly."

"I don't want to fly. I want to be warm. I don't like this place at all. It's spooky."

Sunny pulled her little daughter closer and assured her soon there would be so many people around, she wouldn't have time to think of spooky. Soon she'd have a big family. "That's what you said you wanted. You said you were tired of it being just you and me. You wanted a big family like Olivia Hernandez has."

"I didn't say I wanted to move," Brio sulked. "I didn't say that. You didn't tell me all this family lived in this cold, nasty place. You'd have to be a Huggamugwump to live here. Is this where the Huggamugwumps live?" she asked, referring to a tribe of small, furry creatures who had endless adventures at bedtime and whose domestic arrangements included rolling themselves into balls and snuggling all together. "Is this 'Deepest darkest Alberta, by the shores of beautiful Lake Huggamugwump'?"

"No, that's much further north. This is Isadora Island in the Puget Sound, and right around this bend and up a bit, you'll see Henry's House."

"Who's Henry? Who's Sophia anyway?"

"They're both dead. Oh, long ago."

"Then why is it still her beach? And why is it still his house?"

"The house isn't really Henry's. It's Celia's and it's not really a house you would live in. No one does. It was a school to begin with, once a long time ago, but now it's a B-and-B."

"What's that?"

Sunny did her best to explain that a B-and-B was a sort of hotel. People came to spend the night. Lots of people. It was a famous place.

Thank you for calling Henry's House at Useless Point, Isadora Island, Washington. Henry's House is open from April 1 to November 1. If you would like to send a fax, just press your start button now. If you are calling about a reservation, we are booked for summer weekends, but we have a wait-list and we still have weekday openings. If you would like to be wait-listed, please punch 1. If you would like to leave a message, please punch 2. Henry's House can also be reached on-line at henryshouse.com." The voice repeats the e-mail number; it's Celia's clear, untroubled voice, her public voice. Sunny punches 2 and leaves a message that the phone has eaten her thirty-five cents and that she is here, just arrived and wants to come to Isadora Island, that she has returned to the Northwest, to Washington, for good, or if not for good, at least for better or for worse.

Worse seemed to rise now in Sunny's throat, but perhaps it was only the dreadful hot dog at the bus terminal. Certainly, she still wore the mustard stain on her jacket. And on her pants, the stain from the tea she had spilled on herself when Brio—suffering from fifteen hundred miles on buses and the ferry—had heaved up her hot dog on Sunny's shoes. Mother and daughter were both pale with fatigue, varnished with the old travel-patina of grease, exhaust, their hands grayed from the print of tickets and sticky with all the shared effluvia of handrails and benches, bathrooms, stairwells, seats and tables that were the collective property of anyone with the price of a ticket and a destination. Sunny had always envied people with the knack of creating comfy little encampments wherever they went. Celia was like that, Sunny remembered from family trips to Disneyland. Celia Henry could domesticate an airport bathroom. She was like one of those desert nomads adept at setting down their tents, tethering their goats and calling it home. It was a gift, not a practice. Celia seldom traveled and yet she had this gift. Sunny had been to all the great cities of the world and she did not. Sunny traveled badly. Worse now.

Catching a whiff of stale vomit off her athletic shoes, Sunny tried to tuck her feet further underneath the black canvas bag. Her narrow shoulders hunched forward with the self-effacing posture of people embarrassed by their own beauty. Like a rose trying to pass as a common weed, Sunny habitually wore sloppy, floppy, unappealing clothes, like the overalls she had on now beneath her oversized jacket. Hers was not a conventionally pretty face of planes and angles, but something more luminous and less standard, a tenderness and intelligence in the direct gaze of her great blue eyes. Her dark hair was cut very short, a stubble over her head, and each ear studded with tiny rings. All her life Sunny had been told she had beauty and talent. Of the Henry girls, Bethie was The Charmer, Victoria was The Smart One, Sunny was The Talented One. She had dazzled Isadora as a kid, starring in every school production, whether she was the lead or not. She had gone to L.A. like so many other aspiring talents, but Sunny was insufficient to the task—and it was a task—of being an actress. To be an actress in L.A., you needed, concealed beneath your beauty and talent, some rough-grained toughness Sunny did not possess. She was perhaps like her father in that regard. She had worked at any number of numbing jobs, and for a while, briefly, ingloriously employed as a model, changing clothes in fluorescent-lit cubicles for cokehead photographers. Finally she got and kept a job, assistant to a cokehead producer. He relied on her to organize his life, tote his coffee, clutch assorted clipboards as he made movies with names like *Dirty Dark Death Blood Angel Fist Sport III,* movies which were dubbed in Asian languages and released in faraway places. So Sunny's name was in the credits after all, at the end, and rolling on screens she would never see.

"Is there a swimming pool at Henry's House?" As a California child Brio was obliged to ask this and when her mother said no, she relaxed into disappointment.

But Sunny tensed as they motored toward Useless Point, Assumption Island in the distance. Assumption was a two-acre rock and no one lived there: it was good for picnics only, and home to a noisy tribe of seals. They rounded Useless Point and Sunny could see the Useless public dock, so beautifully maintained, painted bright white and garnished with hanging baskets of flowers. The baskets were empty this early in Washington's raw uncertain spring. But by April, the beginning of the Season, they would be waving color and holiday promise. The stairs at the end of the dock led up to a tiny, manicured park, complete with pastel benches and more hanging baskets. Oh, it was all too cute for words. Made you want to puke. Or perhaps that too was just the old hot dog.

Sunny could remember when there was no dock, when Useless Point was only a potholed road that dead-ended into Puget Sound, like all the other island roads. Useless Point owed all its abundant charm—and its attendant prosperity—to the zeal of Celia Henry, to her unrelenting pursuit of a mainland bank all those years ago, after the Island Bank had firmly refused to finance the restoration of Henry's House, saying she had no credit, no education, no MBA, no proven business sense. Undaunted, Celia traded on the name Westervelt (a name she refused to wear) and got financing from a mainland bank with the help of Mr. Ellerman. With the restoration of Sophia's school building once underway, Celia had set about rousing the torpid and suspicious Isadorans at Useless Point to form a cooperative to finance the building of this dock. Now, despite the treacherous currents known to swirl in this channel, people would sail all the way from Seattle. In summer, boaters were constantly flocking here, some merely to have lunch at the Useless Cafe, or to buy ice cream at the Useless Store, pottery at Useless Ceramics, or merely to mail their bills at the post office and have them marked *Useless*.

Henry's House, from its proud perch on the hill, presided over everything, the lawns downsloping to undulating gardens, its views unobstructed of Useless Point, the Sound, the other islands rising in the west. Built in the early twenties, it had begun life as a school, on the model of Isadora Duncan's schools, offering interpretive education in the arts. The ceilings were twelve feet tall and all its other proportions equally broad and generous. Two stories high, a long gallery ran the length of the building in the front, its roof providing a balcony for those second story rooms that opened on to it, each with French doors. In one of these rooms, the window was lit. At either end of the gallery, just off the conservatory, and the other just off the library at the other end, dual arbors were gnarled with thickly twisted wisteria vines, leafless now in March. Six brick chimneys, cold, smokeless, lined up perfectly along the roof. Henry's house, painted pale yellow, trimmed in creamy white, greeted Useless Point, Assumption Island, the other San Juan Islands, the Puget Sound, the whole world for that matter, with serenity: a work of art, a thing of beauty, a joy forever, set upon the hill. A cake of vanilla certainty in a world pickled with doubt.

But Celia did not live there. Celia lived in a house you could not see, a house without a water view, a house obscured, tucked behind a small orchard of apple trees, their branches gnarled, lichened and nubbly with the promise of spring. This narrow house, narrow windows, narrow doors, had its own uphill driveway, out of sight, the entrance far down the road beside the Useless Cafe. But on foot, from the dock, the house was best reached by a shortcut, if you knew where to find it. Launch (who did not drive any vehicle, but could maneuver a boat anywhere) let them off at the Useless dock while he went back to the ferry landing to get their other bags. Sunny pulled her reluctant daughter in her wake, while Brio moaned that her knees were tired, that she was cold, that she wanted to go home. "This is home," replied Sunny unsympathetically.

She took Brio's small hand and they started uphill, their feet crunching on the great graveled drive of Henry's House. For a quarter of a mile this drive curved up toward one of the most spectacular views in the Northwest. Thickly wooded with birch and maple on either side of the drive, there were massive rhododendrons set close, which had yet to bloom, but a ragged carpet of crocuses frayed across the ground and the first early daffodils waved at each other across the drive like overeager sorority girls.

Sunny found the shortcut through the rhododendrons and birches to the right, and made her way up to the orchard where she was surprised to find a smoothly curving concrete path weaving through the trees. That was new. Connecting the service entrance of Henry's House with Celia's house, the path had narrow gauge tracks running on one side. Sunny and Brio followed these till they came to an unpaved yard surrounded by outbuildings, garages, sheds, wood stored in tin-covered lean-tos and the house itself. Like many Northwest homes, it had a prim, pince-nez effect, resulting from the windows set too close together and a roofed porch like a narrow mouth. But this house also had several unaesthetic additions appended, tacked on (no doubt in the usual Isadoran fashion without permits or permissions). As Sunny and Brio approached, two nervous mutts bounded toward them, barking ferociously. "Just stay still," Sunny cautioned Brio as she knelt and held out her hand, calling cheerfully, "Here Sass, here Squatch." She could not tell the dogs apart, but Celia's dogs were always called Sass and Squatch and they were all undifferentiated mutts.

With the dogs as excited escorts they walked past Celia's blue 1968 Dodge pickup and a 1986 Jetta. None of these had changed either. They approached the house where crates and boxes, recycle buckets and crab pots were littered and stacked the length of the long covered porch. Additionally there were perhaps half a dozen carts with metal wheels, clearly meant to go along the tracks on the paved path. Someone had cleverly devised this trolley path to ease the burdens of traffic between Henry's and this house, Henry's out-of-sight command post. The screen door hung uncertainly and none of the windows were curtained.

Peering through the window into the kitchen, Sunny watched Celia pacing, cordless phone to her ear, as she restlessly checked the oven, hung up a few miscreant saucepans, picked up the remote and flash-flooded through a bunch of TV images before turning it off. Celia always seemed taller than she was. She wore a man's sweater, wheat-colored, draped over faded jeans, and thick wool socks over feet thrust into ancient Birkenstocks. She had thick hair, blunt-cut, salted with gray which Sunny did not remember. Other than that, Celia too had not changed. Sunny picked Brio up and pointed. "That's Celia. That's who we've come to visit." Turning toward the window, Celia's face lit with welcome when she saw them. Still holding the phone, she hurried to the door, opened it, hugged them both, ruffled their hair, held Brio, embraced her, kissed her, put her down, laughed, and did all this without making a sound or interrupting the flow of her quarrel (and it was clearly a quarrel) with someone named Russell. She pointed toward the five earrings in Sunny's ear and rolled her eyes, carried on with the exaggerated gestures, fluid expression and animated body language of a silent film star portraying unrestrained welcome. Her dark eyes shone with undiminished brightness, and she seemed to Sunny, as always, to have more moods, more zest, more love and wrath, more irreverence, more native exuberance than any three people combined. Her energy was formidable. It wore Sunny out, sometimes, just to watch Celia in action.

"You're being unreasonable, Russell, you are—" Celia drew Sunny and Brio through the service porch past the three institutional-sized fridges, two freezers, a washer and dryer, the washing chugging, the dryer whirring. She rattled and nattered, tried to explain to Russell that she didn't want to have this conversation and certainly not now, but he clearly kept interrupting. She led them toward a large, marble-topped table dusted with flour where some serious baking had been going on. Fragrance wafted from the oven of the massive gas range which dominated the whole room. That was new. As were the three or four food processors and giant mixer, a built-in microwave, lots of other tools of the cooking trade stacked on shelves, hanging from the ceilings. Years ago Celia had knocked out the wall between the kitchen and what had once served as a parlor. She had no use for a parlor and she had never let a wall stand in her way. An unlit fireplace gaped in the wall and near it an ironing board and a basket of linen napkins starched to look like meringue peaks. The place was heated by ancient radiators, and atop them, pots of red geraniums limped through the winter. Over this there rattled the singsong voice of the marine radio. And under all this there persisted the thread of steam from the stockpot, still bubbling away on a back burner. The smell was the same. The stove was new, but the pot was its old battered self. One never knew what went into that stockpot; what came out was always savory and heavy on the thyme.

While Celia paced and continued her quarrel with Russell, or rather tried to extricate herself from the conversation, Sunny took off her hat and jacket. She wore a tank top, two shirts and a flannel work shirt underneath her overalls and she knelt to help Brio, similarly clad, out of her coat. Brio drew from the Minnie Mouse backpack Baby Herman, a battered Cabbage Patch doll of uncertain gender dressed in oversized jammies, and she ministered to its needs. Sunny sank into a chair and looked about. Perhaps all was not as she remembered it. In a small room off the kitchen, an addition, a bank of electronic lights blinked and a blue computer screen glowed. A fax machine dribbled out white paper and the buttons on three or four phones winked red and green, but they made no sound, no ringing at all. Together with the TV, VCR and CD player in the kitchen, the place had the look of electronic heaven. Only the marine radio chattering its inexorable and uninflected information on the shelf seemed familiar to Sunny. Still, there was the same ugly, cracked linoleum from twenty years before. Such light as there was (a precious commodity in western Washington) filtered through the kitchen windows where myriad jars filled with shells and rocks and seaglass lined up, some jars dated, some not; there were beach stones and pieces of petrified wood, and tucked amongst all this, there was a fortune in sand dollars collecting interest. And dust.

"I tell you, Russell, for the last time, I have to go! I have company! Sunny. Yes, Bobby's Sunny. Yes, she's here. I don't know—" Celia gestured, grimaced in a veritable dither of pissedness, but seemed absolutely unable to get him off the phone. Finally she butted in, "No. Tonight stay at your own place. Please, Russell. Tomorrow, yes, yes." She held the phone at arm's length and an anxious male voice peppered out objections and then there was an audible click. Celia grinned at Sunny and said her first actual words of greeting. "Don't you just hate a man who always wants to talk?"

She set about immediately making them comfortable, all of them, including Baby Herman (such was the name of the Cabbage Patch doll who persisted as a female despite the masculine name). Celia listened intently to Baby Herman's catalog of woes and observations; first, Baby Herman's knees were tired and second, she was hungry. Celia clucked sympathetically, she had the very thing: boxed macaroni and cheese. Brio's face lit. Celia put on the water, exclaiming at the surprise of their visit, how beautiful Brio was, asking after their journey, the weather in L.A., the ferryboat, asking after everything (except, directly, why they had come, though she did ascertain that Sunny had not informed anyone in the family, including her father or sisters of their arrival). She filled the kettle for tea and offered a hit of Wild Turkey to sweeten the tea, and all the while surveyed Sunny critically. "You look like hell, Sunny. I have to say it. You're beautiful, you'll always be beautiful, but you just look terrible."

"Travel doesn't agree with me."

"You've traveled everywhere! You sent me postcards from Tokyo and Australia and Mexico."

"I used to. It didn't agree with me then either."

Celia's eyes narrowed. "You're not one of those women sticking her finger down her throat and puking for fashion, are you?"

Sunny shook her head, stifling a smile, never having heard bulimia thus described.

"And you're not into Recovery, are you?"

"Recovery?"

"You know, coming off some dreadful drug and wanting everyone to embrace your pain?"

"What would make you think that?"

"Forgive me. I'm sensitive on the subject." She sighed and turned to Brio and Baby Herman. "I should be beaten for asking Sunny a question like that, don't you think? Just like in the rhyme, right, Brio? 'So she gave them all butter without any bread and beat them all soundly and snapped off their heads.' "

"It doesn't go like that," Brio condescended to correct her. "It's 'sent them to bed.' "

"Well, you will just have to teach me all these rhymes. I've heard them all wrong, I guess. But if you'll tell them to me right, in return, I'll tell you all about the Huggamugwumps."

But Brio was not to be outdone here either and she proudly asserted that she knew all about the Huggamugwumps. She recited the opening unchanging lines about deepest darkest Alberta.

"Celia invented the Huggamugwumps," Sunny admitted sheepishly, never having exactly assigned credit for the original creation of these legendary little balls of fur and muscle. "I just borrowed them."

"Nonsense. I didn't invent them. I discovered them."

"Then they *are* here!" Brio's face brightened at the thought of seeing a Huggamugwump in its natural habitat.

"They were here," Celia sighed sadly. "No longer. But once they were all over this island. They've left artifacts. I'll show you one day, but now it's off to wash your paws!" She included Sunny in this injunction as though she were about ten and hustled them both to a small bathroom off to the back (another addition) to wash up.

When they returned to the kitchen, a tall, solid-looking man in work boots stood warming his hands at the radiator, enormous hands, the long, sinewy fingers lined with dirt. His hair was thick, dark, coarse, curly and unruly, and he wore delicate round glasses with wire frames which gave a scholarly cast to his face, entirely out of keeping with the rest of him. A stubble of beard stippled his jaw and a faded Huskies sweatshirt touting some long-ago Rose Bowl win hung from his broad shoulders.

"You remember Grant Hayes, don't you, Sunny?"

"No, I don't. Sorry." Hunching over this half-truth, she busied herself tucking a napkin in Brio's shirt. The man in front of her was a stranger, but the other half of the truth was that of course she did remember the twin brothers, Grant and Lee Hayes. Nasty boys. She had hated their father. She had hated their mother without ever having met the woman. She had hated Celia as well at the time, and her own father, Bobby too, hated all adults, hated the squalor they created with their sex, with their endless messy coupling and uncoupling, their noises behind closed doors. Now she chewed ineffectually on her thumbnail and listened, because Grant remembered her. Brio listened, wide-eyed as Grant detailed Sunny's childhood exploits, like her knocking on the door of the suicide's cottage. "The rest of us just hung back because it was way deep in the woods and scary, but Sunny Jerome just crashed through and went to the door and saw the ghost who gave her a Hershey bar."

"There was no ghost. I had the chocolate bar in my pocket."

"Then there was this story we heard how Sunny found her little sister crying because some fifth graders had called Victoria a shrimp on the schoolyard." Grant and Celia both laughed. "And Sunny said, 'You just point them out to me, which ones, Victoria?' Sunny punched them out, every last one of those boys. She told them, 'No one calls my sister a shrimp!' "

"I lost," Sunny informed Brio. "My dad had to come get me out of the principal's office. And I was black and blue for a week."

"Oh, Sunny Jerome," Grant ruminated, fondly rubbing his hands over the radiator, "she was just a legend. She jumped out of the swing once on Sophia's Beach because she was convinced she could fly."

"I broke my arm. I could have broken my neck," Sunny explained dryly. "It's very stupid to jump out of swings on a rocky beach."

"Your mother was the bravest girl on this island." Grant pulled a chair up at the table and sat down across from them.

"Now I'm the bravest girl," Brio asserted. "I'm not afraid of anything."

"It's not the same thing, you know," Sunny said pensively. "You can be afraid of something and still be brave. Maybe that's the bravest thing of all." She put her arm around her little daughter. They were the image of each other, or perhaps Brio was the image of the child Sunny had been: an independent girl, sturdy and confident. But all that glamorous readiness for experience had receded in the adult Sunny and she had developed a reserve, calculating constantly the outlay of energy that any given situation would oblige of her. Certainly she did not want her combative self held up to Brio as a glorious model of childhood excellence, even though she could still remember, if not re-create, the imaginative conviction that had impelled her—her whole family watching her—to believe she could fly, get that swing high, high over the water, over the tide so she could jump, arms outstretched and fly. A certainty short-lived.

"You're here for Bethie's party tomorrow?" Grant asked brightly.

"Her birthday's not till May."

"It's for her engagement," said Celia in a deliberate voice as she put three cups on the table and the teapot, a battered tin thing, devoid of aesthetics and long on service. "You got an invitation, didn't you?"

"Oh, I forgot." Sunny stifled a moan. "The invitation got lost, I guess. If I'd remembered . . ." *I certainly would have waited to come. I would not be here now.* But Sunny did not say this, mused only. "So she's really going to do it? Marry Wade Shumley."

"You know him?" Celia seemed amazed.

"I know about him. At Christmas Bethie called me and said she'd met the man of her dreams. She was crazy with love. She said she was going to marry him, to have a real wedding, and she asked if I would be a bridesmaid." Sunny poured three cups of tea and pushed Grant's toward him, making a little path in the flour. Sipping the hot tea spared Sunny having to add that on the phone she had suggested to Bethie that bridesmaids and white weddings didn't exactly run in their family. Probably what Bethie wanted was a witness for a courtroom wedding, right? But this is not what Bethie wanted at all. No, Bethie wanted—and would have—a formal engagement, announced in the Seattle paper, engagement pictures and a diamond engagement ring. And for the wedding: real bridesmaids in pastel dresses, tuxedo-clad ushers, flower girl (Brio), a gorgeous white dress for the bride, long veil, the whole Traditional Event, including a real preacher, Pastor Lewin of Wade's church. Bethie went to church nowadays because Wade went to church. Bethie had declared outright she would not give in to Celia's stupid flower-power notions of bare-foot unions on Sophia's Beach. Nor would she organize her love life as their other sister, Victoria, had done. A year ago Victoria had legally wed Eric Robbins in a judge's office, but never told her mother she had done this Dirty Deed, since Celia was dead set against marriage, against all the social crust and custom it implied. Warming her hands on her cup, Sunny observed that Celia must truly have mellowed. "I can't imagine you giving an engagement party—I mean not for someone in your own family. It's not like you. Didn't you try to talk Bethie out of it?"

Celia paused reflectively. "I tried my best. But you should see Bethie nowadays. She's on the rampage for tradition, for bringing the whole family together—really together." She shuddered. "She's insisted I invite Eric's whole family too. She's absolutely bullying everyone into doing what she wants."

"Even you?" asked Sunny.

"Especially me," Celia replied glumly.

"One hundred fifty people," Grant offered in the ensuing uncomfortable silence, elaborating on the great plans. His account alone fatigued Sunny and she desperately wished she had come a few days later. She should have remembered the invitation and avoided all this. Now she would have to deal with the family in one great, awful mass. As a group, her family always reminded Sunny of a sackful of kittens about to be drowned.

Celia brought the pan to the table and dished up two bowls of goopy over-yellow macaroni-cheese, one for Brio and one for Baby Herman. Sunny declined, feeling still too rocky to eat.

"Why can't Bethie just fall in love?" Celia bristled. "Why get married? It's a stupid legal artifice. I've told her that, of course, but she's besotted." Though the furrows between her brows had deepened, Celia wore her laugh-and-worry lines well and her mouth retained a supple quality, which suggested that life had not yet altogether constricted around her. She had an olive complexion, the more drab for its being March in the Northwest, the long, gray winter behind them, the uncertain spring before. "Why go through all that dry, ugly, legalizing, pulverizing bullshit of the law? If you don't get married, you don't have to get divorced. They don't even call it divorce. They call it dissolution, like you're going to dissolve. Or worse, after the love has all been choked out, people stay shackled to the institution. Marriage is nothing but a property arrangement between people who have decided to consolidate their assets and register themselves as card-carrying dupes to convention."

Sunny was certain that next would come some reference—Shakespearean in its inflection and intensity—to the Unfettered Life or Unfettered Love, something like that, and Celia did not disappoint. "Love is unfettered or it isn't love at all," she added.

"You told that to Russell lately?" inquired Grant without a trace of irony.

Celia shot him a dirty look. "At least Victoria never felt obliged to marry Eric. She knows better than to tether herself, body and soul."

"If you think about it," Grant mused, blowing on his tea, "it's pretty remarkable that Victoria didn't get married. Eric's a nice guy, but he's conventional to the core." He glanced at Sunny, mirth just visible in his eyes, and then he looked away. Did he know that Victoria and Eric were married? Sunny wondered. Did everyone? Everyone but Celia? Or did he just enjoy nettling her?

"Did you get married, Sunny?" asked Grant.

"I got what I wanted." Sunny reached over and touched Brio's head in an affectionate gesture at once reflexive and instinctive, smiled in her self-effacing way. "My sweet girl. Will Bobby be here tomorrow?" she asked, deflecting conversation from herself, though she well knew her own father, Bobby Jerome, would act as father of the bride. "And what about Gary Alsop? Will he . . . ?"

"Be a pain in the ass?" Celia supplied. "Of course. But he's not coming tomorrow. Thank you, Jesus. But for the wedding in November, oh yes, he's insisting on being father of the bride."

He was the bride's father, actually, though Celia was always embarrassed to have been so enamored, to have made serious love with someone who could conceivably do corporate audits for the IRS. In consequence she had perfected a sort of fable about Gary Alsop, a story which ran something like this: in the colorful past, Celia personally had drafted Gary Alsop into the Army of Youth, Peace and Love, and that he did his tour of duty here on Isadora Island, comporting himself with abandon, smoking dope, dancing naked on Sophia's Beach, making love with Celia Henry and accidentally begetting a daughter on her. Celia refused to marry him, and off he went in a huff, back to San Jose and his college sweetheart and the IRS. The fable stopped there and did not indicate how important Gary Alsop had been to all of them. Once a month, they had all adored Gary Alsop. Sunny could remember Celia putting Gary Alsop's monthly support check on the mantel when it arrived, and the family's Ritual Dance honoring the check, Bobby making up the song and playing it on the guitar, Celia and Bethie, Sunny and later baby Victoria, doing an impromptu, not to say Isadorish dance of thanksgiving before Gary Alsop's check. Then they would all pile into the '68 pickup and drive to Massacre to cash the check, and the Henry girls got ice cream cones in Gary's honor. They were all known as the Henry girls.

The timer sounded, and Celia jumped up; the kitchen filled with a burst of sumptuous fragrance and the clatter of bread pans as she opened the oven. She returned to the table with a single loaf and tumbled it out of its pan, saying they could spare one loaf. "I can't wait to see Bobby's face tomorrow when he sees Brio! You are going to adore your grandpa, and he is going to adore you. Oh, make no mistake, all the kids adore Bobby Jerome."

"My grandpa gave me my name." Brio brought Baby Herman closer. "Tell them, Mommy. Tell them the story."

"In music, *con brio* means with spirit, with verve"—Sunny tenderly brushed her daughter's cheek—"and my dad always used to tell us girls to live *con brio!* Whatever you do in this world, he used to say, do it *con brio!* With verve and spirit! So when my baby was born, I thought, What better name? Now I can live always *con Brio*. Your grandpa is going to be so surprised tomorrow."

"Are you my grandma?" Brio inquired of Celia.

Celia pondered this for a while and said she would adore being Brio's grandma, but Brio had better ask Sunny what she thought. "I mean, there's Janice, isn't there?"

"Janice doesn't count."

"Who's Janice?"

They all three unraveled it for Brio. Or tried to. How Bobby and Celia had once been Together, the capital T implied, as opposed to having been merely married (which they each had been before, and which Celia did not approve of and Bobby also did not approve. Though clearly, since Bobby had actually married his first wife, Linda, Sunny's mother, and since he had also actually married Janice, this suggested that he had responded to the strength of Celia's convictions against marriage, responded to her powerful personality and not that Bobby himself held these sentiments). When Bobby and Celia were Together, they had lived on Isadora Island in this very house. They had lived with Celia's little daughter, Harmony (now known by the more prosaic Bethie, short for the queenly Elizabeth) and Bobby's daughter Sunny (*née* Soleil Jerome, daughter of Linda who fled Bobby, fled Sunny, fled Seattle, pursuing her art in Denver). Together Bobby and Celia had had their own little daughter, Clarity (better known now and always addressed as Victoria) and they were all five happy here, Edenically happy for a long, long while. Until they were Not Together. (And in the unraveling, nothing more specific was offered or alluded to, certainly not Andrew Hayes, Grant's father, whose tenure in Celia's bed had predated Bobby's departure.) Bobby and Celia had split up. Bobby went back to Seattle, and naturally his daughter Sunny went with him. Then, later (and several other women left unspecified), Bobby met and married Janice. Janice had a son already by her first marriage and his name was Todd. Odd Todd. That's what they all called him. But they assured Brio she would like him. Todd was a college freshman and most of them were odd anyway. Janice, however, was not sufficiently odd and it remained to be seen how Brio would like her. Janice worked for the State of Washington as a vocational counselor in Workers' Compensation, heading up the office of Chronic Pain. And finally, they all agreed, truly, it didn't matter if Janice insisted on being Brio's grandma because everyone was entitled to two grandmothers after all, so Celia could be one and Janice the other.

Brio might have followed all this, even pretended to be mildly interested, but these complexities, however diluted, towed her under with fatigue. She drooped over the table, over Baby Herman, and Celia said to take her upstairs. "The girls' room is sort of ready, not very well made up, I'm afraid, I only had time to put sheets on the bed when you called. I haven't—"

"It's fine," Sunny assured her. "It will be fine. It's good of you to put us up at all without notice. Especially with all the work you have for this party, and all the other burdens."

Grant picked Brio up. Sunny, carrying the Minnie Mouse backpack and Baby Herman, followed him up the stairs, which creaked where they had always creaked and groaned where they had always groaned. She was surprised to find that no one had ever painted over the flowers she and her sisters had daubed all over the stairwell walls. That was how Bobby had measured their growth; periodically he would give them all paintbrushes and tell them to draw the tallest flower they could draw and then he would date each drawing with each girl's name, so their growth was measured not in how tall they actually were, but how far they could reach. So like Bobby to measure by aspiration, not actuality. At the top of the stairwell there were three bedrooms and a bath. Grant had to duck to enter the low door.

As Sunny entered the room, she was accosted by the Damp. So powerful and pervasive is the Damp in the Northwest that it has a life of its own. Perhaps the Damp even has feet and can paw and crawl into rooms, into clothes, and blankets and drawers and closets, into books and letters. Like a stubborn tenant, the Damp will not be dislodged. Here in this room, the Damp reigned. There were boxes thrust into corners and the odd lamp,

typewriter and old toys Sunny vaguely recognized and two children's beds, one on either side of the narrow window. As Grant
laid Brio down, she murmured something about Baby Herman
and her blanket and Sunny handed them both to her and unlaced
her shoes.

"I'll go get your bags," Grant offered. "Launch probably left
them down by the Useless dock."

"Has Useless changed so little that they are safe by the dock?"

"Nothing changes here. That's its charm." He paused but did
not leave and Sunny could feel him physically filling up the door
frame behind her. "Do you really not remember me?"

She busied herself with her daughter's Osh-Koshes before she
answered. "I remember you. I didn't recognize you. There's a
difference." He offered nothing, so she added, "I'd appreciate it
if you didn't make fighting the boys and jumping out of trees
sound glamorous to my daughter."

"You know, Lee and I had no part in all that. It was our dad
and Celia who—"

"Please don't bring up the past." Then she thanked him for
getting their bags, and bent over Brio, smoothing her dark hair
back from her sweet forehead, and whispering in her ear the
rhythmic and well-remembered litany of the Huggamugwumps,
but Brio was asleep before Sunny even got to their adventures.
Sunny remained sitting on the bed, looking out the darkened
window and listened as Grant retreated down the stairs and shared
an exchange with Celia. She heard his car start up in the yard
and waited till its headlights broke up the blue dusk hovering,
smudging the window.

Returning to the kitchen she found Celia on the phone again,
no quarreling this time, just checking with Lattimer's Bakery in
Massacre, strategy for the delivery of the cake tomorrow. Celia
did all this while she ladled out a bowl from the omnipresent
stockpot, seasoned it liberally and set it before Sunny at the table.
She sliced the fresh bread and buttered it, pointing to the repast
and indicating that Sunny should eat. To the baker she repeated
that she wanted the cake early, even though the party had to be

timed with the ferry's arrival (and its departure). "Angie will come early. Send it with her." Celia signed off with the Lattimers and apologized to Sunny for the uninspired meal. "But it's all I can do right now."

"It's fine. Thank you." Sunny tucked into it to prove it was fine. "How is Angie? Does she remain unchanged like everything on Isadora?"

"Things change here, Sunny. Children grow up, after all. Angie's two boys are teenagers now. They are monsters."

"Really?"

"I mean they're enormous. You'd never think someone little and skinny as Angie would have two such hulking boys. Anyway, Angie says she had her kids so late in life that now she and her teenage sons are growing their mustaches together."

Sunny laughed, "That sounds like her. Does she still run Duncan Donuts?"

"She'll run that cafe from the grave."

"Do you think she might need some help in-season?"

"Angie always needs help in-season. Everyone does on this island." Celia had been mopping flour off the table with a damp cloth, and she flung the cloth, perfect drop shot, into the soapy water in the sink. "Who did you have in mind?"

"Well, me. I'd like to stay on Isadora for a while. For the Season anyway."

"And then what?"

"I don't know yet. I'll take the Season to think about it and decide in the fall."

"You mean you're going to stay up here? You're not going back to California?"

"Yes. I'm here for good. I've come back."

"But what about being an actress? Oh, Sunny, don't give up your talents. You are a marvelous actress! Oh, that Christmas pageant—we were all of us blown away, just sitting in the school cafeteria—you, in your dress with its twinkling lights and your little arms outstretched, the spirit of Christmas!"

"That wasn't the highlight of my life, Celia."

"It was the mother of all Christmas pageants."

Sunny ate silently while Celia resurrected the wonderful Christmas pageant, the dress she had designed for Sunny, battery-powered and dazzling in the darkened cafeteria. Celia had coached her on her lines and Sunny had captivated the whole island. Finishing her soup, Sunny put her spoon down. "I'm old enough now, I mean, you reach a certain point when it's not enough to hitchhike through life and expect a bit of luck or the right man, or both, to pick you up. You spend your youth expanding, but then, one day you start to narrow it all down, to ask, What do I want? What I mean is, you ask, What can't I live without? What will finally matter to my life? And you realize you have to put your own hand to this effort, to your life. Once you know this, then everything has to change." Sunny spoke slowly, as though picking each word from a garden of thought.

"So what was it? What made you realize everything had to change?"

"Oh, no one thing in particular. It was a process, not a moment. Maybe it started when I had Brio. Everything changed when I had her. Change for the better. Your whole vision alters when you have a child. Or at least it should. Mine did." She brought her great blue eyes up from the table and she smiled at Celia. "You know what I mean."

"Yes. Yes, of course."

"It's been long over with Brio's dad. I know you and I haven't kept in touch, but I'm sure Bethie or Victoria, someone must have told you he was already married. It wasn't a secret. He already had a family for that matter. The wife and kiddies and a Bel-Air home. What he wanted from me was that I should be a beautiful ornament on his arm, and I was. Actors are like that. Most people in Hollywood are like that. When I got pregnant with Brio, he counseled abortion, said he'd pay for it. He said I should do it for the usual reasons, but I couldn't, and I didn't want to. But after that I wasn't so ornamental. My breasts were used for nursing and I smelled like baby spit-up. And once I had

Brio, I didn't want a man who believed that an ornament was all I was or ever would be."

"So it wasn't a tragedy, your breakup with him?"

"It was a choice. He's always been regular with the support checks for Brio, but they come from his accountant. And that's fine. He's taken up with lots of different women since me. I wasn't the love of his life. If he needs a family, he can go home to Bel-Air. But if I need a family, I have to come back up to Washington."

"And you haven't told Bobby you're back? Your dad doesn't know?"

"Seattle isn't home. Isadora is." She toyed with her spoon. "I'd like Brio to have some time here. I know there's no good job for me, but I wanted Brio to climb up in the apple trees and have Launch show her how to fish off the Useless dock and be scared of the watch-geese. I wanted her to go over to Assumption Island for picnics with the seals, and to run along Sophia's Beach like we did, go up high on the swing and play with the otters and climb over the rocks and have Boomerquanger duels."

"Oh, Boomerquangers! I haven't heard the word in so long. Who made that up?"

"Bethie. We'd each have to find a stick on the beach, perfect for sword fighting, and there were some that were just sticks, but some were Boomerquangers."

"I'll bet we still have Boomerquangers out in some of the sheds."

"Brio will have to find her own Boomerquanger. No one can do that for you. It's one of the things you have to do alone." Sunny tried to brush the fatigue from her face, and looked to the kitchen windowsills. "You see all those jars full of rocks and seaglass, shells lined up? It's like the past all caught and held. I'd like to line up lots of jars full of Brio's summers, of shells and rocks and bits of glass she's found on island beaches. I'd like to have lots and lots of them, jars full of summers with my daughter. I want to give Brio a place where she can feel like a native."

"Well, Sunny, I'm happy to have you back, but you don't

have to go all the way into Massacre for a seasonal job that pays shit. You can stay right here and work for me! I pay lousy wages just like Angie. Just like everyone else on this island."

"I don't mind working for low wages."

"You will. These are all pay-and-flay jobs, you know. The kind where you get paid, but you feel flayed. All island jobs are like that. They're all service jobs tied up with tourism, or fishing, or logging if you work for the Westervelts. Wages here are so low, our greatest export is our children. Very few come back. Bethie did, now and then, but only between love affairs. Grant's back, but he won't stay. He and Lee are both working construction for Andrew, but Grant has more ambition than that. Did you see that trolley path connecting this place to Henry's? Grant went to Washington State, got a degree in engineering. This was his senior project, this path through the orchard. He told me he'd been planning it for years, ever since he was a kid! He designed the whole thing at Washington State and when he came back, he and Lee built it. They built the carts and everything. It's a marvel! You remember how we used to have to haul everything, however hot, however heavy, rain or shine, uphill through the orchard?"

Sunny dutifully nibbled her bread and butter, drank her tea and listened to Celia wax on about the charms of the trolley system, the carts and how they had made things so much easier, especially for this god-awful engagement party. Tomorrow Sunny could expect to see the whole Isadoran cast of thousands, well, hundreds. All of Useless Point was invited, from the postmistress, Nancy, to the old Isadorans, a term reserved to describe those cantankerous artists whose residence on the island dated from Sophia Westervelt's day when she had imported artists to teach at her school. The school had failed, but the artists stayed on. Because of them, Useless Point was the premiere artistic address on Isadora. There was in fact a sort of rivalry between Useless and Massacre, so much so that Useless people refused to patronize Duncan Donuts for its exploitation of Isadora's name. People from Useless Point believed Massacre was a hotbed of tourist-suckups and crass commercialism. To people from Massacre, the Useless Pointers were truly useless, artsy-fartsy types who threw pots and smoked it too. Sunny wondered now how one island could contain so much variety, vitality and ill will. It was like a little terrarium, Isadora Island, a closed environment where for six months a year everyone courted tourism, and fought for the tourist dollars that kept the island alive at all. Then, off-season, everyone lapsed into a languorous, uncommunicative torpor. Massacre and Useless remained suspicious of one another all year long. Celia congratulated herself for being so democratic, because Massacre was invited, Dr. Aagard, Lester Tubbs, the island librarian, as were the farmers and commercial fishermen who were Celia's suppliers and whose own high standards had contributed to Henry's House's success. "And speaking of reputation! Guess who called this morning—*Joie de Vivre!*"

"Really? That high-class rag?"

"That high-class rag," Celia grinned. "No other Washington B-and-B has ever appeared in their pages. *Joie de Vivre!* writes up places all over the world—and there we'll be. But I can't even think about *Joie de Vivre!* till this terrible party is over. Forewarned is forearmed," Celia cautioned Sunny. Then, at tedious length, she enumerated the number of family hatchets to be buried, the many island feuds that would be soft-pedaled, the number of ruffled feathers that would all be soothed for Bethie's sake.

"I'm sure everyone will be on their best behavior," Sunny replied unconvincingly, especially when she found out Andrew Hayes was coming. Both Andrew and his current wife. As well as, no doubt—Celia pointed out—whoever else Andrew was sleeping with. Celia was a veteran of his infidelities. "You can bet he's sleeping with someone."

"I hope Nona York is coming." Nona was the island's resident romance novelist.

"Nona's the only one Andrew hasn't slept with."

Sunny knew from her sisters that Celia's relationship with Andrew Hayes, though long over, was still rocky. All her other exes had outlived—or outloved—their moment. Not Andrew.

That's what happened with sexual meltdown, Sunny thought. Once you melted down, you could never quite pull yourself upright. At least not with that particular man. Sexual meltdown was not in Sunny's personal catalog of experience. But she had seen it happen to others and it seemed to her that Bethie was deep into sexual meltdown with Wade.

Celia said if their extended family had its way, the family table would take up the whole room. Russell, Celia's Man of the Moment, insisted on sitting with her, and he'd insisted that his kids come too. Janice wanted to join Bobby—and bring Odd Todd. And Thelma, naturally.

Sunny winced. "The Wookie is coming?"

The girls used to call Janice's parents Jabba the Hutt and the Wookie. But then Jabba (Janice's father) died, and it didn't seem right to speak of the dead in those terms. Thelma, however, continued as the Wookie in the family's collective parlance.

"Janice says Thelma is step-grandmother to Bethie. Like Barbara Cartland was to Princess Di." They both burst out laughing. And speaking of far-fetched connections to the bride: Bethie absolutely insisted on having all of Eric Robbins' tribe "to share her joy." Celia's lip twisted painfully. "Eric has three married brothers and his parents, so that's eight people. How can they share her joy if they don't know her?"

Sunny had no answer. Her head hurt.

"Let me live through it, Lord, that's all I ask. Family up the ying yang. Everyone there to watch Bethie flaunt the engagement ring on her left hand and practice her nuptial kiss." Celia sighed. "Bethie says that all the time: Watch us practice our nuptial kiss."

"It could be worse," Sunny offered tentatively. "Getting engaged isn't so very bad. I mean, it's not the Unfettered Life, but it's not the army or the priesthood either."

"Getting married to Wade is like the priesthood." Celia thrummed her fingers in the flour. "He has missionary instincts. Maybe that's what I can't bear. He goes after people just like a missionary goes after people and he bewitches them."

"Missionaries are supposed to convert, not bewitch."

Eyeing an antidote to introspection in the ironing board, Celia walked over to it, turned on the iron and ruffled through a basket of starched linens. "Call it what you will, I just know Wade Shumley makes me want to spit."

Sunny sugared a fresh cup of tea and suggested, gently, that perhaps Bethie wanted someone mature, hardworking, suggested (without ever quite saying so) that given Bethie's upbringing, such a man, might look, well, exotic. Appealing. Even interesting. Certainly that could be said of Victoria's domestic partner, Eric. Sunny was careful to say domestic partner, not husband.

Celia spat on the iron, but it wasn't yet hot. "Wade and Bethie asked us—that is, me and Russell, and your dad and Janice, and Odd Todd and the Wookie—to a potluck dinner at their church because they wanted us to meet the pastor who will marry them, and some of their friends. Wade's friends. Of course, they love Bethie, and Bethie just loves them too. Oh, big love bath. Everyone just splashing around in this love bath. And during the evening—which, I assure you, was a mere coming attraction for tomorrow's festivities—all these people tell me, really, the same story, variations on a theme: how wonderful Wade is, how noble, how remarkable, how willing he is to admit his own flaws. Such bravery for a man. And I said—Well, what does that make him? An Olympic moral athlete? When a woman admits her own flaws, is she merely stating the obvious?" Celia snorted and laid out the body of a resistant linen napkin. "If you ask me, I think Wade is overfond of his flaws. I think he loves his flaws and he wants us to love them too."

"Bethie said Wade didn't have any flaws."

Celia spat on the iron, and this time it hissed and crackled. "He's a former crack addict. Did she tell you that?"

"She said he'd recovered. Eight years ago."

"You misheard her, Sunny. None of them are recovered. They are Recovering. There's a difference. They are Recoverees. That way, it's all still in process. They might slip down that dreadful path again, any minute, and so we're all obliged to be supportive and give them—continually, mind you—great dollops of assurance. We must constantly remember to restore their shaky selves, to build up their wavering self-confidence and polish their poor self-image. Oh, it takes a fucking village all right."

"Well, that's better than still being on drugs. Drug addicts are very unpredictable."

"Wade is predictable, all right. He leads a group called ReDiscovery and they get to embrace all their pain, and, at the same time, they get applause for embracing it." For the sheer pleasure of the hiss, she spat again on the upturned iron. "He's addicted to recovery."

The kitchen suddenly fell silent, no beeping faxes, no whooshing dishwasher, no clicking phones and voice mail, no washer or dryer, quiet save for the marine radio, the steady hum of the fridges and the freezer in the service porch and the thump of Celia's iron as she flattened out the napkins. Sunny took her dish to the sink where houseplants straggled in varying stages of neglect. "Maybe it's just a moment in his life."

"Eight years?" Celia ironed the napkin into a linen brick and stacked it with the others. "I suppose Bethie told you how they'd met. A romantic tale, that one," she added sardonically.

Bethie had indeed told Sunny a romantic tale, entirely in keeping with Bethie's way of looking at the world. Bethie had energy and vitality, great warmth. She was Bethie The Charmer, affectionate, restless, athletic but impatient with anything that required careful reflection. When she spoke of Wade Shumley, however, she evinced passion. Not puppy love. It was sexual meltdown all right. Fusion. And perhaps Celia was right and Bethie was bewitched, but that's what love does to you. Before Wade, Bethie had had different love affairs and different jobs, and always, when one or the other ended, she always bounced back with a bright resilience reminiscent of Celia herself. But Wade Shumley was different. Sunny knew from the tone of Bethie's voice, that first phone call. Breathlessly Bethie had recounted to Sunny how they'd met: she was working at Angie's Duncan Donuts and Wade came in and said he was looking for Island High and did she have a map of the island? Bethie had had a bad day at the cafe, and she retorted that on Isadora Island a map wouldn't do you any good, here, you needed sonar. But she had directed him to Island High and later that afternoon, after he'd finished at the high school, he came back to Duncan Donuts and asked her to go out to dinner. Bethie said he waited for her to finish her shift, just sat there with a cup of coffee and a book, for hours, looking up at her, smiling now and then, till she finished her shift and he took her to the Chowder House for dinner.

"And he missed the ferry," Celia snapped. "So you can guess where he spent that night. Bethie was renting a studio apartment in Massacre, but within two weeks she'd left Isadora and moved in with him. Two weeks!"

Celia's outrage seemed to Sunny rather unwarranted, coming from a woman who had kept Isadora Island enthralled with her sex life for years and years. But Sunny merely asked what Wade was doing at the high school. "Is he a teacher?"

"Oh, Sunny, how banal! Wade, a teacher? That would be too easy, too straightforward! He calls himself an educator, a counselor, a healer, but he's a fucking missionary. He brings people his message—oh, you'll hear it, no one is spared. Please, God"—Celia gazed heavenward—"don't let him tell it tomorrow. But sooner or later, Sunny, you'll hear his sad tale. Everyone hears his stories. He has a counseling service in Seattle and he tells all his clients this story. He gives it out at high schools, to kids in juvie, to troubled families: how his life had sunk to the very pits for drugs! He robbed his own mother to get money for drugs! He watched his best friends shoot up heroin with infected needles and die of AIDS." Celia struck her breast theatrically. "He went homeless, he sold his body, he stole for drugs! He was arrested, tried, convicted, went to prison—and even there he somehow got drugs. *Drugs made my life a living hell—and they made that hell tolerable, yea, a heaven,*" Celia concluded with lionesque gravity. "Don't you see? Wade gets it both ways. He gets to be a paragon of sterling strength and a victim of the cruel world. At the same time." She turned the iron off and rubbed both hands across her forehead, as though chasing a headache.

The lights of a car flashed into the yard and Sass and Squatch set up a great howl and Celia said her dogs would have a coronary going after a moth, but they'd welcome the Hillside Strangler. Grant brought in Sunny's bags and started to carry them upstairs, but Sunny protested.

"Oh, let him carry your bags, Sunny," Celia chided her, waving Grant on up the stairs. "No one thinks the less of you here if you let a man carry your bags. It's not like L.A. You don't have to tip him, and he won't ask you to read his screenplay."

Sunny laughed, "I guess Bethie and Victoria have told you some of my stories."

"And you have all summer to tell me the rest, because if you're going to work at Henry's House, you're going to live here. You and Brio will live with me. You can have your old room and stay all summer. It'll be so much fun—have the house full of people again! And I won't hear of anything else."

She fended off Sunny's protest and vanished into the small room where she could listen to her voice mail messages. Strange voices, preceded by electronic pings and beeps. These sounds followed Sunny as she obediently trudged up the creaky stairs, meeting Grant on the landing. He told her there was a lamp in her room, but no overhead light anymore and Sunny replied it was OK, she was used to the dark and she would find her own way.

She'd brought only the one dress, a loose, unstructured thing, grazing her ankles, almond-colored magnolias on a beige background. The fey young man at the Hollywood thrift shop where she'd bought it had assured Sunny that Jean Arthur wore this very dress in one of her films. Sunny bought it on the spot. Brio had two dresses, but no proper party dress, she complained, and no party shoes. Sunny pointed out she too had no party shoes. She was wearing a pair of platform sandals with knee-high stockings.

"At least you don't have to wear shoes like this," Brio complained, pointing to her high-tops.

"Quit squirming and let me tie them up."

"Olivia Hernandez has a party dress and party shoes. Why don't I? Isn't this a party?"

"Yes, yes, Miss Fashion Plate. You sound just like Victoria."

"Who's that?"

"Your aunt. Mama's sister. You'll meet her today. You'll meet the whole tribe of your family today. All at once," she added with less enthusiasm.

Sunny and Brio were to go over to Henry's House early to serve as Celia's emissary while Angie held down the fort in the kitchen and Celia rushed home to effect her own transformation from General MacArthur into mother of the bride. As Sunny and Brio hurried through the orchard along the concrete path, Sunny nonetheless stopped, turned her face to the fine rain and breathed in the smell of spring near the sea, the old lathe of time turning the year, the earth and season. She wrapped herself momentarily in the silence, pocked by gossiping finches, the starlings rustling in the vestigial leaves.

These trees were full of ghosts for Sunny, and their lichen-scabbed branches supported scaffolded specters, shimmering girl-ghosts, voices echoing, singing, calling out, inviting one another to their house or ship or fort or school, whatever function the apple tree was called upon to fill at any given imaginative moment. Orchard protocol was inflexible: one sister could never climb another's tree without an invitation. Adults too were bound by it; once they were in the trees, the sisters were deemed invisible, and Celia or Bobby, any adult, could only summon them by a generalized call through the orchard, never a direct address to a certain tree. This remembered orchard oozed largesse: apples in autumn, shelter in summer, dreams dreamed and songs sung. Sunny could all but hear, stirred by the damp wind, the verses they had made up, "Man of the Moment," to the tune of "Man of La Mancha," lyrics funny and unflattering to Celia's various men, the term itself indelible and unflattering, especially on the day Celia had caught them at it, had heard them laughing, mocking the man of that moment, Phillip, the marine biologist (the lyrics naturally rhyming with *fishes* and *wishes*). Celia had ordered them out of the trees and they stood before her. They were too old to be spanked and too young to be grounded. Sunny was especially afraid, certain she would be dispatched back to Seattle on the very next ferry. Sunny no longer lived on Isadora, but in Seattle with Bobby, though the sisters spent weekends together at one place or another. Standing there, head bowed with Bethie and Victoria, she remembered the terrible insecurity of her position, not being Celia's actual daughter and so, subject to dismissal. Celia berated them soundly, forbade them to sing that song again, threatened dire consequences if they did. But she had punished them equally, not singling Sunny out for exile. She had marched them all over to Henry's House and put them to work polishing furniture since they had all that excess energy.

Excess energy, thought Sunny, coming upon the back garden at Henry's and the service entrance, too bad you couldn't store it in some liquid form, cork it and swill it when needed.

As she let Brio into the kitchen, Angie cried out her name, embraced them both and introduced them to the high school students—all dressed exactly alike, neat black pants, starched white shirts, black bow ties—who were following instructions left by Celia, Angie there to oversee. Angie was a tiny, nervous woman who smelled of Newports. She had indeed brought the cake from Massacre, a three-tiered beauty, white frosting, blue and yellow rosettes. Escorting Sunny through the kitchen, Angie warned her, the task she'd taken on, working for Celia. "Maybe you can organize her. I've been trying for a hundred years and she still does everything in the same haphazard, half-assed way. She doesn't seem to understand that not every decision is an aesthetic decision. Henry's House is a business."

"Not today," Sunny replied. "Today it's a party for Bethie." Angie rolled her eyes. "Well, they're all here."

"But the ferry—"

"Not them. The old Isadorans."

"Of course they would be here," Sunny laughed. Wherever there was food and liquor, preferably free, the old Isadorans would be the first to arrive. They would submerge their long-standing quarrels and would leave only when the liquor ran out. The bar, bartender and half a dozen tables for hors d'oeuvres had been set up in the enormous dining room and indeed, that's where Sunny found them. In a single arthritic whoop of welcome, they greeted the return of the native and her little daughter.

To Sunny, the old artists were yet more evidence that Isadora Island had somehow exempted itself from human time. Not that the old Isadorans hadn't changed—they had, of course, and some had died—but they subscribed to collective memory, unchanging memory, and for them, time stilled, slowed, stopped and they curled round their old antagonisms and ancient gossip. For them, the Henry Girls remained indelibly Bethie, The Charmer; Victoria, The Smart One; Sunny, The Talented One. Sunny's title was bestowed upon her that night of the Christmas pageant at the elementary school, dancing across the stage in her battery-powered dress laced with twinkling lights. So convinced were the old Isadorans that Sunny was, and would always remain, The Talented One, they all asked after her acting career (after all, she'd moved to L.A.; they knew that). They wanted to know why they had never seen her on TV.

"I've never been on TV," Sunny explained, hoping that answer would suggest what had happened to her acting career as well.

Ernton Hapgood, a difficult old man with a stupendous waxed moustache and skin coarse and mottled as an aging potato, patted her shoulder. "Hollywood has no regard for talent. Talent cannot sleep with Mammon, can it?" Peter and Louise Marchand nodded gravely. Befitting ceramicists, both Marchands looked like porcelain dolls, ivory complexions with bright lips, rouged cheeks and dreamy expressions.

An endlessly eccentric lot, the old Isadorans all had artistic pretensions and many had artistic achievements. Their elderly fingers were still nicotine-stained, or paint-stained, clay-stained or ink-stained, and they lived lives pinched by penury and enriched with art. The men were still inevitably rakish, though bald, with big ears and heavy dentures. The white-coiffed women could not be described as matronly; they were regal, despite their advanced ages, aristocratic in their bearing, weird in conversation. The old Isadorans prided themselves on their *La Bohème* sensibilities and would never have been so crass as to ask after Sunny's husband, or the father of her daughter, Brio—who, they all agreed, looked exactly like her, especially now that Sunny's hair was cropped so short, short as a man's. They frowned to see the five rings punched in her ears, and more than one remarked that at least Sunny didn't have a ring in her nose.

"The girl who bags your groceries has a ring in her nose," Nona York interrupted majestically, joining them and enfolding Sunny in a great, warm embrace. "Ah, Sunny! I'd heard you'd come back, but I didn't dare believe it."

"But I only just got here last night."

"This is an island. News travels at the speed of light. Gossip even faster."

Of all the old Isadorans, Nona York was Sunny's favorite. She was a romance novelist, though not a romantic figure. She always wore Wellingtons or shit kickers, or stout shoes, no-nonsense trousers, thick sweaters, and her still-graceful hands twinkled with many rings. Her hair was cut short (though not as short as Sunny's) and it surrounded her face like a silver Roman helmet. Indeed, there was a kind of Roman quality to Nona York. She took everything seriously, and she had never been known to giggle; she was as astute and inquiring on sexual questions as any diplomat on questions of state. She was not, however, always diplomatic. Listening to Nona extol at length the possibilities inherent in flesh-puncturing, Sunny hoped that for the sake of Wade Shumley and his friends, Bethie had forewarned them about Nona, about Ernton and the Marchands (both of whom rouged their cheeks and colored their lips and kohled their eyes).

"I understand that young people puncture and ring themselves in their nipples and in their belly buttons. Lower than that, too," Nona added ominously. Nona spoke always through her nose which was high-bridged and monumental. "But I cannot help but think that a ring through the nipples, the belly button, much less the clitoris, would not enhance coitus. I speak purely physically, of course, and perhaps I'm missing something in the realm of the imagination."

"You would never miss a single thing in that realm," Sunny offered. The room had started to fill with other guests. The old Isadorans were drinking gin, vodka or whiskey. Everyone from Massacre nursed a white wine.

"Personally I cannot imagine submitting to such an indignity as a ring in my flesh. A ring in the flesh, especially the sexual flesh, smacks of slavery, doesn't it?" Nona was wonderfully imperious. "But the truly significant question is why are young people doing it? What does it mean about the way they perceive themselves? And love? What about love?"

Sunny could feel the old Isadorans, their glasses poised, staring at her as though Sunny alone in this room could answer the question. Their clothes smelled faintly of mothballs and their romantic notions ditto, Sunny thought, but it pleased her to be in their company. Having spent all those years in L.A. amongst slouching cynics, buff skeptics and preening egos, these octogenarians with their watery eyes and palsied hands exuded unfashionable exuberance. "Naturally I've been in love. I have a daughter, after all," she added, consonant with their assumption that a love child could only be the fruit of a love union. "But I don't think about romance or men anymore. When you have a child, other things are more important. My daughter is my life."

Few of them had children. Nona, for instance, had never married though she was certainly the resident expert on sex. Titles of her romance novels often took the form of commands, *Take Me to Heaven, Bring Me Your Heart, Bid Me to Fly,* and so on. A fabulously prolific author, Nona's novels had provided Sunny, her sisters and many another island girl with the rudiments of sex education—or romantic standards, depending on the girl. Nona donated copies of each of her books to the island library and York novels filled two shelves with paperbacks, the jackets mostly in vermillion or royal blue, bold gold lettering. In L.A. Sunny was always surprised to see Nona's books lined up, beckoning, at the checkout counter in the supermarket. Did adults actually read these books? The sex was repetitively rapturous. If the scribes of the Middle Ages were renowned for balancing hundreds of angels on the head of a pin, Nona York was equally adept at balancing hundreds of adjectives on the head of a penis.

"We haven't seen your dad on the island for ages," said Nona, clinking the ice cubes in her empty glass. "Is he still married to Chronic Pain?"

"Janice and Bobby are into double digits for their anniversaries."

Nona clucked sympathetically. "Of all Celia's men, Bobby is the one I liked the best. Of course, it doesn't pay to get too attached to any one man. Celia's quite right in that. Men come"—Nona paused significantly—"and then go. Have you met Celia's latest? Russell Lewis? He is her first excursion into academe since she slept with her English teacher."

"She did?"

"They all did."

Nona nodded toward Russell, a portly, middle-aged man who did indeed look very natty and academic, complete with a little bow of worry knotted between his brows. He blinked frequently in the manner of people with annoying contact lenses. Russell had adopted a professorial stance, including an expressively wagging finger. But perhaps, thought Sunny, that's because he's talking to a man so much younger, a tall man clad in a navy blue blazer and wool slacks. Just then this man winked at her. And for the second time Sunny failed to recognize Grant Hayes, no longer stubble-bearded or sweatshirt-clad.

Celia joined them, sailing into the dining room at that moment like a flagship, having effected a transformation from *generalissimo* to mother of the bride. Although that office usually calls for something in organdy pastel, a frock on the order of a petit four, Celia wore a long, rich red dress, glass beads, the simplicity enlivened by high, laced boots and a fringed piano scarf of Aegean blue silk, befitting her Corinthian posture. The orchid corsage she was to have worn pinned to the maternal bosom was tucked rakishly in her hair. She checked her watch and smiled as the string quartet of high school students, set up in the conservatory, broke into strains of Mozart there amongst the potted palms and wicked bromiliads. The floors of Henry's House were teak so the music reverberated underfoot as well as through the air. "Perfect and on schedule," she commented benignly. "The early afternoon ferry will be pulling to the dock just about now. It's twenty minutes from Dog Bay to Useless, twenty-five with traffic. People should be arriving in about a half hour. I am the maestro of timing."

"Some would say the monster," offered Nona.

"It's a question of perspective."

Russell came over, kissed Celia on the cheek; she tucked her arm through his and introduced him to Sunny Jerome, Bobby's oldest girl. Russell was courtly to Sunny in his professorial way, though consternation crossed his face when Celia announced that Sunny and Brio were back for good, that Sunny would be working for her for the Season, the two of them living at Celia's. Nona thought this delightful news, as did Grant who joined them informally, and whatever reservations Russell had, he mastered them quickly and said he looked forward to knowing Sunny very well.

Grant excused himself, wandered over toward his brother, Lee, who waved happily at Sunny from across the room. She did indeed recognize Lee's wife, Robin; they'd gone to elementary school together. She was brought back to the conversation when Nona asked her what her father was doing these days. "I can't remember," Sunny admitted. "I haven't kept up with anyone the past couple of years."

"Whatever he's doing," Celia volunteered, "you can bet it's

something with lots of potential. Bobby is potential personified and I'm sure Janice is getting him vocationally rehabbed—again."

"Bobby has a vocation. He needs a job," Nona declared. "Bobby Jerome will never do anything in the workaday world."

"He certainly never has," commented Russell dryly.

Sunny felt obliged to defend him. "My father is very spiritual."

"So was St. Peter," offered Celia, "but it didn't keep him from working."

Sunny winced on Bobby's behalf and kept her eyes on the floor. Bobby had tried the patience of everyone who ever loved him, including Sunny.

Celia glanced at her watch. Abandoning Russell to Nona, she took Sunny's arm. "They'll be here almost instantly, and I'll need your help. We'll take their coats and reassure this lot."

"Reassure them of what?" asked Sunny, as they walked down the long central hall.

"These will be mostly all Wade's friends. You'll see exactly what I mean."

Celia, the maestro (or monster) of timing, was absolutely correct: the ferry guests began to arrive en masse, their cars pulling up the graveled drive in a sort of sporty cortege. And, since Henry's House had begun life as a school, it had a walled cloakroom off the foyer and Celia tossed people's coats and jackets gaily to a high school student positioned there for that very purpose. As these guests moved into Henry's House, Sunny marveled at the way Celia bathed people in the bright aura of their own importance, paying effortless court to that person's individuality, that individual's personality. If she had met them, Celia remembered their names, their spouses, where they lived, what they did. If she had not met them, they were spontaneously refreshed and refurbished in her presence, made certifiably memorable, engulfed in welcome, awash in warmth. Celia's charm was legendary—if a trifle practiced by now—and she wielded it reflexively rather than reflectively, impersonally as the butterfly who charms the

70

flower. If the flower is uncooperative (and some were), the butterfly moved on, its feelings unhurt, its abilities unimpugned.

"Sunny," cried Celia, peering out the open front door, "hurry! I can see Victoria's car coming up the drive—go find Brio! This'll be such a surprise!"

Sunny found Brio in the conservatory with the string quartet, dancing to Mozart as though the students played for her alone. "I need a new dress," she announced to her mother. "I can tell I'm going to need a dress to live here, and party shoes."

"Yes, yes," Sunny soothed her, took her hand, pulling her down the long hall toward the foyer where Sunny could hear her sisters' voices, her father's laughter. Oh, it had been so long. And as she flew toward the door, Sunny created a wake of excitement behind her as the old Isadorans followed, gathered, listened, watched and collectively held their breath when Sunny burst through the crowd to greet her father, her sisters. She opened her arms to them in a great tsunami of reunion, of surprise, delight, disbelief, of unrestrained emotions, tears of joy, an avalanche of shouts and shrieks, hands flung over open mouths and mascara streaking tearstained faces, people cried and laughed and Sunny was swept into her father's great embrace, breathed in Victoria's rich cologne, felt Bethie's arms enfold her. Brio, clinging to Celia, eyed them all with the grave suspicion of the only child of a single parent.

"And this"—Bobby approached Brio, the look on his face akin to the adoration of the Magi,—"this is my beautiful little Brio. Oh, Brio! Brio! I am your grandpa! Life *con brio!*" And with that he snatched her from Celia, swooped her into his arms and began dancing about the foyer to a tune of his own making, in and out, round about.

Bethie snagged Sunny, hugging her, pushing and propelling her at the same time through the crowded foyer to meet Wade, calling out Wade's name through the crush, bringing them finally face to face. Bethie glowed as she made the introduction, "My sister, Sunny. Sunny, this is my beloved Wade."

From Bethie's ecstatic descriptions of Wade Shumley, Sunny

had always assumed he was her sister's equal in zest and vivacity, that he would percolate sex and energy, so she was surprised to meet a pale, narrow-shouldered, bearded man, flecks of gray at his temples, his thinning hair combed dramatically back from a magnificent forehead where thick brows arched over grave brown eyes, penetrating in their gaze. Lithe and lightly built, Wade was scarcely as tall as Bethie (who had Celia's physical presence) and he probably weighed less.

He wore a sport coat over jeans and a T-shirt with a logo against animal testing and he took Sunny's hands in both of his, consolingly. "Your being here for our engagement is the best present we could possibly have. Elizabeth has told me many things about you, Sunny, but never how beautiful you are."

Sunny murmured that she was glad to meet him at last, flushed and withdrew her hand. Putting one arm around Bethie, and one around Victoria, she watched, misty-eyed, to see Bobby dancing with Brio. Bobby Jerome had acquired bulk with age, but his inborn agility still served him. He had a big nose and twinkling blue eyes, and where Sunny remembered dimples in his face, he now had creases; his hair was almost entirely gray, bristly, caught in an unruly ponytail, as though the hair had been lassoed on his way out the door. Brio's little mouth was wide with laughter and she shrieked with childish delight.

"How long has it been," Nona York asked Celia, "since all the Henry girls have been together?"

Years and years. And yet, anyone could tell to look at the three, that they were united, that they shared some elusive link, an expression perhaps, an energy that translated slightly differently in each of them. Arm in arm, the sisters marveled over one another, over the more obvious changes time had wrought, Bethie and Victoria plucking at Sunny's cropped and stubbly hair, while Sunny commented on Victoria's midwinter tan which testified, it turned out, to a recent week spent at the Robbins family condo on Maui. Victoria walked like a woman accustomed to clay courts and thick carpets. She exuded an informal, mannered chic and she wore a short, smart two-piece suit, mauve silk, matching high heels, gold accessories artfully arranged. Victoria swiftly assessed Sunny's clothes and found them instantly wanting. "You have to come to Seattle soon. I'll take you shopping." Victoria was a marketing analyst at Nordstrom.

"You don't like my dress?" Sunny held out her long skirt, laughing, "It looks like prewar wallpaper, doesn't it?"

"Which war?" asked Bethie as Wade came up behind her. She freed herself from Sunny, turned and put her arms around Wade. "We have to practice our nuptial kiss."

Bethie beamed from every pore. She had arrived at that moment in a woman's life when the present is its own vintage, and will not keep until tomorrow. Bethie had achieved a richness, a succulence somehow beyond the confines of the body proper, a moment that could not be infinitely maintained, but in its midst, even plain women take on a lush orchidean quality. Bethie was not plain. Or perhaps it was not the moment in her life, but the man. Watching Bethie close her eyes, tilt her head, part her lips for Wade, Sunny wondered if anyone had ever been that much in love. She felt like a tourist in a foreign country to witness Bethie's happiness.

Slowly, from the foyer they all flowed toward the central hall, the other rooms, Bobby chiding Celia for keeping Sunny's arrival a secret and Celia swearing she knew nothing before yesterday.

Brio rode high on Bobby's shoulder with the aplomb of a girl who has just discovered the perfect lookout on the world. "Mommy says it's not enough to be a family, you have to *have* a family. I always wanted to have a big family, like Olivia Hernandez, and now I have one. Wait till I tell Olivia," she added with some smugness, under the impression that all one hundred fifty people here were related to her in some indirect fashion, and that she had completely outdone the Hernandez clan. "We're going to live here with Celia."

"You're not going back to California?" Bobby stopped, and turned to Sunny. "You're going to stay!"

Sunny nodded, pinked slightly in the flush of sudden attention, explaining inadequately that she was going to work for Celia.

"You don't want to do that," advised Victoria, as soon as she could pull Sunny from Bobby's ecstatic embrace. "The pay is—well, you know what the pay is. Deplorable."

"Don't stay here," Bethie joined in. "All roads on Isadora Island dead-end into the sea."

"There are no opportunities—like zero—for advancement," Victoria added, taking Sunny's arm. The three sisters freed themselves from the crowd of relatives and well-wishers and moved together in unison, a phalanx of beauty down the hall.

"You don't want to work here, Sunny," Bethie counseled. "Toting laundry? Washing dishes? It's scut work."

"I have other skills"—Sunny paused pensively—"at least I think I do. I was a producer's assistant, after all."

"Listen." Victoria lowered her voice. "Can you use a computer?"

"Of course. Can't everyone?"

"Well then, don't worry. Celia won't have you toting dishes. She's got all that up-to-date equipment, you saw it, didn't you? And she can't use it. It's the truth. She won't admit it, but it's true. E-mail is the end of her abilities. Grant had to teach her that. She says she can't learn the computer, but she's just stubborn and she won't. She's a complete throwback when it comes to the real world. You've seen all those yellow stickies on the fridge and the chewed-up pencils and crazy ledgers. There'll be work for you, believe me."

"Though why you'd want to stay here, I can't imagine," Bethie said. "There are no men on Isadora."

"You found one."

"That was destiny."

Sunny chuckled, "I guess there's always Ernton Hapgood." Ernton was a notorious ladies' man.

"Or, you could always take Russell off Celia's hands," Bethie suggested. "He's pressing her for commitment. Personally, I think

Celia should stick with adulterous affairs. At least with adultery, the man can't make demands on you, can he?"

"That's the theory," Sunny concurred, with an unspoken reflection on her own past.

"I only meant that in any healthy relationship there are mutual demands and obligations, and that's not possible in adultery," Bethie explained. "There's always the imbalance of expectations and the life you share with that person can't ever be a whole life. Not when one person is dividing everything, and expressing anger from one relationship into another, owning both and belonging to no one, not even yourself."

"Ignore her," Victoria advised. "She talks like this all the time now." Though Victoria was the youngest of the Henry girls, she had an incipient furrow between her brows, like an inadvertent slip of the sculptor's chisel on her otherwise exemplary face. "The *simple* way to say it, Bethie, is: if you can't trust a man to tell you the truth, what do you have?"

"A relationship that needs healing," Bethie stated unequivocally. She rattled off lots more phrases, thick and difficult as jawbreakers, they seemed to Sunny, before concluding, "A person who needs to take responsibility for herself, and her actions within a framework of reality, who needs to heal these wounds and recover her childhood, discover her own adulthood, or remain forever a codependent. Come on, Victoria. It's time."

"I don't want to do this."

"You must. You know you must. You have to do this. Today is the day. You want to be an adult, don't you? Then take responsibility for your own choices." Bethie took Victoria's arm firmly, despite her resistance, and marched her off toward Celia. In a nononsense fashion, they collected her as well. The three of them vanished into one of the downstairs bathrooms. The door closed behind them.

"She's going to make Victoria tell Celia she's really married," said Bobby confidentially, coming up beside Sunny, his guitar in one hand, Brio in the other.

LAURA KALPAKIAN

"But it's Victoria's secret, not Bethie's. Victoria shouldn't have to tell the truth till she's ready."

"Bethie says confrontation in the service of healing is justified."

Discouraged from asking any more, Sunny went with him and Brio into one of the smaller sitting rooms, less populated because the food and drink were set up elsewhere. Bobby needed to tune his guitar, readying it for his performance later; he had written a special song for this wonderful occasion. Sunny could have guessed as much; Bobby wrote songs for every occasion, but over the years, they all came to sound the same. He was an accomplished musician with the instincts of a born teacher and patiently he explained to Brio the process of tuning a guitar, though she had no interest whatever in the tuning and awaited only the tunes. Sunny sank back into the comforts of a wing chair and basked in her father's remembered presence, his feckless charm, undiminished, even if it were entirely out of date. He was over fifty, but he retained a youthful disdain for the workday world, for advancement, security, benefits and carpooling. He loved music and poetry, lyrics and children. He had already promised Brio party shoes, Woodland Park Zoo, the Space Needle, sailing this summer, beach picnics and anything else she desired. He tuned the guitar, all the while telling Sunny about his latest songs, his latest lyrics and his conviction that these songs would make him famous, that they would be picked up by big-time stars and sung all over the country. Sunny was the more touched that Bobby's idea of a big-time star was Neil Diamond. She nodded encouragingly, occasionally exclaiming how positive it all sounded, how promising. Bobby was big on promise, and Sunny had long since learned to Let It Be. Let Janice inquire of him *who, where, when* and *what will it cost?* After Bobby's breakup with Celia, Sunny had looked after her father till Janice took him In Hand (this was Janice's favorite phrase and a fair description of their marriage). Janice continually trussed him up with a sport coat, dress shoes, a résumé and vocationally trained him to go out into the real world to get a real job. But Bobby always

76

subverted her, escaped the commute and continued to write music on guitar and piano, continued to give lessons on both instruments to a changing pool of adoring students. Bobby liked dawns and dusks and would sometimes observe these pageants as though the world were his own theater. He was an impossible man who believed all things were yet possible. He clung to his own possibilities, and if potential on the middle-aged looked rather silly, Bobby seemed unaware of any incongruities between his graying hair and his undimmed hopes.

"I'm going to find you a song, Brio, catch you a song just as soon as I can. It'll be called 'Brio's Song.' " Bobby strummed the guitar. "See, it's in here, 'Brio's Song' is inside this guitar and all I have to do is coax it out."

Brio got down on her haunches at his feet and peered into the round guitar and said she didn't see a song in there.

"No? Well, some songs aren't inside. Some just float around, and you have to catch them. They're in the air, melodies, just floating in air, but most people can't hear them. Only certain people. Certain gifted people. Now, Sunny and Bethie and Victoria, they could always hear them. But Sunny was the best. Oh, Sunny could hear a song a mile off. Sometimes she used to come get me and say, Bobby, I heard a song down on Sophia's Beach, you better go catch it! And I would."

"I can't hear any music," Brio pouted, " 'cept for them—" She pointed out the door down the opposite end of the long hall where the high school musicians had abandoned Mozart for Vivaldi.

"You will. You live here on Isadora, and you will hear songs," Bobby promised her. "And when you do, you reach out and catch that melody! Catch it—" He made a swoop with his arm and showed her a closed-up fist.

"Like catching a moth."

"Exactly. You catch it and give it to me and I'll turn it into 'Brio's Song.' "

Preceded by an Altoid pennant on her breath, Janice steamed into the sitting room and found them. "I finally got through to

Celia and we're all sitting at the family table. Todd too, but Celia balked at Mother. Come on, Mother." She waved in the Wookie. "I'll make certain Celia doesn't seat you by Ernton Hapgood. He's already made a pass at Mother," Janice informed them tartly.

The Wookie bawled out a greeting and embraced Sunny, saying how terrible she looked. "Is it the curse, Sunny? The curse used to make me sick."

"Now, Mother. You go sit down and meet your little great-granddaughter, Brio."

Brio gave Sunny a panicked look and ran to her knees, hugged them. "Everything's very strange here for Brio," Sunny explained to the Wookie.

"Everything is very strange here, period," cried Janice. "I don't know who's worse, the ex-addict friends of Wade's or the weird Isadorans. Have you got your speech, dear? Your glasses?" She fussed over Bobby affectionately. Janice was a short woman, short hair, short skirts, short stature, a short, solid sort of woman who wore jewel-tone clothes and high heels on whose narrow stems her muscular calves balanced. Her hair was sprayed until it stood like spun sugar and her mouth pursed in perennial disapproval, or perhaps Chronic Pain. "Really, Sunny, you should have given us some warning, told us you're coming. Why show up at Celia's? You could have come to us. After all your glamorous life, I can't imagine why you'd want to work for Celia. The pay is terrible. It's not what you'd call a career."

"What's Todd doing these days?" asked Sunny, desperate to evade Janice's assertions.

"Todd is going to the community college. With Bobby. Bobby has many gifts but they need updating. He's learning the computer, aren't you?"

"I'm learning on-line."

"You go on-line, dear," Janice corrected, "you don't learn it. What did you do to your hair, Sunny? You don't have any left at all."

"There was an audition for Joan of Arc," she explained, certain that sometime since the invention of celluloid there must surely have been an audition for Joan of Arc. "I was trying to get into character."

Mercifully Janice's place card was not near Sunny's at the head table, the family table which ran the length of the ballroom, facing the mirrored wall. It was called a ballroom, but it had been designed primarily as a practice room for dancers (hence the mirror). In between the beveled windows and all along the walls were elegantly painted murals, opulent Art Nouveau maidens in bleached Maxfield Parrish colors, flowing hair, garlands and Grecian draperies, their breasts undraped, nymphs dancing in the mode of Isadora Duncan—not surprisingly, since the island itself had been freshly renamed Isadora by Sophia Westervelt. (Before she arrived with plans for her school, an Indian name had served this island from the dawn of time.) Sunny's place was between Eric Robbins and Brio, and looking at their collective reflections in the long mirror, she realized only Bethie's people graced the family table. "Where's Wade's family?" she asked her brother-in-law.

"They abandoned him," Eric replied. Eric was a sort of Ken to Victoria's Barbie, good-looking, well-dressed, mild-mannered, unmemorable. "When Wade was a drug addict they abandoned him completely, and they still can't forgive him, even though he's been absolutely clean for eight years. But he's forgiven them."

"It couldn't have been easy, I suppose."

"It wasn't." Eric briefly colored in for Sunny the tale of a man more sinned against than sinning, at least for the last eight years, when, not only had he forsaken drugs, but he had founded ReDiscovery, which was making a huge difference to Recoverees in the greater Seattle area. ReDiscovery wasn't just for addicts. Wade's program had broader applications, but Eric didn't know what they were. Brio tugged on Sunny's other arm, asking her mother to butter her roll. Eric asked Sunny if her daughter were named after the cheese.

The engaged couple had the place of honor, at the center of the table, Victoria beside Bethie, Celia to Wade's left, Bobby to Bethie's right next to Victoria. Bobby rose, put on his half-glasses, arranged his note cards against his water glass and pinged on the wineglass with a fork. High school students moved amongst the round tables, serving the first course, a savory soup, a pale cream of leek, each bowl with a jaunty cap of fresh parsley atop it, and guests leaned forward to breathe in its fragrance, anticipate its taste. The students moved like black-and-white-clad butterflies (a few nose rings amongst them) as Bobby slowly collected the attention of the guests and launched into his speech, announcing this was the happiest day of his life. "To have all three of my girls together for the first time in eight years! To have my beautiful little granddaughter, Brio, here with me at last! My world is complete. My family is complete."

"And Wade," Bethie reminded him in a whisper. "Wade."

"And Wade. Add Wade to my list of blessings. And Eric! Victoria's fine, fine . . ."

Beside him, Victoria murmured that it was OK and Bobby went on to use the actual word, *husband,* creating a tide of surprise amongst the Isadorans present, not that they hadn't already known Victoria was legally married. They had, but they wanted to watch Celia absorb the news. They were disappointed because Celia did not so much as flinch or grimace at *husband.* On the contrary, she actually appeared interested in Bobby's remarks, contexted with quotes from the poets, the Bible and the Beatles, as he came at last to Number Three of his twelve note cards.

"We are all here to celebrate love! True love. Let us say with the poet, with all the poets who have embraced love, that love knoweth no season or clime! Love will defeat the rags of time! Let us celebrate here the love of Bethie and Wade. Love is more important than marriage, though I suppose there are those who would disagree with me."

His wife for one, Sunny noticed, regarding the scowling Janice in the mirror opposite the family table. And clearly, at the various tables, other people disagreed. Eric's mother. What was her name? Victoria had introduced her in-laws to Sunny, but they were a colorless lot, and this wan woman, plucking nervously at her pearl choker, she was . . . ? Dorothy. Dorothy Robbins disagreed with Bobby so vividly, she shivered and her left eye twitched uncontrollably till she put her hand over it. Her husband dozed beside her; Ned Robbins was sporty, corpulent and his bald pate pink from a Maui sunburn. What a disparate crowd they were, Sunny thought from her vantage point overlooking the whole room. Could the marriage of Wade and Bethie truly unite such a group? As Bobby waxed on, eloquent in the service of love, Sunny surveyed the tables, feeling a furtive pang of pity for those Recoverees sitting on either side of Nona York, two young men, their skin still angry about some adolescent outrage. Clearly, Bethie had done nothing to prepare them for the likes of Nona York.

But Celia had carefully placed Grant Hayes beside Launch, as much to protect Launch as anyone else. People always thought him deaf or retarded because he was mute and they often hollered at him cruelly. From across the room, Launch caught Sunny's eye and he waved enthusiastically. He was nicely dressed, no doubt in borrowed clothes, a clean white shirt, buttoned to the neck, though his wild hair and uncombed beard radiated around his face. Grant Hayes winked at her again and Sunny managed a smile in return.

Looking around the gathering, Sunny recognized remnants of her island childhood: Lester Tubbs, silver-haired Ian Ellerman, Dr. Aagard, who had set Sunny's broken arm when she jumped out of the swing, Angie and her sons, two teenage boys who towered over her, over everyone for that matter. There was Nancy, longtime Useless postmistress, the Lattimers from the bakery, and the librarian, Edith Anthony. Though she could not name them, representatives of Isadora's unambitious fishing fleet were easily distinguished, as were the local farmers, who were Celia's suppliers. These men were mostly bearded, burly and uncomfortable in tight-fitting coats and narrow ties, their women brushing wrinkles out of dresses they hadn't worn in years, all of them being exceedingly polite to the high school students serving, who were, for the most part, their own children.

And there was Andrew Hayes—his blond hair gone gray, gone

altogether, lots of it, his big teeth yellowed, his fair skin darkened with age and the weather, his thirty-year loyalty to Budweiser evident in his paunch and the pouches under his eyes. But here he was in a suit, his arm around his wife (Number Three? Number Four?), listening studiously to Bobby Jerome wax on about love. Emollient love. Ennobling love. Bobby said not a word about the old destructive, wrecking-ball love, about sex, about love providing a mere perm for the proverbial beast with two backs. Sunny still thought of Andrew as a beast, blond, hairy, uncaring. She had loathed him, loathed his blue eyes, his big grin, his big hands and the easy lope of his walk, the clank of his tool belt when he came, day after day, to Henry's House, where he was the contractor overseeing its restoration. Sunny had known her stepmother was sleeping with Andrew Hayes before Bobby knew it, maybe even before it actually happened. Subtlety was never Celia's forte. These careless adults had seemed to the children like dinosaurs crashing through the lush world of the Henry girls. Bethie and Sunny and Victoria had all scurried and crouched, trembled like tiny mammals trying to survive this perilous moment, the disintegration of their warm, tropical world, the coming of the cold. Like small, strong, warmhearted, warm-blooded little mammals, furry and fleet, the girls trembled when the dinosaurs thundered, when their footprints gouged the alluvial mud, when they brought massive trees smashing down. And when those dinosaurs succumbed, fell over and died, they crushed all the little creatures below. Sunny wondered if perhaps Celia had come by the notion of the Huggamugwumps, those unlovely little burrowing creatures, by watching children try to evade the fate that giants could impose on them. Sunny put a protective arm around Brio; she would never do that to her daughter. She knew how painful and powerless children felt, remembered the hollow feeling in her heart as she had crouched there under the stairs with her sisters, knowing their parents were breaking up, and they would be severed from one another, their family, their very world.

And look at these destructive giants now. Celia and Bobby, the very picture of the bride's parents, full of rectitude and pomp, not the tiniest indication that all their passion and desire, their lust and hunger had made people crazy and toppled worlds and wrecked marriages and flung children around, yanked Sunny and Bethie and Victoria, Grant and Lee for that matter, in the wake of whoever their parents decided to sleep with next. Look at them all. Middle-aged people for whom all passion was visibly past. They looked contented certainly, complacent probably, boring, no doubt. All tucked happily into ruts. Just as though Andrew never banged Celia blind, never betrayed Bobby, never moved into Bobby's bed, into Bobby's house and eventually inflicted his own two brats on the family. What a lot of wasted energy and emotion, Sunny thought bitterly, all of it squandered so these middle-aged men and women could regard the world and one another cordially, even warmly, as though those old storms had not only passed, but they had never really mattered. Maybe they didn't. Sunny suffered a twinge of envy for these middle-aged people, envied them the time they'd had to put their struggles behind them. To quit caring and call it perspective. Sunny put her lips to her little daughter's bright head, whispered applause for her good manners, her good behavior in the face of Bobby's stupefyingly boring speech.

"We are gathered here today not only to honor the love of Bethie and Wade"—Bobby took a fresh note card from his pile— "but the love of families as well and the achievement of raising children—and those of you who don't think it's an achievement have never had children!" He got a laugh for that and moved on (though not swiftly) to truth and beauty, quoting from Keats and returning to Sophia Westervelt and her idea for the school. How this connected to Bethie and Wade, Sunny did not know. No one did. "Truth and beauty still live on Isadora Island. A haven for unfettered spirits. More in peril now than ever before, since missionaries and technocrats have taken over the world." Bobby took a sip of water.

By now the efficient high school students had served everyone and though there was a general flurry of starched napkins and though wafts of fragrant steam hovered above the bowls of cooling soup, not so much as a spoon was lifted.

"Pity us poor mortals at the end of the twentieth century," Bobby declared ominously, on card Number Eight. "The technocrats have invaded our most private lives! They tell what is Good, what is True, what is Beautiful and prescribe what we must do. They tell us what to eat, what to drink, what to think. Preserve us from the experts who will insist we obey their oppression, and who will call our obedience health!"

Eric bent closer to Sunny. "Does he always sound like he's on the gallows and making his last speech?"

"And the missionaries!" Bobby continued. "They smile and tell us God loves us the more for our repression! They tell us, line up, two by two, one man, one woman, each couple standing before God upon their connubial bed so that we may float into heaven on these little islands of conformity! But I thank God the pagan spirit still lives on Isadora Island! Thank God, poetry and art and music and love still flourish here and pagan souls still dance naked on Sophia's Beach!"

At the mention of dancing naked, Dorothy Robbins shivered violently and seemed to jolt in her chair. Ernton Hapgood leered at the Wookie, and Sunny rather feared the Marchands might peel their clothes off and dance *à la* Isadora Duncan. They had been known to.

"Missionaries and technocrats believe we live in sin, but let me assure you, Dearly Beloved, that the only living sin is to live without love! I hope that Wade and Bethie will live in love always. Make love always. Anyone can have sex. Only lovers can make love. Why can't people say that anymore? *We made love! We make love, damn it!* Why must people say, *We had sex*. Or *We have sex often*, or *They had sex?* It's as though the act of love was a root canal! I don't understand it. I object! To have sex is not the same thing as making love! You can have sex—like you can have lunch. You can have sex, like you can have the flu, or a dentist appointment or an overdrawn check at the bank. To have sex is not a creative act! It's like the difference between Wonder bread and making bread. Wonder bread is a processed product. I might hold Wonder bread in my hand, but that doesn't mean I've made it! Now this bread"—he reached out and hoisted a nearby loaf, held it high—"has been fashioned, created with hands and care and time. The very things you need for making love! One is a creative endeavor and one is not. Only a true lover can actually make love."

Launch jumped up, applauding wildly, grinning, his woolly head bobbing, gray hair waving, white teeth glowing in his leathery face. Beside him, Grant also rose, reluctantly perhaps, but clapping just the same, and slowly the rest of the assembled company rose to their feet, applauding Bobby who smiled, bowed, and in glancing at Janice beside him, received the marital cryptogram that he had best shut up. Raising his glass, Bobby toasted Bethie and Wade and everyone followed suit and Bethie and Wade practiced their nuptial kiss. Bobby warbled more quickly through the rest of his note cards and finally, everyone could eat. The soup was cold.

After lunch, coffee was served in the library at the opposite end of the long hall from the conservatory, but such were the fine acoustics that the music still wafted in. The smokers (including Angie, Nona and Ernton) all bolted outside to smoke on the veranda. Coffee in hand, others strolled through the long hall, the beautifully appointed rooms, though most remained crowded here in the library where the sense of cohesion, conviviality and well-being was augmented by the smell of leather bindings and early narcissus in vases and a bowl of white tulips. The sterling-white tulips waved beneath Ernton Hapgood's oil portrait of Sophia Westervelt, whose clear, gray-eyed gaze went directly across the room to another Hapgood painting, three little girls, Sunny, Bethie, Victoria as children. He had made the girls all look serene and confident.

Sunny came upon this portrait with some surprise, like unexpectedly meeting friends in a place full of strangers. Wade's friends were certainly strangers, and though Sunny did her best to balance their names and faces, there was an unremitting sameness to the

Recoverees. The friends of the groom-to-be were all tentative, subdued, wore athletic shoes, well-washed jeans, and seemed unwilling or unable to make eye contact as they made anxious small talk. Celia was right, they did need reassuring. Strange, Sunny thought, to have her maternal instincts stirred by people who were, many of them, a good deal older than she was.

But odder still was the sensation of seeing Henry's House through their eyes. As she moved amongst them, in a sort of choral unison they enumerated to Sunny the glories of the place: the polished floors and fine rugs, fires burning briskly in the fireplaces, flowers in the vases, the ping of fine china, the ring of silver surfaces.

"You're Elizabeth's sister, so you must have grown up here too," said the pastor who would marry Wade and Bethie. Pastor Lewin was a solid man, perhaps forty, with a doughy complexion, thinning hair and a five o'clock shadow well before five. He had the look of a curator, expertly assessing goods as he turned his saucer over to inspect the mark. "How marvelous it must have been to have such a home."

"We didn't live in this house," Sunny replied. "No one did. No one does. No one's ever lived here. It isn't meant to be lived in." Sunny tried to explain it was meant to be absorbed, experienced, that everything here was designed to affect and for effect, but she seemed to splash and flounder in the effort and Pastor Lewin's attention wandered. He smiled benignly and left for more coffee.

Sunny sipped a glass of water and moved toward the further reaches of the room. She watched the Recoverees as one might watch the seals on Assumption Island. Knowing Celia's true feelings for Wade, Sunny was even more impressed to see her so affectionate to him, absolutely radiating warmth to his friends. Was this reflexive charm, or unmitigated hypocrisy? Sunny rather shrugged at some hypocrisy (believing it to be standard issue for adult life), but Celia was clearly determined to be loved by Wade and his friends, to shower on them some measure of her affection for Bethie. People drew in toward Celia. Her stories had sent ripples of laughter and pleasure eddying through the library, draw-ing people from their own conversations and pulling them into her orbit, a sort of Celia-centric universe where even people she didn't like felt warm and wanted. She did it all so effortlessly, Sunny thought, her warmth expanding, as heat expands.

"I've always rather fancied myself a mother out-law rather than a mother in-law," Celia laughed when someone mentioned how marriage changed people's relations. "But all at once, I find I've got all these new roles. Suddenly I have a granddaughter." She gave an appreciative nod to Sunny, though Brio was not to be found, but off with Bobby somewhere. "I discover today I already have one son-in-law and will shortly have another." Be-hind her logs gave way in the fireplace and a fine pine plume of smoke scented the room. "It just goes to prove that you're never too old to enjoy change. Endure it, anyway."

"Your sister is a very fortunate girl," said a jittery voice behind Sunny and she turned to find an angular young woman with long hair, loosely braided down her back. She introduced herself as Fran from ReDiscovery, noting for Sunny the caps. "Wade is dedicated to doing good in this world. He is a great man. Make no mistake. Wade is dedicated to easing others' pain."

"Well, that presupposes pain, doesn't it?" Sunny replied lightly, knowing she was not equal to hearing, yet again, how lucky Bethie was to be engaged to Wade. Truly, it was as Celia had foretold, and Sunny could certainly understand her impatience with all this Wade-worship. But on the other hand, it didn't necessarily mean he was a pump-sucking pious missionary. "Does Wade require pain?"

"Wade is a good shepherd," Fran replied.

Sunny was about to inquire after Wade's flock, but just then Odd Todd bounded up to her with a burst of brotherly love, hyper-brotherly, as Todd did everything, his awkward enthusiasm exacerbated by an enormous shambling frame, a heavy jaw, thick mustache and great drooping brown eyes. Like the walrus he resembled, Todd too barked and flapped in the crowded library, very nearly spilling more than one cup of coffee as he dithered on to Sunny about North Seattle Community College and his computer classes. Someone had given him the engagement page from the Seattle *Times* for this Sunday, complete with picture of Bethie and Wade looking beatifically happy. When Wade wandered over and joined them, Todd drew his attention to this astonishing coincidence. Wade had graduated from CalState Northridge and Todd's own favorite professor at North Seattle Community College graduated from CalState Northridge! Imagine that!

Wade listened, intensely interested, until Todd, clutching his newspaper clipping, went barreling over toward Janice, who was deep in conversation with Dorothy Robbins. Dorothy continued plucking distractedly at her pearl choker, edging closer to the fireplace while she clucked and bobbed and ineffectually responded to Janice. Nearby sat the Wookie, frowning, indicating approval and disapproval with the same generic snort.

Wade moved a bit closer to Sunny. "It must have been very hard for you."

"Excuse me?"

"I meant, to have had your childhood so ripped up and torn apart, to be split up like that, you and Elizabeth and Victoria."

"Oh, we still saw each other all the time, either here or at my dad's place. Twice a month for sure."

"You didn't feel the pain of separation?"

"Of course we felt it, but—" Sunny stammered, unaccustomed to verbalizing her emotions. "We still had an island childhood. Little savages, that's what we were. That's what you want as a kid. Haven't you ever read *Where the Wild Things Are?* Hasn't Bethie ever told you about the Huggamugwumps?"

He laughed with genuine warmth. "Oh yes, in detail! I've heard more Huggamugwump stories than I care to admit to."

"Has Bethie taken you around Isadora much?"

"Everywhere. She's shared everything with me."

"Well, it's a magical place, especially for a kid."

"Is that why you brought Brio back? Elizabeth thought you'd

never return to Washington, that you had become a real Californian."

"There are no real Californians. There are only people who live there and people who don't. It's not like the Northwest. Up here, to belong, you have to be native. You must know that if you're from Northridge."

A gentle and forebearing smile lingered at his lips. "I'm not from anywhere, really. Military brat. Emphasis on the brat. I'm one of those people from nowhere."

"And no one?"

"My father died a long time ago, when I was just a boy and my mother remarried quickly. She won't have anything to do with me. She has cut me from her life. I'm saddened by that, of course, but I understand her pain." Wade regarded the crowded library reflectively. "Of the many things Elizabeth has helped me ReDiscover, I most value love, friendship and family. You can see I'm blessed with many friends, and Elizabeth is all the family I need."

"Well, in that case," Sunny said dubiously, "you might be getting more than you bargained for." She regarded her extended family, overextended, like credit or debt: Odd Todd ricocheting around the room perilously close to where Victoria's father-in-law had surrounded himself with a bevy of his sons, a sort of circling of the Robbins wagons to ward off Todd. Bethie was showing off her engagement ring to Lee and Launch, and not far distant Celia charmed the socks off rapt Recoverees whose solemn little faces lit with laughter, whose spirits seemed to rise, buoyant with the warm, wood-smoke scented air. Other Recoverees, not so fortunate, were in the thrall of Nona York who was describing herself as the Amelia Earhart of romance novels, and extolling the historical significance of her heroines: the first in their genre to give blow jobs. Grant, pinioned to the bookshelves by Russell Lewis, nodded gravely as Russell described his own wonderful chiropractor, and the groin injury he—Russell—had been cured of, certain that an old football injury of Grant's could be similarly cured. Fascinating material, Sunny could tell, just from looking at the faces of Russell's two wretched teenage children, sitting side by side, their knees pressed together, lips closed over their braces. Bobby bounced in with Brio and his guitar, announced he was ready to perform. Janice had Victoria in the grip of Chronic Pain. The Wookie was fending off Ernton's attentions. Eric fussed over his mother, Dorothy, whose knuckles had gone white clutching her pearl choker. Surely this was what Dante had in mind for hell. Why would anyone willingly marry into this? Sunny shook her head. "I'd take the ferry to Vladivostok rather than marry into this family."

"It was important for Elizabeth to include her whole family in this occasion, in our happiness. She knew that everyone needed this healing moment to accept one another."

"Oh."

"There've been so many breakups and so many hurt feelings and the traumas of so many men in your mother's life, so many surrogate fathers."

"Celia's not my mother. She's my stepmother. Ex-step-mother." Sunny squirmed slightly. "Bethie actually told you all that stuff?"

"We have no secrets. Our relationship is based on complete emotional honesty and responsibility. Elizabeth is my life. She's made me realize everything I've missed in the world. I spent all those years messed up on crack and for the last eight years I've been so fulfilled with ReDiscovery, I've forgotten what it is to be loved. In fact, I've never known what it is to be loved as she loves me—and as I love her. Elizabeth taught me all that, and I'm grateful."

"I can't think of her as Elizabeth," Sunny confessed.

"Elizabeth Ann Shumley," he mused. "The three most beautiful words in the language."

"That's not her real name, you know. They chose those names. Well, Bethie chose them. Victoria was still pretty little, but Bethie just announced one day that they wanted to be queens, and they were changing their names to Elizabeth and Victoria." From the look on Wade's face, she instantly regretted her revelation, but there was no turning back. "What could Celia do about it? When you subscribe to the Unfettered Life, as Celia always has, you can't just deny people the right to choose their own names, even if they are in elementary school. Besides, when Bethie sets her mind to make you do something, well . . ." Sunny's voice trailed off.

"What are their real names?" asked Wade, the genial set of his mouth tightening slightly.

"I shouldn't have said anything. I'm a firm believer in keeping secrets, and I've broken my own rule, haven't I? It's Bethie's secret to tell, not mine."

"Bethie and I have no secrets."

Sunny was spared any reply because Bethie waltzed over, took Wade's arm, practiced again their nuptial kiss. She implored Sunny to come visit them at their condo in the Wallingford district in Seattle, and to see the offices of ReDiscovery, in fact to come to some of the ReDiscovery workshops.

"But I'm not a drug addict," Sunny protested.

"Everyone is a victim to something," Wade smiled.

Victoria bore down on them, again clucking over Sunny's too-short hair, her ill-fitting dress and her unlovely makeup. "For someone who was an actress and a model, Sunny, you have no fashion sense whatever. You'll just have to come shopping with me soon. Really soon," she added, with a critical look, up and down. "The rope-heeled platforms have to go. The Lancôme rep is a friend of mine and—"

"Did you tell her?" Eric burst in on them, interrupting Victoria's plans for Sunny's makeover. "I have to go to the car to get Mom's sweater and her heart pills, but I want to know if you did it. Why won't you tell me? Did she?" he inquired bluntly of Bethie.

"Victoria has to learn to speak up for herself. Go on, Victoria." In the shelter of Wade's embrace, Bethie regarded her sister expectantly.

Victoria studied her French manicure. She indicated in a series of staccato retorts that, yes, she had told Celia they were actually, legally married. There was a tiny chip in the polish of her index finger and Victoria applied herself to it. "Celia wasn't surprised and she wasn't angry. She wasn't anything. She didn't say anything, really. I don't think she cared one way or the other. It was all anticlimactic, and I wish, Bethie, you had not made such an issue of it. I would have told Celia, in time."

"In time? What time!" demanded Eric. "When hell freezes over? When pigs fly?"

"In time. I would have—"

"A year!" Eric lowered his voice. He looked like Ken when Barbie wouldn't let him drive. "I can't believe for a year you never told your mother we were married, Victoria! That's why we went to the judge's office and did it all so fast and hush-hush, wasn't it? So you wouldn't have to tell your mother! Are you afraid of Celia?"

"Of course not. It just didn't seem worth the effort."

"Marriage to me? Marrying me wasn't worth the effort!"

"It isn't you, Eric. It's just the way she is. Trust me. I know my own mother." Victoria cast a look of extreme pissedness to Bethie and tried to soothe Eric who was having none of it.

Sunny wanted to console poor Eric who felt undervalued, even unloved. She thought Bethie was wrong to have pushed the issue, but her heart broke for Victoria. All her life Victoria had fought her parents' romantic values: The Smart One, high school valedictorian, straight-A student, Island Rotary Girl of the Year, Junior Achievement, alumni scholarship to the University of Washington. Victoria Henry (Jerome) had always been an exemplary achiever, and in any other family she would have been the paragon of perfection. In her own family she was completely anomalous. Her father went in for daytime dreaming and ambition unsullied by action. Her mother ran a business like a work of art, ran people's lives, ran through lovers, raised five kids, cooked for hundreds, had had people in and out of her home for years, and yet subscribed to the Unfettered Life. Victoria had not the slightest use, ever, for the Unfettered Life, or Love Unfettered, and she had shed these values and this island as soon as she could. Proudly, bravely and against her family's values, Victoria had gone to the University of Washington where she had picked Eric out of an Econ class, tried him on for size, as one might try on Italian pumps. Like the pumps, Eric was comfortable and becoming, and immediately after graduation, she took him to the judge's office and married him. With her university degree she got an enviable job in marketing, at Nordstrom; she was the driver of a BMW with gold hubcaps, the owner of a lake-view home in Bellevue, not far from her in-laws' gorgeous place. She was a married woman of style, substance and assured upward mobility in the grown-up world. She had fulfilled ambitions undreamed of by the residents of artsy-fartsy Useless Point. Yet she had not had the courage to tell her mother she had legally wed the inoffensive Eric Robbins. And now, since Celia did not seem to care, the keeping of the secret looked pitiful, ludicrous, and Victoria's single failure of courage was public.

"Your mother is a nutburger," Eric muttered. "Everyone on this island is as weird as owl shit, if you ask me."

"Well, Celia's right about one thing"—warning rattled in Victoria's voice as surely as if the marine radio squawked nearby, —"if you don't get married, you don't have to get divorced."

But Eric plunged heedlessly into danger. "What does Celia think happened with her and Bobby? What does she call that? Mint chocolate chip? So they didn't get legally divorced! The effect on you—on all of you—was the same, wasn't it? They are divorced even if they never got married."

"Sunny never got married, did you, Sunny?" Victoria turned briskly to her sister.

"I never wanted to marry. I only wanted Brio."

"Have you ever been married, Wade?" asked Victoria, desperate now for some backup.

He drew Bethie's arm through his and kissed her forehead. "I've never been married. For that courage and commitment, you need someone to love and to teach you love. Now, with Elizabeth, I'm ready for that challenge."

"Wade was waiting to get married till he met me," Bethie beamed. "Destiny. Just like Celia and Henry."

"Oh God, spare me Henry Westervelt!" Victoria rolled her eyes, "I'm sick of all this crap and blather about love. I hate love. I hate hearing about it, talking about it. Look, Eric, I've told my mother. I've done it. What more can I do? What do you want of me? Some belated bachelor party?"

"I want to know why you could not admit you'd married me, why all this time has passed and—"

"Sometimes maturity doesn't always come with growing up," Wade offered, his palms upturned, his face serene. "So we must free ourselves from the old dependencies, we must stand up and be new, rinse off the sources of confusion and abuse, and learn to give ourselves permission to be free. And sometimes that permission itself is painful, and through that pain we recover and discover."

"Oh, balls." Victoria walked out of the library, her high heels clicking on the teak floors, Eric right behind her on his way down to the car to get his mother's sweater and her digitalis pills.

"Misdirected anger only hurts the emanator," Wade commented.

"Victoria will get over it," Bethie laughed. "That's just the way she is. Her room was always neat, her clothes were always ironed and her homework always done. You can't hold it against her. Look, there's Grant. He's going to be an usher at our wedding in November, Sunny. Him and Lee both." She waved to Grant who smiled and strolled toward them. "Honestly, honey"—she held Wade close to her—"you can't imagine Grant and Lee when they were kids. Such nasty snots! They were so mean and always in trouble. They used to pull the heads off our dolls. They stole their father's truck and wrecked it on a logging road. Andrew used to beat them. Tried to anyway. But they got big fast. They were awful, weren't they, Sunny?"

"Beasts."

"But they could be tons of fun. Remember, Sunny, they taught us to smoke cigarettes?"

"First and last time I ever smoked."

"Grant lives on a boat now. I bet he'll take us out in it this summer, Wade. He lives on this boat over in the Massacre Marina, don't you, Grant?" she asked when he joined them. "What is it called? Some funny Greek name."

"Pythagoras."

"That have to do with math?" asked Bethie.

"With symmetry."

No one knew quite what he meant and he did not elaborate, but he turned to Sunny and asked if she would like to dance.

"There isn't any music."

"Listen."

From the conservatory and over the voices came the sounds of the string quartet. "You can't dance to Mozart," Sunny replied.

"You can if you live *con brio*."

But Sunny excused herself to find her daughter, and Bobby strummed his guitar and announced he'd written a special song for Bethie and Wade's engagement and he would now perform. The happy couple practiced their nuptial kiss.

PART III

The Maid of Dove

Dorothy Robbins was cold. Exceptionally cold these days and she didn't understand why. Long since finished with the indignities of menopause, Dorothy was annoyed, of late, to be so inconvenienced by her body which was generally so cooperative. She had sent her son Eric to the car to get her sweater and her digitalis pills, but her hands were so cold, they were beginning to ache, and she could hardly chafe them vigorously in the library with all those awful people about. Someone might think she was applauding Bobby Jerome's singing. Far from it. What a wretched lot they were, Victoria's family. Imagine, quarreling, talking about groin injuries at a party, discussing blow jobs to Amelia Earhart. Disgusting. Dorothy decided to warm her cold hands under hot water, but three or four women were already waiting in line for the downstairs bathroom, and had been there for a while, judging from their chummy conversation. Thank you, no. Dorothy went upstairs. Far better. Even had there not been a line, Dorothy preferred to undertake all bathroom activities, however innocuous, far from the madding crowd, so to speak. She had always been like that. Even as a college student at the University of Washington, she would never enter a stall directly adjacent to one already occupied. To do so seemed to her, if not a breach of etiquette, at least a lapse of taste.

Climbing the gleaming staircase she came to the second floor of Henry's House which was unheated, chilled actually, but she found a bathroom that suited her. She was gratified too to escape the party. Though she did not need to pee, she did so anyway, remembering some wordless edict of her mother's. Turning on the hot water, Dorothy chafed her hands over and over, rubbed them, ran hot water over them. It must have been the long ferryboat ride over to the island which had penetrated her bones with cold. She made a mental note to wait for summer, high summer, August, before she went on the boat with Ned and the boys.

She thought of them as boys, but all her sons were grown men now. Eric, the youngest, was the one she most doted on, perhaps because he was her unexpected gift in middle age, or maybe he truly was the most winsome of the four. Or perhaps it was merely a process of elimination. The other three all seemed strangers to Dorothy, like colleagues of her husband's, colleague-clones she might have met at professional parties of like-minded stockbrokers in similar Seattle firms, and not at all like boys she once had snuggled and adored. Moreover they were not adorable, her sons. She had to admit it, to herself alone perhaps. Dorothy's regard for the truth kept her honest, if not candid.

Like her other sons, Eric had married young, but unlike them, he was not eager to drop his old affection for his mother, to trade his love for his mother for an exclusive allegiance to his wife. In fact, Eric's wife didn't seem all that interested in staking out territorial claims to his affection, not like Dorothy's other daughters-in-law had done. Why, those other boys were all but picketed and posted *no trespassing* within months of their marriages. Victoria was different. You wouldn't have known it to look at her. She looked like all the other daughters-in-law: pretty, chic, groomed, coiffed, plenty of exercise at the gym, vitamins, fresh fruit and vegetables, mineral water, poached fish. That sort of thing. And, like them, Victoria was a professional. Were all young women professionals now? When Dorothy was a young woman, she and the other wives talked of their children, their husbands, their golf game, their bridge game, but young women now talked incessantly of the Workplace, talk in which Dorothy could not share, and in truth, had no interest. Victoria too talked of the Workplace. She was a buyer, or in marketing or some such thing for Nordstrom. Handbags, wasn't it? Accessories? She always gave Dorothy accessories for Christmas. So yes, Victoria looked like all the other girls, wives to her sons, and she sounded like them, and seemed yes, very nice, and though her parents were divorced (divorce was common enough. Fine. And remarriage, well, that was a fact of modern life), there was nothing upon meeting Victoria that would have suggested to Dorothy and Ned—never mind to Eric!—that she came from such a revolting tribe of noisy and licentious weirdos.

The poor girl. No wonder she kept her distance from her mother and father. Such an awful father. That ponytail! And he brought his awful guitar everywhere and wrote awful songs and played them. Sang them, even. He wrote poetry too, he told Dorothy this afternoon. Though Dorothy's facial expression had never changed, inwardly she had murmured, *Spare me, spare me.* He gave piano lessons, though not for a living, a living was provided by his wife, Janice. Janice, Victoria's stepmother, was not at all *simpatico* to Dorothy. Too brusque and too ready with confidences. Dorothy did not approve of unwarranted confidences, in short, gossip, but she had listened, nonetheless, in the library, coffee in hand, to Janice's *sotto voce* tales of Victoria's mother, Celia. Celia was overbearing, always believed she knew best, inflicted her views on people. Celia was a great bully, Janice said. Celia was the island slut and everyone knew it. Janice pointed out Russell Lewis and said he was sleeping with Celia now, poor slob. Janice in fact, pointed out half a dozen men she was certain Celia had slept with, or would sleep with if the occasion arose. Moreover, Celia had a real loaves-and-fishes complex. And when Dorothy had inquired quite what a loaves-and-fishes complex might be, Janice retorted that Celia thought she could feed the five hundred and make magic at the same time; Celia thought Henry's House was a work of art instead of a mere B-and-B, a commercial establishment for tourists.

Perhaps. But here in this upstairs bathroom Dorothy's eye fell on a tiny vase of snowdrops tucked in a corner where a guest would come upon it as one would a work of art, a gratifying surprise to the senses. The towels were stacked and arranged so that their individual textures were evident and eye-pleasing, and on the shelf just above the inviting claw-footed tub, a whole array of bubble bath bottles gleamed and twinkled, the light somehow caught liquidly within.

Leaving the bathroom, Dorothy paused momentarily as voices and laughter from the first floor, applause for Bobby floated up. But rather than rejoin the party, she turned right and wandered down the long hall, ambling, taking her time, regarding the framed pictures—prints, watercolors, a few photographs—which drew her attention, and rewarded her, each in some distinct way. She fondled the satin fabrics on chairs which stood like little sentinels along the hall and touched the polished wood of small tables with curved and graceful legs. She opened doors as she passed along the hall, glancing into bedrooms. She found even a small sitting room created from a space too small to be a bedroom and too big to be a closet, and in here she saw library shelves half filled with old volumes and two leather chairs, a table in between. Pausing, Dorothy breathed deep: pipe tobacco, a smell wholly masculine. Indeed a pipe stand sat upon the table, pipes with blackened bowls. She sniffed from each, as though they were flowers, *Daddy, Daddy,* as though her father might yet be there, snoozing over his evening paper, as he had when Dorothy was a child, her parents' only child, beloved by and of them. Daddy had owned a small newsstand, a little shop in downtown Seattle till urban renewal put him out of business, and then he worked for others, long hours, low pay and no respect. But Daddy never complained, asked only to have his pipe and paper at the end of the day, and a smile from his wife and daughter. She could all but see Daddy, so Dorothy closed the door softly, not to disturb him, and proceeded along the hall.

It was all very lovely here, but Dorothy reserved her especial admiration, her downright wonder, for the floors. The floors were dazzling. Of course everything at Henry's House was meant to be nice (it was, as Janice pointed out, a commercial establishment, and that was its job to be nice, to be lovely) but these polished teak floors, these voluptuous ribbons of gleaming wood, alongside pale, thick rugs, these floors were dazzling!

In making these judgments, Dorothy Robbins had reached her frontiers of expression. For Dorothy virtually everything could be slotted, described, adequately invoked as *Nice,* or *Lovely,* reserving *Dazzling* for the Vatican which she had seen with Neddy on their honeymoon. Admittedly, on occasion, when honesty and candor were at odds, Dorothy had been known to use *Dazzling* to conceal patently false statements, but in general Dorothy Robbins preferred to keep the carriage of her conduct behind those two well-known dapple-gray words: *Nice* and *Lovely.* The floors at Henry's House, however, were dazzling.

Dorothy often judged people by their floors, knowing full well that she shouldn't, that it was impolite, politically incorrect and probably very narrow to do so. After all, there were people who didn't have enough money to keep up their floors. There were people who didn't have enough time, who worked long, numbing hours at wretched jobs for paltry pay, processing fish in canneries or processing checks in banks, people who had delinquent children or unfaithful husbands, people who had been beaten down or cracked up, who were strung out, or hungover, people who couldn't possibly keep their floors up. Dorothy didn't disparage them for it. But an unpolished floor always seemed to her to betray a lack of—well, perhaps only a disregard for detail, pointing to some larger lapse. Dorothy had always kept her own floors polished. She had kept her own house and reared her own children and cooked the family's meals and paid the family's bills and mowed the family's lawn, unlike her daughters-in-law who all had housekeepers, nannies, accountants, lawn services and someone to do the floors and carpets every three months. No, if Dorothy could judge Celia Henry by her floors alone, Dorothy would be—in fact, was—rapt with admiration. She and Celia might have been very good friends indeed.

Bobby Jerome must at last be finished because she could hear the string quartet launch into an exuberant Vivaldi which wafted upstairs. Dorothy would have gone back down, but there were too many people, a hundred or more, and they were all too weird: those people in jeans recovering, discovering and sharing their ill-bred pain. Those people were completely foreign. They all talked in phrases, a language Dorothy didn't exactly understand, and it was too exhausting to translate. Talking to the Recoverees reminded her of the time she had had to use her high school Spanish in Vera Cruz, Mexico, explaining to the pharmacist that she needed something for the diarrhea. Dorothy shivered. And those uniformly queer old people! The couple who both wore lipstick and eye shadow. The old paint-stained artist leering at the women. The novelist nattering about blow jobs! Novelist? Too kind. A scribbler of trash pandering to low instincts in ill-bred female readers. Pity the trees that died to provide that woman with paper. And then, then there were the silent fishermen and the taciturn farmers. In short, there were too many people who were not from Bellevue.

Dorothy would not go back downstairs. She went into the bedroom at the very end of the hall and opened the door, walked into a large room, of pale pink and green, its colors reminiscent of that moment in spring where the cherry tree blossoms fought their valiant, losing battle against the leaves. Thick matching rugs on (dazzling) floors echoed these tender sentiments and though the drapes appeared to be white, actually the faintest nuancical green tints hovered in their folds. Dorothy closed the door behind her, breathing deeply, suddenly out of breath, desperately chilled and weak, her heart racing violently, as though she had run up-stairs, run and run. She would collect herself here, and then go downstairs to get her sweater and her digitalis pills from Eric.

When she opened her eyes, Dorothy's glance first fell upon minute sprigs of pink azalea in a crystal vase which sat atop some books on a nightstand next to the big brass bed. A straw hat perched upon one of the bed's four brass knobs, as if some glad-some girl had just breezed in, left her hat and breezed out. In search of adventure, Dorothy thought, a girl in search of adven-ture. With the image of the gladsome girl in mind, it was rather a shock to turn to the mirror and see her own face.

Dorothy toyed with the pearl choker she habitually wore. An involuntary tremor rattled her left eyelid. She peered more closely into the mirror, strained and leaned toward it. She should have brought her handbag upstairs for a refresher on the lipstick. Was it the gray afternoon light that made her look so pale, chalky? Or was it her old self in contrast with the spring evoked here, the ineluctable pinks and flirtatious greens in this room? With both hands she smoothed her short, dark, curled hair. Dorothy had had her hair colored the same color, her natural color, in the same salon and by the same hands for the past twenty years. Maybe twenty-five. All right, maybe more. She always thought of the hair-coloring process as the Triumph of Art Over Nature. But could it be—she frowned at the woman in the mirror—that Nature had played a nasty trick on Art? She had kept her hair its natural color, but it no longer looked natural. She realized with a little start that her dark hair atop her gray face made her resemble one of those ice cream cones at Dairy Queen, pale vanilla, all soft and conical, dipped into dark chocolate, the chocolate sitting on it like a cap. That's what her hair looked like atop her white face. The effect was neither nice nor lovely, dazzling only in the negative. Slowly she sat down on the bed and shivered.

She might have lain down, gotten under the covers to warm up, but it smacked of Goldilocks and no grown woman could do such a thing. Lying at the foot of the bed, though, she saw a beautifully handworked afghan, a creamy pink color with green highlights, and in the center of it, flowing letters, the name *Clara*. She wondered fleetingly who Clara might be, but she wrapped the afghan around her shoulders, hugging it for warmth. She took off her shoes and chafed her cold feet before padding about the room in her stockings.

On the writing desk Dorothy was delighted to find another little vase with tight little apple blossom sprigs, and to see there was real ink in the capped crystal inkwell, blue ink, and thick writing paper with blue letters. Neatly stacked, the paper awaited only the pen which also lay nearby, a real pen with a steel nib. At the top the writing paper was embossed with blue letters:

HENRY'S HOUSE
USELESS POINT
ISADORA ISLAND
WASHINGTON

No mention that it was a B-and-B, a commercial establishment. No phone. No zip code for that matter. Dorothy sat down at the desk, picked up the pen, dipped it in the ink, consumed by the need to feel the pen in her hands, to see letters flow from its inky nib, words formed and absorbed by the paper, to write tenderly to someone, oh, to write to someone. Who? Mother. *Dear Mother*—Long dead. So very long dead was Dorothy's mother, but in the quietude of this room, Dorothy knew her mother would have been comfortable. Happy. Daddy would have been happy here. Dorothy was happy. She regarded the carriage clock on the desk and it ticked comfortingly. Of course. How caring of Celia and what an eye for detail! All the clocks in Henry's House ticked. They had to be wound. There were no electronics. No beeping microwaves, no glaring numbers flashing *12:00* from the VCR. No VCR. No television. Was that possible! And no radios either. No ubiquitous telephones, no fax machines or computers burping and tweeping and chirping their electronic chirps. In these rooms people were obliged to talk.

That was the great pleasure here, wasn't it? Dorothy turned

back to regard the room afresh, reassess it altogether. Beautifully hung pictures in perfect frames. Old books on the little table beside the brass bed. Books so well used and loved, their bindings were gray at the ends like the stubble of beards on old men's chins. People in these rooms must talk or read—or make love, came the thought, unbidden. She remembered Bobby Jerome's dreadful, windbaggy speech, but at the conclusion he was right, wasn't he? Making love was a creative endeavor. Talking could be a creative endeavor. Reading could be. And these rooms were full of such endeavor, thought Dorothy, rising and going to the French doors. Here, in a room like this, you would make wholesome love, love unsullied by time, uneroded by doubt, untarnished by lies, omissions or innuendo. True love. Love that would endure. Or, if it did not endure, at the very least, love you would not forget. You would think of these things in a room like this. Even if you came here alone.

Clutching *Clara* to her shoulders, Dorothy looked out the French doors. The roof of the long veranda formed a sort of balcony for those rooms opening on to it and in the cobbled driveway far below, Dorothy could see Eric engaged in what was clearly a quarrel with Victoria. Dorothy waved energetically, but Eric did not see her and slowly her wave died a self-conscious death. She felt silly. Like a ghost her own best-beloved son could not see.

She turned and walked to the window that gave out, not to the drive and the lawn, but to the Sound alone. There was a lamp on the table in front of it, and the lamp was turned on. The drapes had been parted and tied back. Was this the famous window of Victoria's story? Victoria had told the Robbinses Celia's story, in fits and starts. And stops, Dorothy remembered rather sourly. The story hadn't come out until after Eric had married Victoria and by then, Dorothy was already convinced her son had engaged his affections unwisely. But it was too late. Poor Eric. Allied to a family like Victoria's. Though Ned did not see it the same way. It raised Victoria in Ned's eyes that she was related to the Westervelts, even though Dorothy reminded him—

over and over, really got impatient with him, the number of times she had to tell him—that Victoria was *not* related to the Westervelts. Ned always bit back, yes, yes, he understood, he wasn't a fool, was he? He understood that the late Henry Westervelt was Celia's first husband, not Victoria's father and not the father of the other girl either. No one's father. And yet, Ned maintained, you couldn't deny there was a certain *connection*. Victoria herself had said so, words to the effect that Henry Westervelt was part of their lives and in strange ways, he was like a father. They were known as the Henry girls. All of them. And then there was this window. Dorothy was certain it was this very window. Look at the lamp, burning away in mid-afternoon.

Victoria had told them that in the off-season, Celia kept the lamp lit in a window that overlooked the bay and Useless Point. She did it for Henry. In case he needed the beacon, needed a point of light to find his way home, to Henry's House.

To leave a light on for a dead man had struck Dorothy as inefficient. It had struck Ned as crackpotted, hairbrained and stupid, until Victoria had added that the dead man in question, her mother's first husband, was named Henry Westervelt. "But not Victoria's father," Dorothy reminded Ned tartly, though he was not here to accept her correction. Oh, the name Westervelt just slew Neddy to pieces. Admittedly, it would have done the same to any Northwesterner and the Robbinses were native Washingtonians—and proud of it. How could you live in Washington and not know the name Westervelt? Westervelt logging had made the Northwest great long before Boeing ever came to Seattle and started building planes, and a century before Bill Gates started manufacturing his little chips of electronic whatnot. For a hundred years, more, the Westervelts were logging their way through the Cascades, through the Olympic Peninsula, through the San Juan Islands. Their lumber operations had helped build railroads and shipping lines and their mills kept whole towns afloat all over the Northwest. Honestly, as Ned had pointed out, you couldn't go to the toilet without thinking of the Westervelts since their mills manufactured the toilet paper you wiped your butt with.

Dorothy thought this allusion less than lovely on Ned's part. It was in keeping, however, with the mind of a man who would name his boat *Strumpet*. Dorothy disliked the boat, but she loathed its name, *Strumpet*. She felt it always as an indirect insult, a sly jab at her. He had chosen the name, Ned had, without telling her and when she saw it brazened there across the bow, she felt always that it was an indictment, public notice that Dorothy had not given Ned what he wanted, that Ned had—or would have liked to have had—a strumpet to pleasure him in ways his wife wouldn't do. He called the boat a pleasure craft, though it was a 40-foot Tollycraft powerboat. Power more than pleasure. The *Strumpet* gave Dorothy no pleasure whatever. People made jokes about the name and when they did so in Dorothy's hearing, she felt these jokes were jibes at her, stabs at her inadequacies, those inadequacies publicly alluded to, and made the butt of jokes. "Wipe your butt indeed," she snapped at no one. No one here.

From the advent of the *Strumpet* into her married life, Dorothy had drawn away from Ned, oh, not so pointedly that he would have noticed, but drew away nonetheless. Since she had been first and foremost a wife and mother, and since her children were grown and gone, and *mother* was ended, when she drew away from *wife,* she found she had no other avenues for her affections, or her energies. Such as they were. And so, Dorothy had redoubled her efforts on her clean house, a perfect home, perfectly clean. Perfect. And she had the most dazzling floors in Bellevue. In all Washington State. At least that's what she'd thought until she came here to Henry's House.

Ned had asked Victoria why her mother didn't call it West-ervelt House and Victoria had replied that Celia detested the Westervelts, quarreled with them after Henry's death, so bitterly she would not even wear their famous name, called herself Celia Henry, and that Victoria had been actually Victoria Jerome, though everyone knew her as Victoria Henry. Now, of course, she was Victoria Robbins. Eric's wife.

Oh, Eric! Darling Eric! Dorothy clutched *Clara* tighter to her shoulders and walked back to the French doors overlooking the drive, hoping for another sight of her beautiful son, but he had gone. Now Dorothy knew why Victoria had not planted her little wifely stakes all over Eric like all the other daughters-in-law. Just a few days ago, Eric had told Dorothy that Victoria confessed to him she'd never told her mother they were married, legally wed. Celia had been conveniently left with the impression that Victoria and Eric were living in sin, domestic partners, as Victoria so coyly put it. Eric had told Dorothy all this, confided in his mother how it hurt, really, to know that Victoria had not told Celia she had married the man she loved. Dreadful. *Dreadful,* said Dorothy. But she was secretly touched; his telling her this proved that Eric had not altogether left his old mother, that he trusted her with his feelings and his confidences. This made Dorothy proud and happy, though she was sad for him at the same time. *Now I understand,* Dorothy had said soothingly to her best-loved boy, *I understand why you went to the judge one afternoon and had no proper wedding at all.* (Though she had not added, wouldn't want to hurt Eric by saying that she, personally, had been heartbroken that her dear boy, her favorite, should call her from a downtown phone booth to say he'd gotten married in a judge's office on his lunch hour.)

When Victoria had declined Dorothy's offer of a wedding reception (wouldn't hear of it, *would not, would not, would not),* Eric just thought his bride was delightfully unconventional. But now they knew the truth of it, didn't they? Sweeping *Clara* up in her arms, Dorothy paced the room hoping to get warmer, admitting to herself at last (honesty if not candor) she was glad she didn't have to give them a wedding reception. So hard on the floors, guests were. Scruff and scrape, the high heels making nasty little jab marks in the wax. But to let a year go by before Victoria told her mother. Really! And at that—Eric's sweet voice had trembled—Victoria wouldn't have said a word to Celia, but Bethie made her! The sister who was getting married said this lie could not continue: Victoria must tell Celia. And she must tell her this very day, at the engagement party. Eric told Dorothy he was crushed, hurt beyond words. *You'd think she'd be proud, Mom, proud I married her instead of just living together. I made a commitment, Mom. What did she make?*

For this Dorothy had no answer, and though she tried to comfort Eric, it remained a thorny question. Why: what made Victoria so reluctant to acknowledge to her mother the fact that she had gotten married? Why wouldn't she tell Celia? And slowly, it came out. Or rather, slowly Dorothy came to understand that Celia did not believe in marriage, hated marriage and thought anyone who committed it was a fettered prisoner caught in the shackles of society's twin claws, Custom and Oppression. Celia in fact had refused to marry any man after Henry. That meant Celia had not married Bobby Jerome. The bar sinister crossed Dorothy's mind. Victoria might well be, was in fact illegitimate. Victoria's illegitimacy was implied, if not assured, since Eric went on to say that Celia believed in something called the Unfettered Life, or Love Unfettered, something like that. These were values Victoria had been raised with. *This is incredible, Eric!* No, Mom, it was the truth. And there was worse. Worse? *I am ready,* she had declared to her sweetest son, though she sat down now to catch her breath though there had been no exertion to speak of. She tucked her cold feet underneath her in the chair and pulled *Clara* closer and sank into the welcome of the chintz-covered chair by the cold fireplace. *Tell me the truth of it, Eric.*

The truth was, though Celia did not believe in marriage, she believed in love. She had had lots of lovers and lots of weddings. (*Patently unfair,* sulked Eric, *we didn't get to have a wedding, but she does?*) Well, several weddings, all on Sophia's Beach: that is, weddings, as in celebrations to formalize relations between her and her lover, *The Man of the Moment,* according to the girls. Clearly, however, they were men of various, indeed, many moments: at least two before Bobby Jerome and after him, others. Several, certainly, of whom the most notorious was Andrew Hayes. There was no end of upheaval with Andrew Hayes. Andrew had lived with Celia and brought two boys with him, or rather two boys were dropped off at the Useless post office by their mother who said they were incorrigible and they had ringworm besides. (Ringworm? Dorothy shuddered even now.) Poor Victoria and her sister, young girls obliged to live in the same house with ring-wormed brats who were not even their own brothers! Victoria and her sister had to share their mother with these boys who were in trouble continually with the family, the school and the law. They had to share their mother with these boys' father who was repeatedly unfaithful, cheated on Celia for years. Not till everyone had already lived through years of tantrums and tears did Andrew move out. The brat boys were so pissed off with their dad they wrecked his truck on a logging road. *Imagine, Mom.* But Dorothy couldn't. After Andrew left, upheaval continued, ongoing anguish because Celia was emotionally on all fours. That was Victoria's description. Wretchedly vivid. Later, there was a guy named Phil. A marine biologist who had come to Isadora Island to study marine life and enjoyed a few happy years in Celia's bed and actually believed she'd leave with him and go back to Woods Hole, Massachusetts. *(Ha ha ha,* Victoria had said, *Ph.D. or not, you could see how stupid he was.)* No wonder Victoria wanted to escape Isadora Island! Eric had commiserated with his wife. No wonder she had vowed she would never return. Of course she had to escape! How could you live someplace where everyone knew that your mother was a great slut, a—Eric cast about for some word equal to his outrage—a strumpet.

The word *strumpet* had set off in Dorothy a pang of alarm then, did so again now as she sat here, feet curled up and going to sleep, tingling, and *Clara* around her soothingly. And yet. And yet—Dorothy felt a sudden seizure of conviction, or some-thing very like it—the woman who could create this room, this house, could not be a strumpet, not with everything that nasty word implies. It was not possible. There was, there must be, in that woman a well of reverence, a deep chord of caring, an instinctive understanding. What had one of those girls said? The pretty girl, the skinny one from California (the husbandless one with the fatherless child), she'd said that no one lived here at Henry's House, and now Dorothy knew why. It was a museum of inspiration, this house. The woman who had created inspiration could not be a strumpet. And whatever Celia might *say* about the Unfettered Life, Unfettered Love, she clearly *knew* that not all fetters were equal. That much was evident to anyone with eyes, with imagination, with heart. Dorothy was pleased to include herself in this elect.

She roused out of the chair, slowly, because her feet had gone to sleep and as she walked, gingerly, her feet sent jagged zaps of pin-like pain radiating up her legs. She walked and walked and when the pain finally passed and her feet had woken up, she found herself at the bureau where, on a starched lace dresser scarf there were perfume bottles. Empty, but with the labels still on and in some cases, sticky amber still glopped in the bottom of the bottle. *Chanel Number Five.* Oh, who was that? Enid. Enid Brislow and Cousin Lucy, too. *Joy!* Oh, she breathed deep in *Joy* because that was Barb Binton, Madcap Barb, so daring, so confident, Madcap Barb was full of *Joy.* And *Estée Lauder,* oh, Mary McAslund was all but in this room. *Tabu.* Ugh.

She corked *Tabu* and rubbed her nose against its after-scent as she tugged at the top bureau drawer, expecting to find it empty (Henry's House was a B-and-B, after all, not a real home, but a commercial enterprise), but even as these thoughts occurred, the drawer yielded, and in it Dorothy found pressed linens. In the next drawer she poked through all sort of miscellaneous junk, the sort of untethered flotsam whose worth is entirely in the eye or mind or heart of the beholder. Foreign coins. A key without a corresponding lock. A plastic fat baby of the sort to top a christening cake. A Christmas angel in wax, which might once, forty years ago, have been a candle that no one ever burned. A pin that said *Have a Nice Night.* Silly. A tiny silver-plated bud vase. Turning this in her cold hands, Dorothy noted little rosebuds worked round the rim and on the base and on the two tiny handles so that the vase looked like a small urn or trophy, something one might win or earn. She pressed the silver vase in both hands to warm it, perhaps to warm her own hands. She put it back in the drawer. Then she picked it up again, and put it in her pocket.

Never had she done such a thing. She could not do it now.

She chided and lectured herself, wrangled and hectored, but she did not put it back. The sight of the little silver vase, so nice, so lovely, there amidst all that junk, it just spoke to Dorothy: *Rescue me,* it said. *Rescue me from the tawdry trash of this world, the detritus, the orphaned keys and geriatric angels. Rescue me. Liberate me.* So she did. Then she went on down the bureau, opening drawers to see if there might be any other items in need of rescue, but nothing else spoke to her. At the bottom drawer, however, a whisper wafted up in the form of fragrance, over, around, eluding the usual Damp (ever-present, everywhere pervasive). In this drawer she found lacy dresser scarves ironed with a whiff of ironing wax. Lemon-scented ironing wax.

Oh, did people do such things anymore? Dorothy's mother always used ironing wax, lemon-scented, on all her clothes, lingerie especially. *It gives things such a nice finish, Dorothy,* Mother used to say, *and it's just a little luxury, not an indulgence.* As a girl all Dorothy's slips had been ironed with lemon-scented ironing wax, and sometimes she could feel the fine finish crack slightly along her legs, not altogether unpleasant as a sensation. And the ironing wax in her slip had not cracked, but melted on a summer day, hot, especially hot for Seattle, temperature in the nineties, wilting heat, heat unabating that afternoon when she was a college girl and she had wilted under heat and his welcome weight and the ironing wax in her slip had melted under, with the lovely heat of that dazzling boy who was not Neddy. Before Neddy.

She closed the drawer abruptly. Feeling rather wobbly, she pulled herself up with one hand on the dresser, using the other to keep *Clara* tight against her. Clutching *Clara* she lurched slightly back toward the window where the lamp was lit in broad daylight. The lamp lit for the dead man. Perhaps it was not so very inefficient after all. Perhaps, if you loved someone, even if the love had not endured as marriage, it endured in some other form, underwent some slow change over time, but it remained recognizable, at least in the eye of the beholder. Beholding now Useless Point and beyond, Assumption Island, that gorgeous gray rock, Dorothy felt happy here. Behold the outer islands: great blue bolsters, the sea quilted, an undulating bed of fog, and the lovely gray and granular light Dorothy had known all her life, loved all her life. She had hated Rome if the truth were told. (Which it had not been: candor disconnected in that instance from honesty.) On her honeymoon she had followed Neddy and their nasty, grasping guide all around the Eternal City, eternally hot, too much heat in Rome, that terrible unabating heat and all those beggars and bright colors, swarms of both and all that ancient dust and Old World decay, dust and dirt and desiccation everywhere with no proper saltwater breezes, just a corrupt old river winding nearby. No, for Dorothy, the beloved Northwest patinas were dearest: moss, old, thick, fuzzy, gooey, napping moss growing under cloud-clotted skies, moss and lichen, ferns, rocks in all those shades and strands of gray and green evading nomenclature, fog all grainy, stippling every distance and the air so thick with dampness you could taste it; the trees in huge stands, creating thick, black shadows, evergreen trees with ever-black shadows. The Northwest coast, the saltwater Sound, the freshwater rain so ever-present it felt like a friend. Dorothy had a friend here in Henry's House. Maybe two. *Clara* and Celia. Celia kept dazzling floors and she kept a lamp lit for a man long dead. Dorothy understood both.

A touching story. That's what Ned said. It was a touching story about the lamp kept lit off-season and Henry Westervelt. It would have remained merely that, a touching little story, except for the gory details, and Ned had blamed Dorothy at the time for having elicited the gory details, for having asked Victoria all those tender questions and pressing her for details which turned out to be gory. When he blamed her, Dorothy had cried a little, and Ned had said, *There, there,* but she cried a lot now, just let go and wept noisily, wiping her nose with *Clara* and smudging mascara mucky with makeup, because she had only pressed for details to be nice to Victoria because of Eric. Because she didn't want to lose Eric, and she could not tell Ned that. She loved Eric too much. Maybe she had loved everyone too much, because certainly no one had loved her back, not as much as she had loved them. Few to love, and no one ever equal to her love. Dorothy blubbered outright to remember that Wordsworth poem she had read in college. She had cried even then in the dorm room she shared with Barb. She cried because the poem had described, warned her what life had in store for her. Barb Binton had chided her, *Get hold of yourself, Dot, it's just an old poem, quit your crying.* And, in honoring Madcap Barb, Dorothy tried, even now, to get hold of herself, but it was hard. Hard not to sob outright, great heavy swells coming up in her throat, choking and constricting tightly in her chest, tears running unheeded down her face and dripping off her chin because

> *She dwelt amongst untrodden ways*
> *Beside the Springs of Dove*
> *A maid whom there were none to praise*
> *And very few to love.*

Very few. Very, very few. Eric maybe. Maybe Eric had loved her as much as she loved him. So when he had married this inoffensive, pretty, polite and otherwise unremarkable girl, Dorothy had tried to be *extra, extra* nice to Victoria because she didn't want to lose Eric as she had lost the other boys to grasping wives. Dorothy had made every effort to love Victoria so as not to lose darling Eric, to prove to Victoria she had a warm heart, a willing ear and open arms. And so as Victoria had told her story, Dorothy had inquired concernedly, *How did he die, dear? How did Henry Westervelt die that your mother should leave the lamp burning night and day for him in the window overlooking Useless Point?*

Gory indeed. Victoria had told them how Henry was sailing with Celia, just the two of them one summer afternoon on a boat called *Deo Volente. Really,* Victoria had said, *wasn't that awful? A boat called, really, God Willing,* and this awful accident happened because Henry and Celia were stoned mindless, tripping away, naked as the day they were born, both of them. Celia lay on the deck and drifted off to sleep and she woke because something rolled and hit her, roused her and Henry was gone. The boat

pitched, nearly tipping over, the boom flailing crazily and unsecured, swinging back and forth, the sail flapping, snapping. There
she was, Celia, naked and alone, sunburned, stoned silly and no
idea of how to sail or what to do, save for keeping her head
down and out of the way of the boom, and crying out for Henry,
crazy with fear, with grief, crying out as the boat lurched and
limped and listed, rocked madly in the open water, Henry! Henry!
The boom, still unsecured, might have killed Celia too, might
just have swept her, stoned as she was, right off the deck as it
had swept Henry off. Help! Help! Her voice carrying across the
water till some other boaters rescued her. *Celia hates boats,* Victoria
had added. *For a woman who lives on an island, she is singularly
unfond of boats. You can see why.*

But in fact, in their collective imagination, the Robbins family
saw this: a completely naked woman, arms outstretched, sunburned, stoned and stunned to wake and find herself alone. A
woman incapacitated by marijuana and LSD, incompetent in any
event. And culpable? Ned and Dorothy both remembered the
story in the newspapers: Mr. Westervelt had tried to have criminal
charges brought against Celia, and there was a sort of inquiry,
but nothing more, not even a coroner's jury because there was
no body. Despite Mr. Westervelt's paying for divers to go down
into the waters of the Sound, no one could find the naked body of
Henry Westervelt which remained, caught, rocked by the current,
resting at the bottom, the cold waters of the Puget Sound.

Certainly after that little recital, the Robbins family did not,
ever again, ask after Henry Westervelt, or how he had died.

But Dorothy knew that whenever the Westervelt name came
up—yes, even in the bathroom—Ned felt a tiny thrill of kinship.
He sometimes trotted the story out at parties when he thought
Dorothy wouldn't overhear him, the whole story, including the
gory details, in fact relishing the parts about Celia and Henry
being drugged mindless, stuporifically stoned and buck naked.
And in the telling of the story Ned always managed to leave the
oblique impression that his youngest son, Eric, had married the
late Henry Westervelt's daughter, adding that Victoria didn't have

much to do with Westervelts, and the Robbins family was too modest (or too proud, depending on Ned's audience) to trade on her family connections.

Animated voices echoed down the long hall and Dorothy turned abruptly from the window, her eyes on the door. Her eyelid trembled involuntarily and she played with the pearl choker. Women's voices coming down the hall. Victoria's was one. She recognized Victoria's voice and the other one, the girl who had just gotten engaged to marry the man who looked like a saint. So forebearing. Not handsome really, but gentle and fore-bearing. You could tell that just to look at him. Wade. Wade made you think of Jesus. Even if you didn't want to. And another voice, the girl from California. The other ex-half-stepsister, the one with beautiful blue eyes. And Celia. Oh yes, Celia's bold voice and throaty laughter. But really, they were going to one of the bathrooms, weren't they? They must stop at the bathroom. Dorothy pulled *Clara* tighter around her shoulders and mopped the mascara from her face, or tried to. She wished vehemently that Art might instantly triumph over Nature and she would be turned to stone. She wished to become a stone statue because the voices seemed to be coming, were coming, all the way down the hall to this very room. Dorothy stood still, chilled, silent, hoping she wouldn't be detected, wishing to become a statue, to be or become an inconsequential artifact, to die or dissolve. Or both. They were coming here. Their feet. Their voices. A hand on the door. Dorothy could not move. She could not evaporate, nor turn to stone, but neither could she move before they crashed into the room, where they would find her with *Clara* and the silver bud vase. They would know she had taken it. Stolen it. They must not know. Dorothy's heart pounded on the walls of her ribs, she could feel it pound through her bones, the bones in her head, the bones in her feet, the bones in the hand clutched round the silver vase at the very moment the door opened and Celia Henry burst in, her face stricken with surprise, then alight with something else. Concern? Caring? Friendship? Affection? Could that be possible? A friend in Celia Henry? Dorothy tried to mouth that word—or any other—faltered, couldn't. Dorothy's lips were open, but soundless as her own heart attacked her, as Celia Henry swept over her and caught Dorothy in the curl of her embrace, like the curl of a wave. Aegean blue, this wave, silken, inescapable, and for a moment Dorothy knew what Henry Westervelt must have felt like, as a force greater than himself drew him down down down into the sea, as Celia broke over Dorothy and drew her into a connection altogether new and rich and strange.

Staff at Island Medical went to work on Dorothy Robbins like she was a bed they were stripping. They plugged her in and shouted shorthand commands at one another, forcibly untangled Dorothy's hands from Celia's as Dorothy cried out. But the staff pushed Celia out of the cubicle and closed the curtain. Celia stood there, stupidly rooted, not knowing what else to do, except murmur, "*Deo Volente,* don't let her die," over and over until an orderly thrust through the curtain Dorothy's clothes, rolled up in the afghan *Clara.* He pointed Celia down the hall, to the door at the far end, the door with portholes, the waiting room. Under her breath, as she walked past pale walls, empty gurneys, under buzzing fluorescent lamps, she said over and over, "*Deo Volente,* don't let Dorothy die."

Opening the door with portholes and walking into the waiting room, the Robbinses swam at Celia like a school of fish. Like those great old groupers, their sad eyes, half-lidded, their mouths open, shaping words that will not come, the Robbinses pulled Celia into currents she could not resist, in the depths and shallows of *Calvin Klein for Men.* Celia bobbed and floated till finally Eric anchored her, his head against her shoulder, weeping, thanking her for saving his mother's life.

Ned, freckled, corpulent, mopped his face and bald pate with his handkerchief; the sons and all the sons' spouses pressed their hankies and Kleenexes to their lips and noses, and as a family they thanked her for saving Dorothy's life.

"Dr. Aagard saved her life," Celia protested, "I just . . ." It was hard, quite, to say what she had done. She had caught Dorothy when she fell. Then, in the mad cross-island dash, Eric at the wheel, Dr. Aagard in the backseat with Celia and Dorothy, Dorothy had refused to relinquish her hand, had held on to Celia. Even when Ned and Eric reached for her, reached out to her, Dorothy clung to Celia and the wild terrified look in Dorothy's eyes implored Celia not to relinquish her. And so, Celia held Dorothy in a grip so insistent Celia could feel the pain in her own chest. Not until the medical staff pried open Dorothy's fingers did they part, and at that parting Dorothy cried out, *Maybe my floors didn't need to be that clean!*

"What did they say when you left her?" the family beseeched Celia. "Did the doctors tell you anything at all?"

"Did Dorothy say anything to you?" Ned implored. "What did Dorothy say?"

Celia frowned. Paused. "She said maybe her floors didn't need to be that clean."

"What?"

It was a collective question, deservedly so because certainly Dorothy's cry had also seemed to Celia one of the strangest possible things anyone could have said under life-threatening circumstances. "She said, maybe her floors didn't need to be that clean," Celia repeated to their still gape-mouthed incredulity. The Robbinses regarded Celia as though she had spoken in tongues, as though she had personally dealt them an axe blow to the base of the family tree. So Celia added, "Then she said how much she loves all of you, and you're not to worry and she'll be fine and she loves you." This was a lie, beginning to end, Dorothy had said no such thing. But Celia felt better for having told the lie, just to see relief draped across every Robbins face, even Victoria's.

"Mom loves everyone too much," Eric sobbed, "and it's just like her to always think of others."

The family retreated to chairs placed along the waiting room walls, chairs lined up church-fashion and bolted together before a TV set placed up high and raining down CNN. Island Medical Center was a small facility in Massacre (it could not possibly be called Massacre Hospital, could it?), one floor, two wings, better resembling an elementary school from the fifties. This waiting room had been last redone in the early eighties and its once-blazing Southwest colors, peach and turquoise, had faded, splotched here and there in the Northwest damp. Framed prints on the wall looked like they had been cut from Kleenex boxes. Celia leafed through old *People* magazines and *Sunset*. She closed *Sunset* quickly, unable to bear all that implicit ambition, all that remodeling you could do in your spare time.

Eric's brothers and their wives were huddled each in separate little corners, cell phones pressed to their heads, and Celia realized she ought to call Henry's House and check on things there. She hadn't so much as a quarter, no purse at all. She was about to ask Victoria for money, but a single glance over to Victoria and Eric convinced her not to intrude. For all the public nature of this place, Victoria had somehow closeted herself with Eric, creating a space exclusive to themselves. With one hand on his knee and one on his back, Victoria talked in a low voice, a just-audible murmur for Eric alone. Celia remembered how Bobby used to do that with the girls when they were sick or hurt, sometimes just when they were angry. He would close the door and sit on the bed, hold that child, recite poems, sing songs, tell stories, his arms around her, his attention hers alone, his assurance calming, his love palpable.

One of the Robbins brothers (Raymond? Roger? Robert? Celia—whose memory for names was legendary—struggled to separate them) offered her the use of his cell phone. Sunny picked up at Henry's House, assuring her that she and Angie would oversee the cleanup and she was not to worry. Was there word on Dorothy? "Not yet," Celia replied, with a glance round the waiting room. "We're waiting for the doctor, but you better check that the beds are made up at Henry's because it's safe to say, Sunny, we're going to have people there tonight. Nine, I'd say. No one will be going anywhere till there's word on Dorothy."

"When will that be?"

Celia didn't know. It seemed strange to her to be in this waiting room on such a dire errand. She thought of Island Medical more like a garage, a place where you'd bring something to get it fixed. And she often had brought kids who worked for her, her own kids, step-kids, and here they had broken bones set, burns salved, cuts or gashes stitched up, had tetanus shots and assorted vaccinations. It was a place where someone might be born, as Bethie and Victoria both were. It was not a place where someone might actually die.

She took a seat beside Ned, offering her hand and such comfort as she could. Ned took her hand and began to weep, his shoulders shaking seismically. Celia said quickly, "Dr. Aagard called the cardiologist on his cell phone, so he was here when we arrived. I'm sure Dorothy will be fine, will get well."

Bursting into tears, mopping his face, Ned blamed himself. Dorothy had had heart trouble now for a long time and he blamed himself for not taking it more seriously, even though it was just a condition. "But you know, both her parents died of heart attacks and so did her best friend, Madcap Barb, five years ago, and she was devastated, really devastated by these deaths. It's all my fault. I shouldn't have brought her. I should have seen this coming."

"You can't blame yourself, Ned."

"But she didn't even want to come to this stupid engagement party! I insisted. I said we had to go because of Henry Westervelt." He wept the more.

What the hell was he talking about? But Celia didn't query, or ask him to clarify, just held his hand, listened, nodded as he told her all about Dorothy, their years together, their honeymoon in Rome, their perfect marriage, their perfect home, their successful sons (Roland? Richard? Ralph?) and their successful daughters-in-law (Kathy? Kristi? Kelly?), their successful grandchildren, two of whom were UW students, all UW alums, their family, their view of Lake Washington from their beautiful home, their boat, the 40-foot Tollycraft powerboat, *Strumpet*, how he loved Dorothy and couldn't live without her.

"You won't have to," Celia assured him over and over, wishing someone in the family would come and comfort Ned, but though they had put away their cell phones, Dorothy's sons and daughters-in-law had picketed themselves off in couples, sharing their sorrows intimately, like a picnic lunch for two.

At long last the cardiologist emerged through the portholed doors and called out their name and they all rose and moved toward him like he was a law of gravity.

"Mrs. Robbins is out of immediate danger," he began. Everyone sighed with relief and Eric began to cry again.

"When can we move her to Seattle?" asked Ned.

The doctor looked at him with some surprise and said Dorothy could not leave Isadora, not even to go to another hospital. "Not till her condition has stabilized."

"But she has to go to Swedish Hospital or University Hospital!" Ned protested. "She has to have Bellevue doctors."

With a show of concerned impartiality, the doctor listened to Ned for a bit, then he said in a peremptory fashion, "Out of the question."

"We can airlift her to Seattle. I can pay for it."

"It would do more harm than good. She's out of danger for the moment, but she can't be moved. Now, Mr. Robbins, you can go in and have a very few moments with her. She's been given some sedatives and she'll sleep. The rest of you, well, I guess we'll see you tomorrow."

But he did not see them all the next day. After spending the night at Henry's House, the sons and spouses, Victoria too, returned on a morning ferry. They all had jobs and homes and lives which could not be ignored, schedules already stretched thin, irate nannies, irate clients, irate assistants, irate supervisors. Their cell phones had been ringing off the hooks. If they'd had hooks. Only Eric and Ned remained on Isadora. On his cell phone Eric called

Microsoft and told them to limp by without him. "I'm not leaving this island till I can bring Mom home to Bellevue."

Eric hung up and turned to Celia sheepishly. "Can I stay? I mean, I didn't ask. I don't need to stay here, this beautiful place, Henry's House. Just a sleeping bag on the floor, that would be fine."

At her own home Celia readied the other little room at the top of the stairs for the Robbins men. There was only one bed in it and Eric gave that up to his father and slept on a cot set up in the kitchen. He endeared himself to Celia by being generally very handy around the house. Especially her house—which, unlike the showcase Henry's House, was unkempt, untidy. Things lounged about in a sort of congenial squalor. When he was not at the hospital, those days of Dorothy's recovery, Eric borrowed a pair of Russell's sweats and spent his time organizing the silverware drawer, cleaning out under the burners on the gas range, polishing all the copper. In looking for the copper cleaner, however, Eric discovered in the cupboard under the sink a small empire of mold, a place where the Damp had built itself its own little kingdom by the sea. When Celia came back, the smell of Clorox was dizzying but the mold was gone. Chagrined that Eric had gone under her sink at all, Celia told him please not to bother. "But how else could I repay your hospitality?" he asked.

All in all, Celia could see why Victoria had married him.

Ned was a different story. Ned whipped out his checkbook at every conceivable juncture. Celia declined, wondering how he could be continually so obtuse. Couldn't he understand that Celia felt personally involved in Dorothy's recovery? Catching her like that, Dorothy's embrace on the ride to the hospital, the cryptic remark about the floors, the look in Dorothy's eyes. "Please, Ned." Celia laid a steadying hand on his arm. "Don't even think about money, about paying me. After all, we're all family, aren't we?"

Ned paled slightly at this, but he capped his Montblanc pen and put it in his pocket with pleased finality. He took the cup

of coffee she offered him and had a long, intense discussion with
Russell about the stock market.

So it was a considerable shock to Celia, a day or so later, as
she walked down the corridor at Island Medical toward Dorothy
Robbins' room, daffodils in one hand and a gift box with a blue
ribbon in the other, to see Ned burst out of Dorothy's room and
stalk down the hall, puffing like The Little Engine That Could.
When his gaze fell on Celia, he flushed furiously and wagged his
finger at her, hollering all the way down the hall, "I suppose you
think this is funny!"

"Funny ha ha?" asked Celia as he propelled past her. "Or
funny peculiar?"

But Ned refused to reply and, still barreling down the hall,
nearly collided with a high-wheeled cart of used lunch trays, and
yelled that he would not have it! No indeed, he would not!

All the rooms at Island Medical were doubles, but Dorothy
had hers to herself and Celia walked in on an unguarded moment
between mother and son, Eric's hand clutching Dorothy's and
Dorothy stroking his cheek. She stepped back out in the hall to
give them privacy, but from the very tone of their voices, Celia
could hear Dorothy soothing her son while Eric protested vehemently. When he came out of the room, into the hall, the young
man who had been so warm, so sweet, so helpful walked past
Celia with scarcely a word.

All was not well in the world of Robbins, that much was
clear. But when she entered the room, Celia was surprised to find
Dorothy looking rather perky. Her skin was so fine and frail that
blue veins showed at her temples, but her lips had lost that tight
pucker of pain and her eyes were a serene blue. She was sitting
up, all IVs removed from her arm. She smiled at Celia, and then
busied herself smoothing out all the wrinkles on her bedsheet, so
it lay nice and flat, an even, white band across her lap.

Celia asked how Dorothy was feeling, bracing herself for the
obligatory litany, knowing she would have to endure the charts,
medications, EKGs and CAT scans, the whole opera of medical
opinion. Celia was impatient, bored with illness, taking her own

good health for granted and everyone else's besides. Unlike Bethie, who fell absolutely captive to anything sick, lost or forlorn, Celia would cross the street, cross town, cross Isadora for that matter to avoid having discussions with people recently obsessed with cholesterol, Pap smears, mammograms and all the other accoutrements of middle age. No thanks.

So it came as considerable surprise to Celia when Dorothy scarcely alluded to health in general, or the heart attack in particular. She replied to Celia's inquiry about how she was feeling with the single word *fine,* and went on to compliment Celia on raising such a lovely girl as Victoria and how glad she was Victoria and Eric were married and had brought their two families together.

"I said more or less the same thing to Ned," Celia replied, for lack of any better response, and wondering what the hell had set Ned off.

"And your other daughter, the bride-to-be, such a vivacious girl, so, well, so luminous! And your other girl is a stunning beauty."

"Other girl?"

"The one with the very short hair and the fatherless—the one with the little daughter."

"Oh, that's Sunny, Bobby's daughter by his first marriage."

"And where is Sunny's mother?"

Under the circumstances *dead* sounded terribly harsh. "Passed away," said Celia, "long ago."

"Sit down, please."

She gave Celia one of those smiles associated always with the Girls' Vice Principal: inscrutable, patronizing and correct. The smile of the Mrs. Digbys of the world. An injunction against spitting must surely follow, Celia thought, but she sat down, first passing to Dorothy the gift box with its big blue bow. "I brought you a present."

"You have done so much for me already, Celia. This is surely above and beyond the call of duty."

"No, no, you're meant to have this. Really."

Celia smiled as she watched Dorothy undo the bow and withdraw from the box the silver bud vase, lifting it from the top of the folded afghan *Clara*. Celia, poised, ready for Dorothy to say, *No, I couldn't possibly,* to blush, or flush with dismay, to try to explain how the vase came to be in her pocket at all. Celia was all ready to interrupt and assure Dorothy that things like the bud vase, she actually put in the drawers so people *would* take them, so they have some visible token. Dorothy shouldn't feel the least embarrassed. Celia was ready to say, *You must keep it* before Dorothy even objected.

But she did not object. She did not show the least dismay. There was no mention of stealing, shoplifting or how, exactly, the vase came to be in her pocket. Instead, she looked as though she'd been reunited with someone dear to her. Dampness gleamed at the corners of her eyes. "Who's *Clara?*" she asked at last, with a little smile.

"I don't know. I never did. This afghan was part of a big purchase I made over in Snohomish. People do that a lot, when there's going to be an estate sale or something, they let me know early on and I buy stuff by the lot for Henry's House. It's none of it sentimental, at least not for me. I keep it all at Henry's House so people will feel like it's a home."

"Oh, I know why it's there. And I know *Clara*. I know her very well. And this vase . . ." Dorothy wrapped it in her hand and gazed serenely out the window which gave on to the Island Medical parking lot. "Has Victoria ever told you about my house?"

"Victoria tells me very little," Celia admitted. "Anyway, it wouldn't be like Victoria to notice a house. She's not that sort."

"Oh, you're wrong! When Victoria came to my house, that first time, when the kids were still in college and Eric brought her home with him, Victoria noticed everything. She commented on my floors and I thought, What an astute young lady."

"Hmm." Could it be that Victoria had a whole life of which Celia was completely unaware?

"From my house in Bellevue, right on Lake Washington," Dorothy went on dreamily, "we can see the lake and the skyline across the lake, the boats in summer, the whitecaps in winter. It's lovely, absolutely lovely. But I realize that when I picture it, I see it like a postcard from a long-ago vacation. Rome, maybe. I don't picture the lake as though it is there every day, and the reason is, I didn't see it at all. I didn't look out the window. I didn't look up. I don't know how many years have passed since I looked up. For years I've seen nothing but my floors. What does that say about my vision? My eyes have been downcast"— she paused, as if searching for the rest of some lyric, some old hymn perhaps—"but my floors! Oh, if my floors were violins they would be Stradivarius! If my floors were roses, they would be in the White House garden! If my floors had law degrees, they would be Supreme Court justices! Really! My floors were so polished I could see my own reflection in them. Like Narcissus. You remember the story of the young man who so loved his own reflection he died of it?"

Celia nodded, wondering how *Clara* and the bud vase had brought this on.

"My floors were the most dazzling in the world—so I thought. That is, until I came to Henry's House and saw your floors, Celia."

Celia winced, and she pasted an insincere smile across her lips. She loathed housekeeping discussions. She quickly offered the name of the firm who stripped Henry's House floors for her once a year, hoping she could cork this conversation before it got started. No such luck. Dorothy rattled on about her floors, rhapsodized about care and feeding of her floors, and how they were inferior to the floors at Henry's. *O God of the New Disciples,* Celia prayed inwardly, *spare me Olympic Housekeeping. Spare me events in Downhill Mopping, the Five-Hundred-Meter Bed-Making, the Ironing Board Slalom.* Is there anything worse than women assessing, asserting superiority in a field so incredibly trite? Ordinarily Celia would have bolted right then, but she was stunned by the web of banality she'd flown into; she felt pinned to the chair and tied up in dust ruffles. Then she remembered Dorothy's own dying words. What Celia thought were her dying words. To hell with good manners. "Maybe your floors didn't need to be that clean."

"Well, that's exactly right, isn't it?" Dorothy exclaimed enthusiastically. "And more than my reflection was in those floors. My whole life—oh, Celia, it was terrible. A terrible loss of a life, don't you see? I have squandered my life in the service of my floors. Not in the service of an idea or a principle, not even an institution, like a library, or a law firm, or the University Women's Club—Madcap Barb gave them her life and service and they revere her name at the University Women's Club. You would have adored Madcap Barb. But me? What have I to show for my life? I didn't even waste it on a man. Women who squander years of their lives on worthless men, they're better off than I am!"

"That's probably not altogether true." Celia spoke with some experience.

"I would be better off in Pioneer Square, stinking drunk with my bottle in a bag, panhandling tourists. That woman, that raving drunk, that slut—that strumpet!—at least she has a story to tell. What have I been doing all my life? A housewife! Shocking! Oh, don't you think that's shocking?"

"Not all that shocking," Celia soothed, fearing for another siege of chest pains.

"But don't you see? To be a housewife implies you were married to the house itself, doesn't it? The wife of the house. The companion, the lover, the lifelong partner of the house! Ghastly! Horrible. Terrible. What have I got to show for my life? Other than my floors," she conceded.

"You raised four sons."

"That's not an achievement. Children grow up no matter what you do with them. Neglect them altogether and they still grow up, don't they? And it's not even a question of how they turn out. Whatever you do, you can't control how they turn out." She lowered her voice confidentially. "Some of the best mothers in Bellevue have drug addicts for children. It's the truth. Wonderful mothers, but their children as unlike them as day from night. Why, look at your own daughter. Could anyone be more different than you? Look at Victoria."

This was so indelibly true as to defy denial and Celia started to offer the usual drivel, the conventional wisdom she assumed Dorothy wanted to hear, phrases about respecting differences, etc. etc.

"God gives you children to sharecrop," Dorothy interrupted her. "You rent this piece of ground and you till it, plant it, work yourself old and ugly worrying about it and then, if it brings in a good crop, you get none of the credit. If it's bad, everyone blames the mother. So children are not an achievement, more of an accident. I can't count on my sons to give me a sense of self. But I must have something besides the floors. Don't you see? If I look up from the floors I have no reflection at all. I have nothing. I'm invisible." In her thin hospital gown Dorothy's shoulders slumped and she seemed to diminish visibly. "Like a ghost."

"Not yet. You're not a ghost yet. You're alive."

"I knew you would understand. Everything. I knew the woman who could create Henry's House would understand completely. Neddy doesn't. He thinks I'm mad. He knows you saved my life, he just doesn't know how."

"Dr. Aagard saved your life."

"When you caught me when I fell, it was for a reason. Don't you see? I have so much to learn from you, Celia!" She pressed the little bud vase in her palms. "You have so much to teach me and I assure you I'm an excellent student. *Cum laude.* I graduated with honors from the U. Neddy didn't."

"I'm not a teacher," Celia protested.

"You are, you just don't know it. A teacher and an artist."

"No, that's Sophia. You've got me confused with Sophia Westervelt, who built the place as a school. What I run is a business like any other."

"That's not true," she retorted with Mrs. Digby-ish certainty. "If it were true you would not leave the lamp lit in the high bedroom. I know all about the lamp. Victoria told us about you and Henry Westervelt and how he died. All the gory details. Terrible. So young. Imagine how his mother felt. But Henry's House—oh, Celia! Henry's House is a work of art. It's like walking into a painting—with all those textures and colors and the way the light plays off the past—all that experience is waiting to be collected, gathered up and held close, as though—as though—the chairs are still warm from the bodies that we've loved in the past and the flowers will never die. You've painted a place where the flowers are real and fragrant as those daffodils, but they will never die. That's improbable, isn't it?"

Chagrined that she'd forgotten to give Dorothy the daffodils, she handed them to her. Dorothy unceremoniously thrust them in the water pitcher where they lolled forward like gossips not wishing to miss a juicy word. Celia said yes, it was unlikely that flowers could live forever, adding thoughtlessly, "Dying is a condition of life."

"Not in art. *Ars longa, vita brevis.*"

"What?"

"Life is short—oh, don't I know it?—Art is long. Art remains, but we're all just flowers." She reached out and touched the trumpets of the daffodils. "It's so sad. Neddy thinks I've lost my mind. He said, Dorothy, you've lost your mind, but I tried to explain to him, Yes, I have lost my mind and I must find it. I shall not return to Bellevue until I have found it. I shall not go back without my mind. Neddy was—well, you probably saw him. You must have heard him."

"He was very upset."

"Ignore him. He's like an old dog with a shoe. It will take him a long time to come around because he won't make the effort. That's entirely up to him, isn't it? I am not responsible for Ned. It's all finite, Neddy—" She called out as though he might be lurking in the hall, waiting to contradict her. "Once you know it's finite, everything changes. Everything must. You ask yourself not what do I want, but what can't I live without. What must I do before dying?" Dorothy wept. "I was at death's door, I tell you, Celia. And there was none of that embraced by the light, or any such heavenly crap! It was hell! I mean it was horrible to see—how near death I have lived!" Dorothy began to mop her nose with the sheet. "My whole life was *in* those dazzling floors and not just *on* them. Isn't that pathetic?"

"Please, Dorothy, you'll break your heart again." Celia went to her and put a consoling hand on her shoulder.

"But I have lost my mind!" she sobbed.

"And you'll find it. Just like you told Neddy. Ned, I mean. You'll find it and when you go home, your floors will still look good," she added to soothe.

But Dorothy sat bolt upright and cried, "I won't care by then! Isn't that marvelous? I told Neddy! Do what you want with the floors. Flood them! Freeze the water, ice-skate on them. Bring on the grandchildren and their Rollerblades. Little barbarians, my grandchildren. Let them skate all over the floors! Neddy said, Dorothy, you're mad. Mad, mad, mad! But the freedom of it, oh, the freedom of peeling my reflection out of those floors!" She used the sheet to polish very quickly the silver bud vase, and Celia understood where her son had gotten his housekeeping skills. "I could say that to Neddy—to hell with the floors!—because I won't be there to see it. I'm not that strong. Not yet. But I will be. And I will be happy. When I find my mind, my sense of self, and some new reflection, I will be happy. I have not been happy for a long time. I told him at last: Neddy, I have not been happy for a very long time. Not since Eric was in high school. Maybe before that. Do you know what Neddy said? He said at my age it was stupid to want to be happy. He said it was enough to have health and money. That's all people our age should ask for. Oh, thou heartless husband! To be told to narrow down my every expectation in life to health and money! Health and money are fine, in their way, necessary—and, well, you can see, I certainly have more of one than the other—but what of passion and triumph? What of the past? The future? What would I be if I had died the other day?"

"Dead?"

"I would have been a broom-wielding ghost, a mopping specter, a waxing ghoul."

"I've met ghosts with brooms."

Dorothy pulled the pitcher of daffodils swiftly to her bosom and inhaled passionately. "I said, Neddy, the floors did not have to be that clean—and you know what he said, Celia? He said yes, they did. They needed to be that clean and I told him, Well, fine, then you do it, Ned. You keep them up. I'm not coming home to look at the floors. I'm finding a new reflection." Tears streaked down her face and she clutched Celia's hand as she had the day she fell into her arms. She pressed the bud vase against her narrow chest and the thin hospital gown. "I knew you would understand! I'm staying here with you, Celia. I've told Ned. I've told Eric. I'm staying here and I'm going to learn everything you have to teach me."

"What?"

"I've misspent my life but I have another chance. When this vase spoke to me, cried out, *Liberate me, Liberate me,* I thought it was speaking of itself, but it wasn't. It was speaking not just to me, but of me! You know what it was saying? *Liberate through learning!*"

Three days ago Celia had scarcely known Dorothy Robbins existed, except as a vague reference in the life of her daughter. She scarcely even knew that Eric had parents, much less brothers, sisters-in-law, nieces, nephews. On meeting the Robbins family briefly at the engagement party, her first impression was that Ned was an insufferable prig, that Dorothy was a gentle nebbish, that Eric's brothers had all attained Black Belts in Boring, that their wives had brooms up their butts, straw end first. And now she was about to become responsible for the liberation of Dorothy Robbins? Celia was less alarmed than curious. "You think the vase was telling you to stay here," she inquired, "on Isadora, with me?"

"Liberate through learning," Dorothy insisted. "I can't go home until I have a new reflection, something beyond the floor, until I have learned what you need to teach me. I was *cum laude,*" she repeated, lest Celia should have missed the implication. "And

I'm eager to learn. If I go back now, you know what will happen to me."

Celia considered. "Narcissus' fate?"

"He drowned in his own reflection. He died in it. That's what would happen to me. What almost did happen to me. But I am determined to live! To experience happiness. To expand and learn. It's not too late, is it?"

"It's not Bellevue either," Celia cautioned her. But she had not been asked for her consent. Dorothy had already assumed it, already told Ned she wasn't coming home. And Celia could not have sent her back. She heard in Dorothy's outburst, echoes of her own rebellion, over lo these many years—pushing fifty years—rebelling against the men in her life, beginning with her father, and probably not ending with Russell: her ongoing quarrel with those male voices, authoritative Elders, repeating no doubt Adam's advice as far back as Eve. *Don't bother looking up and don't bother looking ahead, keep your hand on the pot and process. Let men deal with the products. The processes of daily life will suffice for women. The products of achievement are for men.* Men lived on those Assumption Islands and women just made Useless Points. "Sometimes," Celia said slowly, "when you look up from your Lot in Life, you can tell it needs to be completely plowed up and replanted."

"The curse," Dorothy declared, smoothing her sheet again, "gives way to the change."

For a woman fond of quoting Wordsworth, the poem about the Maid of Dove, the girl whom there were few to praise and none to love, Dorothy Robbins brought into Celia's life a cast of thousands. Not only was Henry's House booked every weekend that spring, but so, in a manner of speaking, was Celia's. Day-trippers everywhere. The dogs loved it. Brio loved it. Baby Herman loved it. Russell hated it. Modesty, of course, forbade him to go naked, what with Sunny, Brio and Dorothy living there. Often reservations were required for the upstairs bathroom. No shirt. No shoes. No service. To Celia the house now felt pleasantly crowded, lively, full of noise and voices as it did in the days when there were lots of kids and their friends, indeed the days before that, when Henry was alive, and friends came and went like tides upon Sophia's Beach.

Dorothy's was the other small room at the top of the stairs which had been cleared of the accumulation of years, stuff donated to Island Thrift, or carried down to the basement. In her small room Dorothy kept her narrow bed meticulously made, with *Clara* folded neatly at its foot and the bureau always dusted, the silver bud vase refreshed always with some token of the progress of Isadora's spring. She had assured Ned she needed nothing from Bellevue but a few clothes, but he brought lots of family pictures anyway, most of them taken in the days before their sons had married. The men all looked like the later Elvis.

Ned came faithfully, every weekend throughout the spring, persistently flinging out deadlines by which time Dorothy must return home. The deadlines passed, each of them without the dire consequences he predicted, and he reminded her she could not always rely on his indulgence. To this Dorothy replied she had never asked to be indulged and she did not do so now. Their reunions were rocky.

Her sons, as well, arrived in droves and hordes with a squadron of spouses, battering ram by blood tie, brandishing the pikes and arrows of family, insisting that Mom go home to Dad and cease all this foolishness. They even brought their children, the youngest of whom were about Brio's age. These children amused Brio until they began to play catch with Baby Herman. Then Brio, Baby Herman under her arm and Sass and Squatch right behind her, went into the orchard and like her mother before her, selected a favorite tree, climbed up and said she would not come down till those "bwats" were gone.

Ned and sons and spouses had thought that the grandchildren could work a maternal miracle on Grandma. Each one had urged her to home to Grandpa. After the first such assault, Dorothy suggested that they not all come at once. Of course she was happy to see them, pleased that they cared about her well-being, but they should stagger their visits and call first. "It's too much for Celia and Russell and Sunny and Brio. It's not my home, you know."

Oh, they knew all right. All too well. They came separately, but each time they left they exuded collective indignation, blaming Celia for Dorothy's bizarre decision to stay in a little room at Useless Point when she could have a lake-view house in Bellevue. Clearly, Celia had done this to Dorothy. Though what Celia had done, they could not say, much less how this transformation had been perpetrated. They knew only that their mother was somehow held hostage by the Infidel Celia and, like great lords on the Crusades, they gnashed and stormed the Useless citadel, Robert the Insufferable, Richard the Intolerable and Roland the Unendurable. Robert the Insufferable once took Celia aside and, on behalf of his family, threatened legal action if there were any changes made to his mother's will.

Eric came every weekend with Victoria. He bought a small RV which, with Celia's permission, he left in her yard so he could be close to his mother often. He was patiently obliging when Dorothy explained that she had not left Dad, that she thoroughly intended to return to Bellevue. And Eric did admit that Mom actually did look better, that she was contented and alert in ways he did not remember. The little twitches and grimaces that had so often disfigured Dorothy's face had all but vanished. Still, in some wordless way Eric blamed Celia for breaking up his parents' marriage.

The only Robbins who did not blame Celia for Dorothy's weird transformation was Victoria. Victoria's attitude to Dorothy was less than sympathetic. Victoria blamed Dorothy for the complete upheaval of her own life. Victoria blamed Dorothy's near-death encounter for having set in motion those forces which now drew Victoria back to the island, those slow, alluvial forces that pulled her, inexorable as the tides, back to Isadora, back to Useless

Point, back into her mother's orbit, to the Celia-centered universe which she had so successfully heretofore escaped.

Pulled back into the past, Victoria endured ambivalence, excruciating for a woman whose life had achieved a Tinkertoy regularity. Victoria's public description of her having fled Isadora was to laugh lightly and say, Oh, I contracted island fever. Everyone did. You could not live forever someplace where all roads dead-end into the sea. To live forever at Useless Point? To gaze always at Assumption Island? Worse, imagine living in a town called Massacre! No—Victoria would always add blithely—either you got island fever and left, or you went mad. To make her point, she usually brought up Launch, evidence clearly of congenital weirdness if you stayed too long at Useless.

But now, the past, the old ambivalent past, embraced Victoria, enveloped and upset her every week because her sister and her father were there too. Sunny was utterly changed, Bobby completely static. There were all the old recollected pleasures of life with Bobby, walks they took, had taken, would always take, along Sophia's Beach, the girls playing on the swing he made; that swing was Bobby's bit of immortality. Victoria had the sense of encountering her own young self in her little niece, Brio. She and Sunny unraveled for Brio all the remembered pleasures of their island childhood, Bobby's penchant for sunsets, his belief that each girl ought to have her own day to skip school and ride bikes around the island with him, his impulse-buying. Victoria remembered his having bought her a toy once that made her so happy she could not even eat ice cream: she was already too happy. Bobby made Brio that happy, spinning for her endless songs and stories, some of which Sunny and Victoria knew and some of which were wholly fresh and *con brio.* They took picnics as they had in childhood, all of them, Celia too sometimes, out to Chinook Lookout, wading through the ferny forest to come to the high cliffs, to see clear across the Sound, where on a good day a tiny lighthouse was visible on a neighboring island, a toy, a chess piece in the hand of God. Never mind all this, Victoria still breathed more freely to feel the ferry pull away from Dog Bay.

Determined to make up for time lost with his granddaughter, Bobby Jerome came to Isadora faithfully that spring. Those first few weekends in April he brought with him Janice, Odd Todd and once *(Oh God,* thought Sunny and Victoria in silent unison) the Wookie came too. But these efforts to cobble themselves into a stepfamily were not successful. Amongst the Jerome women—Victoria, Sunny, Brio and Janice—relations could be most cordial at a distance, and after these first ill-fated weekends, Janice spent her Saturdays at home resenting the time, money and enthusiasm her husband lavished on the women at Useless Point. She suffered chronic pain which she refused to treat. Bobby of course refused to acknowledge Janice's pain. He had not acknowledged the pain of any of his women. Ever. Life was sweet. And at Useless Point, he was determined to be loved.

He came accompanied always by his guitar, and usually a teddy bear or a little toy for Brio and often a little something for Celia and Dorothy, Brach's chocolates, pansies in plastic pots. He was courtly to Celia, and as for Dorothy, he seemed to want to slay her with kindness, to surround her with warmth, to inundate her with his charm.

Bobby's was not the sort of charm to which Dorothy responded. In truth, she thought him a silly sort of man. In Dorothy's experience grown men did not act like Bobby Jerome. Grown men acted like Ned and her sons. Grown men were—well, bristly. Befitting their whiskers. Grown men were not enthusiastic over little children, but reserved their displays of excitement and avid affection for the Sonics, the Mariners or inanimate objects like the *Strumpet.* Grown men certainly did not have tea parties on the porch with Brio and Baby Herman, or snatch songs out of the air for a child's amusement. When the weather was bad, Bobby sat at a small wooden table near a window in Celia's kitchen and played Go Fish with Brio and Sunny and Victoria. He lost endlessly. Ned never lost at cards.

Indeed, for a woman who had raised four sons and been married for forty years, Dorothy got a real education in the ways of men while she lived on Isadora. She had never met a man so silent as Launch, so buoyant as Bobby or so jealous as Russell. From Dorothy's bedroom, contiguous to the one Russell shared with Celia, she could not help but overhear Russell complain endlessly about Bobby.

"There's no reason for you to be jealous," Celia would tell him. "I haven't slept with Bobby for years. I'm not going to sleep with him now. Bobby is as much a historical part of my life as Watergate. Just because I enjoyed it once, doesn't mean I want the rerun."

"I know that," Russell snorted. "I'm not questioning your fidelity."

"Then what is it? I'm not jealous of your wife. Of course you slept with her! You had a family with her while you were married to her, of course you should see her when you go back across the bay. Your children live with her. Well, why shouldn't Bobby come here? His children are here."

"Why? Why are they here? I don't mean Victoria, I know she comes with Eric, and I know why he comes, so don't rattle on about Dorothy—"

"Hush, Russell—"

"But Sunny—why did Sunny come back here?"

"To help me. You've seen what she's done for the business! I don't know how I ran it without her."

"That's what she's done since she got here. Why did she come in the first place?"

"I don't know. I don't care. Keep your voice down. She's welcome to stay here as long as she likes."

"There's something she's not telling you, Celia."

"Fine. I'm going to sleep."

"I don't like Bobby here all the time."

"It isn't all the time."

There was a long silent pause. "Isn't it enough that you run a B-and-B at Henry's House, why must you run one here? All these people, Celia! What happened to the time we used to have, just us together?"

Dorothy heard the bedsprings squeal.

"I like all these people," Celia replied. "I like having a house full of people."

"Don't you ever need time alone?"

"I get up at five a.m."

"Don't you ever need time with me?"

"I don't want to have these conversations."

"You never want to talk."

"You know what my life is like in the spring and summer. It's the Season, Russell. You live on this island. The Season shouldn't be news to you. This spring, all right, things are a little more crowded—"

"A little more? A little?"

"OK. A lot."

"Bobby shouldn't be here every weekend."

"Well, if you can't hack it here on weekends, you have your own place."

And he did. On weekends Russell left early Saturday morning and returned late Sunday night. At first he moved back to his apartment in Massacre, but it was lonely there. Without admitting as much to Celia (and she didn't care, he told himself) Russell took the ferry back across the bay to visit his own children. They lived with his ex-wife, Shirley. Shirley asked how things were and Russell told her. At length. Shirley thought Celia insensitive, truly thoughtless—no, cruel—to allow all these people to move in and traipse through the house without so much as asking Russell what he wanted. What would suit him? Shirley bristled to know that though Russell lived there too, thoughtless Celia had just altered their whole lives without so much as a *What do you think?* Domestic decisions ought to be made together during quality time while you worked on your relationship. And she (Celia) not only allowed people to move in, but welcomed their whole families every weekend? The son-in-law had an RV in the yard so he could spend time with his mother? No, seriously? And Celia tolerated without so much as a flinch the presence of her ex-husband, Bobby Jerome? (Not to put too fine a point upon the legalism, *ex-husband*.) Unthinkable, really, that Celia should treat Bobby just as though he had every right to be there? It was Russell's home, not Bobby's. What? Bobby missed the ferry one Sunday night (likely story) and Celia made up a cot for him in the kitchen, so there they all were when Russell came home on Sunday night, just a jolly little family group? What was wrong with Celia? Bobby Jerome should see Sunny and Brio somewhere else. Why were they living with Celia anyway? Sunny wasn't Celia's own child? Sunny was only an ex-stepdaughter? What was she doing there? Why did Sunny come to Celia's?

Dorothy thought she knew why: Sunny came because there was something prodigal about Celia; she strewed possibility in your path and made you believe you had the energy to bring those possibilities to fruition. Certainly she had that effect on Dorothy, though she would not hear of Dorothy's taking up any real work till she had the doctor's OK. So for the rest of March and April Dorothy did what she could around Celia's house, carrying on the clean-and-polish work that Eric had begun, till finally Celia forbade her from picking up so much as a broom or a brush. "A dishcloth, fine, Dorothy! A dustcloth, OK, but please, I can't bear it! You're putting me to shame!"

"That's unfair, Celia," she remarked with Mrs. Digby's inflection. "No one can put another to shame. One incurs shame oneself."

"Well then, allow me to go on being indifferent to this house. Really."

"Very well. But I must have something to do."

"Get better. And when you do, I'll put you to work if you like. You see what I've done to Sunny." And she would fling an affectionate glance over to Sunny who was reading to Brio and who looked up and smiled.

"On the contrary, Celia, I see what Sunny has done for you."

Within six weeks of her arrival Sunny had revolutionized Henry's House. No minimum-wage bed-making-dish-toting job for Sunny Jerome. She became the Lieutenant Uhura of the electronic addition. With the help of Lester Tubbs, she invested in software that allowed her to computerize everything, including menus, recipes, reservations.

From that spring forward, out went the old pencilled ledgers and recipes stuck on spindles and yellow stickies pasted on the door frames. Suppliers that had taken Henry's House for granted were rudely awakened. Sunny closed their long-standing accounts—for instance, with Isadora Landscape and Garden Supply—when she discovered they were charging a fee every month just to carry Henry's House on their books. Instead she issued a credit card to Launch so he could shop around for the best price of things he needed. She paid the credit card off every month. Moreover, at Sunny's suggestion, Celia installed in the employees' bathroom behind the kitchen (and unseen by guests) a time clock for workers to punch in and out. In this way, Sunny kept more careful track of their wages and hours. And minutes. This annoyed the students since Celia's bookkeeping had usually worked in their favor, and when it did not, Celia usually assumed herself to be in the wrong. Sunny was not often wrong.

Among the three of them, Sunny, Celia and Dorothy, there came to be a kind of mutual reliability and camaraderie that annoyed Russell during the week, perhaps even more than Bobby's presence annoyed him on the weekend. He told Celia flatly he did not like sharing her with so many people, that they never had quality time to themselves. Not only was the house itself crowded (and, he reminded her, he and she had both raised their children and should not be obliged to endure a four-year-old again) and a zoo on weekends (Eric and Victoria and Ned and Bobby reliably, other assorted Robbinses on a need-to-know basis), but also the place was continually crawling with old Isadorans, who, after her heart attack, had adopted Dorothy as a sort of ward, extending to her their geriatric guardianship, which meant they were forever dropping by and asking after her health and well-being, asking her to tea at their various studios, and filling her with tales which Dorothy repeated. Only Russell was heartless enough to tell her everyone had already heard these stories about a thousand times.

But Dorothy was an entirely new audience for the old Isadorans. So, the hoary anecdotes got trotted out, refurbished and bandied about, new and untarnished. Oh, the old days with Sophia! Her vision in founding the school, her teaching methods! Her belief in the melding of art and nature! Her days in Paris at the turn of the century, her hair grayed by the First World War! And how (this was a favorite) Sophia had beseeched her dear friend Isadora Duncan—Isadora the Great, Isadora the One-and-Only—to come to her island namesake and teach a class in the summer of 1927. Isadora Duncan had agreed, booked her tickets for passage to America and to Washington for a date one month after the day when she had her fatal encounter with the scarf and the Bugatti, tossing a long scarf around her neck as she rode out in the dashing Bugatti, the scarf catching on the wheel and Isadora choked to death. Dead of gesture.

Dorothy was charmed. Never had she lived around such people. With such stories! The closest she'd come to such variety and delight was Madcap Barb, but after Madcap Barb died, Dorothy's zest waned and she let her University Women's Club membership lapse. Madcap Barb was about the only story Dorothy had in trade for the Sophia Westervelt legends, but just talking about Madcap seemed to Dorothy to bring her more vividly back to life, to re-create Madcap's effect on Dorothy's life. She had long since ceased to talk to Ned about Madcap. Her family was bored with Dorothy's memories. What a pleasure that Celia and Sunny and Nona, Ernton, the Marchands and the other aged artists loved Madcap Barb stories.

For her part, Dorothy never tired of hearing how in 1919 Sophia Westervelt had talked dear old Pa into giving her a huge tract of land on this island which wasn't even Isadora then, but a Lummi name with a small settlement called Massacre. The island had had a Lummi name in the late 1870s when it was bought, more or less in its entirety, by the first Henry Westervelt, a failed 49'er who had taken up the rather more certain occupation of selling dry goods to the gold fields of California. He moved north and was well-established in Seattle by the 1890s when gold fever hit the lower reaches of British Columbia and moved up to the Yukon. Henry Westervelt made his name familiar anywhere men would pay $5 for an egg. Westervelt bought huge tracts of land, timberlands prodigal with forests, and he cozied up to the railroads and they snuggled back, building tracks to reach docks and mills where Westervelt lumber was processed, logs cut from Westervelt land, shipped to ports on Westervelt-leased ships. All that wealth and power notwithstanding, they remained a scruffy lot; the Westervelt men still picked their teeth with knives, and their women's lips cinched up in Protestant disapproval, not one of them with any vision beyond their bankbooks or their Bibles. With one exception.

Sophia Westervelt must have risen from the genetic silt of some long-dry family channel. At the age of eighteen Sophia talked dear old Pa into letting her study art in Paris if chaperoned by her aunt. Once in Paris she dumped the aunt and moved in with a Montparnasse artist, counting on her doting Pa to supply her with money. Which he did. Oh, the artist's life! Her copious diaries suggested she slept with Picasso, with Braque, with Juan Gris, and indicated that she was more than a little friendly with Gertrude before Alice came on the scene. But the artists and the life Sophia had loved impaled itself on barbed wire in World War I, their bodies in uniform turned to tatters, their dreams decayed with their flesh. World War I broke Sophia's heart, but not her spirit. Determined, indeed vowing to undo the work of murderous men, she would build a school and use education as her tool, convinced that art and education alone could save the world from annihilation.

It was not Sophia's intention to become a hermit, but to become a magnet. Not to lose herself but to find others. She attracted to her beautiful school, both as students and teachers, an array of like-minded painters, poets, musicians, dancers, naturalists. No doubt there were a few charlatans too, but for the most part, the people drawn here were an extraordinary group, and though the school failed, hit first by the Depression and then by World War II, Useless Point retained its eccentric cachet. It was said that the people of Useless Point were two-thirds misfit and one-third mad.

Nona York, for instance, was known to walk the beaches and the woods, alarming summer people unaccustomed to her working methods, which included a sort of books-on-tape in advance of books-in-print. She would narrate her novels into a tape recorder (breathless dialog and all) as she strolled the woods and beaches with her dogs and her dish towel, the relationship of dogs to dish towel not immediately apparent. Nona's were a bevy of small dogs, canine shrapnel who would explode, tear madly about and pee on every bush and post, yap and run after people, biting their ankles and barking ferociously, ignoring Nona's every command until she took the dish towel and began hitting herself with it, calling out *Doggy doggy doggy*. And to this curious conditioning the dogs responded. The faster Nona thwacked herself with the dish towel, the faster did the dogs obey her. Islanders of course were used to this. During the course of Dorothy's recovery, on her many walks with Nona, Dorothy got used to it too. She and Nona became the best of friends.

When Dorothy had first returned to Celia's after the hospital, Nona brought over a half dozen of her novels. "Just what the doctor ordered," she said.

Looking at the covers of these books, Dorothy rather blanched, and would have declined, but she had promised herself Liberation through Learning, and, well, the first step was to take the garters off your mind.

For Dorothy Robbins, Nona's novels were as much an education as Wordsworth had ever been. More. They kept her awake at night, reading, pondering, wondering. They gave her insight that more closely resembled oversight: how could Dorothy have gone through her whole life and felt nothing of the vehemence chronicled in these pages? She had been married all her adult life and had borne four children, but she had never felt, could never have imagined, could never have approached such passion. *Passion*. Dorothy savored the word, *passion*. Dorothy felt certain Celia Henry had actually lived like a Nona York heroine. She admired

Celia the more, though she would never have dreamed of trying to emulate her.

But when Celia offered to take Dorothy to Sophia's Beach, along with Brio, to teach them both to spit, Dorothy agreed. It was too early for watermelon, so Celia brought sunflower seeds and as they walked up and down the beach, a tattered shawl of barnacles and seaweed, Celia demonstrated. Brio and Dorothy practiced. It was a leap for Dorothy, but once encouraged, she could spit, perhaps not *con brio,* or even very well, but there did seem to be something liberating about standing at the tide line and raising your chin, focusing your attention and spitting, getting it out. Letting go.

Also, it helped that Celia, too, told stories of the old days on Isadora, how years and years ago Sophia's was a nude beach, even when the kids were little. "Oh, everyone came down here, jumped out of their clothes and jumped in the water. But you can't stand it for very long. The girls looked like naked little savages. They used to get brown as little berries and fight their battles with their Boomerquangers." Then she had to explain what a Boomerquanger was.

"I have some difficulty imagining Victoria running naked with a Boomerquanger," Dorothy confessed.

"Well, she wasn't always naked, of course. Isadora Island got more respectable and people didn't take their clothes off anymore. Isn't it strange, Dorothy—you raise them up, your children, you think you know them better than anyone and then, once they're grown, they are a complete puzzlement to you, both my daughters. I used to think Bethie was most like me, but not now. I can't imagine myself ever mouthing all that junk Wade puts in her mouth and Bethie swallows." On this note, Celia spat. "Every time I see her, or talk to her on the phone, she's just full of this pious bullshit. Even in love, I don't think I could have done that. Even for a man who turned me to sexual mush."

"Sexual mush . . ." Dorothy considered the phrase and then spat a sunflower seed with an ineffectual trajectory. "What is sexual mush?"

"The agony of the breakup is in direct proportion to the ecstasy of the affair. It's loving a man who scrambles your brains, no matter what he's doing to your body. When your brains aren't congealed with lust, they're fried with pain."

"Sounds like a Nona York novel," Dorothy observed. "That's what the sex is like in her books."

"I love Nona—but her books? I don't even try. I couldn't read them any more than I could watch soap operas."

"I used to watch soap operas. When I was done with my floors."

"Well, Dorothy dear, spit on! There'll be no soap operas for you, and no more reflections in floors. Are you ready to go to work? The pay is shit."

"But the rewards are great."

That was what Dorothy told Ned when he arrived the following Saturday. She told him he would have to stop coming on Saturday because she was starting work at Henry's House. "The pay is shit," Dorothy said, coloring slightly, "but the rewards are great."

"Work!" he cried, ignoring everything else. "Work? You've never worked a day in your life!" They had walked through the woods to a fabled Isadoran point, Chinook Lookout, high up over the rocks and the Sound, with the view across to the faraway lighthouse. The view was especially astonishing because coming through the woods one never had the sense of climbing, so on a sunny day, the effect, coming out of the deep woods to bare, moss-thatched cliffs, was—in Dorothy's lexicon—dazzling. She had spread out a picnic blanket and poured them each two cups of hot tea from the thermos while Ned flustered and fluttered, bludgeoned and begrudged the notion of Dorothy's new job. "You don't have to earn your keep here, Dorothy. I offered to pay Celia while you stayed here. I offered! I had the checkbook out and she refused. She refused just to make me angry."

"She refused because she knows there are some things money can't buy."

"Like?"

"If you don't know, Ned, I can't possibly tell you what they are."

"Are you getting minimum wage? Benefits? Social Security? I'll turn her into the feds if she's abusing your naiveté!"

"I am not naive."

"You've never been out in the world. You don't know what it's like. It's . . . It's . . ." Words failed Ned and he huffed and puffed and blew himself up into a dither. "You've never worked a day in your life!"

"That's not true, Neddy, and it's not fair and it's not kind." She sugared his tea for him.

"But it's true, damn it! I've supported you since the day we got married."

"And I've supported you. For better or for worse, I have supported your every endeavor."

"What the hell kind of work can you do?"

"I have lots of experience."

"At?"

"At supporting you, Neddy. Think of it, all those years, advancing your career—and I did a very good job, Ned. Look where you are now, how successful and important. All the things you wanted from life I helped you to achieve."

"I thought we both wanted those things, Dorothy."

"Well, we did, and we both worked to get them. I worked being kind, being nice, being interested and accommodating to people I scarcely knew and cared nothing for, keeping house, keeping everything running smoothly at home for you. That's a skill. That's a talent. I was a good mother. The children annoyed you and I spared you all that, well, messiness. I'm putting all those years to some use at last. I have something more than my floors to be proud of. They didn't need to be that clean," she added with dreamy finality.

Ned's round face and balding head suffused with color and choler, but he made an especial effort to soften the words he wanted to hurl like rocks. He reminded his wife she had had a heart attack. She was supposed to be recuperating. "You're not supposed to take your first job—ever—when you're recuperating from a heart attack. You're supposed to take it easy and stay at home."

"I'm not ready to go back to Bellevue. Not yet. I'm not strong enough to face the floors. I must be cured first, not of the heart attack—which is a condition, not a virus—but of being a floor-o-phile. That's what I was, Ned, I loved my floors. When Bethie was here last weekend with Wade, he said I was a victim of my floors and caught up in very bad addictive behaviors."

Ned peered at her weirdly. "I pay a woman to come in once a week and keep the floors up for you, Dorothy. I take my shoes off now, Dorothy, just like you always wanted me to do."

"Wear your shoes if you like, dear. It's all right. I'm weaning myself away from the floors. I'm looking for a new reflection, but I'm not going to ReDiscovery. I shall do this my own way. When I am ready, dear, I shall go home, but I shall not go back." She leaned over to rummage in the picnic basket and bring out the sandwiches, neatly wrapped. "Celia doesn't think like anyone I've ever met. Such imagination, Ned. Really. Look here. Olive sandwiches. Who else but Celia would think to make olive sandwiches? Mother always did ham or baloney, cream cheese and pimento on your birthday. But olive?"

Ned held his olive sandwich disconsolately, as though it had anchovies and escargots. "What's wrong with your hair?"

Dorothy reached up and touched the crown of her head. "It's gray, dear. You're bald and I'm gray."

"You didn't used to be."

"That's because I was having the Triumph of Art Over Nature. Once a month."

Ned's whole face strained into a frown. "What are you talking about?"

So Dorothy nibbled on her olive sandwich and tootled on about the restorative aspects of art and how it could be used, often was used to remedy nature, to prettify nature, to tease us into believing that our lives could be picketed against nature. She understood at last that art was garnish, fine in its way, but once it came to substitute for life's roughage, then something was amiss. All nature was cyclic, all art was static.

"Oh, Dorothy, Dorothy," he groaned. "You didn't used to talk like that." Here in the afternoon sunlight she did look decidedly different from the woman who had collapsed just a few months ago. The gray radiated out from the crown of Dorothy's head in a lengthening swirl, softening her complexion and visibly underscoring her conviction that her life had taken a fundamental turn, a change as certain as if she had crossed into a new country.

Perhaps she had. Beginning in May, on Fridays and Saturdays Dorothy greeted guests who arrived at Henry's House. This was her new job. Checking the reservations list (and the method of payment) unobtrusively against a master list that Sunny gave her, Dorothy invited people in, advised them where to hang their coats and hats, to leave their bags in the foyer and to come have tea. (Credit cards were not discussed till people had refreshed themselves.) She directed one group to the library, another to the conservatory, one to the wisteria arbor in good weather, and while they meandered off to absorb Henry's House, Dorothy took a set of color-coded tags (her own invention) from hooks in the cloakroom and put them on bags to let Launch know which ones to take to which rooms.

Occasionally the sight of Launch, his wild hair and mammoth beard, gray-flecked and wiry, his grinning and bobbing, dismayed guests who saw him hoisting their bags. These people Dorothy calmed with the observation that it was a little like having their bags carried by St. Jerome. "Launch is silent of spiritual necessity," she added, "but he's not mute."

Then Dorothy would smile. The sort of smile that had so endeared her to the University Women's Club, the Dahlia Society of Greater Bellevue and the Republican Women of King County. She had indeed a wealth of experience. To be greeted by Dorothy Robbins was like being greeted by your own mother, someone exuding undeserved maternal approbation and—equally undeserved—implicit criticism. Dorothy was not above straightening a cuff or collar, brushing a bit of dust (or dandruff) from the shoulder, or even righting a brooch, the sorts of actions by which mothers always let children (especially grown children) know they are fine on the whole, but some little detail could yet be improved. There is always some impossible maternal standard which can never be attained. She was priceless beyond rubies.

And she was not *cum laude* for nothing. Though some forty years had passed since her graduation from the University of Washington, her unswerving attention to detail—which she had once bestowed upon her studies and then upon her sons, then upon her floors—still served her. From the modest set of responsibility she took on early that spring, Dorothy moved into larger arenas, found reflections that were not in the floor, and in her cool, unflappable way, she rose to the occasion. And while she was at it, she always put the lid on the toothpaste, folded the bath mat and dried the water spots from the chrome fixtures at Celia's.

In her married life Dorothy had had a house key and two car keys, but now she carried a key ring noisy with implied responsibility. In fact, the larger measure of both, since that summer the whole edifice of obligation associated with Henry's House fell on Dorothy. It became her responsibility from that June day she came out to the wisteria arbor, drawn there because she heard the sound of human weeping, sobs, perhaps not even human, sounds so utterly bereft she thought, feared, perhaps she had disturbed ghosts who needed a less stately mansion in which to spew their anguish. But what she saw was Celia Henry, sitting on a bench, broad shoulders heaving. To see Celia decimated with sorrow surprised Dorothy more than if she had come upon her in the throes of passion, à la Nona York. *Has someone died? Has someone died?*

As that terrible summer progressed—and though no one had died—Celia could not recover her old equilibrium. For the first time in her working life, her energy, imagination and stamina failed her, or failed to resuscitate and her endless elasticity could not remain forever supple. Into this void (because Henry's House must go on; once created, the place had its own demands and urgent needs and could not be denied because a place dedicated to the proposition that family could inspire and comfort you must never hint that it could also destroy you) came Dorothy Robbins. Dorothy's equilibrium had never been better.

The very summer that Henry's House graced the pages of *Joie de Vivre!* (its own bit of immortality), guests—who had read of *Sesamied Salmon* and *Chicken Grilled with Peppers and Vermouth*, who might look forward to *Linguine with Almond Pesto* or *Chicken Poached in Lavender Water*, to *Lemon Rice with Basil*—found themselves at dinner confronted by meat loaf and mashed potatoes. Salad with thousand island dressing. Rice pudding for dessert. Dorothy's mother's favorite cookbook had always been *The Wonders of Cornstarch.* The book itself long vanished, its coarse pages flaked and fretted, crumbled into the collective memory of generations of people like Dorothy, and their children and their children's children for whom gravy was sacred, Velveeta sublime, to whom 7-Up salad (lime Jell-O and canned pineapple) was an everlasting delight and no culinary problem so profound it could not be addressed, enhanced or concealed with a can of Campbell's mushroom soup. *It's good for you,* Dorothy told people who prodded at the meat loaf, looking perhaps for pâté de foie gras. *Eat up,* she said in a voice that had raised four boys to manhood. Extolling the food at Henry's House, the article in *Joie de Vivre!* had headlined:

CUISINE AT THE CROSSROADS OF MEMORY AND IMAGINATION

Dorothy Robbins came down rather more firmly on the side of memory. Under Dorothy's regime, judges, surgeons, airline pilots, TV personalities, politicians and Microsoft executives, the successful men and women of this world, retreated into the wary watchfulness of well-brought-up children presented with Brussels sprouts on their plates, their mother's eagle eye attending them, lest they should slide those sprouts under the rim of the plate, leaving, at the end of dinner, a little green halo on a gray Formica table.

PART IV

Dying, Egypt, Dying

A dandelion in March is more welcome than a lily in June, and despite the unremitting rain, the cloud-clotted skies, dandelions yet dotted the hillsides and roadsides before March surrendered to April. Wet, misanthropic April relented unto May. But spring on Isadora Island is coy and unreliable, and—like a coy and unreliable lover—on those days when it was not false, it felt somehow supremely true. People came out from under their raincoats and stretched their bare, mushroom-colored arms to the sunlight, closed their eyes and turned their pale faces skyward.

That's what Brio and Sunny Jerome did one afternoon on the sloping lawn before Henry's House. In summer, the lawn was dotted with wicker furniture and wooden deck chairs, but it was too early for such amenities, and Brio and Sunny had spread their jackets out beneath them on the damp ground and lay down, their overalls rolled up to the knee, eyes closed. That's where

Grant found them when he paused at the top of the drive. He meandered downhill, sitting down beside Sunny and making a sign for Brio to be quiet so as not to wake her mother. Sunny between them, Grant and Brio looked across Useless Point to Assumption Island's gray rocks. At this distance the seals looked like rocks themselves, differentiated from the rocks only because they barked and moved now and then, grossly clumsy on land. Sunlight gleamed and rippled in the bright and intersecting circles of water where they splashed.

Grant had come to Henry's House to help Launch lift and stack some heavy timbers for a raised herb garden bed just beyond the kitchen, but dressed in ironed shirt and jeans still stiff from the clothesline, he did not look like a man here to do heavy work. A few nights before, Launch had motored his small boat over to the Massacre Marina where Grant lived on the *Pythagoras,* a 28-foot wooden sailboat he was restoring. With pen and paper Launch communicated what he needed. As Grant had watched Launch gesticulate, he realized that Launch himself was a reliable barometer of the change of season. Merely by looking at him— shorn or unshorn—Isadorans knew that the earth had turned again and some balance struck between the day and night, between light and darkness.

This warm May afternoon was the island's prize for having endured a sulky April. And not until a thin cloud veiled the sky, casting an imperceptible chill, did Sunny wake up with a start, surprised to see Grant Hayes. She hoped she had not snored. Collecting herself with some difficulty, she inquired what had brought him to Henry's House and how long he'd been there.

"About fifteen minutes. Ask Brio."

"Brio can't tell time."

"All the better."

Sunny fluffed her short hair which had grown out a bit in the last few months and now seemed to her uncomfortably long.

Grant chatted about Launch and the timbers that needed lifting for the kitchen garden, one more thing that needed to be ready for the *Joie de Vivre!* editor whose arrival on Wednesday was the current focal point of all Useless activity. He did not say that none of this had brought him round to the front of the house, or mandated the clean, neat clothes. He did not say that Sunny Jerome was the most elusive and interesting woman he had ever met. Warm, but not always approachable, Sunny carried before her some bright independence, like a candle, or a sword for that matter. Having heard her joke once about trying out for Joan of Arc, Grant thought perhaps that wasn't such a bad analogy. She rather reminded him of Joan of Arc. Even thinking in terms of analogies was new for Grant. By nature and training he thought in geometric terms, and his experience with women had, for the most part, been with women who were themselves of a geometric turn of mind. They geometrically took the shortest distance between any two points. Say, between the front door and the bedroom. They were not aggressive, the women he was accustomed to, but efficient. They liked to get the sex out of the way, so as to arrive more quickly at the essential questions, like, if they liked him. They believed and said plainly that if you got the sexual tension relieved, you could decide if you liked the guy, your vision unclouded by anticipation. Grant always agreed this made sense. Oh, eminently sensible, but not altogether fulfilling—a word he was reluctant to use because he was never quite sure what he meant since it could not be described with axioms. And as opposed to the geometric women he was used to, Sunny Jerome seemed an enigmatic spiral.

They sat together on the grass and watched as Brio delighted herself, rolling downhill, coming to a stop at the edge of the lawn where dandelions shone, golden buttons in the shadows cast by lavender rhododendrons. She stood up and waved at them.

Between Assumption and Useless, a single sailboat came into view, struggling with the stiff currents and unruly wind. Sunny lay back down, arm draped over her forehead, but Grant watched with interest, admiring the way the sailor tacked. "I still think *Pythagoras* could beat him though."

"Why do men always think of competition first?" Sunny asked. "And who was Pythagoras?"

"One of those old Greeks, the father of geometry, but he's also supposed to have come up with the notion of the transmigration of souls. A Renaissance man. Before the Renaissance."

"Tell me about *Pythagoras*," said Sunny, pleased just to lie there and feel the wind and hear his voice. "The boat—not the transmigration of souls."

"Fifty years old, all wood," he said, relaxing into one of his favorite subjects, going on with the technical descriptions, till he thought her even breathing suggested she had gone back to sleep. "The last owner let it go to hell, so I got it cheap. But it was a mess. I'm restoring it while I live on it. A sailboat is the only kind of boat to have. It tests everything you've got, your strength, your savvy, your coordination, your senses, everything. I don't have any use for the other kind of boats, those big powerboats like the Robbinses' *Strumpet,* that's nothing but an RV on water. A bus. But a sailboat—well, that's a combination of art and science and nature. People have been using the same principles to sail for thousands of years, maybe millions. Think about it. Think about the first man who stood on a beach or a high cliff and saw a place far away, a distant shore he wanted to get to. Wind and water. Boats and kites. I love the way they use the wind. It's, well, poetic." He flinched slightly at the word.

"Shakespeare thought so too." Sunny sat up. *"The barge she sat in, like a burnished throne, burned on the water; the poop was beaten gold, purple the sails and so perfumed"*—she opened her arms up wide—*"the winds were lovesick with them."* She laughed. *"Antony and Cleopatra.* I played Cleopatra once. You know, the great lines, *I am dying, Egypt, dying.* That's all anyone remembers."

Grant did not remember, would not have known *I am dying, Egypt, dying* from the menu at Little Caesar's Pizza. "When were you Cleopatra?"

"A gala theatrical experience at Santa Monica City College." She lay back down. "I'm done with acting, though, and I'm certainly finished with roles where women kill themselves for love. In books and plays, love motivates everything. Greed and revenge are only close seconds."

"And in life?"

She regarded him critically. "You're an odd sort of engineer."

"I'm not an engineer. I have the degree and I could have had the job. Fat salary. Benefits. Vacation. 401K plan. The whole American dream, tied up in a great big bow, handed to me right out of college, the rest of my life laid out like the white line on Route 5. That's what was wrong with it." Boeing had offered a similar job to his girlfriend. They had been living together their senior year in Pullman, and her idea of the glorious future, the possibilities in life, was to move to Seattle, get an apartment, start their jobs with Boeing and work there forever. "I'd been jumping through hoops for years, taking courses required of me, turning in assigned work, all that. Why would I want to graduate and keep on doing the same thing? Different hoops, that's all. I didn't want to spend my life, my energy, fretting over some little kink that eighty other engineers were fretting over too. So, I just declined the job—and the girl who wanted me to take the job," he added obliquely, "and I came back here to Isadora. I knew I could always work for my dad. Lee was here. I could have a sailboat here. And besides, I had this idea for a path through Celia's orchard, connecting her place to Henry's." He laughed ruefully. "So look at me, I could be wearing a tie, bent over a computer, or selling something to the unsuspecting. As it is, I'm sitting here on this lawn with you and we're watching the crazy currents between Useless and Assumption."

"And you get to live on a sailboat." Sunny sat up and stretched.

"Once *Pythagoras* is seaworthy I'm going to sail her all the way down the west coast to Baja. To Costa Rica maybe. I hear it's great down there. That's the real challenge for any sailor, to do it solo."

"Only men think it's so romantic to go it alone. Look at you—you're off with your boat—you and no other. Man against the sea! Why do men think you can only be a hero by yourself? Man against Nature! Man against Society! Why don't men ever acknowledge that keeping something together can be just as heroic as being all alone? Men are always against something. Why can't they be for something?"

Grant seemed to ponder this. "What are you for? World peace? An end to hunger? Human brotherhood?"

"I'm not committed to universals." She drew her knees up close and wrapped her arms around them. "I'm for very modest, particular things. An ordinary life. Watching my daughter grow up. Making a home for us. A living. Nothing very grand or ambitious."

"To be without ambition doesn't sound like you."

"How do you know?"

"You're The Talented One, aren't you?"

Only the wind rustled between them, carrying Brio's bright voice, and off-shore, the seals barked in response. "Talent isn't enough. Talent by itself is a poor thing, like a seed with no dirt or water to make it grow. If it's going to flower, then you need more than a seed, more than just talent. You need a kind of grit and willingness to sacrifice. I'm not like that. Linda—my mother—was like that."

"Where is she now?"

"She died."

"I'm sorry to hear that."

Sunny shrugged. "It was a long time ago and I didn't know her very well anyway. She left us when I was little, went to Denver to pursue her art. She had lots of talent, fancied herself an artist, like Bobby fancied himself a composer. They were bound to break up sometime. All marriages do, I suppose. Although I think Janice and Bobby will probably last. If you can accept chronic pain, you can accept anything."

"Bobby is still a composer."

"He writes songs. And he loves music," she said affectionately. "He's a fine musician and his students love him, but he never took on the world and he never will. Linda took on the world. But to do that she had to leave us. Since Brio was born, I've kept wishing I could ask Linda, *How could you do that? How could you leave me, your daughter?* I could never leave Brio. Just walk away from her? I moved back here because I couldn't live *con brio,* because they were eating up my life in L.A. My little daughter stayed with the neighbors and I only saw her in the morning when we were rushed, and in the evening when we were tired. Even when I wasn't off on location, there was always someone on the phone needing me. There was always some crisis or another, something that couldn't wait. The stress was intolerable finally, and I thought, This is the only life I have, the only life I'll ever get and I'm giving it away to people who don't really matter to me at all, who flatter me by saying, Oh, Sunny, you're the only one who can do this or that, fix this, or answer that question. Really? And if I died tomorrow? Wouldn't someone step in and fill that void? Of course they would. My daughter will not grow up without me. Not if I can help it. I don't understand how my mother could leave me. Giving up your family, your child, to pursue your art? Maybe it makes a difference to the rest of the world if you turn out to be Picasso, but it doesn't help the family, does it?" She scoffed lightly, "Whenever my dad wants to explain their youthful aberrations, he gets misty and says, *Oh, it was the sixties,* like that should explain everything."

"My grandmother would excuse crazy things she'd done saying: *Oh, it was the War.*"

"Exactly. Too bad for us, huh? What can we say? *Oh, it was the nineties?*"

Grant chewed on a dandelion stem. "Why would anyone go to Denver? I mean, for art?"

"Who knows? When I was little I used to picture Linda pursuing her art and all I could see was this lovely woman, arms outstretched, chasing after a paintbrush or a palate or something she couldn't quite touch, calling out, *Wait! Stop! Wait for me!*"

"Did she catch it?"

"I know almost nothing about her life. Denver, Taos, Tempe, Phoenix, she would always send me hand-painted postcards and packages. They always had a sun on them, a great big sun with shining rays and the address in the center. So I knew they were for me. That's my real name, Soleil, French for sun, or sunshine, a lovely conceit, I guess. Bethie and Victoria, their real names are Harmony and Clarity."

Grant laughed. "Hard to imagine, isn't it? What was in the packages your mom sent?"

"Decorative vials from all these hot, sunny places with bright-colored water, each one with a hand-lettered label, *Eau de Soleil*. French, for Sunny's cologne, something like that."

Grant nodded, as though secretly pleased or amused. "What did they smell like?"

"Paint. They had that wisp or whisper of paint, or maybe food coloring. They didn't really smell, but they were always lovely colors and beautiful little bottles, corked or capped. *Eau de Soleil*. I used to line the bottles up on windowsills so they would catch the light."

"Where are they now?"

"Oh, I don't know. Lost. Bobby and I moved around a lot for a while. I probably left some at Celia's."

"You did," Grant said after a time, and with a suppressed laugh. "When Lee and I moved in with Dad and Celia, Bethie and Victoria had to double up so Lee and I could have a room. And I found some of these little bottles in a shoe box in the closet."

"It must have been my old room. The one Dorothy's in now?"

"Yes. I found a box of them on the floor of the closet, *Eau de Soleil*. Well, I didn't know what the hell that meant, but they looked inviting."

"Inviting?"

"I drank them."

They both burst out laughing, so much so that Brio, hearing their voices, looked up from where she had been pelting Baby Herman with the torn-off heads of dandelions and she raced back up the hill.

"I drank them and I kept waiting for something magical to happen."

"Did it?"

"Well, I threw up once."

The alchemy of the moment worked its magic on Sunny—the happy child running up the lawn, this sun-drenched lawn, the unruffled Sound in the distance, the barking of the seals and even the man beside her. Part of Grant's appeal, she decided, was his own contentment; people whose lives are fundamentally satisfying are always attractive. They suggest about themselves a sort of leisure and generosity that hungry, driven, dissatisfied people can't fake or emulate. Was that the difference between Grant Hayes and all the other men she had known? Even if he was off to Baja sailing solo, his life was not bifurcated like the men in L.A. who were all writers/directors, actors/models, waiters/producers. Grant seemed all of one piece, though the scholarly glasses were at odds with his calloused hands. She thought he must look like his mother, the woman who had abandoned him and his twin brother, just as Sunny had been abandoned, the lot of them raveled back together by Celia Henry. They were alumni of the Unfettered School.

She touched his hand, turning it so she could see his watch. "I've been here too long. I have to go up to the house. I'm expecting a delivery and I have to make sure everything's there. Celia always just signed her receipts without counting anything. Then, if she finds she's short, she'd have to go back through the whole order to find out where it had gone wrong. It was always too much trouble. She lost money."

"Maybe so, but she's doing all right by this place."

"She overcharges." Sunny called out to Brio, insisting she leave the dandelions in peace. "I don't know why she agreed to this *Joie de Vivre!* thing. Prestige, I guess. I'll be glad when it's over. Celia's been quarreling with them ever since she agreed to do it, grumbling. Endless upheavals with Diane. That's the editor."

"Celia doesn't like people telling her what to do."

"Diane made her submit her guest list and then complained about it. *Joie de Vivre!* insists on couples. You should have heard Celia. She was in a cursing froth, telling Diane that it was a party, not goddamned Noah's Ark where we all had to get on two by two. That's why you got invited," she informed him crisply. "So there'll be an even number of men and women. It'll be Russell and Celia, Dorothy and Ned, Victoria and Eric, and Bethie and Wade. Then, after all that, when Diane heard Nona York lived on this island, suddenly she didn't care about couples anymore. Diane went into a swoon, and told Celia how much Nona would enhance the shoot and how the whole world reads her books."

"Really? What whole world reads Nona?"

"The whole world that buys their literature at the checkout counter with batteries and disposable razors and chewing gum. Have you ever read one of her books?" Grant had not. "They're very instructive if you're ten or twelve."

"You mean like what-goes-where?"

"What-goes-where! That will never appear in a Nona York novel. It's all described in terms of sensation. The breathlessness of it is so convincing that when you close up one of her novels, you are certain you will never be a whole person until someone loves you just like that. The kissing is rapture and the sex is so exquisite that you ache. It's silly."

"It doesn't sound so bad."

"It isn't if you're ten. But for an adult?"

Grant thought of the women he'd known best, of their sexual directness and ungarnished candor. They were athletic women, full of endurance and strength, and the bed always seemed a sort of diving board from which they could spring and exhibit their form. "Maybe people read Nona York's books because even though they know what-goes-where, they can't describe the sensation. They need the words. Maybe there is an experience where you do feel whole, but most people can't express it."

Sunny rolled her eyes. "This is the nineties, Grant."

"Not for long. Pretty soon it will be something else. Something entirely new. The turn of the century."

"You'll be sailing solo to Baja by then." She stood, shook out Brio's little jacket, and smoothed her hair. "See you later."

Grant plucked the dandelion stem from his teeth. "After I

finish with Launch, you want to go to Sophia's Beach? You and Brio. Ride on the swing? Ice cream afterwards?"

"I can't," Sunny said firmly.

"Tomorrow?"

Sunny flushed. "I'm sorry, Grant. I should just tell you, so there's no hard feelings, but I don't date people."

"Oh." He rose and dusted off his backside.

"Goodbye then." She started uphill.

"Gnomes?"

"Excuse me?"

"Do you date gnomes? I could grow a beard and wear a pointed cap and floppy shoes and hunch over if you think you'd like me better. Get a big fake nose. Brio, would you like me better if I were a gnome?"

"Yes." Brio's face puckered. "What's a gnome?"

"Like a Huggamugwump," Sunny explained, "only not so furry."

"And taller," Grant added quickly. "Better-looking. Smarter. Talented. Oh, gnomes are really talented. Notoriously talented. They are the champion kite flyers of the world."

"I thought you lived on a boat. You can't fly a kite off a sailboat."

"Last time I looked, Moonless Bay was right across Massacre, about half a mile from the Massacre Marina. Moonless is low and flat and treeless. I build kites and fly them, but I'm tired of flying kites solo. Man against the wind, you know. Tedious, really."

Sunny said goodbye and left him, going up through the orchard to Celia's. She could see the Swan's delivery truck already there in the yard. She had lingered too long on the lawn. Dorothy was showing the driver where the freezers were. Sunny quickly got her clipboard and inventory and checked each item and quantity off in her methodical fashion as he loaded the two freezers. Brio went out to play, and Dorothy returned to her Nona York novel.

After the deliveryman left, Sunny found Brio in the orchard, in her own favorite tree. Since Brio was supposed to be invisible,

Sunny called out only generally, "I'm going to Henry's and I'll be back in a bit!" Approaching Henry's, she could hear Grant and Launch, the sounds of their hammers ringing, their voices, just out of sight. She went in through the kitchen, calling out for Celia, who did not answer.

She found Celia finally in the foyer using the electric buffer on the floors, dancing to the music in her headphones, Motown girl-groups, Sunny suspected. She stopped the buffer, the noise died and the headphones sounded tinny. "I can't believe Dorothy used to do floors for fun."

"Maybe she'd do them here."

"No floors for Dorothy. Not anymore." Celia turned down her headphones. "Anyway, she should just be getting her strength back now."

"She takes long walks with Nona every day."

"Yes, and we have to keep a careful eye that she doesn't snatch dish towels and start flagellating herself with them, don't we? Ned would think it was all my fault."

Still moving to some Motown rhythm, Celia unplugged the buffer and carried it back to the kitchen. "The spring is my favorite part of the Season. The work doesn't all have to be done on a tight schedule, and we can relax a bit. The weekends are crowded, but during the week, we don't usually have many people."

"No one tonight."

"It's nice we're booked through September. I like a house full of people." She put the floor polisher by the back door. It would go out in one of the small neat sheds where Sophia had once raised chickens for the school, and where now (the chicken smell entirely gone) they kept appliances out of sight. The kitchen itself was high-ceilinged like the rest of the house, with long windows, walls painted a pale vanilla color, and blue tiles behind the stove and sinks. Blue and pale yellow accented everywhere, from the ceramic handles on the ancient spigots to the knobs on cupboard doors. Along one wall there was a huge, five-foot-long cooker, too big to be called a stove, black metal with brass fittings, ovens large and small, grills, the whole of it overhung by an enormous hood at either end of which copper pots hung. For all the versatility and expanse of Henry's kitchen, the truly messy work got done at Celia's kitchen, so that this place should always look as though all meals cooked themselves, and phantom hands were ever-present to clean up.

"I need Friday off next week," Sunny began. "I have to go to the doctor. In Seattle. Dr. Aagard said the best doctor he knew was there and I made an appointment."

"Are you pregnant?"

"Haven't you ever been to the doctor for anything other than pregnancy?"

"I had an ear infection once. Hurt like hell." Celia turned on the tap high over the soapstone sink. "I have to be at death's door to go to the doctor."

Sunny took a deep breath. She knew that Celia loathed illness, hated talk of illness, knew how impatient she was with people who rattled on about their health, their bodies as topics of conversations or competitions, but that was not Sunny's situation. "I'm not pregnant," she said flatly as Celia continued to echo some deathless doo-wop. "You remember my mother, Linda?"

"Of course. I never met her though. She was, well she was gone before Bobby and I . . ."

"You remember what she died of?"

Celia turned off the tap and the headphones, turned to Sunny. "She died of cancer. Breast cancer."

The fear is worse than the feat, Sunny told herself. "Linda didn't give me very much, my blue eyes, I suppose, and these rotten genes. I had a radical mastectomy of my left breast, Celia, well up into the armpit area. They took out thirteen nodes and of these, ten were malignant."

Celia paled and sat down, sank into a chair, knotting her hands one over the other.

"But that was two years ago almost and I have been OK—not altogether fine, maybe. I don't have a lot of stamina and I have to be careful, always get rest and all that, but so far the cancer hasn't returned. And that's really miraculous. Even the doctor said so. Miraculous."

"Why didn't Bethie or Victoria tell me?"

"They didn't know. Don't know. Still don't know."

Momentarily speechless, Celia finally spluttered, "Still? You were diagnosed with cancer, had a mastectomy, chemo, recovery, you went through all that alone?"

"I wasn't altogether alone. I had friends. Good friends and support in L.A., and I tried, really, more than once, to call home, but it was just too terrible. Cancer was too awful to say. I knew my dad would dissolve—he fell apart when Linda died and he hadn't even heard from her in years. I knew Victoria and Bethie would be on the first plane to L.A. and that the whole family would be all over me. I couldn't bear it. And if they came, Brio would know I was really sick. And even if I could have told them"—she bit her lower lip and swallowed hard—"I couldn't tell Brio. There are no words to tell a child that."

"Oh, Sunny—you should have let us help you. You should have turned to us."

"I told myself, I'll wait. Till after the surgery. If the doctor says to me: You're doomed, you're finished, you are dying, Egypt, dying, I'll call my family in Washington. But he didn't say that. I have a chance. Five years."

"Five years to live?" cried Celia.

Sunny sat down and slumped forward. "Five years to stay clean."

"They make it sound like alcoholism."

"Standard advice for cancer patients. And that's after all the really terrifying stuff, after the mastectomy, after I'd been drained and post-op'd and taught to sleep with pillows under my left arm, after I'd been therapied and dosed with tons of meds, after aggressive chemo. Five years was the good news. I get tests every three months—that's why I'm going to Seattle. Dr. Aagard said he was only a family physician and the best doctors were in Seattle—and take my meds, and if the cancer doesn't come back in five years, I have a good chance for a normal life. Whatever that is."

Celia wiped her eyes with the back of her hand and struggled against tears. "That night, when you just showed up before the engagement party, you said you'd reached a point in life when you asked yourself what you couldn't live without."

"Doesn't speak much for my maturity that I had to undergo breast cancer, a mastectomy and chemo before I asked the question, I suppose," Sunny conceded sadly. "I had to wait for someone to tell me I was going to die. Of course, everyone's going to die, but people don't think about it, don't wake up in the morning and say to themselves: I'm going to die one day so I should leave nothing undone. I should embrace every moment because all this—life—is finite. People always say you should live intensely, like every day will be your last, but you can't. You'd go mad. No, you need to be able to believe you're not going to die. You need to believe you'll live forever and your days will ripple out endlessly. You have to believe in your own life. Once you believe in your own death, you ask questions. Difficult questions."

"That's exactly what happened to Dorothy with her heart attack."

"Cancer isn't like a heart attack. Cancer is a long drawn-out process and in all these years, it's Brio I embrace every day. I try not to think: If I die now, she'd scarcely even remember me. I hold her and love her and I ask God, Just let me live to see her grow up. But if He doesn't—" Sunny toyed with the buckle on her overalls. "What I mean is, I couldn't live without Brio, but I couldn't die without knowing she was safe and protected and raised by someone who would love her." Sunny rested her gaze on Celia's well-known face. "You said I should have let you help me. I'm asking for your help. I need your help. That's why I came back here."

"You want me to raise Brio."

"Yes. Please. If I die—"

"I'll raise Brio. I'll love her like my own. She'll be my own."

"If I die, you'll raise my daughter?" It had to be said, outright, attested to.

"I promise. You won't die, but whatever happens, yes, you have my promise."

"Please don't cry, Celia. I just had to do this now while I have the time and the strength. I can't count on either. I had to bring Brio back to Isadora so she could get to know you and you would know her, and if things went badly, if I got sick again, if—"

"This is your home. Both of you. For as long as you want. Always if you want."

"Can we ask Mr. Ellerman to—"

"After these *Joie de Vivre!* people leave, we'll both go to Seattle and see Ellerman. I'm honored, Sunny, especially since I know I haven't been the best of . . ." She sought some phrase that would encapsulate all the complicated past. "You and I haven't always—"

"It doesn't matter. We haven't always gotten along, you and I, but what mother and stepdaughter do? What's important to me now is that you always accepted me here, like I was your own."

"And you are! Bobby feels the same way about Bethie. Bobby and I have done some harm in our time, but we always agreed that the girls were all sisters and should stay that way. We tried, anyway," she added.

"I was happy here as a child. When I came back a couple of months ago I wanted to be certain that I hadn't remembered it all wrong, or just through the veil of nostalgia. I wanted to live here for a while and see if you were still the woman I remembered and Isadora was still the place I knew."

"Nothing changes here. Very little anyway."

"You've changed. You have. You're more tolerant."

"That's old age. I'm pushing fifty, you know. I hope I die before you do, Sunny." She opened her arms to Sunny and they cried silently against each other's shoulders.

"You gave me my dreams, Celia. The famous battery-powered dress. The Spirit of Christmas." Sunny sniffed, drew back and wiped her nose. "You made the dress. You coached me in my lines. I stood on that stage and I thought: I want to do this to audiences for the rest of my life. The fact that I've let go of those dreams doesn't reflect on you. That has to do with me, my health, the way things turned out. All I want now is to see my daughter grow up and if I can't do that, then I want to know she's loved."

Celia looked up to see Launch gesticulating that she should come see the work that he and Grant had done. "You have my word," she said to Sunny.

"And you won't tell anyone else? Not Bethie or Victoria or Bobby?"

"I think you owe it to them to be honest, Sunny. I do, but you should do it in your own time, and at your own moment."

Sunny well knew what her own sisters would say when she told them. They would be hurt at being excluded and critical of Sunny's decision to make Celia Brio's guardian. They would pull from the trough of anecdote endless stories of Celia's being generally impossible, occasionally unfathomable, often unrealistic and always stubborn. But the difference between Sunny and her sisters was that Sunny had not needed to assert her adolescent independence from Celia. To be a stepdaughter was to be, in its own way, independent. Sunny understood that however impossible she might otherwise be, Celia's generosity was a great gift in a stingy world. Celia's insistence on experience, her wish to be loved, her willingness to crash through life, to gnash and weep when love broke down, to make mistakes and to make up stories, these were aspects of a life writ large on an island that was small. Celia had offered Sunny what no one else, including Sunny's own mother, had offered her: a childhood, a tiny island of time where she could count on being loved, rooted, connected. And if these things turned out to be ephemeral, that did not make them false. If you'd once been given these things as a child, no one could ever take them from you, and if not, no one could ever adequately fill that void.

After the initial flush of pride, the massage to her vanity and a spasm of self-congratulation, Celia regretted having anything to do with *Joie de Vivre!* The undertaking had thrust her into downright intimacy with Diane Wirth, the *Joie de Vivre!* editor who was constantly telephoning from New York to set things up to her own specifications. Diane believed that *Joie de Vivre!*, having bestowed the honor, should dictate the menu, the guests, the occasion, and the weather if that were possible. There had been several major differences of opinion. Celia was in a state of pissedness.

Sunny stood with Celia and Dorothy, awaiting the rented car that would bring Diane and her crew from the ferry landing to Henry's House.

"How many are they, the crew?" asked Dorothy.

"I don't know. I could never get an answer out of her to those simple kinds of questions." Celia sighed, "I dread this whole thing."

But when the car pulled up and Diane Wirth emerged, she hugged Celia, like they were old college friends; she was introduced to Dorothy and Sunny and she hugged them too, enthusiastic embraces all. If this had been an athletic contest of effusive charm, Diane Wirth blew away all other contenders. With Diane as a sort of cheerleader, they all agreed this experience was going to be wonderful! Diane exclaimed in joyous bursts: How lovely was Isadora Island! Henry's House a jewel! Useless Point so delightfully quaint!

Sunny distinctly thought she heard one of the men with Diane mutter, "Fuck quaint," but she couldn't be sure. He was a surly man, a good deal younger than Diane, and she did not bother to introduce him formally, only waved her hand in his direction, said he was the photographer, Woody, and behind him, the general gofer, a kid named Scott.

Since cooking for the dinner party would absorb all of Celia's energies, Dorothy undertook to supervise the housekeeping during *Joie de Vivre!*'s visit and Sunny volunteered to be *Joie de Vivre!*'s island guide and liaison. Almost immediately she wished she'd changed jobs with Dorothy. Diane was a tyrant of the worst kind, and expected Sunny to succumb instantly to her demands. Clearly, Woody and Scott had, though not gracefully or willingly. The two of them exuded a dogged churlishness, reminding Sunny of medieval serfs. Woody, especially, grumbled continually, profanely under his breath. Diane Wirth failed to hear or notice. She paid no attention whatsoever to his Brooklynese under-mutterings, perhaps because Diane was all Manhattan, with a dash of Albuquerque.

A sleek, fastidious woman in her early thirties, Diane Wirth had great green eyes polished by contacts, clothes of casual silk, and turquoise and silver jewelry that clanked and rattled with her every gesture, of which there were many. She was *Joie de Vivre!*'s answer to Cecil B. DeMille and a self-confessed control freak. "I've already had a few little differences of opinion with Celia," she told Sunny, "but trust me, I've done this before. I know how it works."

"It might not happen that way here," Sunny cautioned her. "Celia takes Henry's House very seriously. It's her own personal work of art."

"Of course it is! That's why *Joie de Vivre!* is here!"

While Celia, the maestro of timing, worked according to her carefully laid plans in her own kitchen, Sunny guided Diane and crew all around Henry's House, inside and out, down through the gardens (though not through the orchard, or over to where people really lived). Diane wanted to know all the famous artists and writers and musicians who lived here, past and present, but other than Nona York, she knew none of the names Sunny offered. The luster of the old Isadorans, Sunny realized, had dimmed considerably over time. Diane was even more disappointed that Henry's best-known celebrity guests were a couple of Seattle TV personalities and an ex-governor. Sunny could see the place diminishing in Diane's Manhattan eyes. "The most famous guest here was Isadora herself," Sunny volunteered. "Isadora Duncan. She and Sophia were best friends. Sophia named the island after her and she came here to visit," said Sunny, traipsing lightly around the summer of 1927, and leaving out the Bugatti. And

Diane asked no difficult questions, apparently unaware who Isadora Duncan was.

"Tell me all about Nona York," Diane said in a low intimate voice.

Sunny paused and faltered. What was there to say? "She writes her books into tape recorders." She did not mention the dogs or the dish towel.

"When I was a teenager," Diane confessed as they walked, "Nona York's books were my first introduction to sex, oh, long before I had a boyfriend. After reading Nona York, I couldn't wait to have sex. It all sounded so—so—so exquisite, so passionate, so breathless."

"We all read her too."

"But then, when I actually did have sex, it was—well, it wasn't like Nona York at all. I was disappointed. Depressed, really. I'd expected so much more. And for years, honestly, after I'd had sex with a man, I used to have to go home and read Nona York novels. To even out the experience. You know? Like needing to masturbate because you haven't been satisfied. You know what I mean?"

"Hmm," offered Sunny, taking the conversation quickly elsewhere. "Nona used to have us to tea when we were kids, my sisters and I. She always treated us like young ladies even when we were little girls. The old artists around here would often invite us to tea, and Celia would always send us with some little gift and we had to have our hair combed, clean clothes, all that. It was a sort of education, I suppose."

"I'm surprised your mother would let you go to Nona York's house. Was she actually *having* that kind of sex?"

"I don't know. Anyway, Celia didn't read Nona's books."

As they walked, Woody and Scott behind them, Diane would stop here and there and point out what she wanted photographed and Scott would place little markers in those places, and when they were all done, hours later, Diane blithely excused herself to go to her room (the apple-green-and-pink one so beloved by Dorothy) and take a hot bath and have a nap while Scott and

Woody (muttering continually) spent the rest of the afternoon meticulously setting up shots. They took, in one day, perhaps two hundred photographs, in two days some five hundred.

The day of the party, all of the food that could be photographed in the morning was to be laid out and Woody and Scott busied themselves in Henry's kitchen and the dining room, setting up their equipment while Celia fumed. Timing was everything. If these shots took too long, or the lights were too hot, the whipped cream peaks of Henry's Trifle would melt. Moreover, no one had ever ordered Celia about in Henry's kitchen. She pushed a yellow bowl of green apples back onto the table.

Diane removed them again, instructing Scott and Woody to do exactly as she said. "Let's get back on track here," she upbraided Celia. "The point in *Joie de Vivre!* is not real life. Our purpose is to make *Joie de Vivre!* readers believe that with less money, less time, less talent and less taste than you have, they can do exactly what you do here. That it can be reproduced. In total."

"But that's not possible. It's not just the recipes, it's—"

"Look, Celia, you've done what you do best. Now let us do what we do best. The party's tonight, why don't you have a lie-down and a cup of tea?" And with that she shooed Dorothy, Sunny and Celia out of Henry's kitchen.

"To hell with tea," Celia muttered as they walked through the foyer, "I need Wild Turkey."

Most of the guests for the *Joie de Vivre!* dinner came to Isadora on the 4:10 ferry. Victoria and Eric, Ned, Bethie and Wade. Russell escorted Celia, Sunny and Dorothy along the concrete path. (Launch was baby-sitting Brio, endlessly listening to her recite *Goodnight Moon* and *Where the Wild Things Are.*) Nona had picked up Grant and they all assembled, by prearrangement, in Henry's library.

They looked, for the most part, rather uncomfortable, but perhaps that was the clothes as much as the occasion. Grant, in the same fine clothes he'd worn to the engagement party, fidgeted with his tie. Nona had traded her shitkickers for sensible shoes.

The assorted Robbinses were at ease in casual finery. To Victoria's dismay, Sunny had not updated her magnolia-wallpaper dress or the rope-heeled platforms. Sunny thought that Wade and Bethie looked less like lovers and more like allies, soldiers in a common cause, wearing the same uniform: black pants and T-shirts with ReDiscovery's colorful new logo, the R and D boldly imposed in red and blue over words in a clean, crisp script, *Discover Your Life . . . Recover Your Strength . . . ReDiscovery*. The shirts sold for $20 each, said Bethie, "but everyone on staff gets one free. We wear them in the office. And anyone who signs up for a seminar, those people get one free."

"How much are the seminars?" asked Grant.

"They're three hundred fifty dollars for a two-day session."

"But three hundred dollars for students and seniors," Wade added.

"A bargain," Grant agreed, with an unobtrusive grimace.

Diane breezed in from the dining room, calling out to Woody, and abusing Scott. "More wax on the salmon, Scott, more—"

"Wax!" cried Celia, nearly dropping her glass of sherry. "Wax?"

"Oh, Celia, it has to *gleam*." Diane pursed over the word, then gave a bright gasp of pleasure and went straight to Nona York, took her hands and exclaimed over her wonderful books and the hope that Nona was still writing and would go on writing.

"What else would I do?" asked Nona.

Diane moved right along, through the rest of the family, her scarf and palazzo pants fluttering around her and her thin wrists weighted with jewelry. A thick silver and turquoise necklace hung from her neck, reminding Sunny of a ball and chain. Victoria, however, wanted to know if that's what they were wearing in New York nowadays. "Oh, don't ask me about New York! Impossible place! Impossible. Ask me about Albuquerque!" Diane greeted Eric like her own dear nephew and told Dorothy she could see where her son got his looks, then just as swiftly, to Ned, she implied that those good looks had come from dear old

Dad. "Hello, handsome," she joked with Grant. On meeting Russell she asked Celia if she'd kept this gorgeous man a secret on purpose. When Diane's back was turned, Celia rolled her eyes and made a gagging reflex, and so she missed what Diane said to Wade and Bethie, but then she heard them decline.

"Sorry," Diane said blithely, "the T-shirts have to go." Wade and Bethie again refused to follow her instructions. So she repeated, "No T-shirts."

"We were never told this was a formal party," Wade stated coldly.

"Yes, but you knew it wasn't a beach picnic either. Anyway, that's not the point. It's the logo."

"I don't mind what they wear," said Celia.

"*Joie de Vivre!* minds."

"This is what we're wearing," said Wade stubbornly.

"Sorry, Wade. No can do."

"These are our clothes."

"Not the point. *Joie de Vivre!* cannot be seen to be endorsing any product that doesn't pay us for advertising."

"ReDiscovery is not a product," stated Wade, "it's a program. Recovering the self means discovering the life denied. It's an unfolding program and it treats the whole abusive personality, not just a single substance."

"I don't care if it makes gold bricks out of cow shit, *Joie de Vivre!* cannot endorse it," Diane interrupted, urbanely immune to his sincerity. "I'm sure it's all very worthwhile, don't get me wrong, but *Joie de Vivre!* can't be supporting one group over any other. Personally, I don't have anything against T-shirts. I love T-shirts. I wear them all the time. And I think Recovery is great. Some of my best friends are recovering whatevers. But *Joie de Vivre!* is a magazine and can't be making political statements. You know how awful politically correct can be. But, well, we're all prisoners in victimville and it's a dirty little war."

Celia laughed out loud at the image.

Wade unhooked his elbow from Bethie's arm and spoke to Diane in his low, compelling voice. "I don't think you understand. This is a program. This is a set of principles, like a theology. This is—"

"Look—" Diane combed her ringed fingers through her glossy hair. "I really can't get off track with this issue. I have a deadline to meet. This is supposed to look like a family party, but it can't *be* a family, see? Let me put it this way. You and your fiancée can change clothes, or you can't be in the pictures. The pictures are the point of the exercise. Like it or lump it."

"We're not giving up our principles."

"They're not principles. They're T-shirts," Diane corrected him. "People don't wear principles. They have them, or they don't."

Grant stepped forward and took off his sport coat, putting it around Bethie's shoulders, as though she might be cold. "There," he said, as much to Bethie as to Diane. "There. You keep your T-shirt. You wear the coat."

Victoria shifted her body weight slightly and Eric immediately knew to take off his sport coat. He handed it to Wade. Wade put it on.

"Cool." Diane flashed them a smile as sterling as her jewelry. "Now, where were we?"

The dreadful evening passed into photographic history, Bethie and Wade stung into frosty reserve, everyone else, their good manners dwindling with advancing exhaustion and galloping anxiety. All the guests pretended this was just the sort of delightful occasion they so often enjoyed together and they were so fond of one another's wonderful company that they did not hear Diane Wirth carping and sniping, abusing Scott and dictating to Woody, who muttered *Fuck, shit, piss* under his breath while he took pictures of everyone having a lovely time.

PART V

Some Remembered Eden

The *Joie de Vivre!* pictures, when they arrived in my post office box about six weeks later, were awful. The salmon looked better than the guests, and he'd been poached. In these pictures there was no soul to Henry's House. Nothing invitational, just cute. The place looked cute. We all looked like we suffered from obstructions of the gut. In her note, Diane chirped and bubbled, reminding me I could not reproduce these shots without the express written consent of *Joie de Vivre!*, and that I had already signed documents to that effect both for the pictures and for the recipes which were now property of *Joie de Vivre!* magazine. I didn't read on, but put all of it back in the envelope. I turned to leave the post office when Nancy called out that she had two envelopes, one for me, one for Sunny, that looked to be identical and both had postage due. She took my IOU because I hadn't brought any money.

I'd walked down to get the mail this beautiful Friday morning just to savor the weather. We were booked, of course, but guests couldn't check in until the one o'clock ferry. Lots of time between then and now, so I wandered toward the dock. A cloudless day, the sky rippled out from some bolt of heavenly blue and gazed at itself fondly in the waters of the Sound. The trees all round Useless were no longer stippled with green, but so thickly leafed they seemed to ripple, a wind-driven green current. Bursts of amethyst and scarlet rhododendron, the last of them, flamed between the Useless dock and Henry's House, but I'd no sooner reached the road when I saw Bobby's old Subaru bounding toward me. He must have left Seattle at dawn to be here this early. And I gulped slightly because it was Friday. Russell was home.

Russell still regarded Bobby as a competitor for my affections and loyalties, and since I couldn't make him understand anything to the contrary, I'd given up trying. Rather than endure Bobby's presence, Russell moved to his Massacre apartment on Saturdays and stayed there till Sunday night when he and his laundry came home. But now it was a Friday morning and I'd left Russell at the table with a cup of coffee, Dorothy deep in a Nona York novel, Sunny at the computer and Brio playing school with Baby Herman.

Bobby's car trundled to a halt. "Hello, Celia! Isn't this the most glorious morning?"

"Isn't this the wrong day, Bobby?" I ventured. "You always come on Saturday."

"Un-dim your vision! How could this be the wrong day for anything? But, if you are referring to Russell, you have my solemn word, there will be no further incidents, no further arguments. Even if provoked, I have vowed not to respond. I will tie myself up and light my own faggots first. I have not come to make trouble with Russell. I embrace Russell! In this weather, I embrace everyone. So glorious! I called Sunny last night and I said weather like this cannot be squandered in work! I'm coming on the early ferry and you are going to play hooky. I told her I'd write her a note, just like I used to do when she was in high school and we'd go play hooky."

"Did you convince her?"

"I convinced Brio. She was easy. But don't worry about Russell. I can't answer for his moods," Bobby added with a tinge of malice, "but I will be the soul of sweetness. I'll just pick up my girl, Brio and leave. Russell won't even know I'm there."

"Oh, I think Russell will know you're here."

"I will not be crowding Russell's space. I'm taking this class now that explains all about territorial imperatives between alpha males. You should play hooky with us today."

"And who would do the cooking?"

"Let them eat cake. Feed them all Twinkies and put them to bed."

"What about your piano students?"

"I gave them all their freedom. They were delighted."

"And Janice?"

"I turned on the Crock-Pot and threw in a chicken before I left."

"Yummy."

"I tried to talk Todd into coming with me, but he's too much Janice's son. What's that you've got from Bethie?"

"Probably bride stuff."

"Bethie doesn't seem to talk about the wedding as much as she used to." His expression darkened. "Whenever I call, Wade says she's never home and I keep hoping, well, maybe she's *not* home. Maybe she's found another lover and she's having an affair. Wade seems a little stuffy and serious for Bethie."

"She wouldn't be living with Wade and sleeping with someone else. That's not like Bethie, but I have to admit, I haven't talked to her much. I haven't seen her since the *Joie de Vivre!* fiasco."

"Sunny and Victoria told me how terrible it was."

"Well, it was, but the T-shirt business, that was stupid really. I called Bethie the next day, and I said what did it matter? I wish I'd never heard of *Joie de Vivre!* I said Diane Wirth was shallow as a dog dish, but Bethie was just sort of silent, a little grunt now and then. Then Bethie said she had to go. She couldn't talk to me. And since then, sometimes she talks to me when I call, but sometimes she doesn't. Sometimes there's lots of interference and other voices on the phone."

I declined Bobby's offer of a ride and he threw the car in reverse, backed up a few hundred yards and burned up my drive-way, leaving a great cloud of dust and exhaust. Bobby always did drive like a fool and he believed in seat belts only metaphorically, convinced they constricted his freedom. I might have shared his ideas twenty-five years ago; then, lots of things seemed metaphori-cal, significant, pointing always to some larger Truth. Maybe that capacity for discovering meaning—or inventing it—diminishes with age, like your close-up vision. But Bobby still concocted metaphors and believed in them. In that regard, I guess he re-mained relentlessly true to his young self. When we were first together, lovers, Bobby's great charm was his belief that in making love we could create Eden without the sin. And now I'd found, seeing him every weekend for months, his appeal is that we both remembered the past that way and it did not tinge the present.

I knew within the hour, Russell would be on his way to self-imposed exile in Massacre and if I stayed away, I could avoid his anger or hurt or whatever it was, so I walked up to Henry's the long route, by way of the Useless dock and the sloping lawn. I don't often see it from this perspective. In this light and from this distance, the house has a lemony glow and the white wicker furniture dotting the lawn looks like bits of frosting, rosettes, artful and accomplished. I had my keys, but didn't go in the front, rather round to the side, to the wisteria arbor where the fountain was silent. I plugged it in and my feet ground over the husks of all the spent wisteria blossoms carpeting the flagstones. I sat in the rocker there and tore open the envelope from Bethie. The other one, to Sunny, was exactly the same weight and heft.

But in this envelope I found no wedding froufrou. I held in my hand twenty pages, notebook paper, handwritten, hand-scrawled, the writing slanting hard to the right, like a skiff in a stiff wind, the letters growing tinier and tinier against the implied horizon of the lined paper, words flattened by the force of the emotions. It had been stapled again and again so that these pages should not shift or fall from order, tumble or spill, once dropped—as they surely would be dropped, as I dropped them to read

I am recovering my childhood, reclaiming my memories; it is better to see it, to say it, to speak it, even if the pain it brings me is unendurable. Pain is a path. Pain is the path to healing and there is no healing, no wellness without pain, but horror and the sickness are [illegible]. I won't be silenced any more. I was a child. I was alone. No one protected me. I was abused by the men my mother slept with. The men she slept with came to my bed when they were done with her. Bobby Jerome came, called himself father, lover and I could not speak or cry out and when I whimpered, he told me it was pleasure. Oh God, he smiled when I whimpered because he thought I took pleasure in his hands and his fingers. He would come to the bed and sit there and hold me and poke in me and make me hold his thing [scratched out] penis and work him with my hand.

What is this? Impossible! No! I crashed on through the thicket of accusation.

Celia knew what Bobby did. She didn't care. She didn't care about anything except smoking dope and having lovers. She even sent me to his house later when she didn't have to. She could have protected me, but she didn't care. She was jealous of me. She let him be inappropriate with me.

My daughter molested? My girl abused? A helpless child wounded? *No.* Her youth betrayed? *No.* Her innocence corrupted? *No.* Bobby Jerome in Bethie's bed, Bethie's body? *No! No! No!* I crumpled the pages in my lap, in my fist and took several steep breaths as though going under, sinking into unimaginable depths far, far over my head, but I read on, blinded by tears and nausea, tore through the other pages—more of the same, more vivid, till at last I somehow got to the end.

I am sick of lies, sick of lying and pretending and keeping your secrets for my family and their lies. They are all so fattened with lies they cannot know the truth. The truth is hard and dry and brittle as old bread and I have eaten this hard, dry bread and my pain is unbearable. I have eaten dry bread while my family chews on meaty lies.

I thought of Sass and Squatch chewing, gnawing their way through the rag ends of ham bones, the sound of it terrible, abominable. The blood and bone of it. I felt like it was the flesh of my flesh, the bone of my bone. Disemboweled. Nuclear family? Wrong phrase. Isn't that what I'd always blithely maintained? Family needs some Darwinian grisly food-chain imagery? I could all but hear the shred and sunder of my family. I began to cry into my hands, to sob and gasp, shoulders heaving.

"Celia?" Dorothy startled me as she came through the French doors. "Has someone died?"

This time it was Dorothy's turn to catch me, to hold me, to embrace, to try to stand between me and the abyss that yawned. I clutched the pages and sobbed against Dorothy.

"Read it," I said finally, bitterly, handing her the letter. "Read it and weep."

She did read it and weep. So did Sunny when we went back home. Sunny read and wept and gasped, plummeting through these pages one by one, going finally to

Bobby loved me better than he loved his own daughters. If I told anyone what he did, they would know he loved me better and

how it was good for me and didn't hurt and didn't hurt me even though I cried and Mommy didn't listen and didn't come to me. He would not let me cry out to Mommy. He told me he did it to me because he loved me best, and if I told, no one would love me ever. I would be alone. But I am alone. Mother lets him. Maybe the others are alone too, maybe he does it to them too and she lets him use his fingers to

Sunny dropped the stapled pages and they fell to the floor and she sat paralyzed in her chair, head thrown back, hands clenched. "How can she say this? How can she *lie* like this? How can she think this!" Sunny's voice spiraled up into a screech and she gulped the glass of Wild Turkey Dorothy offered her, a shot glass. The three of us sat at the table looking and not looking at the two duplicate letters in front of us. "Who else got one?" Sunny asked at last. "Do we know?"

"Victoria, no doubt."

"Victoria and Eric are in Portland this weekend," said Dorothy. "She won't see it till they come home Sunday night."

"Bobby. Bobby will have one waiting at home." I was sure of it.

Sunny began to tremble and she covered her face with her hands. "Bethie was as much his daughter as I was. Every time Bobby came to get Victoria for visitation, Bethie always came too. We were all three sisters, all Bobby's girls. *You're my girl, Bethie,* that's what he used to say." Sunny mopped her face. "It's all so sinister now. So ugly. My father never hurt anyone. No child. Ever. He could never hurt a little girl. Brio!" And Sunny clapped her hands over her mouth to stop herself from saying the worst thing there was to say, from thinking the worst there was to think. The most terrible.

"It's unthinkable," Dorothy maintained, her voice cracking, "unthinkable."

I looked at the letters, forced myself to reread swiftly: Bobby skewered for perversion and me impaled for collusion and cowardice. As my fingers scraped down the pages, under my fingernails there collected not paper and ink, but flesh and blood. Mine. Flesh of my flesh. Bone of my bone. Bloody, all of it.

"Bobby Jerome"—Dorothy stroked Sunny's short hair—"is a good man. A good man. Maybe not the most responsible of men, but not . . . " In the silence, shadows shifted uncomfortably around the kitchen, the wind outside stirring trees. "Never this unthinkable accusation."

"It's been thought," I said slowly. "So, it's not unthinkable."

"How can you take any comfort in that logic?" Dorothy asked.

"I don't. There's no comfort to be had. Now that Bethie has sent this—and God knows, these are copies, God knows who else received this same letter—once the indescribable has been described, then it has a life of its own. It has form. It has the possibility of truth. Once something has been thought and someone has said it"—I pushed the twenty stapled pages away—"then it can be true or false. But it is no longer unthinkable. It has been thought. Written. Said. Now we have to fight or deny. Or whatever people do. What do people do?" I asked. No one knew.

"We're all made ugly, guilty," Sunny said at last. "Bobby molested Bethie. You didn't care. The rest of us were stupid and ignorant, victims ourselves, or uncaring."

"This is going to tarnish and shatter everyone it touches. Even you, Dorothy. No one living here will be spared."

"Really, Celia"—Dorothy drew herself up—"I am not the sort to scurry back to Bellevue at the least sign of trouble. I will not desert any of you when you need me. Besides, you do need me—it's almost one. I'll go on over to Henry's. I'll take care of everything. You stay with Sunny. You need to be here when Bobby comes back with Brio. I've never heard anything so vile and ugly in all my life," Dorothy added, taking all our glasses to the sink.

After she left us, Sunny and I sat in the silence, or as much silence as there ever is in my kitchen, marine radio, fax machine, all of that. Sunny got up and turned off the radio, unplugged the fax from the wall, and we sat for hours asking ourselves questions we could not answer, anger congealing into defeat, a pool of pain.

Later, hours later I guess, we heard Bobby's Subaru come into the yard and stop and Sunny's face, her whole body seemed to contort in anguish for her father, her sister, her daughter. We heard Brio's voice.

Brio waltzed in full of news about the fox they'd seen. A real fox. A pheasant too, a mother pheasant with her little ones. They saw all this on some back road or another when they'd got lost. " 'Cept Bobby says you can't get lost on an island. All the roads just go dead end at the sea, and you have to turn around and go back. The way you came."

To go back the way we came was so impossible that big tears rolled down my face. Brio didn't notice. Bobby did.

They'd gone to Massacre for lunch, Brio said, and met Grant at the Duncan Donuts. Grant said it was a good kite flying day, insisted they must have a kite. He finished his lunch and took Bobby and Brio back to the sailboat at the Massacre Marina. "He gave us one of his kites. Handmade kite. Grant said girls should always have the things that made them happy. But we broke it," Brio confessed.

"Oh, Brio—" Sunny cried, swooping her up in an embrace and weeping against her sweet neck.

"Don't cry, Mommy," consoled Brio. "Don't cry. Bobby says Launch can fix it and Grant will never know we broke it."

"Somebody die?" asked Bobby, looking at me.

"Grant told Bobby you were boo-ful, Mommy," Brio volunteered. "He said I was pretty boo-ful too, but you were really boo-ful, didn't he?"

"Of course she's beautiful," Bobby scoffed. "Anyone can see that. He must have thought he was Einstein or something to notice Sunny is beautiful. He's as bad as his father."

"Brio, sweetness"—Sunny pressed her close—"you go take the broken kite and find Launch. And he will fix it."

"I'm hungry."

"You go over to Henry's and ask Dorothy for something to eat. Dorothy's there. She'll feed you and help you find Launch."

"Why aren't you at Henry's, Celia?" asked Bobby. "What's wrong?"

I waited for Brio to leave, for the door to close, for Sass and Squatch to bound after her through the orchard path. Then I went to the cupboard and got another shot glass and I poured him some Wild Turkey. Sunny and I sat on either side of him and said he should drink it.

"What's this for? I thought you said no one croaked." Bobby tossed off the Wild Turkey and laughed. "Kills the pain. Give me another, Doc. Give it to me straight, the whiskey and the word. A leg cut off? No, only a foot? Amputation? No, Doc, no! Save my foot, Doc! Save my foot!" He swilled a second with more hokey dialog from Westerns, expecting some response, some laughter, but we just listened. "Well, give it to me straight, ladies. I'm a man. I don't need liquor in my system to have a good time, or to get through a crisis. Give it to me straight. Is it cancer?"

"Dad . . ."

"Dad! Whoo! This must be really bad! She never calls me Dad, Celia. The whole world calls me Bobby. Even my grand-daughter calls me Bobby. OK, not cancer. Gangrene. Right?"

"Dad, we have something you have to read."

"What's the matter with you two? If you're not going to laugh—" Bobby fell suddenly sulky and said, whatever it was, just get it over with.

Sunny pushed one of the envelopes to him. "It's from Bethie."

"I don't get to be father of the bride?"

Sunny started to cry again.

Bobby frowned deeply. "This letter is addressed to you, Celia. I never read other people's mail. I haven't read your mail since Andrew Hayes started billing you for his services. Remember? When you were offering bed and breakfast before there ever was a Henry's House? No offense," he added slyly.

"You have to read it, Dad. I know you don't want to."

"Have you read it? Did you need Wild Turkey?"

"It is a kind of amputation, Bobby," I said slowly, carefully, when Sunny was silent. "In its way, it is an amputation."

Bobby Jerome pulled the twenty pages from their envelope and placed them on the table. He began to read, but slowly, and unlike me or Dorothy or Sunny, who had flung ourselves headlong through the swamp, the muck, the mire and misery, Bobby read slowly. After the first paragraph, he took his reading glasses from his pocket and put them on. He read even more slowly with the glasses.

"What does she mean?" he asked at page two. He seemed to disintegrate like newsprint left in the rain, going gray, volitionless. "What does she mean? What is she saying?" he said over and over and over, long before he reached the end. "What does she mean? What is she talking about?"

They weren't the same question, I wanted to tell Bobby. What Bethie meant and what she was talking about, they weren't the same question at all. Besides, there were lots of other questions, tugged, plucked from this cesspool, like pulling skeletal forms from the tar pits, dinosaur bones long submerged in the sticky medium of the past, caught there after some terrible calamity. That's what it felt like to me. Like someone had died. But Sunny and I, every time we had to enlist help that afternoon, that evening, we kept saying *No one has died, but* . . . To Dr. Aagard, to Launch, to Grant, to Janice—*No one has died, but* . . . It came to have a kind of Biblical rhythm, a kind of reliable punctuation. *No one has died, but* . . .

Bobby collapsed as though he'd had a heart attack, fell forward, slumped finally and slid to the floor, the letter beside him. Sunny and I, imploring, comforting, talking nonstop, *Impossible, impossible, no one will believe this,* could not get him to move, nor could we move him and that was how Brio found us: Bobby between us, all three on the floor, when she stumbled back into the house and stood in the doorway. Over her face there was pasted excruciating confusion, but before she could even open her little mouth, Sunny whisked Brio up in her arms and carried her back to Henry's House where Dorothy promised that the staff would keep her busy till Sunny returned—whenever that might be.

While Sunny was gone, Bobby's condition worsened, and he seemed to me to have gone into acute physical shock, not just a condition of the body, but of the heart and mind. I knew we had to get him upstairs, to get him into bed and keep him warm, but he remained inert, immovable. When Sunny returned, I asked her to go find Launch, to say to him, *No one has died, but* . . . I stayed, kneeling on the floor, Bobby cradled in my arms, me crying and trying to soothe, protest, protect, and then Grant walked in, kite glue in his hand. He flung it down and came to my side. *No one has died,* I said, not believing it, not at all.

Sonofabitch, Grant said over and over, *sonofabitch,* reading Bethie's letter. It had taken the four of us, Sunny and me, Grant and Launch to get Bobby up to my old room, the old bed which Bobby and I had once shared. Sunny sat beside him, his hand in hers, while I closed the curtains against the dappling afternoon light. He shook with chills and shock and I told Sunny to keep him warm and I went downstairs to call the doctor where I found Grant reading Bethie's letter. Launch, in his mercifully incurious way, had gone back over to Henry's.

"Sonofabitch! This is impossible." Grant spoke not so much to me (I was on the phone trying to get through to Dr. Aagard, leaving messages for him), but as a generalized curse. Other words failed him as he read on, finishing the twenty pages at last and sliding them back in their envelope. "Bethie always loved Bobby. If she wanted to destroy someone, if she wanted to strike out, strike back at someone, it should have been my dad. She always hated him. My dad moved in here and broke up the whole happy family."

I declined to comment. It would have been disrespectful of Bobby's suffering to remark that it wasn't such a happy family by then, that Bobby and I had long since ceased to fulfill each other's hopes and expectations by the time I met Andrew. What had once struck me as youthful and unfettered about Bobby came to be childish and vapid. He wanted to dream. I wanted to work. What did the girls want?

"Bethie was always taunting me and Lee, telling us how wonderful Bobby Jerome was, what a great father he was, all the things he did for kids, and how pathetic my dad was, I mean, as a father, how she hated him, and hated us. Lee and I didn't even stand up for him when she'd say how awful he was. Lots of times we hated him too. Our mom hated him. Even when she lived with him, she hated him."

"He has that effect on women, your father," I replied neutrally. Before Andrew Hayes came into my life, I had not understood how sex could be a weapon, or that your physical need for a man, a certain man—Andrew—could propel you through the ruins of a relationship and keep you in those ruins, reduce you to a ruin yourself.

"My dad and women—" Grant shook his head. "But he's indifferent to kids. We envied those girls, Bethie and Victoria, because Bobby was so involved with his girls, so interested in what they were doing. Just like he is now with Brio."

Dryly, I explained as best I could that because Bobby loved the girls—volubly, demonstrably, effusively—that's exactly what made this terrible accusation thinkable. Imaginable. I saw, in my mind's eye, again, Bobby on the edge of the bed with Bethie, or Victoria or Sunny for that matter, in his arms, Bobby playing hooky with one or the other, lavishing himself on each girl so she felt special and enhanced, sharing sunsets with the girls in a way that, certainly toward the end, he could not do with an adult woman. Women get harnessed to necessity. Eve herself had no time for sunsets after Eden. But a child, oh, Bobby and children . . . I started to cry and Grant rose, put his hand on my shoulder and said no one would believe anything so vile of Bobby

Jerome. He said this knowing, as I did, that some would. Some would believe Bobby had it coming. Word inevitably would percolate all over this island and some would believe.

But on an island, because we are broken off from the whole, physically adrift in the Sound and difficult to negotiate in emergencies, some things yet remained possible, like Dr. Aagard coming to your house if you had an emergency that didn't require hospitalization. He came to my house. He gave Bobby a shot, gave instructions, wrote out two prescriptions, and then he asked, if no one had died, what had done this to Bobby Jerome? I gave him Bethie's letter to read. When he finished he said it was a sorry fact, but that this was the avenue some kids took, that it was a way for them to grow up, fast and finally: to smite down the parents in one terrible blow. "It's like the old myths and tales, Celia. Some kids, this is their path to adulthood and they feel they must maim or destroy the parents, the authority figures, or they don't believe they can ever be adults themselves. I'm sorry to say it, Celia, but this is not as uncommon as you'd think."

"Are you telling me I should take comfort from Oedipus?"

"I think you should take comfort wherever you can," he replied gravely. "Does Bobby's wife know?"

Not yet. But that night—that long, loitering June evening, the earth unwilling to relinquish the sun—Janice called. Sunny and I, sitting at the kitchen table, our hands wrapped around mugs of cold tea, we never went near the phone. We let the voice mail pick up. First Angie called. She had gotten a letter like ours. Then Nona. Both were stunned, but we still didn't pick up. Across from me Sunny remarked that Bethie should just have posted it publicly. "That's what she has done," I said.

Finally, at nine o'clock Janice called and she demanded to speak to Bobby. When no one picked up the phone she hollered, "I know you're there, Celia! I want to talk to my husband."

Sunny finally picked up the phone. "Bobby can't talk, Janice." She listened a long time, holding the squawking phone at arm's length. "No one has died, but you should come on tomorrow's ferry, Janice, and you should bring Todd with you. He'll have to drive Bobby's car back." Refusing to say anything more, Sunny remained calm, while Janice protested, raged, threatened, demanded to know what was wrong with Bobby. "No one has died. I can't talk any longer, Janice, and I can't listen." Sunny put the phone down and turned to me, observing, "Fortunate that Janice has had lots of experience with chronic pain."

I called Russell's apartment, left messages, but he never called back. I might have made up the cot for myself in the kitchen, but I was too broken and exhausted, so I just went to bed that night beside Bobby, lay down beside him. Heavily sedated, Bobby slept noisily, his breath straggling up from his lungs, fluttered across his lips. No one had died, but bits and pieces, phrases, accusations from Bethie's letter exploded in my head like shrapnel, ricocheting painfully. Beside Bobby's familiar bulk, I wept against his back, great racking sobs. And it came to pass that, though I had put the New Disciples behind me, I wept and winced, writhed under the onslaught of all the old sinners' questions: *What did I do, Lord? What did I do that Thou should so smite me? What sin? What error? What omission?* Could Bobby Jerome, this man beside me, a man I had loved for years, *could he* have committed these crimes against a child? *Did I* ignore, neglect and fail to protect my children? *Was I* too stoned, dippy and wayward to notice that my children were hurting? *Did I* abandon them to the mercies of the men I slept with? *Did I* countenance or merely ignore the pain Bethie had felt as a child and exhumed as an adult?

Childhood is a gift, after all, like a basket of memory and that basket a gift of the parent. I prided myself on the childhood I'd given all my kids. I'd always thought my kids so fortunate to live here, to revel in the beauty of the place, the freedoms I could give them, the time to dream, to daydream, foggy mornings waiting for the school bus, rainy afternoons curled up with books or dolls, art projects spread all across the kitchen floor, girls practicing violin for the middle school orchestra, those free and wild summer days at Sophia's beach where the girls found dragons and slew them bravely. Oh yes, an island childhood. An island idyll. Was it an imagined past? Some remembered Eden?

Bethie had blighted that past. There was now no summer day without tarnish. No winter evening without rot at its core. Bethie had destroyed the past, the collective past anyway, the thing that families have to assent to, more or less, agree upon in some general way. If they can't remember the same things, they're not a family. With these pages, we had been cast out, expelled from our past. We had been driven from that warm collective place that we could all agree *was* the past. Bethie destroyed all that with what she claimed was the truth. The monstrous truth. Or monstrous lie. All Edens are remembered. Bethie's charges barred my return like angry angels wielding flaming swords.

Drifting in and out of sleep, unable to distinguish one from the other, I moved from sleep to waking, from dream to thought, all echoing the voices of my children, piping, thin and plaintive. And when I did finally wake, I saw that dawn etched alongside the shade, framing the window, the light unconvincing and fluorescent. At least it was overcast, and not another glorious June day.

Beside me, Bobby groaned, woke, rolled on his back and turned to look at me, though he said nothing. He did not seem surprised to be here, in this bed, this room, or beside me. I took his arm in mine and he took my hand, but there were no words possible. We gazed wide-eyed at the ceiling where years before he had painted flowers, all of which had faded now. We lay there, side by side, like a dead knight and his dead lady on marble slabs in a medieval church, discredited relics of our own past.

PART VI

Eau de Soleil

With Todd in tow, Janice Jerome arrived on the morning's first ferry, the one that docks at Dog Bay about seven. Her Honda rumbled along island roads toward Useless Point, scaring the bejesus out of early morning cyclists and rousing the very cows from their bovine stupor. She tore into Useless Point. The Honda spun gravel getting up the hill. Seeing Bobby's car parked there beside Celia's truck, Janice scrambled out of her car, slammed the door and stalked toward the house.

Just then Sunny emerged, a protesting Brio in hand. Sunny was pale, eyes ringed with sleeplessness and her color drained. Brio, by contrast, was in a fine fury, amounting to a tantrum, refusing to go over to Henry's House. "I'm sorry," Sunny said firmly, "but you have to go again today. Dorothy will look after you." Brio stomped and pouted as Sunny said a weak hello to Janice.

"What's happened to my husband?" Janice wore a sort of track suit and running shoes. The ferry ride had disarrayed her short and highly lacquered hair.

"No one has died, Janice."

"Where is Bobby?"

Sunny nodded toward the house. "You might want to go more gently, you might—"

But Janice walked in without knocking and when Sunny returned from having installed Brio with Dorothy, she found that Janice had not heeded her advice. In fact, she could hear Janice well before she got to Celia's and she surmised, correctly, that Janice had read, or was in the throes of reading Bethie's letter.

"You bitch! You slut! You whore!" Janice flew at Celia, the twenty pages clutched in her clenched fist. Todd sat helplessly by, his great mustache trembling. "You've done it, haven't you? You always wanted to destroy Bobby and now you and your slut whore daughter have done it! You destroy everyone, Celia. Love unfettered? The unfettered life?" She virtually spat out the last phrases and Celia sank under the weight of their implied silliness. "You broke Bobby's heart. He loved you and he was a father to your fatherless brat of a girl who has turned on him now, betrayed him, betrayed every affection he ever showed to your brats. Bobby is innocent. You are the guilty one, Celia. Bobby loved and trusted you, but you jumped into bed with everyone, you screwed anyone who took your fancy. You threw Bobby out when he wasn't of any more use to you. You needed a builder for your stinking great hulk on that hill, so you went to bed with Andrew Hayes. Did he take it out in trade? Or did you pay him? Did he pay you? You're a whore. An unfettered whore living the unfettered life."

"Did you receive a letter like this, Janice?" Sunny held up her own envelope, but Janice ignored her, returned to her reading.

"Yes," Todd replied, rocking his whole body. "No one opened it though. It was addressed to Bobby." Todd's long gaunt face mirrored the confusion all around him and his bony hands writhed round one another as Janice read and wept, cursed and sobbed her way through Bethie's twenty pages. There was no marine radio with its comforting litany of weather, no washer and dryer, no dishwasher, and in this unaccustomed silence only Janice's periodic shrieks sounded.

When she'd finished, Janice flung the whole twenty pages on the floor and wiped her feet on the document. "That's what I think of you and of your daughter, Celia. She's right about you, of course. You were a rotten mother, stoned and promiscuous. She's lying through her teeth about Bobby."

Retrieving the letter, Todd read it with difficulty.

"How will he survive this?" Janice wailed.

Perspiration beaded along Todd's forehead. Nothing in his well-ordered life prepared him for the terrible pages in his hand. Moreover Todd was shocked, unnerved to see his mother so undone, screeching and violent. Never in his life had he seen this virago. Even when his father had left them, Janice had maintained control of her chronic pain. Now, delinquent clumps of her hair had unstuck themselves and they trembled, as Janice trembled, took deep hyperventilating breaths. She quit crying. She snatched Bobby's prescriptions from Sunny's hand, and ordered Sunny not to tell her how to take care of Bobby Jerome, that she was doing the job that Celia wasn't woman enough to do. She rained more abuse on Celia, going back as far as the death of Henry Westervelt, and when Todd tried to calm Janice—not to protect Celia, but because he feared for his mother's heart—she shook him off. Sass and Squatch cowered and finally scratched at the door to be let out of the line of fire, but Celia was not so fortunate and absorbed the full barrage, as Janice accused her of wreaking destruction on everyone she'd come near, including her own daughters.

"That's why Victoria didn't tell you she'd got married," Janice jabbed, "she knew you destroy everything you come near and she didn't want you anywhere near her marriage. Victoria told Bobby she got married. She told Sunny. She even told your precious Bethie, but not you. And it wasn't because she knows you don't approve of marriage. You'd like to think so. You'd like to think people look at you like a great iconoclast. You'd like to think you have the admiration of the world. Just because *Joie de Vivre!* fawned all over you, you think you can do whatever you like without risk or consequence—" Janice spied the offending letter on the table, swooped it up, and shook it in Celia's face. "These are the consequences, and by God, Bobby will not pay them! Bobby is never coming here again, and Sunny, if you want to see your father, you'll have to come to him. Once I get him off this wretched island, he will never come back."

"Can Sunny come with us?" asked Todd. "Sunny and Brio. Maybe they should come with us."

Still bristling, Janice ordered Sunny to pack up her things, Brio's things—they didn't have much; everyone knew they'd come to Isadora with little beyond the clothes on their backs—and return with her. "Bobby is your father and your place is with him, and with us. You can't stay here with her, with this homewrecker. You can't live here."

In her slow, deliberate fashion, as though calculating the outlay of energy to the possibility of achievement, Sunny picked up a sock of Brio's that had been left on the kitchen floor in the morning flurry. She looked over at the stricken Celia, sunken and undone, made ugly by the accusations on the page and those in the air. Sunny said quietly, "My place is here with my daughter."

"And Celia?" snapped Janice. "What has Celia Henry ever done for you that you would betray your own father to stay with her?"

Sunny's great blue eyes widened. "I could never betray my father. Isn't there enough destruction here, Janice? Isn't there enough anger out of Bethie? Shouldn't the rest of us be trying to help each other? Shouldn't we try to protect Bobby?"

"How can we protect him from this?" Janice eyed Bethie's letter.

"He's always needed protecting," Sunny appealed to her step-mothers. "I knew this when I was younger than Brio. From the time Linda left, I took care of him. I have always taken care of him. Someone has to. He needs a woman who'll look after him.

You both know that. He's just one of those men. But he doesn't need me right now. He needs you, Janice. He needs your love, not your anger. You love him, we all love him—"

"Celia doesn't."

"I do," Celia protested, weeping. "I'd do anything to spare him this anguish."

"We all have to help him survive this, Janice. But it wouldn't serve Bobby for me to go with you and Todd. I need to be here with Celia, with Brio. I have to think of Brio too." Sunny hurt all over, back, shoulders, arms, like she suffered from whiplash. "This is a grotesque lie Bethie's written, and I intend to prove my father's innocence."

"Where do you think you are, Sunny?" Janice cackled. "Traipsing in front of some TV camera with your stupid lines? This is not a lovely little sitcom where it will all be resolved and tied up in twenty minutes, when saying something funny makes it OK. This is the world, girl! Get real! This is not something that *can be* disproved. Don't you understand? Accusations like these, rumor, nastiness like this will go all around, and it will ruin him. Bobby is a piano teacher! He works with kids all the time. How do you intend to prove his innocence? Put an ad in the Seattle *Times*: Anyone accusing Bobby Jerome of molesting children, please come forward and prove your case, or he stands vindicated? You astonish me, Sunny! You wear this pseudo-LA sophistication like a costume! You come here, show up here out of the blue, no explanation, with your illegitimate child, you admit you had affairs with married men, but then, of course, you're in Celia's great tradition of illegitimate children, and sleeping around! What else can we expect? Look at your own mother. She deserted you and Bobby altogether."

"I think we can leave the dead out of this." Sunny went to the sink and stayed there, staring out the window, looking past the dusty jars with all their bits of seaglass and sand dollars, their remembered summers. "I don't see how the dead have any bearing on this at all."

Janice sagged visibly. "I'm angry at anyone, at everyone who has ever hurt Bobby." She began to weep into her hands and Todd took her in his arms and let her cry. But she was not a woman to weep her way through any thicket, be it bureaucratic or the tangled skeins of a broken heart. "I love him so much and I know what this will do to him." Janice freed herself from Todd's embrace and mopped her eyes. Resignedly she asked Celia if Bobby was upstairs. "In your bed, I take it."

By the time Janice, with Todd's help, finally got Bobby Jerome downstairs and slowly to her car, Saturday morning had waned into Saturday afternoon. Todd drove Bobby's car back to Dog Bay and Janice followed him, a fact which could not have passed unnoticed in Useless Point. Just as it would not have passed unnoticed that Dr. Aagard came last night, or that Dorothy Robbins was directing the operations of Henry's House. Too, everyone employed at Henry's House noted that for several days little Brio was the staff's responsibility. The fact that Bethie Henry had sent the same letter, postage due, to Celia, Sunny, Nona and Angie slowly rolled round Useless and beyond. The slow perk of island gossip began.

Afternoon shadows laced the kitchen floor, Janice long gone, but still Sunny and Celia stared at one another, distraught, debilitated, unable to pick up the phone, unable to stir. They heard Nona's car and her dogs barking, Sass and Squatch in a frenzy. Nona entered without knocking, said a grim hello, and flung her envelope on the table, pulled out a chair and sat down with Sunny and Celia.

Nona fumbled for her cigarettes, then remembered she couldn't smoke inside. "You come off very badly here, Celia," she said at last. "Abusive, irresponsible, manipulative and uncaring. Have I missed anything? But did you really read this letter? I have. Over and over. And I tell you *abusive* is the quilting verb here. It covers everything. If you spanked her and sent her to her room, it's abuse, and it's abuse if Bobby forced her to make him jack off."

"Don't say it—" Sunny implored, "please—"

"Of course it's vulgar! Awful! And we know exactly what she

means, but she doesn't actually *say* it, does she? Does she ever call it vulgar? Horrible? Criminal? Wretched? Disgusting? No— everything in here is *inappropriate*. This cotton candy vocabulary has allowed Bethie to say the truly unthinkable without the weight of its being unbearable. Do you understand?" They looked at her blankly. "The iniquitous is submerged here into the impolite. You and Bobby are accused here of the worst crimes any parents can commit against a child. The letter is completely incoherent. But look at this." Nona held it up by the staples. "Neatly stapled. All the pages numbered. These are *copies* of an original! Someone had to take these to Kinko's! Rouse yourselves," Nona shouted. "What does that mean? What does that tell you?"

"That Wade has his hand in this does not make it hurt any less," Celia replied quietly.

"It means you will never get through to Bethie without knocking down Wade. Have you called her yet?"

"No. We hadn't the heart to call. Or the stomach."

"Has Victoria read this?"

"She and Eric are in Portland."

"I'm a writer," Nona began more gently, "and I know how words work and I think you ought to call Bethie. I think we need to hear the voices as well as the words. It's not so important that you talk, Celia, as it is that you listen."

Wade answered on the first ring. His voice utterly without rancor or resentment, he told Celia that Elizabeth had decided not to speak to her, to any of her family, until she was able to move beyond this terrible, painful point, the recovery and acknowledgment, the expression and inventory of abuse, repressed childhood traumas which are the first steps of healing and redefinition. Elizabeth was doing her work through the ReDiscovery Program, yes. In a tone so low, so smooth, so emollient, Wade described Elizabeth's therapy, adding, "If you could see her suffering, your hearts would break."

"Our hearts are already broken, Wade, but we're not calling to inflict more pain on Bethie. We're calling because we love her. Her sister and I are here, and we love her and we want to talk to her." Celia glanced at Sunny who held one extension, Nona on the other.

"Is Victoria with you?"

"Victoria is in Portland."

"Oh. I thought you said her sister."

"Sunny's here."

"Sunny is not Elizabeth's sister, not by any real measure or standard of kinship. Sunny is the daughter of the abuser. So is Victoria, of course, but at least Victoria is a half-sister to her."

Struck dumb by his pedantry, Celia looked up to see Sunny scrawling on the message board, *No anger. Move on.* Celia cleared her throat. "I can help Bethie. I want to help. I have to help her. I'm her mother."

"Elizabeth has identified you as part of the problem, Celia. She doesn't want to talk to you. I'll take her a message this time. Don't call again. What is the message?"

Knowing, fathoming somehow that Bethie herself was on the phone, sharing it, as Sunny and Nona shared hers, Celia went on, at once astringent and imploring. "I want to tell Bethie that I love her. That she should know I will always love her. I want to ask her why, how—why," Celia stuttered and stumbled, "how she could make these brutal accusations against me. Against Bobby."

"Are you calling Bethie a liar?"

Leaning against the doorway for support, Sunny exchanged pained glances with Celia, and Nona sat at the table, lips cinched.

"Surely," Celia ventured reasonably, "it's more complicated than that."

"I'm afraid it is. In freeing herself from the comforting restrictions of denial, Elizabeth has to discover the pain. Pain is often masked by rage and fear and resentment she has repressed for so long. As a victim of abuse, she has to find the truth before she can begin the healing. You must discover the truth of your abusers within your own family and confront them. Writing that letter was a great step forward for Elizabeth, but it was just the first step. As Elizabeth heals she will discover and recover. If this means you have to share her pain, well, then share it. It's time for all of you to take responsibility for the pain you have inflicted, and for the lies you have told. Elizabeth must forgive herself for becoming a victim and living all those years with reduced self-esteem. The victim must discover, recover. Then she can forgive you for the lies and abuse you inflicted. If you want me to tell her you're sorry, I'll take the message."

Nona scribbled hastily on an old receipt, *Say nothing. If you apologize, it means . . .*

"We love Bethie, Wade. All of us. Bobby too. We have never done anything to hurt her—"

The phone clicked off. Since none of them moved to hang up, shortly thereafter came on the dreadful Midwestern twang advising them, *If you want to make a call, hang up and dial again; if you need help . . .*

"We need help all right," said Celia. She hung the phone up, went upstairs and closed the door to her room, denying Sass and Squatch entrance.

Nona rose slowly. She patted Sunny's shoulder. "Well, it's going to be ugly around here for a while, Sunny. Celia's always said she doesn't care what people think about her. This is her chance to prove it, isn't it? Of course she's had thirty years' experience at that, and you haven't."

"It's like dying, Egypt." Sunny fought tears. "I don't know what to do."

"I don't know what to do either. Romance, that's my forte. Sex and love."

"That's what this is about," said Sunny. "It's about sex and love."

They burst against the sky, great blossoms of fire and light, color dappling the dark waters of Moonless Bay, fire-points dripping down into the night, dissolving at last into the reluctant sunset. Isadora Island's Fourth of July festivities, renowned all over the Northwest, culminated in this fireworks display which could be seen from neighboring islands, and depending on the weather, from clear across the Sound. The Fourth—Isadora's finest moment—was calculated to bring tourists flocking, to attract flotillas of pleasure crafts that docked at the island marinas and dotted the bays, to fill every room, restaurant and campground. Hordes of day-trippers went back and forth on the ferries. Along the horseshoe-shaped beach of Moonless Bay, where the fireworks were actually set off, prime seats had to be secured early on in the day because by six o'clock (the show didn't actually start till ten) the rocky beach was carpeted with blankets, lawn chairs, barbecue fires, and as darkness slowly fell, people readied themselves to *oooh* and *aaah* and cheer in unison.

The tribe from Henry's House had their blanket on Moonless Beach, as they did every year, but the strains and tensions, the divisions inflicted amongst them by Bethie's terrible accusations were everywhere apparent: on their faces and in their relations, reactions to one another. Launch and Brio alone were excepted, and Brio sat on Launch's shoulders, sated with pop and hot dogs, shouting, "More and higher!" with every burst of fireworks across the summer sky.

In the welter of noise and explosions, Sunny wished now she had sent Brio with the others and that she had stayed far away from the smoke, the bursting fireworks, the explosions and crowds. Isadora's public festival made painfully clear what Sunny had long suspected: that everyone who lived on Isadora knew of Bethie's allegations against Sunny's father, knew of Celia's presumed passive acquiescence in the outrage. A great vein of gossip had opened and people took sides. The largest share of island sympathy fell to Bethie. She was, after all, The Charmer, better known than Bobby Jerome and better liked than her mother. Too, it was terrible to hear of her emotional breakdown, news of which floated back to the island via a few people connected with ReDiscovery. The extent of Bethie's heartbreaking crack-up reached her family slowly and by the alluvial channels of sneers and whispers. Bethie's breakdown, along with intimations of darker deeds at Useless Point, the whiff and stench of child molestation, all this came to be laid at Bobby's door, at Celia's door, which was also Sunny's door. And Dorothy's. And Russell's.

Sunny could scarcely abide Russell. Not his presence in the little house, or even on the crowded beach (much less the two sullen teenage children he'd brought with him for the Fourth). When he had come home that terrible weekend in June and read Bethie's letter, he suggested offhandedly that perhaps Bethie's allegations held an element of truth. Oh, not that Bobby was malicious or pervy necessarily, nothing that corrupt, just that Bobby was often stoned and touchy-feely. Everyone was into hugging in the old days. People didn't know then that all that hugging stuff, bodily contact, was often non-consenting, and frequently undesired. Bobby might have done it, unknowingly. A man who loves children, well—Russell indicated in his learned way—if you look at the Greek roots, it's *pedophile*.

Dorothy Robbins had completely discounted, dismissed and refused to hear these gross infamies, especially as they related to Celia's shortcomings as a mother. Ned, however, sitting next to her in his lawn chair on Moonless Beach, nursing a beer and scowling, thought his wife a great moth-head. Once apprised of these disgusting rumors, Ned urged Dorothy to give up her silly job, ordered her home, insisted she must escape people who were mired in this, the worst sort of sexual taint. *Never,* Dorothy had replied. Never would she be disloyal. Ned had pointed out to her that Celia Henry was not her sister or her wife, not her ally, not her family, not anything at all requiring loyalty. But Dorothy steadfastly replied, *She saved my life. I owe her that.* No very great intellect or intuition was needed to see that Ned detested all of them. He detested as well his own impotence and inability to extricate Dorothy from this cesspool. He loathed above all his daughter-in-law, Victoria, whom he blamed for bringing this catastrophe down on the Robbins family.

Sunny, glancing over at Victoria, felt her estrangement from all of them. Victoria sat in a chaise with headphones on, listening to Books on Tape and watching the fireworks impassively. Sunny felt the breach between herself and Victoria as poignantly as the breach between herself and Bethie, save that this one was even more difficult to understand. The crisis occasioned by accusations against their father ought to have brought the daughters of Bobby Jerome together. They ought to be united in denying any such things could have ever taken place. But instead Victoria withdrew. She had little to say to anyone, even to Bobby. When Bobby would not take Victoria's calls—Janice said he stayed in his room all day, watching cartoons—Victoria gave up and quit phoning. Victoria wore her emotions like accessories and took them off whenever possible. Sunny could not do this. She had tried to reach, to reach out to her father, in every way, phoning, writing, even going over to his house, taking Brio with her. A disastrous visit. The Wookie was there. Bobby would not come out of the bedroom and Sunny had to endure both Janice and the Wookie heaping deprecations on Celia, her failures as a mother and a woman, on Sunny's failures as a daughter.

This family tragedy had eroded or wrecked nearly all Sunny's ties, save for Celia. Celia and Sunny clung to one another. Together they obsessed over what they could not change or understand. They taxed their every friendship because they couldn't talk or think about anything else. They were unrelievedly immersed in the devastation Bethie's accusations had wrought. They wondered persistently what they might do about it, trod over and through Bethie's motivations, discussed how they might combat the rumor, innuendo and ruin. But since there was no obvious path and no discernable tactics, they obsessed in the way that divorce obsesses the people going through it—and finally bores everyone else.

Sunny often wished she could take to drink or drugs, some easy palliative to pain. Bobby had clearly retreated into a twilit world enlivened only by the color TV. Bethie had clearly turned into a sort of emotional burn victim. Victoria retreated from any contact whatsoever. Celia's sorrow took the form of being unable to work. She could go over to Henry's in the morning, rising very early as she always did, but by noon she was spent, wrecked, and Dorothy took over. Sunny's work suffered too and her health eroded. She lost weight and sleep, and even Brio was not immune to their unhappiness.

I ought not to be here, Sunny told herself, watching Brio joyfully greet a rocket as it rained down light and fire. But there was no leaving. The smoke from beach fires, the sounds from dueling radios, swirled around her; each burst of light against the sky, each echoing boom exploded inside Sunny's head. Underfoot, the thundering report of each blast inched audibly into the bones of her feet. Her legs ached and her head throbbed. Like being transported back to the days as the producer's assistant on the *Dirty Death* pictures when fires and explosions and battles and men screaming filled her life day after day, etched themselves into her sleep night after night. And now, smoke from beach fire battles clouded her eyes and choked her and the noisy crowds shifted into a many-faced, multi-voiced phantasm and Sunny fell forward, inadvertently jostling one of Russell's children, the son, who turned to her with a hostile stare and gave no reply to her mumbled apology. Shivering, in spite of the July heat, she stepped back into, rather than against, a presence, felt rather than seen. Everyone greeted Grant Hayes who declined a beer, stayed put, planted right behind Sunny and when she flinched, he came closer, so close she could feel the warmth of his body through her overalls, like an infusion. By degrees she leaned into him. Carefully, lightly he brushed her shoulder with his hand. But when Sunny winced again from the booming overhead and the thunder underfoot, in a wordless gesture, Grant turned her toward him, pressing her head against his chest, covering her other ear with his hardened palm. She trembled against him, chilled and shaken, and she tried not to cry.

Quietly, Grant got Celia's attention and she brushed Sunny's hair from her face. Celia herself looked worn. "It's been intolerable," she said glumly, "but worse for Sunny. She takes everything to heart. She always has. She's like Bobby in that respect."

"I'll take her home. But she has to leave now."

"Don't worry about Brio, Sunny. I'll take care of Brio."

"More and higher!" cried Brio from her perch on Launch's shoulders, her attention successfully diverted, while Grant, his arm around Sunny's shoulder, led her away from Moonless and toward the town.

Massacre itself straddles a neck of land, and walking through town could be very quickly done, especially since there was no traffic on this night and nearly every business was closed. Those few still open (including Duncan Donuts and the Chowder House) were empty, their cooks, clerks, waiters and patrons on the sidewalk watching the fireworks. Less than half a mile from the town, on the opposite shore, the Massacre Marina was lit, every slip filled on this holiday weekend and people watching the show from the decks of their boats. Music, laughter, rippling conversation and loud drinking echoed out over the marina. Recognizing Grant, some people called out to him. He waved, but kept a firm guiding arm on Sunny all the way to the back of the marina, to the last slips for small boats where the *Pythagoras* was moored. He stepped on board and drew her after him, leading her back to the stern.

Sunny collapsed in the stern, and wept. Finally, she willed herself to stop crying, tried to concentrate on the sounds around her: water slapping the hull, noisy exchanges from the distant docks, the sputter somewhere of an outboard motor. When she next looked up a buttery square of yellow light fell at her feet as Grant turned on the cabin lights. There were more immediate sounds, Grant pumping water, firing up the stove, filling the kettle, the sound of the marine radio. Sunny smiled and eased. How did he know the weather could be so comforting? That it was like having someone tell you an old, old story, the singsong weather voices on the marine radio. Then she remembered she and Grant were Unfettered alumni, so naturally the marine radio's weathery song consoled. She and Grant had a shared past, though they had not had the same experience. She flinched with yet another burst against the night sky and Grant came out with a light blanket which he put around her. Sunny thanked him. He was not by any means a beautiful man, certainly not pretty, like so many of the men Sunny had known in L.A. But where their beauty was altogether visual and attracted only the eye, something about Grant Hayes made her want to touch his cheek, to put her fingertips on his face, as you would touch a piece of wood to explore its grain.

"They'll end in a bit," he said. Red-white-and-blue lit the sky overhead, dripped down in glorious chrysanthemum formations. "They won't go on much longer."

"I don't know what came over me. Smoke or something. The explosions."

He sat down next to her. "I'd say it was pretty damned self-explanatory what came over you. I'm surprised you and Celia have held up as well as you have. And Bobby? Celia says he's still really broken up."

Sunny bit her lip. "He never went back to the community college and his music students are drifting away and he doesn't care. Sometimes when I call, he won't even talk to me, just hands the phone to Janice. Bobby doesn't have a grain of toughness. He never gets angry. He just gets hurt. Janice is beside herself, desperate to rouse him, but even she can't."

Grant watched as the last of the fireworks flared in the sky. "At least if you're accused of embezzling, you can find records that will testify to your innocence, but this kind of thing just leaves a stink in the air."

"It doesn't get better, either. It gets worse."

"It's taking a terrible toll on you."

"I'm all right."

"Are you?" He invited her into the cabin, apologizing in advance for what she'd find. "It's all still in progress, this boat. It sails round these islands just fine, but it's not ready for Central America."

She asked where the bathroom was. Since he'd just installed a new marine toilet, he had to call out directions for flushing it, adding that it might not yet be wholly reliable.

In fact, when she came back out, refastening her overalls, her face still damp from having splashed it in the sink, Sunny noticed that for a sailboat named after a geometric theorem, the *Pythagoras* was not at all shipshape. A rumpled unmade bed lay in the bow. Along the couch (which made out into another bed if need be) there were navigation charts, balls of string and dowels for kites. Under the table lay several pairs of work boots and an open tool chest, and from hooks along the port side there hung a variety of jackets, sweatshirts and work shirts. Crowding the shelves were books which all had the words *nautical, marine* or *sailing* in the titles, save for a book on kites, and a handful of architectural tomes.

From a tiny dish rack Grant pulled a single cup, joined there by a single plate and a few pieces of plastic flatware. He rummaged on a shelf for another cup and a box of tea bags. The diminutive size of everything in the low-ceilinged cabin seemed further diminished by his broad-shouldered presence and Sunny wondered how he and Lee had both lived here before Lee moved in with Robin. On the wall there hung a plaque, first place for a bridge building competition which Grant had won at WSU, and a single framed photograph, a snapshot of two bald children, their heads painted a brilliant orange, and a Halloween-fiendish expression on their faces. Clearly these boys were looking for a fight.

"Me and Lee." He passed her a mug of hot tea. "Right after they shaved our heads and painted us up for ringworm. Celia took the picture. She said it was priceless."

"It's a pretty unforgettable story, your mother leaving you off at the Useless PO." Sunny slid along the bench behind the table.

"Too bad it's true. But even the Useless PO beat the hell out of living in Yakima. We were island boys, me and Lee, and when our folks split up, Mom took us back to Yakima where she was from. Lee and I thought we'd died and gone to hell. It was hell. Her family was hell. My aunt, she was really hell! My mother was fragile."

"Her health?"

"She wasn't strong," he said, without actually clarifying.

"She's fine now, but she was fragile in those days, and the breakup with my dad tore her up." Grant talked obliquely about his mother, Sharon. When she would lose a job, or lose another man, she would somehow dissolve, and when she was breaking down, he and Lee had to go live with her sister. Enough to make him shudder even now. "We gave them plenty of trouble. We gave the whole family trouble and finally we were just too much for Mom, so she brought us back here and dropped us off and went back to Yakima."

"Did she ever remarry?"

"Oh yes, finally. She had another family too. I've got a half-brother and a half-sister in Yakima." He shrugged and took off his glasses. "I don't know them too well. By the time she remarried, Lee and I were too old to go back to her, and her husband didn't want us anyway. I have a good relationship with Mom now. She's happy, I think. She came to my graduation and she came to Lee's wedding. But she still doesn't deal too well with my dad."

"Your father seems to have that effect on women."

"Professionally, my father is in the construction business. Personally he's destructive. I'm not like that, Sunny," Grant said levelly, not taking his eyes from her.

Sunny bent her head, blew on her tea and turned over a dog-eared little paperback on the table, surprised to find *Antony and Cleopatra*. "I wouldn't have thought this your sort of reading. It doesn't have anything to do with sailing."

"How do you think they got around the Mediterranean? But I didn't buy it for that. I bought it after you said you'd played Cleopatra. I wanted to see if I could imagine you in the title role."

"I was too young. To play Cleopatra, you need some internal grit, some strength, suffering, some sense of loss and grandeur, to want something passionately and to be denied." Sunny did not add that she could now play the role; such strength as she had grew out of suffering and a sense of impending loss.

"A lass unparalleled," Grant commented. "That's what they said of Cleopatra."

"She was dead by the time they said that."

Sunny asked him for an aspirin and he brought her two and a glass of water. Outside a couple of kids went down the dock, by the *Pythagoras,* singing. Then they passed, and only the marine radio murmured in the cabin.

Grant sat back down across from her, his great hands dwarfing the cup he held. For all the time he had spent with Sunny this spring and summer, he could not, he had never dented the shell in which she wrapped herself. But this evening she had leaned into him, leaned against him and neither flinched nor resisted when he'd pulled her up close to his body and held her. And now she was back to flinching and resisting. "What did she die of?" Grant asked at last.

"Suicide. I thought you read the play."

"I did. Twice. I didn't mean Cleopatra. I meant your mother. A long time ago you told me she died, but you never said what she'd died of."

"An accident."

"Car accident?"

"No—not really." She fluttered the pages of the little book. "It wasn't an accident. She got sick. Nothing very grand or interesting. Not a great life and not a great death. Just an exit. It was not *I am dying, Egypt, dying.* It was not heroic. It was a long time ago."

"Is that the hurt you're still toting? There's something. What is it?"

"You're mistaken."

"Tell me what mistake I keep making with you, Sunny, and I'll quit. Honest, I will. I'll quit, but tell me my mistake. I won't even try anymore if you want, but tell me what I keep doing wrong."

Sunny brought her enormous blue eyes up to his gaze. "All I want," she said carefully, "is to bring my daughter up, to make a life for my daughter. I don't want to be distracted from that."

"By loving someone besides Brio? Let it go, Sunny. Whatever it is, let it go. From the minute I saw you, I could tell, I just knew you were carrying around some loss or misfortune, something that has colored the way you look at the world."

"You want too much from me," she bit back. "Please. Don't ask too much of me."

"All I ask is that you look at me, see me for the man I am. I had no part in what my father did, ousting Bobby and you out of Celia's place, any more than you were to blame for that snapshot of me up on the wall. Our fathers were once in love with Celia Henry. They slept with Celia Henry. They lived with Celia Henry, in liaisons that felt like marriage, like family, at least to the kids. Then they broke up. The kids got scattered, pulled by their biological parents into new families or houses, or whatever. That's what happened. It happens to lots of people. But I am not Andrew Hayes any more than you are Bobby Jerome. Just look at me for who I am. That's all I ask. I don't think it's too much."

"I have to concentrate on Brio. I don't have time for anything else. I don't have time," she insisted. Having spent the greater part of her love life scuttling about in the shallows with the tadpoles of the movie business (all of them eager to be frogs), Sunny knew what it was to be attracted to a man because of his power, his connections, his looks, for the sheer reflection of being seen with him. When she had outgrown all that and broke with Brio's father, she was never sure what to put in its place. When she was diagnosed with cancer, nothing else mattered except treating the disease. When slowly she had emerged from that, she thought only of Brio, of Brio's future. She was a one-breasted woman with a child to think of. She did not think of men. Did not want to, but in the past months, slowly Grant Hayes roused in her reluctant longing. He would not settle for an ornament. That much was clear. His very presence was demanding. Sunny hunched over. "Please. Just leave me alone."

"Alone? Why is it that men think it's so heroic to be alone?" He quoted her ironically. "The unfettered life. Is that what you want? Gloriously alone?" He thought perhaps he'd gone too far. He thought she might cry. Short of an apology, there was nothing to say, and he knew if he tried, then she would cry and he would feel like an oaf stomping on ground where he'd been told not to tread. So he murmured something about taking her home and rose, turned off the marine radio. With the loss of the weather—the chop of the sea, the wind from the northeast, the tides all over the Sound—the two of them seemed oddly abandoned, as though the *Pythagoras* rocked far out at sea and not here at the Massacre Marina where laughter echoed amongst the slips. "The car's in the marina parking lot. I'll wait for you on deck. Take your time."

"Thank you."

"Turn off the lights, OK?"

"Yes." After he left, she sat, looking around the cabin. She wished she had paid more attention to Nona York's novels. There were sensations in those novels she could not identify or remember, but maybe—the thought struck her—maybe Nona's exuberant tripe held some truth. Maybe there was in fact a moment that made you a whole person. Perhaps you could live your entire life just fine without that moment. But maybe you couldn't. Maybe if you once complicated your life in that fashion, you looked always for some experience that would duplicate it, replicate that sense of life thickening, expanding. If you'd once had that—as Celia had with Henry—you believed it was possible forever. Sunny feared that whatever she did now—or failed to do, decided or decided against, accepted or refused—was and would be crucial. The fear, Sunny reminded herself as she turned out the lights, is worse than the feat. The feat could only jell into regret, but fear could become defeat. There was a difference. And besides, she told herself, to be brave at the same time you are afraid, well, that's the true test of courage.

She found him on the dock, kneeling in the dark, tightening the lines which secured the *Pythagoras*. He offered to help her jump off the boat, and she took his hand, but once on the dock, she did not release him. Sunny lifted both arms, as though she might dance with him, and lifted her face to be kissed. And he kissed her tenderly, and then more urgently. He murmured her name. He held her so close she could feel his heart pounding percussively in his chest.

"I could disappoint you terribly," she said.

"I'll take the risk. We'll go just as fast or as slow as you want, Sunny. Just let me love you, will you? In your own fashion. In your own way."

"I have to tell you the truth, Grant."

"The truth can wait."

"No, it can't."

"Whatever it is, it doesn't matter to me. Honestly. Tell me later, Sunny. Give me, give us some time."

"I don't have time. I can't count on having time." Silently Sunny took his hand in hers, brought his hardened palm softly to her lips and kissed it, and then slowly she laid his outstretched fingers across her cheek, as though on her cheek some message were written in Braille which he must and should discover. And like a blind man Grant closed his eyes, his dry lips wordless as Sunny led his hand down her throat, over her shoulder and the cold metal snaps of her overalls and lower, to the swell of her chest, holding his hand against there, letting his warmth penetrate through to her very flesh, down to her bones. She willed her own heat to warm him as he warmed her. Though flushed with desire, she nonetheless paused, pressed his hand more closely, held it there over her heart. "Don't open your eyes," she whispered, "just feel. Feel me, Grant. What's missing? Can you feel what's not there?"

Grant's hands caressed her, stroked over her ribs, over her back and then round again to where her left breast had once been. Then he did open his eyes. "Is your heart still there, Sunny? That's all I care about. Did they surgically remove your heart?"

She thought they had. She told him, later, in the milky dawn as they tangled, tossed in each other's arms in the bed near the bow of the *Pythagoras,* water lapping audibly underneath, the sailboat rocking gently with the love they made. Sunny had slept beside him, slept briefly but deeply, and when she woke she felt ripened, enriched, his arms around her, their voices low, they talked inconsequentially while dawn seeped in through the open windows along with the harbor smells and cries of the ceaselessly marauding gulls. And then, for a woman for whom candor was not her native element, Sunny did her best, pieced together for Grant, in a jigsaw fashion, how, for a long time, she thought they had removed her heart along with her left breast.

Her mother had died of breast cancer when Sunny was nineteen, already living in L.A. and attending Santa Monica City College while she worked as a waitress, auditioning for every possible role, sharing an apartment with three other girls. She had got a call from Linda's third husband, a man Sunny had never met. He called to say her mother was in a hospice, dying. "I went to Phoenix right away, of course, thinking she wanted to say goodbye, but there was more than that. She wanted to warn me, she wanted me to know her mother had died of this same terrible disease and it was a curse on the women of our family. Our family? I listened, and I comforted her as best I could, but I did not think of Linda as my family. It had been too long ago, and I was too young when she left. Besides, I was nineteen, and at that age you want to find out who *you* are, not who you're hauling around in your chromosomes. Linda knew I didn't feel related to her, so she kept insisting, *I am your mother, I am your mother.* I said *yes, yes,* but I didn't believe it and she knew that. She kept holding my hand and saying, *You are my daughter and I am dying of what may kill you.* She was very bitter. It seemed really pathetic to me, to both of us, I think, that I should watch her die, though I had never really seen her live." And some years later when they found a lump in Sunny's breast, she felt first rage against Linda and, more heartbreaking, fear for Brio. "I was afraid Brio would only be able to watch me die, and never see me live."

"How old was Brio?"

"Not yet three. I was allergic to something on the set and I had these constant respiratory problems, went to the doctor and she's running a stethoscope over me and she stops. She says, *What's this?"*

It all happened very fast after that, the doctors, tests, hospital, surgery, shunts for draining, therapies, medications, chemo. Sunny felt like a prisoner of her own body, but she had kept her own counsel, telling no one, not Bobby, not Bethie, not Victoria. "At first I couldn't tell them because it was just too awful to say, and I knew once I said it, I could never take it back and my family would be all over me. If the doctor had told me I was going to die, I would have called my father and my sisters, but he didn't say that. He said I needed surgery immediately. My friends in L.A., they were great, very supportive. The producer was great; he kept me on the payroll for the benefits even when I couldn't work. That surprised me. Then after the chemo was over, and that went on forever, the doctor told me, five years. If I took my meds, had tests every three months for a while, if there were no recurrence in five years, I had a chance at a normal life span. But I know—I know from Linda, from watching her die—that this disease, it isn't something that can be cured. It's something I carry. Like a death threat. After I faced that, the likelihood of death, there was only one question: if I die, what will happen to my daughter?"

The answers were inadequate. In L.A. Sunny had loyal friends, but they were young people like herself, who had their own lives and their own careers; supportive as they had been, they were not people to whom she could entrust Brio. While Sunny was sick and hospitalized, the Hernandez clan next door had taken Brio in, but that was an act of casual generosity on their part, and not an answer to the question. Brio's father? His wife tolerated his infidelities in exchange for her own securities and those of her children, but she would never have welcomed his orphaned illegitimate daughter. "And I suppose if I made no other arrangements, that's where the law would send Brio. He was her legal father. Can you imagine anything worse for a little girl?"

"Losing your mother is terrible, no matter how it happens. You already knew that."

"At least I was nineteen. I wasn't at the mercy of others. Brio is a little child. I fretted and wept and stayed awake nights, afraid for my daughter. Who would love Brio like I wanted her loved? Bobby and Janice? Never. Not Bethie, she's too footloose and, well, unfettered. Victoria's too rigid to deal with a little girl. Who was there? One name came back to me. The same name. Celia."

"That's why you came back to Isadora."

"Yes. It was all just that calculated. I only told her a few months ago, and no one else knows. She promised she'd raise Brio for me, love Brio. We went to Ellerman's office and drew it all up. I know now I could die, if it came to that, and not fear for Brio."

He wrapped his arms more closely around her. "Don't talk of dying, Sunny."

"It doesn't bother me anymore. I'm used to it. I can say it without buckling under the prospects. That's the difference between you and me, between me and everyone else my age, they don't think about dying and I do. They count on their lovely good health and when that health fails them, they're betrayed and anxious and angry. My body has failed me so many times and in so many ways, I have accepted it finally. I've lost a breast. You saw the cesarean scar—"

"I love the cesarean scar." He laid his hand across her belly and his lips moved against her cheek. "Don't talk of dying, because—five years or fifty—what really matters is what you do with your years. From that first night in March when I met you, I was dumbfounded. I couldn't believe you were the same girl who'd sometimes showed up here on weekends. You were the most beautiful woman I'd ever seen. And you hated me."

"I didn't hate you."

"You did. Admit it." He nudged her affectionately. "I about gave up altogether on making you like me, or even notice me till you told me about the bottles of *Eau de Soleil*. Then I understood. I'd drunk *Eau de Soleil* as a boy, so of course as a man, I

would have to fall in love with you. It was the fault of *Eau de
Soleil.* That's why, even when I saw you that first night and you
looked so tired and undone, I could feel my old life breaking up.
It was the oddest sensation, like running the *Pythagoras* aground
on Assumption. The life I'd had, oh you know, a few beers after
work, my friends, my brother, building kites, restoring the boat
on weekends, fishing in season, a date or a party now and then,
all the unfettered life, you might say, I knew that it would never
again be that satisfying. Without you, nothing would be
satisfying."

She brought her lips to the slight bony indentation on his
chest and kissed him there, and put her cheek against him, thinking oddly of Nona York's novels of romantic sensation. Sensation
Sunny still had no words for. And maybe she would not have
enough time to find those words. She had this moment for certain. It could not last forever, nor be preserved in the sticky amber
of sex, but perhaps it could contribute to some larger design.
They had a shared, though not contiguous, past, and so perhaps
she and Grant could angle out to a hypothetical future, balance
their geometric relationship to create some sturdy whole, as
though the theorems of Pythagoras could be understood, applied
to the old uncertainties of flesh, never minding the transmigration
of souls.

The rest of July must have suited the English roses. Presumably
they have a genetic affinity to summers cowled with clouds and
slivered by rain. And perhaps these English days affected the *Pythagoras,* because there was no more talk of taking it to Central
America. The sailboat was outfitted now for picnics with Sunny
and Brio, and went all the way to Assumption Island, where the
three bundled against the damp, climbed the rocks and barked
back at the seals. If the weather cleared, they might go as far as

Rosario on nearby Orcas, or Friday Harbor, but those were all weekend jaunts and did not involve the coast of Baja. Even some weeknights in the long dusk, the *Pythagoras* might sail around to Useless dock where Sunny would be waiting. Then they would sail just out of the reach of the rest of the world and anchor there for the night, motoring back to the Useless dock at dawn so Sunny could run back to Celia's, take off her overalls, get in her nightie and be in the bed beside Brio's when Brio woke up.

Celia assured Sunny she was happy to watch Brio on these evenings and the arrangement suited Brio because Celia let her stay up late (except on Island Preschool days). Brio became quite the fixture in Henry's kitchen, and a big help to Celia in hers. Brio was especially good at testing frosting. This was her forte and Celia declared she could not possibly make a cake without Brio's expert opinion. Her favorite was chocolate orange frosting on chocolate orange cake.

"I'll remember that on your birthday," Celia assured her as they walked back through the orchard early one afternoon, holding hands along the concrete path. In her other arm Celia carried a bag of oranges. The rain had stopped without quite clearing and the trees dripped all around them. As they approached Celia's, Sass and Squatch yapped with happy apprehension and Celia was surprised to see Russell's Saab pulled up in front of her house, its doors open and its trunk gaping open like a mouth awaiting root canal.

The door to the house, too, was wide open and Russell came out hoisting two suitcases which he threw in the trunk. "Hey, Russell!" she called out brightly. The bow-tie crease between his brows had knotted itself into a bulge and his mouth was stitched in grimness. In the car she could see his things, his books, his clothes, the computer he had kept in their room, his framed picture of the two teenage children. She sent Brio inside. "What are you doing? What's going on?"

"Will you marry me, Celia?"

"That isn't a very romantic way to ask," she chided, hoping

to soft-pedal, deflect his righteous anger, and anger it was. It rolled off him in waves.

"I've asked romantically before. Will you?"

"Why can't we just go on, Russell? Why does marriage have to be the automatic end result of a love affair?"

"Three years and it's just a love affair to you?"

"What's wrong with that? We should be proud of that."

"I want," Russell drew a deep, exasperated breath, "I have always wanted, a real relationship. Marriage."

"Is that the only real relationship possible? Aren't there lots of others? And do we have to talk about it out here in the yard? Can't we go inside? Upstairs, maybe?" A bauble of anticipation twinkled in her voice.

Russell was having none of it. "Why should we? There's no more privacy there than here in this yard. I wanted a home, Celia. A home for you and me. A place for us to be together, to build a life together, but you wanted to run a halfway house for runaway wives like Dorothy and runaway drug addicts like Sunny."

"Don't you say that about Sunny!"

"That black bag she takes everywhere with her. It's full of drugs."

"Oh, Russell, you're so judgmental. You don't think!"

"Me? I think all the time. I'm paid to think. You should think, instead of encouraging this sick relationship between Grant and Sunny. It's like incest, two stepchildren sleeping together. And you should never have let Dorothy just move in here either. She has a home. How can you possibly have a real relationship with me when your in-laws, your steps and exes are popping in and out all the time? This was supposed to be our home."

"It is," she assured him, afraid suddenly: losing Russell, what would that mean? He was part of the fiber of her life. "It is our home. I love you, Russell."

"I loved you, Celia. I love you still. I wanted to be with you, with you always. Spend our lives together."

"Then why are you leaving?"

"I'm leaving Isadora altogether. I've given up my apartment in Massacre."

She peered at him more closely. "You've got island fever, don't you?"

"Good God! Why are you so blind and stubborn? Why don't you ever look at anyone except through the lens of your own needs? I'm not some Diane Wirth you have to charm! I'm the man you love."

"Then why are you moving out? Because I won't marry you? Wait a minute." Celia paused, peering into the car. "This isn't spontaneous, moving out because you're just pissed off, is it? If you've given up your Massacre apartment, you must have a place to go. If you have a place to go, you've thought this out." Russell gave her a look of consummate distress in which Celia thought she saw the man he would become one day, the aged Russell, fretful and under-loved. She wondered if he could see in her the aged Celia, The Hunchback of Isadora Island, terminally eccentric, weird as the currents between Useless and Assumption. "Where are you moving to, Russell?"

"I'm going home. To Shirley." He said this without any particular angst or anger, as though Shirley's was a simple destination for which he had a ticket. "She's my wife and we have a family. We have a life together. It was interrupted, but we've put it back together. We're getting remarried."

Celia took this news on the solar plexus and momentarily she was stunned. She managed finally to eke out the question: When? When was he getting married?

"Remarried. Soon. I don't know exactly. Next month, I guess. Late September, before the term starts."

"That's where you've been going every weekend, isn't it? To Shirley's. All summer. You haven't been going to Massacre at all."

"I could hardly stay here with your ex moving in."

"My ex did not move in. He spent a couple of nights. He hasn't been back since that terrible night when he collapsed."

"You slept with him."

"Oh, Russell, I slept beside a man who was wounded. I was wounded. We—"

"If you would marry me, I would stay."

"Medicinal marriage?" Celia inquired sardonically. "Marriage that tastes like mouthwash—it's nasty so you know it has to be good for you? No, I won't marry you. I don't want to live like that. I never have and I never will."

"Some things change, Celia. Things change as you get older. They must change. Life changes. The things that made you happy at twenty-four don't make you happy when you're pushing fifty. You're not unfettered, Celia. Look at you. You're the most fettered woman I know and you don't know how to be otherwise. You've got that hulking place over there that keeps you tied to it day and night for six months of the year, and if that weren't enough, you keep a whole menagerie of weird friends in and out all times of the day, Launch, Nona, Ernton, Grant, then you let people just come and camp here, like Sunny and Dorothy. How can you possibly talk about the Unfettered Life? You're deluding yourself."

"Well, I guess I'm unfettered now," she said evenly, meeting his gaze. "You'll be gone."

"Your key is on the table." Russell slammed his car doors resoundingly, got in and drove downhill.

So *goodbye* had not needed deconstructing after all. *Goodbye, Russell.* It ended up being as simple as her feelings for him were complex. She picked up the bag of oranges and went into the house and there indeed on the kitchen table was the key to her house, none the worse for wear.

When Sunny returned, she was flushed, a little breathless, her face slightly windburned and her hair damp. She and Grant had spent Saturday sailing to Friday Harbor and back and she was full of tales of things she'd seen and done. She took off her cap, shook her hair like a puppy, left her damp jacket by the washer, her shoes by the door, and cried out, "I'm back!" She dashed into the electronic addition, hit the computer so it would come on and made a beeline to the bathroom. "The toilet on the boat," she called out, "is not very reliable." When she came out she was surprised that the marine radio was not on, and without its ongoing story, the place seemed disconsolate. "What's wrong?"

"Russell's moved out," Celia said simply, turning off the water and picking up a towel. "He got island fever and he left. They all do get island fever. They think by moving off island they'll be connected to some great enterprise, but in truth, people live in tiny little islands anyway—the route to work, the route to the store—they seldom go outside that island. But when it's physical, when it's bounded by the sea, they think, Oh, the great world out there is waiting for me, if only I could get to it."

"Did he give you any warning?" asked Sunny, surprised. She thought Russell was as much a part of the house as the wallpaper, although unlike wallpaper, of course, he left on weekends.

"He wasn't a tenant, Sunny. He didn't have to give a month's notice and get his deposit back. No. He just left this afternoon."

"Oh, Celia, I'm sorry to hear that."

"Well, so am I," she confessed. "Sometimes I wanted to be rid of him and sometimes he drove me into a froth because he could be so pedantic. We were very different in lots of ways, but you know, whatever else, he was part of my life. He was comfortable. Is that such a bad thing to want? I just wouldn't marry him. It didn't mean I didn't love him. I did love him and it had become like marriage. At least for me. Clearly, not for Russell. My life is breaking up, Sunny." Her eyes lit with sadness. "Bethie is lost to me, won't talk to me, returns my letters unanswered. Victoria is so distant, so cold, she might as well be calling from Turkestan. And now Russell's gone. I guess I'm not as elastic as I used to be. All this loss, it breaks my heart."

"Maybe Russell will be back."

Celia shook her head. "He's going back with his ex-wife."

"Shirley? I can't believe it!"

"Oh, I can, but I don't think they love each other. But maybe they didn't want to be loved. Maybe marriage is more important than love. At least to them. Not to me."

"Did he move out because of us, Brio and me and Dorothy? Russell hasn't much enjoyed having us here, from the beginning. I knew he resented us."

"It was the idea of all of you he objected to. Russell thought his world ought to be two by two, like the Ark, and this place has never been like that. There are almost as many people in and out of this house as Henry's. There always has been. Bethie would come back and leave again. People like Nona and Ernton and Angie, Lester, they're always in and out. Launch is always here and Grant, well, Grant and Lee were here building that path before you came home. Now, of course, Grant—"

"Do you think Grant will get island fever?" asked Sunny, suddenly fearful.

"Only if you do."

Sunny smiled, breathed a great sigh of relief and tossed a bundle on the table, saying she'd picked up the mail. "Look, Celia, it's *Joie de Vivre!* We're in here, but we're not the cover story like Diane promised."

Celia regarded the glossy magazine with no particular interest.

"Aren't you going to read it?"

"I don't really give a damn anymore. *Joie de Vivre!* So fucking what? I keep hearing in the back of my mind Diane's chirpy little observation, that we're all prisoners in victimville and it's a dirty little war. Too bad Bobby's in such a terrible state. He could put that little ditty to music and we could go around humming it. Happy prisoners."

"You know, Celia, the other day, I was working on the computers, I was e-mailing a supplier in Renton, and I started to think that with computers, e-mail, you don't hear an actual voice, but you catch a tone in the words on the screen. I thought, really, maybe we ought to e-mail Wade. We could concoct a really careful e-mail to Wade and ask for a meeting with Bethie. We could make it work on the screen and be very, well, humble and conceal what we really feel about him."

"Tut-tut, Sunny. Lying to Wade?"

"I was thinking not of lying, but acting. Cleopatra at the computer."

"She died."

"I meant only that she knew how to get what she wanted from men. And what we want from Wade is that he will let us see Bethie, talk to Bethie."

"Which he won't."

"So maybe what we need is not a way to talk to Bethie, but a way to talk to Wade. A way that he will have to respond to."

"I want to hear Bethie's voice, touch her hand, hold her, Sunny, not spew my heart and guts out in some blinking, blipping electronic machine."

"But that's the point, Celia. If you spew your guts out, you'll lose. Wade never spews his guts out. He's got a ready-made language. It's all predictable, like an order form, an invoice. His words are all like cans on a shelf. He just keeps his phrases in cans and then when he needs one, he pulls it from the shelf. So if we were to deal with him, that's how we'd have to do it. In his language."

"I could never blather all that bullshit."

"But you could write it."

"I can't."

"All right, you write it however you want it—you call him a class-A bastard if you want and then you give it to me. I'll cool it down. The computer is a cool medium, Celia. You can keep things crisp, refrigerated in a way. You can use all Wade's phrases, use his lingo as you never could if you saw him in person. We have to get past Wade before we can see Bethie."

"I'm not a writer," she protested. "I'm a doer. I need to use my hands."

"You write it out," Sunny insisted, "and I will chill it down and we'll send it to him through e-mail. We'll go at it slowly, formally, arrange for a meeting."

"You think it would work? We could see her?"

"It's Wade we need to convince. We could say, well, we could say—confrontation in the interest of healing is justified. We could say we need to recover the truth. We'll let him think we really have subscribed to ReDiscovery and then when we get there . . ."

"What?"

Sunny didn't know what. She said they'd have to get there.

So in this very modern fashion—through this electronic medium—Sunny posted e-mail messages that she had groomed and cooled. At first she had to completely rework Celia's language, not merely excise confusion, but dim all Celia's passion for Bethie. But when at last Wade actually replied, Celia was thrilled. The horizon brightened.

Together, Sunny and Celia learned to use the phrases Wade was fond of, phrases he could hardly discredit or deny, phrases he was obliged to respond to. It was its own language, like Latin, and as Latin had once served Christendom, uniting disparate peoples, so Wade's lingo allowed the disparate family to commence negotiations. These proceeded with diplomatic finesse, so fine-tuned they would have impressed seasoned UN observers. Carefully, slowly, over a couple of weeks, using Wade's phrases, indeed plucking their phrases from his replies, they negotiated *where, when, what* and *how. Where* first. Sunny and Celia had hoped for Isadora Island. Out of the question, said Wade, who also squashed the hope they could meet in Bethie's favorite Seattle eatery, the Queen City Grill. Elizabeth was not strong enough for a protracted public outing, Wade said. The only possibility was their Wallingford condo, his home turf. He was inflexible on this. This delicacy once resolved, consideration moved forward—through the ether—to questions of *when*. That was easy compared to the thorny path toward *what* could be discussed and *what* could not. Diplomatic amenities were scrupulously observed on both sides, but there was no question as to which party was the supplicant. Negotiations reached a nasty stall when Sunny e-mailed Wade (and it was all Wade; Bethie had no part in this) that Grant

wanted to drive them to Seattle: could Grant come? Finally Wade conceded that Grant could drive them and be present, but he could not participate; it was not Grant's place to say anything. Grant himself had to e-mail back that he agreed to this. Victoria too was required separately to e-mail her signed understanding of the conditions agreed thereunto. It was all excruciating, empowering and conducted in code.

And so, the usual family avenues of expression, family means and methods of communicating in a crisis, channels by which families have always addressed disagreements and difficulties, however base or lofty, all these traditional means of dealing with the other parties in an intimate dispute—which is to say, anger, insults, sulking, silence, tears, tantrums, hurt feelings, low gossip, irrational arguments, ill will, overt attacks, name-calling, backbiting, going for the throat, betraying secrets, withholding confidences, striking at well-known weaknesses and the like—these well-trod paths which families have taken since the days of Cain and Abel, all that was jettisoned. In its stead (and begging the pardon of Leo Tolstoy) unhappy families began to be unhappy in exactly the same way. Unhappy families now speak a new language, a lexicon of dysfunction, a lingo corseted, laced, prim, downright Victorian in its insistence on rectitude, yea, devoted to the understanding that each individual commits to affirmation. Positive construction only is allowed; nothing negative or critical will be permitted. There will be only serious discussions. Everyone must subscribe to the proposition that thou shalt not disrespect anyone else's feelings, even covert disrespect, even disrespect implied, or cast in such a way as to carry this lightest whiff of humor. Forbidden. No violations of the right to get your feelings hurt will be tolerated. Do you have a problem with that?

PART VII

Prisoners in Victimville

There is a Starbucks in Wallingford not far from Wade's condo and we met Victoria there. She was early. We were late. We were, all of us, tense unto terrified, though I still believed if I could just put my arms around Bethie, hold her, see her face to face, that nothing was impossible.

But face to face Bethie Henry was scarcely recognizable. The Bethie we knew—spirited, exuberant, resilient, affectionate—that woman was like a tiny pilot light somewhere in a stove gone cold. She came to the door, her tread heavy, the shuffle of a prisoner in victimville. She wore gray sweats despite the summer day, her coloring gray too, but queerly lit by a thick smear of lipstick, like a paint slash across a pale canvas. Sleepless rings framed her eyes, and her hair, hanging listlessly, was uncut, unkempt. Reflexively, Victoria volunteered the services of her own hairdresser, Charles.

"What's hurting is inside my head," said Bethie, closing the door behind us. There were no hugs. She showed no particular interest in any of us, save perhaps Grant. "Wade's in the study working with Fran." She left us, went into the kitchen. We stood there.

Nearly a year ago I remembered coming to this apartment after that awful church dinner with Pastor Lewin. At that time, I remember thinking Bethie had no presence in this place. But I also told myself it takes time to insinuate yourself into a living space, especially if it's been lived in by someone else. But now, after a year, there was still nothing except for the engagement picture, framed and sitting on a bookshelf, to suggest that Bethie Henry lived here too. It seemed to me still Wade's place entirely. The curtains were closed against the sunshine and the room was airless and oppressive. The books, nearly all paperbacks, were stacked around the TV, well-thumbed volumes, many with broken spines, a veritable archive of self-help going back as far as Elbert Hubbard and Norman Vincent Peale with lots of cheerful titles from the seventies like *I'm OK, You're OK*. If they were going to reprint this volume in the nineties, it would be *I'm Pissed Off and You're Full of Shit*. But when Wade entered, we were all just as cordial as could be, assured each other it was nice to meet again. Wade said we must surely remember his assistant, Fran.

We all stepped forward and pumped hands up and down, agreeing that Fran was unforgettable. An ageless mind imprisoned in a thirty-something body, angular, swathed with a batik shift, Fran's eyes were a glowing gray. After the introductions, Fran and Wade made last-minute confirmations about upcoming speaking engagements for him, and then Fran set her briefcase down and she went into the kitchen to say goodbye to Elizabeth. The sound of Bethie's muffled weeping reached us, along with Fran's low drone of comfort and support. A terrible metallic taste rose in my mouth, a kind of nausea, dread, the sudden intimation of certain defeat.

"Nice to see you all again," Fran said acidly on her way out the door.

"She's been like a sister to Elizabeth," Wade explained.

He gestured that we should all take seats, directing the four of us to a ring of kitchen chairs arranged in a semicircle around the coffee table. Wade sat on the couch, one of those low, marsh-mallow sorts, comfy and consuming. By contrast, the chairs, of a Mediterranean cast, all had wrought-iron backs and red leather seats, like we should all sit here with pikes up our butts. Wade busied himself silently rearranging some notes on the coffee table. God help us, I thought, note cards with today's date.

Victoria and Sunny and Grant studied the prints from the Seattle Art Museum, and looked wistfully at the engagement pic-ture on the shelf. Beautiful Bethie. So much in love. So vibrant and charming. A great void Bethie seemed now. Another void occurred to me. Cats. That's what was missing from this apart-ment, why Bethie felt absent. Bethie had never met a kitten she didn't like and she had never had an apartment without its feline contingent. "There are no cats," I said. "Bethie always has cats."

"I'm allergic to cats," replied Wade, looking up from his note cards. "It's one of the ways I know Elizabeth truly loves me. She gave up her cats to live with me. Greater love hath no cat-fancier." He smiled sadly.

"Is the teddy bear a substitute?" asked Sunny, pointing to a Pooh Bear on the couch on its back, its expression blissful and unseeing.

Wade reached over and picked up Pooh, righted it. "Pooh was my Mother's Day gift to Elizabeth. To help her learn how to parent, to cherish and discipline the inner child within herself. You have to learn to parent yourself before you are ready to fulfill yourself as an adult. You have to be committed to responsi-bility, but still recognize the need to give ourselves room to play sometimes, to be protected as well as responsible." He wound the bear's crank and "Deep in the Hundred Acre Wood" came plaintively from its innards.

Bethie came in from the kitchen, her lips pressed in a seam, and she collapsed on the couch next to Wade, seeking out his hand. Wade scooted slightly forward from the doughy white cush-ion. He suggested it would be best if he began by reviewing the rules we had all agreed to. This was the first of his note cards. All of us nodded soberly and in unison: we were here to heal and to empower.

Pooh's song wound down, stopping in mid-measure. I twitched and bristled in my spiked chair as Wade tediously covered ground we'd been over. On and on. I watched as Bethie seemed to recede altogether. "We know all this, Wade," I blurted out. Lowering my voice to a virtual Vaseline smoothness, I turned to my daughter. "Bethie, we are here because we love you. Because we're your family and we have known you longer and love you better than anyone. We are worried about you, Bethie, and we're sorry to see you so, well, so, so unhappy. We worry about your health and your well-being. You don't look well."

"How could I be well? How could I be well or whole or happy after what's happened to me?" And indeed, her mouth was pulled so queerly down, you could all but see a bit between her teeth.

"What exactly has happened to you, Bethie?"

"I have to discover before I can recover."

I hadn't expected something so short, emphatic and declarative. In the ensuing silence, I said, "And?"

"What don't you understand? How can I make you understand if you won't listen?"

"I am listening, Bethie. We all are. We have come here so that we can listen—" I nodded toward Victoria, whose brows were pinched in a tiny tent of anxiety over her nose, to Sunny, wide-eyed and closemouthed, and Grant, whose battered hands rested one on each knee. "We're here to help. We want to see you get better. So talk to us, Bethie. In your own words," I added without looking at Wade, "tell us."

I asked for it and I got it. Bethie launched into a forty-five-minute recitation, a veritable New Testament of hurt and anger and ugliness, of abuse and neglect and denial of her feelings, of cruelty implied and cruelty inflicted, of deceit and abandonment. A child crying in the orchard because her mother was banging away in the bedroom with some man or another. A child forced to live with the wretched and unkind relatives of men who were bedding down with Mom. A child, a girl, sent off once a month to stay at the home of a man who molested her, who had molested her for years, who had continually broken the most basic trust an adult can be given. A child whose mother was uncaring at best, malignant often. We heard our past, our collective past, dug up as though it were a graveyard. Bethie exhumed all the corpses, resurrected new instances of uncaring, injustice and abuse. And when I would cry out to correct her, when Sunny said *no no no,* when Victoria gave little high-pitched yelps of protest, Wade reminded us of the protocol here: this was Bethie's turn to speak, to release, to tell her truths and recover her past.

Bethie vomited up for us great toadlike chunks of memory and the old remembered Eden was destroyed. That tropically warm place, that confectionary country we all return to, that was all tarred and tainted, every anecdote soured, and the whole gone vile, venal and thuggish. Oh, I had asked for Bethie's own words and they came on me like shrapnel. Wounded, I wept, strangled my Kleenex, *I'm sorry, Bethie, sorry for not asking your permission if we could all skinny-dip in front of you on Sophia's Beach, I didn't think.* Stunned at the enormity of the betrayals she perceived, I gulped and stammered, *Forgive me, Bethie, I didn't think about the secondary smoke of joints passed round amongst the adults.* Stabbed with remorse, I could only wipe my nose and blubber I was sorry I hadn't dealt with her childhood tantrums and hurts myself, but sent Bobby in to her, sent her out with Bobby to watch sunsets instead of taking the time myself. *Forgive me that I gave my attention to Andrew Hayes while little Bethie wept somewhere. I didn't know, Bethie . . . I didn't know . . .* In my own defense that was all I had: ignorance. The humiliation was killing. Ignorance. I thought I would dissolve, slide right off that spiked kitchen chair and puddle at my own feet. I sat there bleeding. And slowly I recognized the weapon. I had been impaled on the past.

I cherished Bethie's childhood more than she did. What parent doesn't? In that childhood the parent too is always young, hand in hand with a beloved boy or girl whose charm, whose laughter, whose tears and joys, whose very brattiness become the occasion for smiles. Parents wrap themselves in a sort of warm shawl of that childhood, the pattern fashioned of anecdotes, fringed with vignettes, tasseled with *When my girl was little, she . . .* The daughter grows up, moves on, sees herself as a fully fashioned adult, the product. But the parent remembers the process. The parent cherishes the process. And now, everything rendered wretched, Bethie led us through a gallery of evils. Some greater than others.

When at last she wound down, rather like Pooh Bear, in mid-measure, Bethie still remained tearless, she and Wade alone tearless. The rest of us, un-recovered, still weeping, wiping our eyes, wincing, unable to collect ourselves.

Finally Sunny spoke, her voice low and uncertain. "Bethie, no one wants to see you breaking down. No one wants to see you haunted and unhappy. You were always The Charmer, Bethie."

"People-pleasers act that way because they need validation outside themselves. It's not enough for them to be self-sufficient and personally empowered, they're always looking for applause. They need others to be good to them because they don't know how to be good to themselves. They get stripped of their own validation and have to go outside themselves to seek it." Bethie's lower lip thrust out petulantly. "Besides, what do you care? I'm nothing to you, Sunny. An ex-step."

"I wouldn't be here if you were nothing to me, Bethie. You're my sister. We're all three sisters. Death or divorce can't touch what we are to each other."

"Celia didn't divorce Bobby," Bethie corrected her. "She slept with other men and threw Bobby out."

"That's a rather harsh way of putting it," Sunny said, to my surprise.

"She slept with his father"—Bethie nodded toward Grant—"and he and his nasty brother moved in with us." Bethie chewed her lip and her eyes narrowed. "There's something between you and Grant, isn't there, Sunny? I can always tell when people are having sex."

"We didn't come here to discuss ourselves, Bethie," said Grant, his first words. "We came to make things better for you."

"You can't discuss yourselves or anything else. You agreed not to talk," Wade reminded him.

"Grant and I both love you, Bethie. We all love you."

"You and Grant are having sex. My ex-stepsister is sleeping with my ex-stepbrother," Bethie mused bitterly. "That's a pretty weird combo, isn't it? Serial incest?"

"They never lived together as children," I shouted, surprised at myself. "They never had any connection at all, except—well, me." I simmered down. "And that was a long time ago."

"You seem to bring sex into everyone's lives, Celia," Wade observed coolly.

Before I could say *I'm pissed off and you're full of shit,* Victoria put a hand over mine, a gesture so tender and unlike her, I nearly cried out loud. She spoke earnestly to Bethie. "We're asking everyone to be brave, Bethie. Even you. You remember last spring? Making me tell Celia that I had married Eric? Remember how you insisted I be brave? I was brave for you then. Be brave for me now and talk to us in something besides accusations. Please. There has to be something other than—"

"You had to admit you got married for your own well-being. You had been living a lie."

"It was my own life, Bethie, and I was happy the way things were. You convinced me to tell the truth. Now I want to convince you to tell the truth."

"I have." Bethie twitched and squirmed beside Wade. "I still think it's really weird and, well, really weird that Sunny should be sleeping with Grant. It gives me the creeps. Grant and Lee give me the creeps. They always have. They've always made me feel terrible. If you knew, Sunny, how awful they were and how awful their father was, how horrible it was to live with all of them, you wouldn't have anything to do with him." She burst into cathartic tears and signaled somehow permission for everyone else to join in. We all wept. Even Wade took a few Kleenex before passing the box on to Grant.

"What can we do, Bethie?" I blew my nose. "Please, honey,

just tell us what we can do to help you. We're sorry you're so unhappy. We love you. All of us. We want to help."

"But you don't believe me. If you want to be in a relationship with me, you have to believe me."

"We *are* in a relationship with you. I am your mother and these are your sisters."

"No." Bethie shook her head, willing her tears to dry. "That's a kinship. You can't help kinships. Relationship is something different. Relationship you have to choose and go on choosing. In a relationship everybody has to agree and everyone has to respect. If you want to be in a relationship with me, then you have to believe me. I'm not a liar and I won't be in a relationship with anyone who thinks I am a liar. If you choose not to be in a relationship with me, I will respect that."

"What?" I mopped my eyes.

"If you love me, then you believe me. You believe what Bobby did to me."

I glanced over at Victoria, and at Sunny whose shoulders had narrowed, hunched protectively, rolled forward. "I don't think it has to be either/or—" I began tentatively.

"It is either/or." Bethie's voice was steady, her tears all dried. "Either you believe me or you don't."

"We can love you without believing that Bobby Jerome is a monster. Any man who would do those things to a child—"

"Why would you want to be in a relationship with a liar?"

"We don't, but—"

"You see! You do think I'm lying!"

"Of course, you're lying!" Victoria screamed, departing from the rules. "My father loved us! Loved all of us, loved you! He was the only father you ever had! You wanted him to be the father of the bride you loved him so much!"

"He didn't love me," retorted Bethie. "I was nothing to him. A stepdaughter and a sex object. Anyway, I have my own father." She regarded me coldly. "You look surprised, Celia. You kept me from Gary all these years. You wanted me to have to trust every man you went to bed with, so I'd be prey to any old person who slid under your sheets. You kept me apart from my own father so I'd have no one to protect me. None of this would have happened if you hadn't sent him away, my real father, Gary Alsop."

"Oh, Bethie. I didn't send him away. I wouldn't marry him, that's all. I wouldn't marry anyone. He left because he wanted to get married and work for the IRS."

"You sent him packing. He told me! We called him up. He said he always wanted to see me, all those years, and you wouldn't let him. You told Gary, Just send money and shut up."

"Bethie, I never—that isn't . . ." Husked inside this patent misrepresentation were the little rattling kernels of the truth, tiny, percussive and insignificant, and Gary's thwarted interest in Bethie was the stuff of fiction, but I shut the hell up. I willed myself to clear my head, to kick my way to the surface, not to drown in this widening, deepening cesspool.

"We're going to San Jose this fall, to meet my dad, Wade and I are going. We talk to him a lot on the phone. I won't be cheated out of having a father. My father would never do to me what your father did." She turned, eyes blazing, to Sunny and Victoria who wilted under the onslaught.

I had to stand up. To breathe, to walk around this kitchen chair and brace myself, to hold on and hyperventilate because I suffered a sort of burning in the chest, a stab to the heart, a sort of blinding clarity across my line of vision. We had been brought here under entirely false pretenses. There was not, there would not be any understanding reached—much less reconciliation. We thought we'd been so clever arranging this meeting through Sunny's cool medium. But this was not a meeting to resolve family issues. This was not an attempt at understanding. This was a kind of slaughter. There came to my mind the chickens my father used to kill. He would chop off their heads with a couple of well-aimed blows and all us kids would laugh to watch the chickens run around, headless, squawkless, still terrified, frantically searching for what they'd lost, until at last they fell over, surprised to be dead. But if we were the chickens being slaughtered, it came to me, Bethie had been faith-healed like a goat. "Go to San Jose,

Bethie. I wish you well," I said slowly. "I wish Gary Alsop well. I think I speak for all of us?"

Sunny, Grant, Victoria nodded slowly and in unison, watchful, wary, uncertain, knowing with the instincts of children (however grown) that the adults are suddenly dangerous.

"But we need to be really clear here, all of us do. Even you, Bethie." I took a deep breath. "You are giving us an ultimatum, right? You will consent to be in the family with us—to be in a relationship, as you put it—only if we believe that Bobby Jerome sexually accosted you, molested you."

"It's the truth! He is a monster!"

"And if we don't believe that, if we believe Bobby Jerome is incapable of those acts, then you are finished with us forever."

"Until you believe me."

"Well then, Bethie, what if I say, I believe you *believe* these things happened, that you have been told they happened and you believe it."

"I'm not a liar!"

"The worst thing is a liar," Wade observed evenly, "whoever the truth might hurt—you, Celia, or Bobby, or any of you—whoever individually the truth might hurt, the lie hurts everyone. If you want to go on believing Bobby's lies and denials, then that's your choice. And your responsibility."

I studied the man on the couch, noting for the first time that his trimmed beard obscured a weak chin and the mustache obscured the defect of an overbite. For once his eyes were not brimming with beneficence and empathy, the suffering of a man who has gotten himself off crack and so knows firsthand the sorrows of the flesh. They were interested eyes, but not benign. Rather than be ingested by the spongy couch, he extricated himself, moved to the edge, alert.

I clutched at the back of the chair. I started to salivate like you do before you're going to heave. I have misunderstood everything. I see that now. I had taken it all personally. *Boo hoo, Wade shattered my past.* But I was only a casualty. Bobby was only a casualty. Sunny and Victoria too. Bethie was the target. The intended victim. The destruction of my past was incidental. It was Bethie's past Wade wanted to destroy. That whole part of her life that did not involve Wade Shumley. That past will now be closed to her. She can never return to that old warm place— Isadora, Useless, Sophia's Beach, girls in the orchard, Huggamugwumps, Boomerquangers—all that is lost to her, suffused with pain, with bitterness and betrayal. She could never go back, only go forward. With Wade. And as for Gary Alsop, he was an unsuspecting dupe in this. Wade would use Gary as long as it suited him. Wade Shumley had kidnaped my daughter. Her face ought to be on a fucking milk carton. She was a prisoner in victimville. It was a dirty little war. Wade might have already won, but I would not go without a fight.

I said to my daughter, "Wade has thought all this out, Bethie. Wade knows exactly what's happening here. What Wade has done is unconscionable." I drew myself up and addressed him directly. "I understand now. I understand what you've done, you sanctimonious, manipulative bastard—"

"You promised," Bethie shouted, "no name-calling, those were the rules!"

"Listen to me, Bethie, you gave us an ultimatum. We leave and then? Then you will have no one but Wade. You will have no one at all who is your family, no one who really knows you, who knows not only who you are, but who you *were*. When we leave here, he will become the mirror of your whole identity. That's why he changed your name from Bethie to Elizabeth. You didn't do that. He did. At that awful engagement party, he could see we had claims on you, long-standing ties that he could not match or meet. And so he had to destroy us. But he's stealing your past, Bethie. It's Wade who's making you sick. He's feeding you off his own sickness. No one man can be a family."

"Wade's given me everything! Work, love, support and a program for my recovery."

"That's bullshit. That's not your work. That's his job." I brought down the fucking kitchen chair and it spronged along the floor.

"Wade loves me! You never think of anyone but yourself!"

"You better leave now, Celia." Wade rose. "You've done more damage to Elizabeth than you can possibly guess at."

"But not more than you can guess at," I snapped back. I turned to Bethie imploringly. "Without your own past, without your memories, you're empty. You're a vessel for him to fill up. You can never mention your past again because it's so ugly now. Don't let him do this, steal and destroy. You can lose everything else, you can give everything else all away. But your past can only be stolen from you, Bethie. Don't let this sniveling, hypocritical, pump-sucking bastard steal—"

"Get out! Go away! All of you! I hate you. You've ruined everything!"

"You've broken all the rules," Wade declared. "Get out. Your relationship with Elizabeth is over."

"You're full of shit, Wade! There are no ex-mothers! This is a family fight and not a teatime relationship. We *are* in a relationship, Bethie. I'm your *mother,* damnit! I pushed you out of my body! I loved you from before you were born! How much more related can you be?"

Wade told us to get out, all of us, told us repeatedly, though he did not raise his voice and he did not look at Bethie, sobbing, curled up fetally in the fleshy couch, pulling at her hair and moaning. Sunny moved toward her.

"Don't go near her," Wade ordered, his temper rising. "Just get out. I should never have let you come, especially you—" He spoke to Grant as we all moved toward the door. "She's told me about you and your brother, about the cruel boys you were, torturing her cats, the brutality you inflicted on her and Victoria while you lived with them, the physical abuse."

"What? Physical abuse? Bethie? Bethie?" Grant reached out to her like a ballplayer, to catch what would otherwise be a home run for the opposing team.

"You know you did it!" she burst out harshly. "You did it! You and Lee—you did it to me. You tortured my kitty. You tore the head off my doll. You cheated from my homework. You poured my goldfish into the toilet, and left him there for me to pee on. You used up all my good soap, my lavender soap, and left it floating in the tub. You kept me in the closet and you made me—" Bethie broke into a fresh paroxysm of weeping.

But it was Wade who clarified and expanded, graphically, how Elizabeth remembered that often, when Grant and Lee's father had been upstairs in bed with me, the two boys had trapped Bethie in a closet and made her take down her pants before they'd let her out.

And with a single expletive, and a single blow, Grant decked Wade with a furled fist. Wade doubled over, crumpled at Grant's feet, hit his chin on the coffee table and bit his lower lip, which began to gush blood. And as Wade turned, he caught his temple on the edge of the table, opening another gash while Bethie screamed, scrambled and clung to him.

Wade shook Bethie off and got slowly to his knees. He wiped his lip with the back of his hand and regarded his own blood with some affection. "You see, Elizabeth, what did I tell you? You are well rid of them."

Once outside in the brightness, and after the sunless apartment, the four of us blinked at one another while our eyes tried to adjust to the light and our minds to adjust to what had just transpired. We could hear from inside the apartment, crying, weeping, a kind of keening wail that would have broken a heart of stone. Sunny started back toward the door, but Victoria stayed her. "It's over," she said. "You can't do anything. No one can."

"It was a lie," said Grant, the cords in his neck still visibly taut. "I shouldn't have hit him, but it was a lie."

"It's all been a lie," I said as we walked slowly away. "But we can't go home yet. We have to go to see Bobby. Now we know where the lie is coming from and why, and we have to tell him or he's going to stay sunk in this cesspool Wade created. We can't help Bethie, but we can help him."

"I don't want to see anyone," said Victoria. "I'm exhausted. I want to go home and cry, or take a Valium, or drink or something. I hate all this."

"Fine, Victoria. But I'm going and Sunny and Grant are going. We all came in the same car," I reminded them. In truth, Sunny looked ashen and Grant was badly shaken, but this had to happen now. "Bobby is living in a hell he did not create and does not deserve. And I think we need to tell him so. All of us together."

"He won't want to see Grant," Victoria objected. "Bobby won't much like it that Sunny and Grant are, well, sleeping together. It's a pretty strange—"

"I'm not asking permission." Sunny stiffened.

I rode to Bobby's with Victoria, the terrible silence between us made somehow the more oppressive by the new-car smell in her BMW, by all that expensive quiet. Finally I couldn't bear it, and I asked her what had gotten into her, or out of her, or whatever was eating at her.

"Do you think you're the only one who's suffered? This has been hell for me too."

"I'm not talking about all this, Victoria, about what Bethie's unleashed. You have not been yourself since Dorothy's heart attack. Since the engagement party when you told me the truth about you and Eric. Why did you keep your marriage a secret anyway? I didn't care. Really. But I'm hurt that you felt you had to lie to me about marrying Eric."

"Oh, God—please just can the hurt feelings, will you? I don't want to hear another word about hurt feelings. Anyway, I didn't lie. I waffled and qualified. There were tiny omissions. You knew I was living with Eric and that much was the truth."

"Eric is a wonderful man. Really, a fine husband."

"Please stop. Please. You sound just like Dorothy. She must be rubbing off on you."

"Your life is your own, Victoria."

"It was."

Bobby and Janice lived in a split-level in North Seattle, a comfortable-looking house with a postage stamp of a yard and a chain-link fence in a neighborhood of small children, judging from the pink bicycles littering the sidewalks. Todd was mowing the front lawn. He looked pleased to see Victoria, looked less pleased to see me and downright alarmed when Sunny and Grant pulled up behind. We said we wanted to see Bobby and he glanced toward the window where his mother and the Wookie stood scowling at us.

Our struggle with Janice was predictably full of recriminations and accusations and anger, but after what we'd just been through, this was a mere toxic picnic. Occasionally the Wookie punctuated Janice's condemnation of all things Isadoran with aspersions on me in particular. Bobby finally straggled out of the bedroom, and he looked as though the noisy altercation had woken him from some dream. Like Bethie, he was a physical wreck and it was terrible to see accused and accuser suffering in such parallel ways. He was unshaven, and his gray hair untrimmed; he'd lost weight but not flesh and his skin seemed to flap unhappily about his jowls. He was wearing shorts that hung on him and a T-shirt from an old Grateful Dead concert. Shocking to see him, to see how the man of such buoyancy and spirit and charm uneroded by age could have drained out of the body of Bobby Jerome in so short a time. But to see Sunny and Victoria, his face lit, and after that, Janice could not deny us.

Sunny especially fussed over him and I could imagine her as a girl fussing over him when they had lived together till Janice took him In Hand. Sunny had a special voice for Bobby, a voice unlike any other in its tenderness, a voice she used perhaps for Brio, but no other. He wanted to know all about Brio, why she hadn't come and if she missed him. So Sunny told him all the news of Island Preschool and Baby Herman and how much Brio missed his music and their games. "She wants you to come back and do all the things you used to do. She wants you to live *con brio,* Dad."

Bobby regarded Grant curiously, coldly, as though seeing him for the first time. He asked what Grant was doing here.

Sunny interceded before Grant could answer. "I'm in love with Grant, Dad. We're in love. Aren't you happy for us?"

"I am not my father," said Grant. "I love Sunny and Brio and I'll always do right by them." And he stepped behind Sunny, as I'd noticed he often did, like a mast or ballast.

Sunny reached for Grant's hand, held it. "You see, Dad, it's going to be OK."

"You never call me Dad unless it's dire. Is it dire?" He looked at Janice, at Victoria, at me.

Slowly, in a kind of chime and spiral, repetition, revelation we told him why we'd come and where we'd been and what we now understood. "Wade can only deal with weak people," I said at last, "people who are hurting and in pain. He can't bear strength, so he had to put Bethie in pain to make her weak. He told her a sort of story about you, about me, about us in the old days over and over. He told her that story till she believed it."

"Like the Huggamugwump stories," Sunny volunteered, "one of those chilling stories kids love, where there's peril and adventure and a safe harbor at the end. He told her those lies like stories."

"Of course these are lies!" Janice interrupted. "What else could they be? Vile lies. This is not news, and you are not helping Bobby."

I went to Bobby. I took his hand. "There is a kind of chronic pain," I said, "that we will all have to endure. We have lost our daughter to Wade and Wade's lies. But you have to get well because we can't let Wade destroy you too. We have to protect the past, Bobby, our past, even though it was not perfect, not all golden, but it's worth protecting. Think of us, Bobby, remember back, all of us, remember us on Sophia's Beach. No matter what's happened to you and me, or that the girls have grown up, something of us remains on that beach. Just like those old Indians who died there, anonymous, long dead, you know? But no one's ever been able to change the name of what happened to them at

Massacre. Some memories are so powerful they cling to a place. Time itself clings there. You go to that place and you meet that time. An island in time. We can't let Wade corrupt that. We can't lose each other. All of us, Janice. I mean that." I glanced at her and she had started to cry. I looked at Todd whose great mustache sat so awkwardly in his young face, and I told Bobby he still had children to think about, Victoria and Sunny and Todd and Brio. "We have to keep ourselves together, Bobby, and protect that island in time. We can't let Wade steal across Moonless Bay and slaughter us all in silence."

I insisted Janice bring him over the following weekend for a picnic on Sophia's Beach, and to my surprise, she did. The Wookie stayed in Seattle, sulking, but Janice made the effort. Give her that. And Bobby was better, visibly so, not entirely his old self, but the sight of Brio seemed a tonic to him. And because Bobby was better, Janice was better and Todd relaxed, bounded along Sophia's Beach barking at the seals, crashing into the cold water where Eric joined him. Briefly. Everyone took a turn on the swing and when it was my turn, I went high into the air and over the water and looked up and down the beach at my family, not just Sunny and Brio, Bobby, Todd and Janice, but Grant too, Victoria, Eric, Dorothy and old begrudging Ned. I laughed out loud. For the first time since all this anguish had struck, I laughed. Maybe for the first time since Bethie's wretched engagement party and dreadful Diane Wirth. I laughed now to think how strangely we were all related. Nuclear didn't describe families. How could it? Dry physics was not equal to that task. In the twentieth century we needed a biological metaphor, Darwinian in scope, to suggest the gnash and crash of carnivorous life in the family gene pool. But for the twenty-first century, the new century, I think the metaphors must be chemical. Molecular. In the molecular family people are connected without being bound. They spindle themselves around shared experiences and affections rather than splashing in the shared gene pool. Families like ours created from the rag ends of other families, molecularly connected to make something entirely different, combined to create a new whole.

PART VIII

Island Fever

Does suffering, unjustly inflicted and patiently endured, make you a martyr? St. Sebastian came to Victoria's mind. Joan of Arc, perhaps. But what about the less literary? What about those masses of victims, suffering hordes, like the Slaughter of the Innocents in the Bible? Or the hollow-eyed proletariat crying out for bread and revolution. Were they martyrs? Or does suffering, unjustly inflicted and patiently endured, simply make you a stupid shit?

Victoria Robbins struggled all summer with these questions, feeling like a stupid shit, though slowly she came to believe that the answers hinged on accountability. I ought to have resisted Bethie, she thought on a more or less daily basis, nibbling around the edge of her French manicure as though it were a baby slug in the middle of an otherwise adequate salad. I ought to have said: *Bethie, do what you want with your own life. Have the Great White Wedding. Flower girls, ushers, blue garters snapped and flung to* groomsmen, *flowers tossed to the bridesmaids, and shove the whole thing down Celia's throat and make her pay for it. Do what you want, but leave me be. I know best how to balance my marriage and deal with my mother. I will tell Celia in my own good time. Or not tell her, as I see fit. I do not need to make an Issue of my marriage. I will come to your engagement party. I will be your bridesmaid. But it is not your place to tell me when or what to confess to Celia.* Victoria practiced this speech over and over till she had finally got it right. It took her all summer. An exercise pointless beyond belief.

Pointless, yes, but it offered some comfort, because though her sufferings remained unjustly inflicted, at least she could actually blame someone else. Hold Bethie accountable for everything. Bethie had insisted on inviting the whole Robbins tribe to the engagement party. Bethie had assured Victoria inviting *all* of them was the only way to get Celia to accept her marriage, to get Celia (famously stubborn) to see that Victoria Robbins was truly a married woman with in-laws.

But if Dorothy had stayed decently home, none of this would have happened. And why hadn't Bethie (so eager to confront in the interest of healing) considered what a prolonged dose of Celia (or Bobby, for that matter, or Nona and Ernton and Launch) might do to Dorothy Robbins? Poor old Dorothy, so undone, she nearly croaked. She fell, literally, into Celia's lap. And stayed there. And now Victoria's adult life, her very own unclouded life, was being infiltrated all over again. Celia was again coloring up Victoria's life, moving through it like a sort of plume of dark ink slowly dropped in standing water. Every weekend Eric dragged Victoria back to Isadora Island to see Mom. Both moms. Every weekend Victoria suffered island fever all over again and vowed she would not return. Every weekend she did, drawn back like the tide inexorably pulled by an otherwise innocent moon. She returned to Isadora Island, with its great brooding mountains, thick shadows, its obscure bays and tangled undercurrents.

Even Victoria's weekday life had been completely altered by that fateful party in March. With Dorothy camped at Celia's and refusing to leave Isadora, Ned now swooped down every night on Victoria and Eric. Eric, the more fool he, had given Dad a key to their house (without asking Victoria's permission) and so now Ned never even knocked, but showed up each evening in his usual funk. Poor old Ned. Having insisted that Dorothy do all his emoting for the last thousand years, Ned had no resources to deal with the crisis. Which was, of course, that Dorothy wasn't there to emote. Dorothy would not come home. Ned dissolved under the hurt and dissatisfaction, and visited it on Victoria and Eric. Nightly.

"I don't see why you care if my father eats dinner with us," Eric complained one evening as they were changing after work, expecting Ned at any minute. "I don't ask you to cook. We almost always go to a restaurant, or get Chinese takeout. If he didn't eat with us, Dad would be alone."

Inevitably in the course of these conversations, Eric gave his wife a look she found increasingly annoying, a great bruising of the eyes, lower lip thrust out in the tiniest defiance, defiance that could turn swiftly to pout if it met with anything but instant compliance. He looked exactly like his mother.

"I don't want to be your mother. I don't want to be a stand-in for Dorothy, not for you and not for Ned either. It's not fair and I shouldn't have to do it, and neither should you." It had been a particularly long day at Nordstrom's marketing department. Victoria put her heels neatly in the closet, slithered out of her panty hose and into a pressed and belted pair of slacks and an ironed T-shirt.

"All right then, Victoria. I'll take Dad out by myself. You can stay home. But we are all going to have a drink here first. You can do that much for my father, can't you?"

As he had been trained since childhood, Eric hung up his pants, put his shirt and socks in the laundry basket and smoothed the beautifully made bed where his rump had rumpled it. These were things Victoria had always adored about Eric, and watching him now in the shaded sanctuary of their bedroom, she felt a sort of lush contraction of tenderness and desire. She might have moved toward him, opened her arms and pulled him into her embrace, but Ned was due and she didn't want to have to hop in and out of bed like teenagers. She remembered how Eric had made the bed after the first time they'd made love. Now, that was a man you could count on.

"Why doesn't your dad go to one of your brothers' houses?" she asked more reasonably.

"My brothers all have kids. Kids get on Dad's nerves."

"They're not little kids."

"All kids get on Dad's nerves."

"Didn't he have four sons? What did he do when he had four children of his own?"

"He wasn't home a lot. It was always Mom," Eric confessed. "We almost never had to eat with him."

"So what's he doing now? Making up for lost time?"

"Please, Victoria—you know the strain my family has been under since Mom had her heart attack."

"And you think my family hasn't!" Victoria's voice raised to a screech. "My sister has accused my father of child molesting! I'd say that was pretty damn stressful, Eric!"

"If your dad wanted to come here night after night, honey, I would welcome him."

That was a lie, but one so obvious and moot that it didn't bear comment. Victoria sat at the vanity (replete with framed photographs of her and her husband in jaunty poses) and furiously brushed her thick straight hair.

"Anyway, the strain your family is under, is all your own fault," Eric went on wickedly. Two could play at this. "Your sister brought it down on you. My family—we didn't ask for this. My mother had a heart attack. She almost died. And now she refuses to budge off that island. She prefers to live with your mother and her boyfriend—"

"Russell moved out."

"—with people she never laid eyes on before that day," Eric continued undaunted, "rather than come home to her own husband and family. It's your fault, Victoria. What happened to Mom is your fault."

"Mine! Mine?"

"All right then, Bethie's. How was I to know you'd never told Celia we were married? Why did Bethie butt in? Why should she care what you and I did?"

Victoria had so often blamed Bethie for inflicting unjust suffering that not only did she not defend her sister, but joined Eric in heaping invective on Bethie. The exercise brought them closer together. Bethie had made an Issue of everything.

And indeed, this is what Victoria had told Eric when she had returned that afternoon from the ill-fated interview at Wade's apartment. She had told Eric it did not go well there at the condo in Wallingford. She had not said there were further accusations of inappropriate intimacy leveled against Grant and Leè Hayes. She did not want to put that thought into Eric's head. Impossible as the thought was. True, Grant and Lee had been odious boys, but they were not perverts, and Eric already thought her family was weird. They were weird; Victoria thought so too. Living with Celia wasn't even like a home, it was like a tide pool: people and things deposited and withdrawn by the flux of events, by tides of Celia's friends and lovers. Victoria again picked up her brush and brushed energetically.

"All I'm saying, Victoria, is that I expect you to welcome my father into our home. You're part of my family now." Eric paused briefly before adding, "And I'm part of yours. That's what marriage is about."

No wonder Celia avoided it, Victoria thought almost wistfully, watching in the mirror as her husband slid his long, pale legs into a pair of jeans. The very word *husband* used to give her such pleasure. She would say it to herself, adore it, relish, *husband*. The word and the man. She and Eric wanted all the same things: commitment, careers and a lake-view home. The good life. Except for those days when they caught planes for lovely vacation destinations, Maui or skiing at Mount Hood, their alarms went off at the same time every day. Each morning they woke, showered, dressed, ate the same hi-fiber breakfast cereal, rinsed their dishes and put them in the dishwasher, gave each other the same perfunctory, but sincere kiss before going off to the corporate world, into their upwardly mobile lives. They had bought this lakefront home very near Eric's parents, though not as grand, within six months of their marriage. Their lives were regular as heartbeats.

But this summer. This wretched summer. Something had happened. Not to the life itself, but to its desirability. Something Victoria could not quite fathom, much less articulate. It was as if one of those big clocks in Henry's House, those windup metronomes of life's passing hours—tick-tock, tick-tock—had suddenly taken up syncopation, tick-tock tick-tick tock-tick tickety-tock tock-tockety tick-tick.

"What the hell are you doing?" asked Eric, watching Victoria drum her fingers irregularly on the vanity top, endangering her manicure.

She brought her hands together and turned to face him. "Eric, it's not good for us to have your father here every night. It's not good for you. It's not good for me. It's not that I don't like Ned, I do. I adore your parents. I always have. They are the parents I always wanted to have, and they are fine people. But it's not fair, Eric, it's not fair for us to be responsible for your father's well-being and mental health. You should share this responsibility with your brothers."

"My brothers take him out to dinner now and then."

"Two weeks ago. That was the last time any of your brothers took him out to dinner. That was the last time you and I were alone together. I don't want to be responsible for your father," she said firmly.

"I don't care what you want."

This uncharacteristic response was not what Victoria had expected. She thought it best to broaden the venue. "As a family," she began, "the Robbinses all need to deal with Dorothy. You and your brothers need to bring more pressure on Dorothy to come home to Bellevue and look after Ned."

Eric conceded defeat to this with his whole body, slumping

into a chair, his legs splayed, his arms akimbo on the sides of the chair. "You think we haven't tried?"

"Try harder."

"Every weekend we try! My dad, my brothers, my sisters-in-law! They call Mom every weekend. I go to Useless, I tell her, *Mom, Mom, think of Dad! Dad can't live without you! Mom, he's turning into the shell of his former self.* But there's nothing I can do to get Mom away from your mother, Victoria. What is it about your mother?"

Victoria bit back, "You think Dorothy's being kept prisoner by my family?"

"Then what is it? What has my mom found there that's more important than us? What has she found there that we couldn't give her?"

It was a son's plaintive cry, the male's absolute inability, Victoria realized, to grasp that a woman could have any more significant tug on her loyalties than his.

"If Mom had got religion," he went on miserably, "I could understand that. You remember my frat brother, Mike? He got religion and—"

"I don't want to hear about Mike. Anyway, Dorothy hasn't got religion."

"Then what's she got?"

"Something else." Victoria took a measured breath and prefaced her remarks by reminding Eric that certainly she didn't know Dorothy as her own dear son knew Dorothy, but nonetheless, she thought that Dorothy's remaining on Isadora Island, with Celia, had something to do with work. "I think she likes the work."

"She could get a job in Bellevue."

"No, Eric, I don't mean a job. I mean she's found something she does well and something she believes in and something she can be part of. Something rewarding."

"She's already part of a family."

"But a family's not necessarily rewarding. And your brothers aren't exactly captivating, on a day-to-day basis," she added with a little verbal kick.

"What sort of rewarding?"

"A sort of process where you're part of something that's changing and absorbing. Like your work for Microsoft. Like mine for Nordstrom. Work that makes your days contrast, one to the other. Work where you grow and you know you're learning, getting better and more accomplished every year, work where you feel you're contributing your skills to something outside of yourself. Now instead of staying home all day, her days are, well, satisfying."

"More satisfying than Dad?"

"You don't understand, do you? I'm going to have to give you chapter and verse."

"Do it."

"When my mother decided to reopen Henry's House as a B-and-B, she lived like a woman with a mission. I was very little, so I don't much remember those early days, but once the place was up and running, we were, all of us, constantly going between Henry's House and our own house. Our house was this ramshackle, rundown place, cramped, messy and crowded. You never knew when people like Nona York and Ernton Hapgood and the other old Isadorans would drop in. In and out all the time, like Sophia never did die. Like Henry Westervelt was still alive and entertaining them. We had Launch who used to scare the hell out of my school friends because he wouldn't talk, just grin and point. We had my mother's lovers and their children and their families and even their in-laws. Phillip's mother and sister were raving bitches and the sister's kids were lunatics and they stayed, lived with us one whole summer. Phil said we were all cousins." Victoria shuddered. "I found it intolerable. But there was—you had to admit—a rhythm between our house and Henry's. There was contrast and texture. You might get pissed off, but it was hard to be bored. Because right through the orchard, you could go from all that crowded squalor to Henry's House. And there was all of this studied opulence! This measured beauty, everything arranged just so and calculated for gorgeous effect and it was all just lovely. The work was hard, but rewarding because you could watch the results right in front of you. People adore Henry's House. They come back. They write it up in *Joie de Vivre!*, stupid rag that it is. But at Henry's there's always this sense of change and knowing that you're learning. You're growing and getting better."

"Your mother's not a figure skater, Victoria. She's a glorified cook, a glorified bed-maker, a glorified housekeeper," Eric scoffed. "She's made my mother into the same thing. For forty years my mother made mushroom gravy with Campbell's soup and now she's doing it at Henry's House. How is that growth?"

"Be that as it may, Eric, you say they're glorified cooks, but did your family ever glorify Dorothy?"

"We adored her," he replied, without a trace of irony. "My father adores my mother and her place is with him."

"I don't think you quite understand."

But any elaboration Victoria might have volunteered was cut short because they heard their front door open and their nightly visitor, Ned, call out.

"Well, let's go." Eric hove to his feet and went to the door. "Are you coming?"

"Not anymore, Eric."

"You're going to stay here in this room?"

"No, I'll be out in a bit. I'll be nice to Ned. But I'm not carrying your dad around anymore like a baby, listening to him whimper and whine. And I'm not coming to the island with you anymore either. Not this weekend. Not ever, if I can help it. I made my escape from Isadora, Eric. You were my escape. Now you're dragging me back. I don't want to go back, and I won't."

"Fine. I'll go without you. I'm not giving up on Mom."

He left her in the bedroom and she heard him greet his father. She could imagine Ned, his balding pate furrowed with the day's dilemmas which he now rained down on Eric, requiring Eric (and Victoria when she was there) to listen to him, as Dorothy had always listened to him. Dorothy had always said something soothing like *How Nice, Dear* when things went well, or *Isn't That Terrible* when things went badly, or *Humph* when things were really unspeakable. Eric did a fair Dorothy-imitation, allowing for slightly different choices in diction. Victoria did not do it well. Hereafter she would not do it at all. Not ever again. Having refused, she had expected to feel a great sense of relief. No longer would she endure suffering. No longer would she be a martyr and a victim. But she still felt like a stupid shit.

She went, eventually, into the living room, greeted Ned and flopped inelegantly on the couch while Eric mixed them all a drink, gin and tonic in honor of the heat wave. Eighty-one degrees. A Seattle scorcher. Sunlight glinted off the lake punctuated by lots of little sails, pleasure boats puttered about. Victoria did not contribute to the conversation. It was the same conversation every night. Eric handed Victoria her drink and went back to his father. These were the Coming Attractions for the rest of her life.

She'd done it herself, she realized now. In parting with the secret of her marriage, she had tarnished it. The secrecy itself was the romance and the rebellion, rolled into one. How sweet, how exhilarating it had been for Victoria to know she was loved—and at the same moment to defy her mother, to rebel against her parents' every value, to repudiate everything Celia stood for. For Victoria, the *I do's* were part of the storybook marriage, the storybook life. She had blessed the fetters that tied her to her husband. She had what her mother repudiated: a husband.

Moreover, in marrying Eric Robbins she had united herself with a family that represented everything Victoria had longed for, united herself with people as far from the haphazard passions of her childhood as could be humanly imagined. Victoria had embraced, adored everything about Eric Robbins. He was bland and handsome. He wanted a good job, a career. He wanted to get married. Everyone in his family was married, including his parents. His mother doted on him and he was convinced he deserved to be doted on. His family was decently dull, thoroughly accessorized, everything in good taste, understated, less-is-more, that sort of thing. When she had first gone to their Bellevue house, Victoria had endeared herself to Dorothy by commenting on the glorious floors and the gleaming kitchen with its empty counters and shiny chrome. So unlike her own cluttered home (which she left unmentioned). The Robbinses did not have a stockpot bubbling constantly on some back burner, a stockpot into which went God Knows What, and the smell ever-present. The Robbins house smelled like Lemon Pledge. They did not say fuck. Dorothy and Ned were sexless as clams. Having lived her whole life around people who were physically affectionate, demonstrative and percolating with sexual tension or sexual fulfillment, it delighted Victoria that she could not imagine Dorothy and Ned in bed. There was the suggestion about Eric's parents that their children were begot while Dorothy wore white gloves and Ned thought of new ways to make money. Best of all, none of the Robbinses talked about life in general as though everything were a work of art in need of framing and how best to go for effect. The Robbinses cared nothing for effect. They cared for a seemly shallow dignity. They did not believe that charm, slavishly applied, was a substitute for that dignity. They had reserve. They voted Republican. And now everything that had made the Robbinses and their life, Victoria's marriage, so appealing, had corroded and was indelibly stained with the life she had escaped.

Who would have believed that Dorothy Robbins, the very pinnacle of convention, would have succumbed to what passed for charm in Celia Henry? Who would have believed that Dorothy would have gone swimmingly into the arms of Celia Henry and refused to leave her? Dorothy had likened herself to Ruth in the Bible. Victoria had laughed out loud. Then Dorothy added she was learning how to spit. This was not so funny. *Whither thou spittest, there I shall spit?* Even when—if—Dorothy returned to Bellevue, she would never be the same. It was over.

While Eric and Ned continued to ignore her, Victoria rose and walked along the white carpet and through the white billowing drapes, out the sliding glass door to the balcony overlooking the lake. Nothing in her own life could ever be so cleanly picketed again. Island fever would come to get her, no matter where she lived. The fear is worse than the feat, isn't that what Sunny had said? Maybe. But the feat could not be undone. And once confessed, Victoria's marriage, her delight in her own defiance smashed up. The significance of her clandestine *I do* diminished to a tiny little speck of *so what* on the great horizon of life. She wanted to cry. She felt rather like Henry Westervelt must have felt, she imagined, stunned by the blow, then roused by the icy waters, flailing, crying out, going under, coming up and knowing in that final dreadful moment he would not—would not ever again—get back on board the *Deo Volente,* and all the old certainties were forever denied and the old dreams of defiance swept away.

PART IX

A Change of Life

Many mornings, the *Pythagoras,* its sails furled, would be anchored in sight of Useless Point. The boat's varnished wooden hull reflected imperfectly the restless water which in turn reflected imperfectly the dome of sky. Mist thickened in the distant Sound as the sun rose slowly over Isadora's great mountain. Sunny Jerome emerged from the cabin, ruffling her short hair. Eyeing her eagerly, a dozen seagulls, their beggarly instincts roused, left their perches on the rocks, circled overhead, skimming the surface of the water, plumping down eventually, close by the boat, floating, complacently certain that human hands would sooner or later reward them with garbage. Sunny crossed the short deck to the stern, looking toward the larger Sound, a Venus in overalls, the sailboat her half shell. She savored this moment, her favorite of her day. She turned back to Isadora as sunlight like thickened syrup ran down the dark sides of the mountain, and in the distance the day's first ferryboat plied toward Dog Bay, its horn echoing between islands.

"Is that the ferry?" asked Grant, emerging from the cabin, bearing a mug of tea in each hand. Sunny reached for hers and lifted her face to be kissed. "We're running late, sweets. I have to get back to the marina." But he kept his arms around her. "We're roofing and we have to get an early start. You can see what kind of day it's going to be. Sunny. Like you."

He drank the hot tea in quick gulps, and weighed anchor while Sunny started the motor and they puttered noisily through the morning light toward the Useless dock. They kissed goodbye and Sunny climbed up, stood there waving to him while the *Pythagoras* chugged away. Other sailboats and pleasure crafts moored at the Useless dock bobbed in *Pythagoras'* wake, but no one stirred this early.

She started up the dock and the road toward Henry's driveway, stopping momentarily to watch an eagle swoop overhead. She turned to watch it fly out over the Point, cascade downward and in the space of a single breath, snatch from the water a fish whose curiosity had brought it too close to the surface. Writhing visibly in the eagle's talons, the fish mounted high into the sky, out of its element altogether as the eagle soared. Then, suddenly, as suddenly as it had snatched the hapless fish, the eagle lost its grip and the fish plummeted back into the waters of the Sound.

The fall was enough to kill it, thought Sunny, just as screeching brakes made her spin around and an old sedan barreled at her. Sunny jumped out of the way, falling in the process, rolling to the side of the road. The driver too veered, then plunged into the rhododendrons before the motor died. Sunny crawled out of the ditch, shaken, bruised, but nothing broken.

The driver, a woman, hollered out the window. "You stupid bitch!" She tried to coax the engine back to life, without success.

Sunny slowly got to her feet, brushing herself off. Still unsettled, she walked to the car, the front of it obscured in the rhododendrons, but the back boasted California plates. Old ones. I should have guessed, Sunny thought. The woman tried again and again to get the ignition to turn over, while on the passenger's side, the door creaked open and there came the sound of puking. The car that had very nearly struck Sunny was a Plymouth, perhaps twenty years old with a roof that might once have been a leather-look top, but which had peeled and flaked and cracked from the heat, and hung in short tongues, flapping over exposed metal. Of an indeterminate color, everything on the Plymouth had been softened, or battered or scabbed, pocked, mottled into an impression of beige. The ignition finally caught and the Plymouth coughed up a grainy pall of exhaust and protest as it backed out of the rhododendrons.

"I'm looking for Henry's House, Useless Point," the driver called out without so much as a mumbled apology for her name calling or her reckless driving. "Do you know where it is?"

Sunny pointed to the driveway which the woman had missed, overshot completely in her haste. The passenger was another woman, neither of them, Sunny noted with a mother's eye, wearing seat belts. "It's too early though. You can't check in till after one, after the one o'clock ferry docks."

"Check in? Who said check in? What is this place?"

"Henry's House. Isn't that what you're looking for?"

"Yeah. Thanks." With a series of difficult maneuvers, the gears protesting, ground into reverse, the woman backed up and made a left up into the driveway. Curiosity got the better of Sunny and she followed the car up the long drive, choked in its exhaust. Brushing grit from her clothes, she followed the Plymouth into the wide welcoming arc, the graveled drive before Henry's.

The driver was out of the car. "Holy horseshit," she cried, staring at the broad verandas and gleaming French doors, the balconies dripping with leafy wisteria vines and huge terra-cotta pots of red geraniums set at intervals, billowing too with lobelia so blue they looked to have been snipped from the midnight sky. Morning light rising cast long regal shadows on the lawn and across the drive. The driver wore tight jeans and a midriff T-shirt which accentuated her wiry little body. Her hair, in the indeterminate stages of growing out, was yanked into a hard high knot, a sort of ponytail, and not till she turned around did Sunny realize this was not a woman of her own age, not a young woman at all, but someone at least forty, alert, darting eyes set in a sharp-featured face. She was so thin that her skin stretched across her collarbones, attenuating and leaving uncushioned her ribs. The skin on her cheekbones too lay taut, insufficient to its task, frayed into creases at the corners of her eyes and pulled tightly at the mouth. "Henry's House, huh?" she said to Sunny. "Who is Henry? Is he married?" She laughed harshly and turned to her passenger. "Wouldn't you just know? Wouldn't you just?"

In reply the car door squealed plaintively. The passenger got out slowly. Unlike her companion, she was clad in clothes so voluminous they seemed to run off her body like lava and coagulate at her feet. When she turned round, Sunny was surprised to see that her coal-black hair contrasted sharply with her face, a ghastly artificial white, heightened by lipstick the color of a black plum. The eyes were heavily kohled, ringed and smudged in black, and the brows also blackened, plucked to perfection and on the right brow, perhaps half a dozen little rings followed the arch. From the girl's nose there bloomed a huge bouquet of little rings dangling there like metallic mucous. Her clothes too were black, save for a heavy chain flapping against her thigh, and all this against the white of her skin reminded Sunny of newsprint, unrelieved black-and-white telling a story purporting to be the truth. These were by far the strangest people Sunny had seen since she left L.A.

"Are you guests here?" Sunny asked.

"Guests? What is it? A loony bin?"

"Looks like a fucking loony bin," observed the girl, slamming the car door shut and leaning against it. "Like you'd be fucking crazy in quilted rooms here." She gazed out over the Sound, steeping now in the first full flush of morning. "No one'd ever hear you neither."

"I work here. Maybe I can help you. Are you looking for someone?"

"Elizabeth Henry," said the woman. "Says here—" She dug down in the pocket of her jeans and withdrew a much-folded newspaper clipping which carried the indentation of her hipbone. She smoothed it out on the hood of the car. Many times folded, the creases had ripped. "Here. 'Elizabeth Henry, daughter of Celia Henry of Henry's House, Useless Point, Isadora Island, Washington.'" She pointed to the engagement picture of Bethie and Wade, their smiles smudged in the battered clipping now six months old. "Actually we're looking for Wade."

"Shumley?"

"Yeah, but his address just says Seattle. This place was easier to find. What is it?"

"A bed-and-breakfast. Like a hotel, only it's a house."

The woman folded up her clipping and slithered it down in her pocket. "In L.A., you wouldn't let strangers into your house. Uh-uh." Her lips roiled vehemently. "Not in Reseda. That's in the Valley."

"Yes." Sunny nodded. "I know."

"You from L.A.?" The woman brightened.

"Sort of."

"Where can I find Wade? Lucky bastard. What a hell of a place, huh, Jennifer?"

"I have to take a piss."

"Wade isn't here, exactly. Not now, but—can I ask what you want with Wade?"

"A little family matter." She reached in over the dash and drew out a pack of cigarettes, offered one to the girl who leaned across the hood and took it. Then the girl got back in the car and slammed the door. "It's a little matter of twelve years of child support." She reached into her other pocket and withdrew a long tab from an adding machine, folded and refolded, and equally bearing the indentation of her other hip. "I did the math on it, see? I did the math on a machine so there's no mistaking it. Eighteen thousand dollars. Give or take." She folded it again. "I'm Lynette Shumley, Wade's ex-wife."

Sunny nodded, gulped, managed finally to eke out a request

for them to wait here. She would be right back. She would bring someone she knew could help them.

Could I help them? Oh yes indeed. Sunny introduced me as the mother of the bride and I was happy to help Lynette and Jennifer Shumley. They were looking for Wade. Wade Shumley, that lying fraud, had cracked a lot of bullshit whips about truth and lies, confronting the past, and I was joyed-over to know the old bullshit whip could cut two ways.

There was no mistaking the girl. Never mind the metal rings jangling on her upper lip and punched along her brow, nor the fact that she didn't have a beard and a mustache, her face was Wade's face, same overbite, same chin; her walk was Wade's walk and she had the same deep brown eyes. Certainly she bore scant resemblance to her mother. Tiny, coiled, ready to spring, her nerve endings all but extruding on the surface of her skin, Lynette Shumley was at the end of her tether. Jennifer was at the beginning of hers. I reckoned her to be about fifteen or sixteen, though she looked much older in ways not related to time. Pale, pissed off, her hair color out of a bootblack bottle, she was dead-white and dead-eyed when she ought to have been blooming.

I told Lynette and Jennifer to drive back to Dog Bay and get in line for the next eastbound ferry. I'd follow and personally escort them to Wade's house in Seattle. A regular travelers' aid society.

Mine was one of the last cars to get on the 10:10 ferry. I'd forgotten how fast the ferries fill up in summer when the San Juan Islands are crawling with vacationers, campers, boaters and sport fishers. I pulled my truck deep into the belly of the ferryboat, got out and started up the stairs as its horns blared and it cast off from Dog Bay. I went from deck to deck, inside and out, looking for Lynette and Jennifer. In summer these ferries have a carnival air about them—part of the appeal of the islands—large airy decks with booths and chairs and benches and wraparound windows, kids running up and down, keeping an eye out for whales, and being rewarded at least with the sight of seals and otters. Audiences *oooh* and *aaah* as people fling popcorn to the seagulls while they follow alongside the boat, amazing everyone with their stamina and skill at catching food in midair. Regulars on these runs have ongoing card games and young musicians play guitars and draw groups of singers to them. A violinist who keeps a summer home out here does his practicing on the way in. All over the ferry, passengers strike up conversations, even relationships, and in the midst of all this August camaraderie, I finally saw Lynette and Jennifer, huddled next to a window across from one another, talking to no one, not even each other.

I offered to go for a round of coffees from the snack bar, and when I returned, I sat down next to Lynette and handed out the coffees.

"Are you sure this is Sweet'n Low in here?" asked Jennifer. "I don't want to get fat." She blew on the coffee and I could see she had a mouthful of braces and a bolt in her tongue.

"Hot coffee must be hell on that metal."

In reply she stuck her tongue out at me, dug in her pack for her headphones and Walkman, put the tape in and the headphones on, and lay down. She rocked and twitched to a beat so percussive I could hear its bass over the rumble of the ferry and the noise of the crowd.

"Your daughter is the image of her dad," I said to Lynette. "I didn't know Wade had a daughter. I didn't know he'd been married."

"There's probably lots you don't know about Wade. Hell, there's lots I don't know. I haven't heard from him in ten years. I wouldn't have known where he was but Maggie sent me the clipping. Maggie, that's Wade's mother, she sent it to me. Some old army buddy of Arnie's lives up here and his wife saw it and recognized the name and the picture. No great love 'tween me and Maggie, or me and Arnie for that matter, but they used to dote on Jennifer. They were real fond of her when she was little."

I asked who Arnie was. Lynette looked at me quizzically and gave me another version of the tale Wade always told: the troubled young man flung from his home because his stepfather hated him and his mother was too weak to intervene.

"Wade tells this story differently," I said.

"Drug addicts always do."

"He's honest about that." Proud of it, but I kept my mouth shut.

"Do you know what being a drug addict means? It means he owed money. All the time. To everyone. It means he would steal his own mother blind. And he did. Lots of times. Finally, Maggie and Arnie told him never to come back. They were finished with him. Then Wade gave their address to dealers he owed money to, so Maggie and Arnie were getting robbed, sort of every three months. New TV—gone. New stereo—gone. They put grills on the windows and the thieves came in through the doors. It was a bad neighborhood, but not that bad. Finally Arnie bought a gun and shot one of them. The guy didn't die or nothing, but Arnie told Wade, he was keeping the gun loaded and by the door and if Wade or any of his junkie friends showed up again, even if it was in broad daylight and carrying a big bouquet of flowers, Arnie'd shoot him on sight. So, yes, I guess you could say his stepfather threw him out. There's some truth in that. Like there's some truth in this." She pulled her battered engagement announcement out. "Says Wade graduated from Northridge. Well, he went to CalState Northridge for a while, but he never graduated. And here, says his mother is Margaret Nash?" She pointed at the smudged newsprint. "Maggie hasn't been Margaret Nash in fifty years."

Little pebbles of truth in the big ocean of lies, I thought.

"I thought Wade was dead," Lynette went on. "I thought he'd dropped off the face of the earth. Dead, jailed or straitjacketed, that's the only choices junkies have. I got to admit, I didn't think he'd go clean."

"He's been straight for eight years. He's a sort of counselor now, helping others." I wrestled that out with no irony. "He goes all around the Northwest with a sort of program for recovery. He's very passionate about it."

Lynette snorted. "Oh yeah, passion. That was always Wade. Fucking dazzling. Passionate and persistent. Don't get me wrong. It's nice Wade's straight and doing all this good work—" She paused and rested her gaze on her daughter, draped across the bench across from us, mouth open, legs apart. "But really, I don't care. I just want to talk to him."

"How long were you married?"

"Depends on how you count it. From the time he moved in with me and my sister? From the time we actually got married to the time I divorced him, or only to the time when he left us? A long fucking time. Six years? I been raising Jennifer fifteen years plus. Twelve of those on my own. If I hadn't had Jennifer, I could have just said, Well, hell with it and gone on with my life. Men always break your heart, but you move on. First couple of times you think you're going to die of the hurt, but you don't. But when you have a kid . . . And Jennifer was only three. Such a little cutie when she was three." Lynette paused reflectively. "If I'd just been knocked up when he left, I'd have given the baby up for adoption. But I couldn't. She was only three."

"And you never remarried?"

"Who had time to remarry? I had time to get laid now and then, but I been working and bringing up this girl, or trying to. Making beds at the Holiday Inn, slinging hash at Denny's, pushing a broom at the mall. You name it, if it was legal, I did it. Sometimes I had to work two jobs, the mall nights and days behind the counter at the Burger King saying, *Have it your way.* I haven't had it my way." Lynette's lips roiled to ease the strain across her face. Her skin was so tightly stretched, it seemed to hurt. She looked down at her hands and on her ring finger there was a small gold ring with a little bunch of pavé diamonds gleaming dully in the middle. "I have a good man now. A nice guy. He's lived with us the last couple of years. He's carrying the rent, everything alone now because I'm out of work. Between jobs you might say. Between careers," she snorted and her gaze rested on the inert Jennifer. "She's been in juvie so many times—been through three or four probation officers and a string of social workers—I'd have to get off work to go to her hearings. Finally, my new job, they said if I took any more time off—they didn't care what it was for—they'd fire me. So next time Jennifer was picked up—what was it? Vagrancy? Some small shit like that. She was just hanging out with the other druggies, she didn't actually have the stuff on her. But I didn't go to the hearing because I'd lose my job. I lost it anyway. Last hired, first fired. But in the meantime the new social worker calls up and chews my ass out, tells me my daughter is a flake, a drug addict, a dropout and banging gang members because I'm so busy with my career. My career—!" Lynette pealed out a raucous laugh, enough to rouse Jennifer who opened one eye and then closed it, went back to rocking. Lynette lowered her voice. "I had to take that shit. You don't dare call them bastards. You don't dare. But honest to God, those bastards. I did tell 'em, I'm working to support this girl. I'm giving her lunch money. I think she's eating mystery meat in the school cafeteria, but she's giving blow jobs in Reseda Park for drug money. She didn't even go to school after the eighth grade. She's shooting up drugs in the same mall bathroom where I work at night, sloshing toilets full of Pine Sol. She got arrested for shoplifting in the Disney Store! Can you believe it? Her pants were full of Pooh Bears."

I thought of the windup Pooh on the couch at Wade's apartment. A hot Pooh? The mind boggles.

Lynette said glumly, "I done everything I could. I tried anyway. What choice was there? It was me and Jennifer on our own. It wasn't my fault. My sister's kids, they're in trouble a lot, but not like Jennifer. Last month cops caught her giving blow jobs in the park. Cop told me they couldn't bust her for prostitution as long as she was a minor. She was my responsibility altogether and I thought—Oh, God, I got three years! Three years before she's eighteen? Three more years to live like this? Cop said I could have her emancipated. Then she'd be an adult and she could be busted. But think about that—having your own kid emancipated. Just like a slave."

Jennifer roused, both eyes this time. "You talking about me?"

"Hell, no. I'm talking about Abraham Lincoln."

"Fuck off." She sat up, turned off the headphones and made a palms-out gesture toward Lynette who dug into her bag and found a pack of cigarettes. Jennifer took the pack and ambled to the outside deck which is the only place you can smoke.

"I don't think it's fair"—Lynette twirled her ring with suppressed anxiety—"I don't think it's fair that if Wade has been straight for eight years, that he didn't call and say, Hi, how's everything? Of course I know why. Money. That's what I want to talk to him about. Money. When he left, OK, he was strung out. Bad. I was doing a few drugs myself in those days, but I never took it up as a career, like Wade did. I did it for fun, but I could see it was a real fuckup, and after Jennifer came along, I told him I didn't want him doing drugs at home, and not around her. Not him or his druggy friends either. I made it stick too, and pretty soon he just left. Fine. Then, couple of years later, he calls me up one night. Middle of the night. He wanted money. I said, Give me an address so I can divorce you, you bastard. I finally did divorce him, but he never paid a cent. It's funny, you know, because if I'd been on welfare, they would have gone after him for the money. But I wasn't. I was working." From her pocket she pulled a long tabulation, figuring out the months of child support at $95 a month. She went through all the math with me and the way the figures had been arrived at, all that before she put it away. "Last time he called was ten years ago. If I'd known I wasn't going to talk to him again for ten years, I'd have said something memorable. But you know what I said to Wade that last time he called?"

"What?"

"I said—Wade, you're going to miss Jennifer's first day of kindergarten. And he said—Send me a picture."

Through the broad windows we could see Jennifer, her black

hair whipping in the wind, trying futilely to light a cigarette from the butt of another cigarette offered to her by a man, maybe just a kid, also clad in black leather and wearing a long, heavy chain looped from his waist.

"Can you fucking imagine?" said Lynette. "Kindergarten."

I could, actually. I could imagine Jennifer Shumley on the first day of kindergarten, proud of tying her own shoes, and carrying a Pooh backpack, her hair all brushed and barretted. I could see her standing with the other kids while all the parents took pictures and some parents clung to crying children, and vice versa. But Lynette and Jennifer, I imagined, would be very bright and brave about kindergarten, Lynette in her Burger King uniform, knowing that now there were four or five hours every day when she didn't have to pay for child care. Jennifer, I could imagine, greeting all the other little Jennifers and Ashleys and Megans. What trajectory brought that little girl to this kindergarten convict? I could recognize all the signs; I grew up in a town supported by a prison. Jennifer wore clothes that fell off her body and unclasped shoes and this made her walk in a kind of convict shuffle. Prisoners don't get belts or suspenders or even shoelaces because they might hang themselves. She was a sort of understudy jailbird, her clothes so voluminous that shoplifted Pooh Bears were nothing. She could have shoplifted a station wagon and got caught only when she had to stop for gas.

Fifteen years old—all those years to go on living—and this girl didn't have a chance. Wade Shumley was his own Eve of Destruction, wasn't he? Not just my daughter, my family, but he'd cut a real swath through these lives too. And how many others? Wade willingly confessed his police records, his jail time, his many failings, not merely to be deemed penitent and absolved, but to be beatified by suffering. The record of his crimes made his conversion shine all the brighter. What crimes went unrecorded? I only half listened to Lynette; I was thinking of Bethie, worried how I'd find her, and hoping the appearance of Lynette and Jennifer would convince her at last that she had been manipulated by a man who despised the inconvenient truth and invented everything else.

Once you trundle off the ferry, the ride into Seattle is a long one, tedious too, especially since I had to keep Lynette's Plymouth in my rearview mirror at all times. And then we had to make several stops along the way, occasioned, Lynette told me, by a bladder infection Jennifer had contracted, almost cured now. Traffic on I-5 thickened up well before Seattle and I lost sight of Lynette several times, cars cutting in and out of the lanes. Between the anxiety of the drive and the anxiety of what I'd find in Wallingford, my fingers were curled arthritically around the steering wheel by the time I parked the truck and locked it. Lynette squeezed her Plymouth into a space best suited to a VW. Talking nonstop, she had one cigarette in her mouth when she went to look for another. She took her purse and shouldered a black-and-white backpack. Jennifer too hoisted a large, soft-sided bag and followed behind us, indifferent without being relaxed.

Lynette was volubly impressed with the condo. The drapes at Bethie's house were still closed despite the brilliant day. I knocked and Bethie came to the door. Her eyes were vacant, but not as weepy as when I'd last seen her, though little pouches of fatigue gathered underneath. She was wearing shorts and a ReDiscovery T-shirt and she was barefoot. Without so much as a look at Lynette or Jennifer (who were behind me in any event), she said, "I guess you've come to apologize for calling me a liar."

"No, Bethie. I've brought some people who are eager to meet you." I spoke slowly, carefully, so there should be no mistake in this matter of calling people liars. I stepped to the side. "This is Wade's ex-wife, Lynette Shumley. And this"—I drew Jennifer toward the door—"this is your new stepdaughter, Bethie. Wade's girl, Jennifer Shumley. Jennifer, meet your new stepmother."

"Where's the shitter?" asked Jennifer.

"Is Wade home?" asked Lynette.

Wade wasn't home, but Bethie couldn't say so. Couldn't speak at all. She looked from Lynette to Jennifer, to me and back again, and only when Jennifer asked again, urgently, after the shitter did she let us in. The TV in the living room was on, some soap opera or another. There were two people swearing undying love in what looked like a hospital supply closet.

Bethie closed the door and leaned against it. "You really will stop at nothing, Celia. You are absolutely determined, aren't you? You will stoop to any charade to destroy Wade and me."

"Turn off the soap opera," I advised. "This is real life. This is Wade's ex-family and they're here."

"And you—just magically—dug them up—" she began airily.

"No one dug us up," Lynette snapped. For probably the tenth time that day she drew out her clipping again and placed its frayed and tattered self on the coffee table with a glance at the same picture on the bookshelf, Wade and Bethie radiant with happiness. She told the long story again. Arnie's army buddy's wife. All that. Bethie, visibly shorting out by now, was able only to nod. She was mute as Launch and not as good-natured.

"When will Wade be home?" Lynette plopped down on the couch, put her bag on the floor, saying she wouldn't leave without talking to Wade. She'd driven fifteen hundred miles and dropped a clutch in Weed, California. If she was here all night, well, OK.

Bethie cleared her throat. "Wade is at a board meeting of the King County Mental Health Association, discussing educational programs. These are important meetings for the whole community."

"Honestly, I don't care if he's interviewing the pope and the president. Same time. It don't matter to me. I'm not leaving till I see him. It's been twelve years. I'm not here to make trouble, but I do want to talk to him."

I sat down too. We all sat there and watched the TV. The scene had changed to a posh boardroom where the men and women were all wearing smart tailored suits and talking about millions of dollars.

"She embezzled it," said Lynette, pointing to one of the characters. "Dwayne tapes it for me during the day, so I'm pretty sure it's her."

Bethie turned the TV off. "Where have you come from?"

"Reseda. The Valley. I never been this far north before. Never been north of Ventura really. Wade neither. At least as far as I know. As long as he was with me, he'd never been north of Thousand Oaks. He was a Pacoima boy to start with. Then Reseda."

I was interested in this. "Wade told us he was an army brat and had grown up on army bases all over the world."

Lynette's lips curled. "The world of the San Fernando Valley." She drummed her fingers on her knees and said Wade and Bethie sure had a nice place. "Own or rent?"

"It's a condominium," Bethie explained. "Wade owns this apartment."

"Making lots of money?"

"Money isn't important to Wade."

"It's important to me. I rent."

We'd heard the toilet flush a couple of times, but Jennifer still didn't come back. She'd been in the bathroom a hell of a long time. Bethie and Lynette each sat on the edge of their seats, about to catapult toward one another. Finally Bethie eked out the words to ask Lynette how long she'd been married to Wade.

"Long enough to have a daughter. Long enough to get divorced. Long enough to get sick of him and his drugged-up, fucked-up, jobless friends."

"All that's behind Wade. He's been clean and straight for eight years."

"Great."

"No, really. I mean it. He's been better than that. He's dedicated his life now to helping others. That's what ReDiscovery is, a way to empower people to treat their addictive behaviors, not just their addictions."

"That's wonderful, but I don't give a shit." Lynette pawed through her bag, looking for a cigarette and a match.

Jennifer slouched back in; she had re-lined her eyes, freshened her black lip liner, fluffed up the metallic bouquet beneath her nose. The chains looped to her pants clanked and she continually made weird hand gestures, fingers stretched and splayed in a lingo impenetrable to the rest of us. "You got a nice place here. A room just for the computer, two bathrooms. Anything to eat?"

"Go look in the kitchen," said Bethie woodenly. She fanned absently at Lynette's secondary smoke.

"Jennifer has a bolt through her tongue and she gets burned easily," I offered helpfully.

Jennifer stuck her tongue out at me, pushed her black hair back to reveal studs punched all the way up her ears, lining them like little stars along a half moon. "My body is a work of art and a statement against phobes like you."

"Phobes?"

"Phobes hate everything, man. Not just homophobe or Mexophobe or Japophobe, but phobic for everything. Phobes like you have to destroy what you don't understand, everything that isn't picture-fucking-perfect."

"Don't start, Jennifer," Lynette warned.

"Like your picture-fucking-perfect house on your fucking-perfect—"

"Jennifer."

Jennifer collapsed on the couch. "Why the fuck not?" She kicked her canvas bag ineffectually. "It's all going to happen anyway, isn't it?"

"Shut up."

Turning to Bethie, Jennifer seemed to assess her against her engagement picture on the shelf and announced she was better-looking in the picture. "How old are you anyway? You look too young to be with my dad."

"Shut up, Jennifer," Lynette warned. "You don't know what Wade looks like."

"I know what you look like," the girl retorted. "I know how old you are. Forty-one."

"And so is Wade, so just shut up."

"Wade is thirty-seven," Bethie protested.

"Maggie says he's forty-one. She's his mother." Lynette took a deep, glowing drag on her cigarette and launched into an expansive description of Maggie and Arnie, how they'd left Reseda and moved to Long Beach. Now they were retired and living in Hemet. Finding no ashtray, she rose and went to a houseplant and ground the cigarette out there. "It's good for plants," she assured Bethie. "I read it in the *Globe*. It's been proved with science."

Jennifer repeated she was hungry and to prove her point, her stomach rumbled. Bethie told her again to go to the kitchen, but Bethie herself could not move. She sat there, undone by the very sight of these two and the betrayal they implied. For my part, I remarked on the stunning resemblance between Wade and Jennifer, metal boogers notwithstanding.

Bethie cut me off quickly. "You better stop, Celia."

"Stop what? What is there to stop? These people have driven fifteen hundred miles to see Wade. You didn't even know they existed. You've been living with this man for a year now and you didn't know he had an ex-wife. He told you he'd never been married! He lied! When I was last here, in this room, Bethie, I remember a lot of bullshit and blather about honesty and facing up to the past. Remember that? So who is the liar now?"

Lynette's alert eyes narrowed. She said maybe I wasn't too fond of Wade after all. I said nothing. I didn't have to. It was for Bethie to do the talking here.

"What do you want from Wade?" she asked Lynette.

Lynette had a nervous shrug, almost a twitch. "I just want to talk. Of course, I could ask for my eighteen thousand dollars. Give or take." And from her other pocket she pulled out her tabulated figures and I thought how the engagement clipping in one pocket and the adding machine tape thrust into the other for fifteen hundred miles must have given Lynette a kind of ballast, keeping her aligned with the white line on Route 5. "It took me a couple of years to get enough money to divorce that bastard, and by then he was gone, off somewheres. I couldn't find him. He never wrote to Maggie, nothing. When Maggie got this clipping from Arnie's army buddy's wife, she said, Go get that bastard, Lynette. Wade hasn't seen Jennifer since she was three. She wasn't even in school when he left."

"I'm not in school now, so what's the difference?" Jennifer ambled back in, a sandwich in one hand, a Diet Coke in the other. She eased down in the chair and her clothes billowed out around her as if she'd sunk into a pool. "Don't look at me like that," she cautioned Bethie. "This wasn't my idea. I didn't want to come here. I think the whole thing sucks. I wanted to go live with my boyfriend, but no, Mommy dearest over there tells him if he lets me in the door, it's statutory rape—slammer time for him. He's twenty-one," she added with some pride. Finishing her sandwich, she licked the mayo off her fingers and lit a cigarette, and then, still using her finger-lingo to thrust and underscore her anger, she burst into the whole catalog of Lynette's cruelties, a torrent of perceived abuses. Lynette kept jumping in and telling her to shut up, shut up, shut up, but she wouldn't. Jennifer raged and rattled and Lynette, the nonstop talker, fell finally into a grim silence. Jennifer told Bethie (and it was Bethie she was talking to) that ever since the clipping had arrived from Maggie, Jennifer's life had not been the same. Statutory rape cooled off her romance pronto. All her friends got told by Mom that if they sold Jennifer so much as a tab of acid, she would give addresses to cops who would nail them. Very quickly, all doors were closed to Jennifer. Except the car door. They were going to Seattle. Five days in the Plymouth with Mom, six counting the clutch job. "God-awful. God-fucking-awful. But I didn't have any choice. Mom said I could shoot tadpoles up my arms, but I had to do it on the way to Seattle. I had to do it on the road."

Bethie's dry lips parted. "And have you . . . are you . . . ?"

Jennifer rubbed her inner elbow protectively and blew smoke through her nose rings.

"Maybe you can interest Jennifer in ReDiscovery," I offered. "Maybe Wade can help his own daughter to change her addictive behaviors."

"I'm not an addict, you phobe!" Jennifer snarled at me. "It's fun now and then. It's fun to get high, but I'm not a fucking addict."

"At least Wade could give her a T-shirt."

"Shut up! Shut up! Shut up!" Bethie cried, jumping up so fast the blood drained from her face and she wove slightly on her feet. "Shut up, all of you!" Bethie wanted to fall apart, to go on one of her weeping jags, which were probably frequent and refreshing. No doubt as Wade's vassal she'd made a habit of them. But she needed Wade present for it to work, Wade or Fran or some equally appreciative audience.

I saw the little Pooh Bear lying beside the couch. I retrieved it, wound it up and its plaintive tune tinkled out. I gave it to Bethie. "Here. Didn't Wade tell you this was a good way to become an adult?"

Bethie burst into tears and flung the Pooh across the room. "Please. Go away. All of you."

Jennifer got up and went to the Pooh, dusting it off. "I always loved Pooh," she said, brightening, and for a moment she looked like the fifteen-year-old girl that she was, anger fled from her face and her eyes alight with affection. "Remember, Mom, my Pooh? What happened to my own Pooh?"

Lynette could not remember.

"I had Pooh when I was a baby. But I guess it got lost. So when I was nine I shoplifted one," she said dreamily, "and now, I always shoplift Poohs. You won't believe this, but on the street, Pooh and Minnie Mouse sell the fastest. No one likes Donald. When I got caught at that last Disney Store, I had a dozen Poohs in my pants." Jennifer loosed a genuine laugh. "Get it? Pooh in your pants."

"Pooh and a couple of joints," her mother reminded her. "They wanted to do a full body search, if you remember, cavities and all, and I wouldn't let them. They needed my permission.

Now, if you were emancipated, Jennifer, they could do what they wanted."

Jennifer relaxed back into her customary sulk and asked if there were video games on the computer. Solitaire, said Bethie. Not interested, said Jennifer, holding Pooh Bear to her heart.

Lynette excused herself to go to the bathroom and Bethie and I sat staring at one another. She'd shelved the crying jag, and her eyes had gone agate-hard and she breathed in short, sharp gusts through her nose. "You're enjoying this, aren't you, Celia? You think it's all very funny."

"I don't think it's funny at all. I think it's tragic. But not for you. For them, for Lynette and for Jennifer, I think it's tragic. For you, I think it's just pathetic. This man is a liar. Lynette and Jennifer, they are not slips of his memory."

"Everyone has exes nowadays," she protested. "Look at you."

"Ex-lovers, ex-husbands, ex-wives, fine, but not ex-children. Lynette has raised Jennifer single-handedly for twelve years."

"And bitched me out every day, too," Jennifer interrupted. "Told me every day since I was six how she wished she'd put me up for adoption. How we'd both be better off. I'd be better off without her, that's for sure. I could be living with rich people instead of her and old Dwayne. Night cook at Denny's and she thinks he's Prince Fucking Charming."

"Don't you bad-mouth Dwayne." Lynette bristled back into the living room. "Don't you bad-mouth him at all. He is a good man. And for your information, Miss Unemployed Shoplifter, night cook at Denny's is a good job." She turned to Bethie and held out her ring with the pavé diamonds. "You're not the only one with a fiancé. Dwayne and me are getting married. In fact, Dwayne's meeting me in Reno when I drive down from here and we're getting married in Reno."

Bethie was about to offer wan congratulations just as footsteps sounded outside and all of us—two mothers, two daughters—tensed and waited for the key to turn in the lock and for Wade Shumley to walk into his past.

He set his briefcase down, offered some endearment to Bethie and then saw me, came toward me, oozing beneficence. I watched him like a truck barreling down the road, like we would crash any minute because I knew if he tried to touch me, I'd have to scream, or run, but the explosion was averted by a word from Lynette, his name, *Wade*.

At that, he turned to her, looked closely, peered at Jennifer clutching Pooh, and then—more swiftly than you could light a match—he staggered, like a soldier mortally wounded, but still on his feet, he staggered like he might drop. He didn't though. Explosion turned to implosion and he regained himself and Bethie flew into his arms. Then she went on her crying jag, saying how we'd all been mean to her, how we had abused her in her own home. He held her close, patted her back, murmuring, eyes closed. And when he had collected himself—which happened so quickly, I was amazed, astonished. What had I expected? I don't know. Maybe that Wade should shout *Great God in the morning!* and run screaming from the apartment?—he soothed Bethie. Then he peeled her off his body. Peeled her off, left her standing with her tongue out. Wade went straight to Lynette, wrapped her in a huge hug and said how wonderful she looked and how happy he was to see her and how it had been a long time.

And still burbling compliments, and bubbling joy, he went to his daughter and said, "This must be little Jennifer, my baby girl." He hugged her. Big hug. Massive hug. Wiped his eyes and asked to be excused for crying, for being so moved to see them again. He beamed, fondling the rings punched in Jennifer's eyebrow and patted her nose like she was a puppy and said she'd turned her body into a work of art. "You've met my beautiful Elizabeth, I see."

Bethie didn't look so beautiful at that moment. No one did. Except maybe Wade. He had recovered himself in a flash. What a maestro. He listened with unfeigned gravity while Lynette dragged out her clipping and her story about Maggie and Arnie and the army buddy and he asked a lot of questions about his mother, tut-tutting to hear she was still with Arnie, a relationship he pronounced destructive, though Lynette said they had been together for almost thirty years and had left Long Beach for retirement in Hemet. Well, said Wade, that explains everything: now he knew why he hadn't been able to get in touch with them to tell them about his engagement. Where was Hemet, he asked, and how was Maggie? And in the midst of all this long-lost-family-chat, Bethie, standing quite apart from Wade, asked how old he was.

He grinned sheepishly. "I see you've found out my little vanity. Women think they're the only vain ones, but they're not. Men are allowed a little fib now and then, aren't they? It would be sexist to deny us that."

"And what about Jennifer and Lynette?" I asked. "Are they also little fibs? A little vanity you neglected to mention?"

Wade removed his sport coat. He was wearing a ReDiscovery T-shirt too. "I don't think it's your place to comment on my family, Celia."

Bethie burst into loud tears again, and wailed, "So it's true. You have been married. You have children! You—"

"One daughter," he corrected her. "That's not children."

"But you lied to me!" Her voice escalated into a great peal of pain. "You lied! I can't believe you'd lie—you above all people, Wade! You wanted to know everything about me! I had to tell you everything. Everyone I'd ever slept with! All my family! You never even told me you'd been married!"

Lynette rose and wedged herself between Bethie and Wade. "I can see this is going to be a long conversation, so I'll say goodbye now. I'm in a hurry. Time on the meter, you know."

"You have to stay, Lynette. Have dinner with us," Wade insisted, "spend the night. There's so much to talk about. It's been so long—"

"That's right, so long. I'm on my way to Reno to get married."

Wade blithered, asking after the lucky man, but Lynette pulled from her other pocket her much-folded tabulations. She held the paper up in front of his nose. "Twelve years, you bastard! Ten years since you called! And then, you wanted money! Well, now

I want money. See this? See? Eighteen thousand dollars, more or less, and that's not counting what it cost me to get her wisdom teeth out. And braces! Show him your braces." Jennifer bared a mouthful of metal, the tongue bolt notwithstanding. "Years of my life, buckets of my sweat are in those braces. My work. My time at six-fifty, seven-fifty an hour! I paid for a new pair of orthopedic shoes every six months for a year while we waited for her ankles to straighten out, and her spine."

"And she has beautiful posture," Wade said.

"And what about her abortion? Who do you think paid for that? And rehab, you bastard, who paid for that? Twice! She's been in rehab twice! And she's not yet sixteen!" Lynette was screaming now, all that suppressed fury she'd carried for twelve years and fifteen hundred miles came spewing out. She was like a hand grenade with the pin pulled. "Jennifer dropped out of school in the seventh grade. She can't fucking multiply! She has a juvenile record long as your arm! She's been a prostitute in the park for drug money! I work and work and work and do the best I can with this girl and where are you? Where were you ever? You bastard. It's taken me twelve years to find you!"

"I can feel your pain, Lynette," he whispered, his entire body radiating compassion, "and I apologize. I am truly and profoundly sorry. But my life, let me tell you how I have lived all those years on drugs and after. I—"

She cut him off with a short right jab to the gut. Instead of telling the tale that he had told to such effect to community groups all over the Northwest, the staple of ReDiscovery, Wade went *Oof oof* and his eyes bulged out of his head. He had not planned this one (like he had orchestrated Grant's attack on him; I was sure of it) and he bent double, the wind knocked out of him, and fell back down on the couch, Bethie rushing to his side.

"Sorry." Lynette's lips roiled in and out. It was a practiced shot, I thought, because tiny as she was, she'd walloped twelve years into that punch and he was some time recovering. "Do you have my eighteen thousand dollars, Wade?"

"Lynette—" he gasped, "I will make this up to you. I know

I have created pain for you and Jennifer, but—all that unhealthy behavior—is behind me and—I'm committed to making some kind of—restitution, giving back to the world—if it's money that you want from me—"

"It's what I wanted once. But it's no good now." Lynette walked over to Jennifer, and again, with a strength you would not have guessed at, she pulled that girl to her feet and flung her arms around her, weeping, crying out her name. Jennifer remained obdurate, angry, unmoved. I pitied them both.

Lynette released her daughter, mopped the tears from her face and said grimly, "OK then, I'm off."

"Please, Lynette—" Wade reached out beseechingly. "Stay a while. At least give me the chance to know my own daughter—"

"You got time, Wade. Three years. When she's eighteen, she's her own legal responsibility, but in the meantime she's yours. I'm leaving here by myself. I'm driving to Reno and I'm meeting Dwayne and I'm getting married. I'm taking my own life back. For fifteen years I've given everything I had to this girl. I went to the first day of kindergarten, Wade. I went to back-to-school night. I went to back-to-juvenile-detention night. I held her hand after the abortion. I went to family rehab. But I can't do any more. I'm finished. I failed. I admit it and now it's your turn. I hope you do better than I did. But I tried. You got to admit that, Jennifer, I tried."

But Jennifer looked away, unwilling to admit anything.

"OK. So long, honey. So long, Wade. And don't you come to me for child support either, you bastard. If it's any comfort to you, I wish I'd never met you too."

"You can't leave her here!" Bethie protested. "She can't live with us!"

"I'm leaving her with her father. Where you live is up to you."

"You said you only wanted to talk to Wade—" Bethie babbled. "You never said—Wade! Do something! Stop this!—You never said you were going to leave this girl here!"

"Well, I am."

"No, you can't do this. You can't just leave a girl here. Just drive off."

Taking her purse (and leaving both big bags), Lynette told Jennifer to write, to call now and then. But not for money. "I'll see you when you're eighteen."

"Not if I see you first," mustered Jennifer.

Then she was gone. Out the door.

Bethie raced after her, shouting, "You come back here right now! You take this girl with you! You can't just leave this girl!" She ran back into Jennifer, shooing her like an inconvenient pet. "Go on, you go with her. She's your mother! Go on—you can't stay here! You hear me! We don't want you!"

"Elizabeth," Wade said, "don't say that. Please."

"But we don't! Get rid of her, Wade!"

"I have to stay." Jennifer melted back into the chair. "Mom won't have me. Anyway she's ruined everything down there for me. I hate Reseda. I hate Seattle. I hate everything. Everything sucks. Everything's fucked."

"Close the door, Elizabeth."

"She can't live here!"

"Close the door. Of course she can. She must. She's my daughter. I can help you, Jennifer. I can bring you back to life."

"Life sucks."

"Wade!" Bethie strung his name out, like a bell tolling.

He opened his arms. "Now we can be a real family, Elizabeth. You and me and Jennifer. We're a family now. Before we were a couple. Now we're a family."

"But I don't want a family. I want you! Only you! I don't want any children. Besides, she's not a child, she's a—delinquent!"

"She's my daughter, your stepdaughter. You've had lots of practice at this, Elizabeth," he added reasonably. "You've had lots of stepbrothers and stepsisters. Now you have a stepdaughter. It'll be easier for you than for most people. Knowing you, I would think you'd welcome this challenge. We can help bring Jennifer back to wholeness." He gathered pace and conviction, while Bethie stared at the unpromising lump of adolescent flesh that was

Jennifer Shumley. Wade bathed, splashed in his sentiments, enjoying their beauty and promise. "Haven't we vowed to share everything, Elizabeth? Aren't we unconditionally accepting of each other's pasts? Committed to a program of individual betterment within a community of empowerment? What is Jennifer but a victim? This girl needs our help. That she is my daughter only makes her more special."

I wanted to shake Bethie till her teeth rattled, but I didn't have to. Bless God, I didn't have to. She wasn't so completely drowned in Wade's tub of rhetoric. She brought it to his attention that he had lied, never said he'd had a child, that he had another wife.

Wade pointed out his own generosity of spirit. "I don't hold your past against you, Elizabeth."

Bethie blinked. "We've been together a year and you never mentioned you'd been married. You said I was the great love of your life."

"And you are, Elizabeth."

I knew right then what he would do: he'll start to cry, I thought. Bethie had told me long ago how easily he was moved to tears, he could be moved by simple things, by the sadness of a few paltry items laid out at a garage sale. He cried even to tell people the story, Bethie said. Wade had a great, deep reservoir of emotion which he had learned to touch through suffering. And I knew—if Bethie didn't—that experience had clearly taught Wade no woman can resist a weeping man. Everything in that woman's body and her blood, her very chromosomes rushes out to make it All Better. To take the hurt on herself if need be.

And that's what happened. He wept like a baby. And while he was weeping, sitting on the couch, crying into his hands, he said he had not told her about Jennifer and Lynette because he was afraid of losing her, that he loved her so much he couldn't bear the thought of losing her. Fear. Fear was the great crippler. And they weren't lies, they were evasions. It was an evasion because he had wanted to be new and bright and clean and fresh for Bethie like she was for him. In every way. Body and soul.

Fear and evasion had haunted him because he was afraid he would lose the love of his life if he told her the absolute truth. He asked her forgiveness for not trusting her love, for not believing she would love him unconditionally. And as for being married, he added, tears streaming down his face, it wasn't such a terrible thing. Was it? Weren't they going to marry? And having a daughter didn't make him a criminal. "Elizabeth, please don't leave me," he wept.

Even Jennifer (she was female, wasn't she?) stared at him openmouthed, abashed at these gushing tears. And Bethie? Bethie looked like a fish flung upon the land, eyes blinking, gills pounding. But she fought her chromosomal instincts and she did not rush to him to make it All Better. Bethie said, "How could you lie? You above all people? You were always so insistent on accountability. Responsibility."

"He's lied about everything, Bethie, beginning to end," I burst in as Wade wept on. "I bet there's more he's lied about. Everything he's ever said is a lie. You'd better get out of this while you can. Pack up and come home with me. Don't stay another minute with this liar, this fraud."

"I don't need you to tell me about my fiancé," Bethie snapped.

Wade continued to cry, brushing tears from his cheeks. Containing his emotions at last, he reached up, reached out for Bethie's hand.

"Don't stay here, Bethie," I warned her. "Come with me. I mean it. I beg of you. This man has lied about the most fundamental relationship there is. Do not condone this betrayal."

Wade raised his eyes and in his sad voice he said, "Either you love me, or you don't."

It was the same uncomplicated ultimatum Bethie had given all of us in this very room: believe me or don't. No room for texture, shading, no possibilities less rigid. Simple. Inflexible. Appealing.

"Either you love me or you don't. If you love me, you'll forgive me. I'd do anything to keep you, Elizabeth. I have lied to keep you in my life. Forgive me. I did it so you wouldn't leave me."

"Bethie—don't let him turn a lie into an act of love!"

"I'm sorry for my past ineffective behaviors, Elizabeth, and I ask you to forgive me."

"Don't stay with this man! He's turning a gross lie into a plea for love."

"Either you love me or you don't," he repeated didactically, as if this were an exam question. "If you love me you will find it in your heart to forgive me."

She went to him. She knelt on the floor in front of the couch, between his open legs, put her arms around him and they clung together. And over Bethie's head, Wade, with only a momentary flick of a glance to me, beckoned to his daughter. Damned if she didn't go to him too. Still clutching Pooh.

So I left them, the little family unit—the abandoned teenage daughter, the fraudulent father, the woman who'd been crippled and didn't even know it—their arms all around each other in the embrace of love and forgiveness and the spirit of humility and abiding affection. Once outside the door I gave a great spit, but it didn't help.

Westbound, the night ferry pursues the sunset, not with any zest or fervor, just patiently plying toward the tarnished horizon. In the distance the islands rise up like dinosaurs and over them, darkness drips down, absorbed in the Sound. The sky, an inky wash, sinks into night till only a bronzed scar divides sea from sky. Daylight lingers though summer flees. In August it is dark before nine, and the drama of those high unending summer days and short contracted nights begins to close. Late August melancholia sets in. Fog in the mornings. Trees balding, going gold when all the rest of the world is at its green apogee. Autumn is the Northwest's moment, our longest and most reliable season, skies besotted with clouds, and on the islands, trees shimmy quickly out of their leaves and go naked.

Unable to bear the camaraderie, noise and cheer of other ferry passengers, I left my truck and made my way up to the topmost deck and then outside where lights were few and the only sounds were the ferry's enormous engines and the cries of greedy gulls who eyed me expectantly. I had nothing for them. Nothing for anyone. I took my place like some sort of westward-looking fig- urehead, wooden and unmoved.

If you live long enough, your experience melds, mortars so that all rainy afternoons accrue into one rainy afternoon. Eventu- ally there is but one snowy night, one summer morning, one spring day when you lay on your back and through the just- greening trees you saw overhead all the clouds of your life. These singular memories radiate, crackle with such energy, such vivacity that you feel they can live apart from you, that they could touch someone else's memory and graft there. For me, of all the west- ward journeys I have taken, of all the ferries I have ridden home to Isadora, there is only that one ferry ride I make again and again. The ride to Isadora when I did not know it would be home. That first ferry ride with Henry. I remake that significant journey with each inconsequential one. Inevitably. Invariably. I make it even now, having lost my daughter irrevocably.

It was our first ferry ride, but it was not our first westward journey. That was the boat train from the Hook of Holland to Harwich, England, the journey beginning on a huge, ungainly ship, filled, that late summer sailing, to capacity for the overnight journey. We didn't know each other, just two strangers, individu- als in a big tribe of penniless travelers who had booked the cheap- est possible passage, which is to say, we didn't rent bunks, but crashed on the deck. The ship's deck was vast and sheltered, littered, dusty and crowded. There were a few plastic chaises for those travelers experienced enough to grab one immediately. I was not experienced, so I was one of the congregation camped on the floor. Slowly and in a protected corner, a group of us, perhaps fifteen or twenty young strangers, pilgrims thrust into overnight intimacy, gathered. Those who had snagged chaises drew them over. We were a sort of gypsy camp. Young, dirty, united by our high spirits, low funds, carrying backpacks, harmonicas, perhaps a single battered suitcase, we shared what we had in the way of food, cigarettes, gum, wine, water, anecdote and experience, communicating in English for the most part, halting English if you were not a native speaker, and carefully enunciating if you were. A motley and international bunch, we were from all over the world, the Malay Peninsula to Israel, New Zealand to Norway, kids intent on travel, adventure, all to be accomplished as cheaply as possible. The tall, lanky kid with a shock of curly hair and exuberant smile, the one in the purple tank top, the faded jeans, the leather sandals, that was Henry West.

Along with food and cigarettes, people exchanged names and places, the places they were from and the places were going. My contribution was almost nil. I had started sneezing right after the engine started up, not your ladylike, occasional *achoo,* but nonstop wheezing-sneezing, exploding through the nose, using up all my own Kleenex and everything offered to me, reduced finally to trips back and forth to the ship's bathroom to use their coarse toilet paper which tore the skin off my nose. Sitting on the floor of the deck, the ship's deep incessant rumble went through my whole body, rattling especially the bones in my head and shaking my sinuses. The dust raised and mazed caught in my nose and eyes. I could hardly listen for all my sneezing and I spoke only to say thank you to people who offered *Bless you* in perhaps four different languages.

At the center of this shipboard camaraderie was Henry West. His laughter drew people to him, and his zest and intelligence, his generosity and warmth kept them at ease. He carried a backpack, a water bottle and a shoulder bag from which he drew some German chocolate bars. He broke them up and offered them all around, and in this gesture he cemented us, mere passengers, into a group of friends. He had been everywhere and he knew everything about traveling on a shoestring. From Constantinople to

Copenhagen, Henry could tell you where to crash, what to see, how and when best to travel, what was not to be missed and what was overrated. Moreover, how to do this on virtually no money at all. This was how Henry had traveled the world for two years on a pittance, westward, from Washington State. He was still going west. From London, eventually he would fly home to Seattle.

As the short northern night wore on, one by one people dropped, literally, fell over where they sat, fell asleep or tried to. No one could sleep for my incessant sneezing, which punctuated the engine's roar. I had long since ceased to collect *Bless you* in any language whatever, and finally Henry got off the chaise he had snagged and gave it to me, insisted that I take it. The dust and rumble didn't bother him, he said. Besides, he said, it was a humanitarian act; he nodded to the rest of them who were bleary-eyed and sleepless. As soon as I got off the floor, the irritations to my nose eased and the sneezing abated miraculously. I curled up gratefully on the chaise while Henry, using his backpack as a pillow, lay down beside me and we talked the rest of the night.

Docking in Harwich, we shouldered our bags and after a quick cup of hot tea, we got on the train to London, our other new friends in the same compartment, Henry and I side by side. Around us everyone slept, but I wasn't at all tired. We laughed and talked with an ease, even a sort of affection that seemed of longstanding, watched the sunlight shuttling through the window, illuminating his tanned face.

He could pick up his Seattle ticket at American Express in London anytime, he told me, but he didn't know when he was going home. When he'd left Washington two years before, he'd done a leisurely jaunt through the South Pacific, Tahiti, Fiji, all those strange and marvelous islands, through the strange and marvelous islands of Southeast Asia, Sumatra, New Caledonia, making his way (and making friends) through the Mediterranean and the Aegean and all those strange and marvelous islands, Lesbos, Samos, Patmos. And in all these two years he had discovered there was only one island he cared about. Isadora Island in the Puget Sound.

A strange and marvelous island in its own way. As we rattled toward London, he told me the story of Massacre, of the violent deaths visited on those peaceful people and how the name had stayed, their sole monument, and how there were places on the island, like Sophia's Beach, that seemed to resonate with a magic, not altogether benign perhaps, but certainly magic. He told me about his great-Aunt Sophia's school, the vision that had formed it, about its sad demise. Though he had been raised in Seattle, Henry said Useless Point was home to him, and his great-Aunt Sophia, who had died some years before, the beacon of his childhood.

Once arrived in London, I was ready to find a youth hostel, but Henry said it would be hard to find each other again in the city. Hostels have no phones. We'll lose each other if we part now, he said. He grinned. He had a marvelous smile and warmth, an innocence odd in someone so cosmopolitan. He was going to a friend's, a grad student from the University of Washington doing research here in history. The guy had volunteered his floor to Henry whenever he showed up in London. It was a pretty big floor. I could come too. I'm not too good on the floor, I reminded him, but Henry said this one wasn't moving. He hoisted his pack and offered me his hand.

Henry's friend rented an attic room in an Earl's Court house that had been carved into many flats. We found the place with difficulty complicated by our excruciating fatigue (and the fact that we nearly died every time we crossed a street, stepping into oncoming traffic). We got the right bus finally, found the right stop and trudged to the address, only to find that Steve Goldblum wasn't home and the house completely locked up. When Steve finally returned from the British Museum that afternoon, he was surprised to find Henry and me on the front porch steps, propped on either side of the door like two china dogs.

We all climbed the stairs to Steve's attic room. The bathroom was one floor down and if I wanted a bath with hot water, Steve said, I'd better get there fast. When I came back up, Henry was already asleep on Steve's floor. He'd made two makeshift beds from blankets, side by side. Till the day he died I slept beside him, wherever we were, from that night forward.

Over the following days and nights, I learned this much of Henry West: true, he was eager to return to Isadora Island, but he dreaded going back to Seattle, dreaded seeing his father whom he described as the owner of a lumberyard and a man more feared than loved. Three older half-brothers and a sister had all bolted Washington to escape him. They had married and taken up lives elsewhere, one brother in New York, two in the Bay Area, his sister gone to Minneapolis. He didn't resent their having fled, and anyway, it was too late to protest. Besides, Henry was more easygoing than the rest of them, and he had never quarreled bitterly with his father as the others had. As the youngest, he had stayed out of the old man's way. Summers he lived with Aunt Sophia at Useless Point, avoiding Seattle altogether. Nonetheless, Henry had done what his father expected of him: graduating from high school, going to the University of Washington long enough to evade a major in business and avoid the draft. Henry was freed by the draft lottery when his number came up, 324. He was restless and wanted to see something besides Washington. That was when his father offered the bargain: Henry could travel round the world, take as long as he liked and his father would fund it. But on his return Henry would come into the family business. More than that, Henry would dedicate himself to the lumberyard, learn it, eventually take it over, inherit and keep it in the family. For Henry, rudderless and relaxed, the prospect of world travel was dazzling, and as for the lumberyard, well, you had to have some kind of work, didn't you? Why not that?

All that time in London, Henry and Steve and I were a sort of Northwest triumvirate, Henry from Isadora Island, Steve from Walla Walla and me from Colby, Idaho. I had them howling with laughter over tales of the faith-healing of goats, and they were equally full of stories. Henry's were about Useless Point, never his family in Seattle, and I came to know Ernton, Nona and the others long before I met them. Henry was a fearless traveler; he had an unerring sense of direction and he never got lost. Or perhaps he just never felt lost. We went exploring. Intuitive and astute, and very clever, Henry figured out a way to get really cheap theater tickets for us, and we went to every forgettable musical in the West End. While Steve worked at the British Museum, we hung out with the rest of the young and unwashed at Trafalgar Square where the London police seemed not to care if you were stoned and happy, as long as you weren't stoned and obnoxious. On rainy days we wandered the National Gallery or the great tombs of culture in the British Museum.

We became lovers, knowing perhaps from that first night on the ship that we would. This gave the prospect relish without haste, and we became lovers slowly, our minds and hearts coupling as well as our bodies. Though I considered myself experienced, not till Henry did I discover I had never been in love. There was with him a sense of twinning, of feeling—to my surprise—that I needed to be made whole, that to be whole I had to have Henry, not in me or on me or with me all the time, just tendriled somehow. With Henry I felt whole, never having known that I wasn't. Or maybe I was always whole, and Henry just made me aware of it, widened my notions, brightened my vision. I saw the world through both his eyes and my own, and it was a far more colorful place than I had ever guessed. We had parallel reflexes. Sometimes I have seen this sense of common-response in couples long married, their alliance forged of habit. But we had this synchronicity early on, this unexpected rapture. Could that have survived? There's no such thing after all as expectable rapture. Rapture deluges and is not reliable.

We made love while Steve Goldblum studied the public career of Lord Liverpool in the British Museum. Steve was sad when he came home. He said we filled the place with our love and it didn't seem fair that we should be so complete and fulfilled while he was so alone. It wasn't fair. None of it was. That's what Steve said to me years later when he brought his wife and sons to Henry's House. Steve and I fell into each other's arms, weeping, both of us, for our loss in Henry, for those days when the mice scampered through his attic room, the hot water meter swallowing coins, the three of us enjoying meals I cooked on a single hot plate. Cheap wine. Warm beer. Toasts to love, to London, to Lord Liverpool, to life and Isadora Island because by that time I knew I would go back with Henry. I had not seen a tenth of what I'd come to Europe to see, but I had found what I needed to find.

We stayed a long time in Britain, tooting around Wales and the west coast of England, Scotland, sleeping in cheap B-and-B's (no hostels; they separated the sexes and we were lovers and could not be separated). Henry and I slowly approached our future, but he warned me, once back in Washington he faced more than a debt, a disaster. He'd kept careful track of all the money he'd spent (and he had preferred the challenge of traveling on a shoe-string, rather than the upholstered comfort he could have had; his father had not capped his offer at a certain figure, had told Henry to travel any way he liked), but an offer to repay all the money wouldn't satisfy the old man. Henry knew that. His father would expect the bargain, once agreed upon, to be kept. The closer we came to leaving England, the more anxiety dogged him. He could feel increasingly the weight of his father's leaden hand. It wasn't altogether fear Henry felt. It was loathing. He said his father did not recognize love or friendship, only power, adored power, practiced power, was very adept with power. He knew how to bend people to his will. He would surely bend Henry, shackle him to his bargain and the lumberyard. At first I pictured this lumberyard like a fort, a sort of Lincoln Log fort with a watchtower command post overlooking piles of rough-hewn tim-ber on one side and smooth, planed boards on the other. Slowly, over the course of our travels, my Davy Crockett picture changed as I began to realize the extent of his family's holdings. Finally Henry showed me his passport. *Westervelt.* I understood then. He said these two years he'd been Henry West. When I do go back, Henry said, I know an attorney, Mr. Ellerman, who'll help me change my name legally to Henry West.

The islands that we saw along the Scottish coast that summer broke Henry's heart because they were so magical and reminded him of Isadora. As we jostled around Scotland on teeth-rattling buses, he said that whatever happened, he knew he would forever fight his father's notion of success, which was to be the richest man in the graveyard. Henry preferred his Aunt Sophia's definition: to create, to contribute, to touch and move others, to love and be loved, to be part of people's lives. He wanted to be like her. He wanted to be an educator.

My idea of success? He asked me what was my idea and I confessed to him that I thought it was to be memorable. To be able to do one thing so very well that whoever experienced it would never forget it, I said as we sat amidst the ruins of an old castle near Edinburgh.

"Art?" asked Henry.

"I hope not. I can't draw or paint or act or dance, or write a line of poetry, or play an instrument, or hold a tune, save for 'Amazing Grace' and 'Abide with Me.'"

"I think a person can teach memorably."

"Maybe you can, or your Aunt Sophia could," I replied, "but not me. I can type and file, stuff like that, but it's hardly memorable."

The quality that made something memorable, said Henry, wasn't any one thing, but what connected it to some larger experience. "Like the way a perfect frame sets off a painting, makes it more beautiful."

When I set about putting Henry's House together, I remembered that, remembered Henry's wish to touch and move people. I think I have achieved what we'd wanted, hoped to accomplish together in the first flush of our adult lives. Henry's House has touched and moved people, the work done in both our names, Celia and Henry. Everything has been in both our names. Even the men I have loved I have loved as Celia Henry and the daughters I have raised, the Henry girls. And judged by that youthful standard—the things we wanted when we were young—perhaps I have less to regret than many women pushing fifty.

But your standards can't resist time any more than your body can. For all my loud blather about the Unfettered Life, I haven't lived unfettered, and now I begin to understand that I never wanted it anyway. From the first time I put my hand in Henry's, on our way to Steve Goldblum's attic room, it's clear to me I wanted connection. In fact now, I most fear being unfettered. Living alone when they all leave. And they will. The passenger side of my bed empty. Russell was a good man, though not perhaps a good man for me. Anyway, he's gone. My girls are gone. Victoria no longer comes over with Eric. I have not seen her in weeks. She won't see me. Victoria is bone-marrow angry with me, not for what I've done or left undone, but for what I somehow am, and cannot alter. Victoria's loss feels like desertion. Bethie's feels like death. Even after that terrible confrontation last month, all of us at Wade's apartment, I still had hopes, faith that Bethie could, would break free of Wade. She'd come to her senses. Now I know better. She is lost to me. If she can endure a betrayal of that magnitude and still kneel at that man's feet, she is lost altogether. So I am unfettered at last, I guess. But in truth, I am lonely. It looks lonely from here.

Isadora! they called out on the loudspeaker, *Isadora Island!* Thronging the narrow metal stairwells, I joined the exodus of Isadora passengers, down into the belly of the boat where I got in my truck and waited. The ferryboat docked at Dog Bay, making all the usual clangs and rumbles, groans and creaks, engines roaring, the rush of water as they secured the ferry to the pilings, logs smeared with pitch, smelling of homecoming. Chains across the front of the boat were loosed and drawn back; the ferry personnel directed cars up the ramp and off the boat. I turned left, toward Useless, following those few cars in front of me, who one by one turned off the road till my lights alone lit up the August night all the way to Useless Point, where the crazy currents and the desperate rocks of Assumption Island were swallowed up in darkness.

The old truck protested the steep drive up to my house and I pulled into the unpaved yard, lit here and there with moth-mad bulbs. Sass and Squatch roused and barked, and flitting through the patches of light that fell from my kitchen windows

I could see forms and shadows. I'd no sooner stepped from the truck than Brio burst through the door bounding out to meet me, her high, bright voice piping as she waved Baby Herman in greeting and the dogs danced around her. Sunny followed, her shoulders hunched over so that no one would notice how lovely she truly was. And following Sunny, Dorothy came into the yard. With her halo of gray hair, her sweet face, her voice, touch and step all modulated, muted, masking her otherwise steely resolve, oh, you would never guess at the stern stuff that was truly Dorothy Robbins. Launch lounged at the kitchen door, weather-beaten but not careworn, and then Grant came out, with his laconic smile and his calloused hands and his heart full of Sunny Jerome. Their forms and shadows danced about the yard in the uneven light, their voices caught in the August wind ruffling over Useless. They were eager for news of Bethie and though such news as I had was sad, surrounded by all of them, I felt buoyant. Connected. These were in some genuine way—if not the flesh of my flesh, bone of my bone—ties, sinews created out of those human obligations, the ones God put on old Adam and old Eve. Not in the Garden, but as they left.

As they moved east, out of Eden, toward the Land of Nod. Think of them, their figleafs flapping, as the angry cherubim flashing flaming swords prod them toward the future. And what prospects lay ahead? The certainty that they must earn their bread by the sweat of their brows. They must work, so they could eat. And eat, so they could work. The knowledge that their hands and backs and minds must be put to this task or they would starve. Well, they faced death anyway, didn't they? Don't we all? And after Eden and until they died, Adam and Eve dropped each night, fell into bed, their bodies bent, energies spent, the demands unchanging, rolling day after day toward death. To sleep, to eat, to squat in defecation, the woman's flesh penetrated in union and bifurcated in birth. No wonder poets invented love. Someone had to. If we do not dignify our lives with love, grace them with laughter and affection, garnish with pity, then our prospects and obligations are those of vegetables. Are they aware, vegetables, that they bloom and grow, produce, decay? Is it not in part our capacity of love, for pity, for affection and laughter that distinguishes us from the squash blossoms and the pear trees? Not solely and not wholly. When did you last meet an avaricious radish? A vindictive beet? A mean-spirited apple? Still, I don't believe the fruit from the tree of knowledge could have been sin alone. If we are fallen, so be it, but surely our capacity to fall is equal to, and commensurate with, our capacity to rise as well.

PART X

Turn of the Century

Slapping herself soundly with the dish towel and calling out *Doggy doggy doggy,* Nona York stood with her longtime editor, Georgieanne, waiting for the afternoon ferry eastbound. They waited with the outgoing foot traffic, those few people leaving Isadora on a September Saturday, summer's spell long since broken, but the autumn still ebullient. Ordinarily they would have been in Nona's car and she would have driven Georgieanne all the way down to SeaTac for the flight that would take her to New York. But Nona had not volunteered. The shuttle to SeaTac would have to do. The two women, friends of many years, were happy to be rid of one another.

Georgieanne, trying vainly to pretend this wasn't so, chatted away, as though their friendship had not been seriously impaired by the bad tidings she'd brought from New York. Worse, she had to make them explicit now, at their parting, because when she had tried to express all this earlier in her visit, Nona had cut her off. It wasn't merely bad news, but a fundamental difference of opinion separating Nona York, doyenne of Romance, from the rest of the world. Nona's books, it seems, had not been selling as well as they had in the past, even the rather recent past. Georgieanne, in consultation with Great Powers of Publishing, was of the opinion that younger women wanted something else in the way of Romance. Something more. Something different. Women's choices were changing, their roles were changing and their passions as well. The New Romance, Georgieanne had called it.

Nona had scoffed at this. Passions never changed. Nona had listened, foot tapping, and then informed her editor it was all rot. "I am a classic writer. I'm not about to start writing novels where young career women get mugged and then fall in love with the guy in the police lineup." Then she had stubbed out her cigarette and cracked a walnut with decisive strength. Georgieanne had not brought the subject up again.

Until this morning. Just before she was to leave Isadora (and in truth, Nona knew it was coming, this entire visit sadly fraught with what had been left unsaid), Georgieanne blurted out that the House was not prepared to pay Nona her usual advance. Moreover they planned to reduce her print runs and would not feature her as prominently in their ad campaigns. They valued her always, Georgieanne said in a speech which she had clearly rehearsed, but everyone must trim in a scaled-down world. This was the nineties. The House would always honor their long association with Nona York, but in truth, things would not be the same.

No bloody kidding, thought Nona, beating herself all the harder with the dish towel, *Doggy doggy doggy*. The ferry had docked, so this goodbye would be mercifully short. Across the way, foot traffic coming down the ramp began to straggle off the ferry, most of them cyclists wearing colors and outfits that reminded Nona of beetles, black-purple, black-yellow, black-green, helmets with points at the back and bicycle tires that whirred like beetles' wings. There was no terminal to speak of at Dog Bay, just a few lanes for the cars, ramps for the foot traffic, a shelter in case it rained and a shabby picnic ground in case it did not.

While her little dogs encircled her feet, barking at the bicycles across the way, Nona appeared to be listening to Georgieanne's parting thoughts, but actually she was thinking, *Kill the messenger.* She was thinking how fast she would get on the phone once she returned home. How swiftly she would call her agent and tell her to put the word out that Nona York—the Sir Walter Scott of Romance—would entertain Other Offers. But even as she relished the thought of dumping the disloyal Georgieanne, she squirmed inwardly because she was well aware that none of the new young editors knew who Sir Walter Scott was. And that might very well be the problem. Such a problem did not lend itself to solution. What was this New Romance? These scaled-down expectations? How cowardly. Scale down your expectations in life, perhaps, if you must. But in books? All the more reason to praise and polish, to enhance Romance in books. All the more reason for a reader to seize that book, to plunge into a world that was not scaled down at all, but grand and glorious. That's why women loved a Nona York novel. Reliable rapture. Sex with gusto. Love with grandeur. None of that foreordained coupling, groping the usual love handles while the 11 o'clock news droned on the bedroom TV. What women wanted in a book was not what they wanted in life. And why should it be? In life what you wanted was a man, steady, loyal, supportive. A man who would be good to your children and nice to your mother and appreciative of you. Who kept a job. If you were very fortunate, he did the dishes now and then, and took out the trash and could change the oil in your car. In books? Well, any novelist who served up such a colorless stew would be laughed right out of the boudoir.

No, for years, since Henry Westervelt first brought Celia to Useless, Nona had taken as her mini-muse Celia Henry. Not Celia's life exactly, but her seemingly unimpaired capacity for romance, a belief in love uneroded by various rocky unions. Celia's courage had never failed her, though her judgment certainly had. For most people, failures of judgment ended their courage and they retreated. To Nona's professional eye, Celia continued to exhibit a kind of bravery not often seen, or maybe merely an ongoing curiosity about the world, and a certain romantic optimism about men. She lived as though she believed that reward was somehow always imminent. In book after book, Nona had utilized Celia's love life in an oblique manner and no one would ever have guessed, say, that the marine biologist Phillip in any way resembled Anthony St. Julien in *Tie Your Heart to the Mast,* or Edward Sherwood in *The Bold and the Reckless.* Nona had got any number of books out of Henry Westervelt, though in the books he did not die. That was not allowed in romance. The passionate connection he'd shared with Celia, that was fodder, of course, but more intriguing was Celia's ongoing loyalty to Henry while she made love to others. Nona had gotten quite a few pages out of all Celia's men, altering the names and the circumstances (the feckless Bobby Jerome became a brooding concert pianist), leaving the heroines more or less of one cloth. However, not a single resident of Isadora Island had ever so much as hinted that Nona's books bore the whiff of local gossip. That is, until Dorothy Robbins began her Nona York binge, reading novels insatiably throughout the summer. Nona denied it, of course. But perhaps Dorothy's sense of Celia as heroine was due to having heard of Celia's love life as tales, not something she had witnessed over the years.

Besides, Nona had adopted only the general shape of Celia's love life, not its particulars. For one thing, she had left out all children. Children are notoriously unromantic. And Nona had smoothed out the life's nubby texture, which is to say, she left out most of the confusion. Nona York heroines were seldom confused, though they enjoyed or endured every other emotion associated with love, its loss and eventual fulfillment. The books usually ended with wide-eyed wild rapture, Adam and Eve after the snake had slithered away and before God popped in unexpectedly.

Even now, Nona had in her tape recorder a story with a Russell-like character, which did not address Celia's ambivalence about him, nor mention his bald spot, his teenage children, his fretty wife and his tendency to nag. Nona had recast Russell regally, in her own modest opinion, as a passionate cleric. And now here was Georgieanne telling her that such figments were unfashionable, passé and no longer selling.

"Romance is timeless," Nona insisted.

"We don't think that's altogether true," Georgieanne countered. "If it were, we would still be reading Victorian three-decker novels."

Nona returned icily, "I meant, in the most general sense. What's wanted in a romance novel is a heroine whose virtue is in danger, but whose destiny is not."

Georgieanne's perfectly tweezed brows knotted in consternation. "I don't think women believe in destiny anymore, Nona. They're all divorced and working while they bring up kids on their own, or they're living with men who refuse to marry them, or they don't know where to begin to look for a good man. Most of them are going to the gym for romance."

"I never heard of anything so stupid."

"Look at the pages and pages of dating personals."

"Those are all fake! Oh, Georgieanne, surely you knew that? People who run those services, they write those ads so other poor schleps will think they're not alone. They are not real!"

"Perhaps you've lived too long on this island," Georgieanne replied. "Perhaps you've lost touch with the world. Not with the way it works, but with the way women want it to work. That's the function of romance. That's what's changed."

The line of foot passengers started to move toward the ferry and Nona bid a swift and totally insincere goodbye to Georgieanne. Thwacking herself the more with her dish towel and collecting the doggies around her feet, she marched back to her Jeep, muttering under her breath. As she pulled out of the parking area, she saw a single figure walking through the picnic area up toward the road. A young woman, dressed in shorts and T-shirt, wearing running shoes and white socks, sweatshirt draped over her shoulder and carrying only a small purse. She wore thick sunglasses; her gaze was downcast, and her step dogged. Nona drove to the stop sign and turned left toward Useless where the lone woman was trudging along the road. Bethie Henry.

Everyone at Useless Point and most of Isadora knew the story of Lynette and Jennifer Shumley and Celia's escorting them personally to Wade's, knew moreover that Bethie had elected to stay with him despite such clear-cut perfidy. Talk about bad judgment! That was the whispered unanimous opinion all around Useless Point. The only person who didn't whisper about it was Launch. Nona pulled alongside Bethie and offered gallantly, "Do you want a ride, Bethie? Are you going home?"

Without taking off her dark glasses, Bethie stared at Nona. "I guess."

"Just couldn't take the stepdaughter, hmm?"

"She was not my stepdaughter, Nona," Bethie snapped. "I was never married to Wade."

"Well, Celia wasn't married to Bobby either and he was your stepfather."

"Please. Please don't talk about Bobby. Don't talk about any of them."

"So Celia's not expecting you?" Nona asked, knowing full well that if Bethie had been expected, the very seals on the Assumption rocks would have known about it.

"No one's expecting me. I'm not expecting me. I don't even know what's happened. Do you think they'll even talk to me at home?"

Nona shrugged noncommittally, but she leaned over and opened the passenger door and shooed all doggies into the backseat so Bethie could sit up front. Wordlessly she sank into the seat and buckled up. Nona neither asked nor offered anything in particular. Bethie's pain, anger, dismay, all these things palpably filled the car, so much so the doggies felt them; they yipped and whimpered. Nona was less sympathetic. She felt a sort of elation: if indeed there was New Romance, if young women wanted something different, if it were true that Celia Henry would no longer serve her as a mini-muse, perhaps Bethie Henry might. Perhaps Bethie Henry was the very person Nona York needed to see.

The Seattle schools had long since started, but Jennifer Shumley had refused to attend. She had refused to go to work. Refused all offers of ReDiscovery. Refused to do anything except smoke cigarettes and watch MTV, Pooh clutched in one arm. When the roots on her black hair began to grow out to a nondescript sandy color, she had asked her father for money for hair dye, and when he refused, she shoplifted L'Oréal because she was worth it. She slept in the computer room, along with Pooh. This meant that the computer had to be moved and that meant something else had to be moved. The whole process of displacement and absorption began, a sort of food chain of displacement as Jennifer moved in with her father and her stepmother. She used Bethie's makeup and Tampax and razors, shampoo and anything else she felt like appropriating. She would eat nothing except Cap'n Crunch and hamburgers. Wade gave her money for Burger King and cigarettes, and so there were butts and hamburger wrappers, French fry packets all over the house. Between the cushions of the couch, French fries petrified but refused to mold.

Moreover, Jennifer completely absorbed her father's attention during his nonworking hours as he tried to interest her in ReDiscovery and to find some venue—school, tech school, a job— where her skills could be used. Other than shoplifting, she apparently had no skills. Wade spent weeks seeking alternative education within the district, and within the citywide system, but Jennifer refused to budge. He discussed all this endlessly with Bethie, as if she cared, which she didn't.

Left at home together during the day, the two women avoided

each other. Jennifer talked to Bethie only when she needed something, stamps, say, for letters back to her boyfriend in Reseda. When there were no replies from Reseda, Jennifer lapsed into anger, tantrums which she lavished on Bethie all day and on Wade at night. And even Wade—the man of patience and forbearance, the forgiveness of a saint—snapped now and then under the stress. But when he did, Bethie bore the brunt of his frustration. Wholly undeserved, thought Bethie, that he should snap at her, growl at her, say tart, mean things to her when Jennifer was clearly the problem.

There were other displacements as well. Wade's affections, his attention, his goodwill were now divided, the greater portion going to his troubled daughter. The more time waxed on Jennifer, the less time spent on Bethie. But this meant as well that Bethie no longer needed to make lists, long detailed descriptions, discovering all her family's betrayals in the past, did not need to recover these wrongs and present them on paper to be worked out with various therapeutic tools. Bethie's personally tailored ReDiscovery program ended with Jennifer's arrival.

Oddly, despite Jennifer's morbid presence, her black leather and clanking chains, Bethie began to feel stronger. Better. More able to greet the world. She wanted to go back to work at ReDiscovery, she told Wade.

"Jennifer needs you at home," was Wade's reply. "She needs a mother. You can see for fifteen years she hasn't had a mother and she needs you. You are more important to me at home than you ever could be at the office, honey. Please, stay home and help her."

"Why can't Jennifer come to the office?" Bethie asked. "She could help out there. She could stuff envelopes. It wouldn't hurt her to put in a day's work. She doesn't do fuck-all."

"You know I dislike profanity. It's nothing but a shortcut through what is troubling you. You'll have to articulate so we can visualize the pain."

"Fuck-all."

Wade put his arm around her shoulders. "We'll find a way

to get Jennifer into ReDiscovery and entice her to go back to school, and once she has her own friends and some social life, everything will be better. I promise."

Perhaps. But Jennifer wouldn't have anything to do with school. School sucked. People who went to school were suck-ups. Or else they sucked. Everything sucked. ReDiscovery sucked. She wouldn't even wear the sucky T-shirt.

One afternoon on her return from the grocery store, Bethie found the apartment empty and Jennifer gone. She did not come home for three days and Wade refused to call the police. He said she was a resourceful young woman and they would wait for her to run out of resources before calling the police. He didn't want her to have a police record in Washington. He said he didn't want to deal with the juvenile authorities as a distraught and ineffectual parent.

"You're not the only ineffectual parent," said Bethie. "Lots of people suffer with their kids."

"I am not ineffectual, Elizabeth. I am challenged at the moment. Challenge is good. But I have submitted a grant proposal for the city to implement ReDiscovery in their alternative schools, and I can't be calling the police on my daughter."

Bethie suggested they should phone Lynette and her husband and ask if they had any clues where Jennifer could be found. Wade said he wouldn't give Lynette the satisfaction. Besides, Reseda was not Seattle. Still, he drove all around Pioneer Square, the U-district and any other places where the young and the restless were known to hang out.

She worried about Jennifer, missing for three days, but honestly, Bethie wasn't altogether sorry she'd gone. Once Jennifer was out of the house, Wade and Bethie made noisy, passionate love, love as they had not made love in the month since Jennifer had been there, sleeping right in the next room, her ear to the bedroom wall, walls so thin that when she would wind up the Pooh Bear, "Deep in the Hundred Acre Wood" tinkled through to Bethie and Wade.

But Jennifer did return. Hungry, hollow-eyed, dirty, disheveled, an intoxicant's stagger to her walk and the puncture on her nose rings red and inflamed. She slept for two days straight.

"Poor Lynette," Bethie said to Wade when he came home that night and saw his daughter lying, sprawled and fully clothed, on her bed, her heavy key chain slagged on the floor. "Think what she had to put up with all those years."

"The difference between Lynette and me," Wade corrected Bethie, "is that she did not love Jennifer and I do. Lynette didn't care. Lynette told her own daughter she should have put her up for adoption. Lynette is part of the problem."

On the tip of Bethie's tongue was the observation—the obvious—that Wade had bolted. That for twelve years he had never called, never contributed. Maybe Lynette should have given Jennifer up for adoption. Bethie wished she had. At least then Jennifer wouldn't be living with her father.

But she said no such thing. She had discovered since Jennifer's advent that bursts of candor were more likely to bring reproof than to open dialog. And though Wade's reproofs were always gentle—never in the year they'd been together had Bethie ever heard him raise his voice—they stung. Bethie tried very hard not to deserve them.

After the three-day disappearance and when Jennifer finally woke up, Wade went into her room and informed her that she would not be allowed to waste her life in this fashion. He was going to take some definitive steps. Finished with this declaration, Wade left her room, closing the door behind him. Pooh hit the door with a thump, and Jennifer screamed, "I hope to hell you have some fucking Cap'n Crunch in this house!"

Meeting Wade outside Jennifer's door, Bethie put her arms around him. "Love has its limits, doesn't it?" she said sadly.

Wade disengaged her, regarded her with tenderness and shock. "You know that's not true, Elizabeth. Surely you know that's not true."

And that was what made her think it might be true. Maybe Wade was wrong.

Still, she loved him, and Bethie was certain that the strains and cracks in her relationship with Wade were entirely due to Jennifer. Everything that would ease when Jennifer left. But three years from now? *Three years of Jennifer?* Bethie secretly began to hope she would get picked up by the law.

Chances looked good. Clearly Jennifer had found a source, and her behavior and her attitude veered wildly with her ability to score. She was, she could be, Bethie thought, dangerous. She began bringing home dangerous friends, street people she picked up and when Bethie told Wade this, he said it was good Jennifer should have friends. It was the first step.

"You haven't seen them!" Bethie protested.

And he hadn't. He was spending much more time at work now, especially in the evenings when he ought to have been home with his family. That's what Bethie actually said to him on the phone, referring to herself and Jennifer as a family.

"You need to be strong now, Elizabeth. For my sake. For Jennifer's sake."

"Half of the time she's not even here and when she is, she has these awful people with her. Really, horrible-looking homeless types. They smell bad and they steal. What am I supposed to do?"

"Love her," Wade counseled. "Love her if only because you love me."

Then Wade had a call on another line and Bethie was left with the dead phone in her hand. Across the room Jennifer lay on her back in her enormous baggy clothes, dribbling Cap'n Crunch into her mouth, tapping her foot in time to MTV, as faces and butts alternately swam up out of the TV screen in rhythmic little bursts of percussion. Bethie stalked over and snapped the television off.

"Phobe," Jennifer accused her. "Like mother, like daughter."

Bethie burst into tears, knowing that she wasn't well, she wasn't strong, she wasn't ready to deal with this unconscionable burden, wishing, in fact, that she were like her mother. Bethie wished she had some of Celia's casual strength and insouciance, her old irreverence, her makeshift charm and her ability to differentiate (most of the time) between the destructive and the merely distracting.

One night when Wade came home, Jennifer's friends were still squatting in the front room, their bags of aluminum cans on the front porch and a warning from the condo association in his mailbox. He turned off the television. He attempted to talk with them about ReDiscovery which sent them scurrying. At that (and, thought Bethie, at last) even his unflappable goodness began to give way, and all tempers (Jennifer's made shorter by methamphetamines) frayed. But Wade vented his anger on Bethie.

Their reconciliation took place in bed. They made love, and afterwards Wade stroked Bethie's hair and praised her for her good work with Jennifer. He could see a real change in Jennifer and it was all due to Elizabeth's caring, her love for a troubled human being. And weren't we, all of us, in some way, troubled human beings? Elizabeth surely knew that, after all the ReDiscovering she'd done this past summer and all the growth she'd made. Look how Elizabeth had come through and come out of the abuse dealt her by her cruel mother and stepfather, by her whole unbelieving family for that matter. It had made her a stronger, better person. And stronger, better people always made effort to give back to others the redemptive health they themselves enjoyed.

In short, Bethie realized when he left for work the next morning, nothing had changed.

But he didn't stay away from home anymore in the evenings. He began to shoulder his share of the Jennifer-burden and this eased Bethie's responsibilities. When Jennifer was not out riding the city buses and scoring drugs, Wade spent hours with her in her room, having long, soulful talks. He emerged from these sessions spent, but confident that he had done some good, that Jennifer had been sent to him to test his own health and welfare, his beliefs. Through the bedroom wall at night, Bethie could hear Jennifer crying, sometimes muffled weeping, sometimes loud boo-hoos, but she felt not the slightest twinge of sisterly—to say nothing of maternal—compassion. Let her cry and get it out, thought

Bethie. Let her cry it out and get her shit together and get into school where she belongs. Somehow Bethie knew that's what Celia would say, if she could talk with Celia. Which she could not. She was finished with people who thought she was a liar.

Jennifer did not go back to school. But she didn't go out as much either. She spent less time in front of the television and more time sleeping and weeping. Weeping and sleeping. And with Jennifer thus pacified (calmed, said Wade, calmed and getting better), Bethie went back to work at the ReDiscovery office, happy to be out of the house and back amongst the living.

In the time that Bethie had been gone, ReDiscovery had expanded and Wade had had to hire another girl to answer the phone and be the gofer, but everyone was happy to see Bethie, and she got her old job back right away. Fran in particular commented on how good she looked, visibly recovered from the shock and trauma of the summer. "From discovery to recovery," said Bethie, "Wade's program works."

Then there came a Friday morning when she answered the phone and a rugged, masculine voice asked to speak to that bastard fuck-hole, Wade Shumley. Taken aback, Bethie replied in her best professional tone, "Mr. Shumley is in a meeting and can't be disturbed. May I say who's calling?"

"When I'm through with Wade Shumley, he'll be in a meeting with the devil at the gates of hell. We got the letter."

"Excuse me?"

"The letter Jennifer sent us saying that I'd molested her every day for the past two years and her mother didn't care and didn't love her. I never touched Jennifer. I wanted to beat the living shit out of her a couple of times, but I never put a hand on her. Lynette did everything she could for that little bitch. Jennifer's a stupid, drugged-up, nasty little slut and she's not smart enough to write like that. Jennifer didn't make it to the eighth grade. You tell Wade that me and Lynette know who really wrote that letter. Lynette is all broken up, but I'm pissed off. You tell Wade he's full of shit. You tell Wade if there's any more accusations,

I'll tear his balls off and shove one down his throat and one up his ass. Got that? I'll kill him."

The phone went dead in Bethie's hand.

Wade was only in a meeting with Fran, practicing his newest presentation, and Bethie decided to disturb him. It must have been going well because Fran (who liked nothing better than to play Mary and Martha to Wade's Jesus) was pouring him a cup of coffee, her face shellacked with beatitude.

Wade was shocked to be interrupted in mid-sentence. Bethie apologized, "Ordinarily I wouldn't have broken in on your work, but it was Lynette's husband. He said they got a letter from Jennifer. He said he was going to kill you. Graphically."

"In my work there are always angry people, Elizabeth. Please close the door and hold all calls."

That night Jennifer's weeping and sobbing were worse than usual; she not only cried, she howled. Lying in bed, listening to the girl's unhappiness echo through the wall, Bethie knew somehow this was not mere adolescent angst or anger, not even drug abuse, drug hunger or withdrawal. This was heartbreaking. Bethie begged Wade to check her into a clinic. "Listen to her—" An eerie wail pierced the plaster. "Check her into rehab, Wade. She's a minor. You can do it, as her parent. It's the only merciful thing."

"She's getting better."

"She's not. She's getting worse. She's in misery. If that were a dog crying in the night you'd call the humane society. You'd put it out of its misery."

"How can you say such a thing?" Wade turned his back to her.

The next morning, Saturday, Bethie woke late to find Wade gone from their bed. She could hear voices on the other side of the bedroom wall. Voices and noisy snuffling. Jennifer's snuffling. Wade's low, soothing voice. She lay in bed and listened. His voice was so comforting in its authority and calming in its assurance, just as she remembered from her traumas; his words were always a balm to suffering. Bethie got up, made coffee, drank a cup reading the Seattle paper while Jennifer's choking sobs sounded through-out the apartment. Bethie got in the shower so she would not have to listen, but when she got out, the moans and tears, muffled voices had not ceased. Quickly throwing on some clothes and kicking herself—mentally and spiritually and morally—she none-theless went to the bedroom wall, put her ear there and eavesdropped.

As Jennifer gnashed and flailed, as Wade held her while she hyperventilated, while Jennifer struggled with and against him, wept, Bethie heard a story she recognized. Lurching from her stepdaughter's lips there emerged the tale of a girl much wronged by a stepfather, the man living with her mother, sleeping with her mother. A predatory, lecherous man, not content with the woman's body, but lusting after the little girl, a man who bullied and cajoled the girl, who pushed his way into her bedroom, who kept her there on the bed, with fear and promises. He was the father figure after all. There was no help for the little girl. Her mother wouldn't help her. Her mother preferred not to know. The stepfather punished and exacted compliance, threatened and prodded her child's body. Rumbling through the wall Bethie heard Wade's voice. "And he fingered you like that? Every night?"

"Days," sobbed Jennifer. "He worked nights. He's a night cook at Denny's and home days."

"Happy as gnats on jam-day," I said to Brio when she commented on the uneven swarm of black gnats buzzing in narcotic ecstasy. There were little clouds of them hovering over the peaches still in crates, or on those lying skinless and halved near the food processor, those steeping in bowls full of sugar, and over the piles of peach pits soaking through the newspapers on the table. Brio and Baby Herman were zapping peach pulp in the food processor, all three of us clad in aprons stained with years of this sort of cyclic endeavor. Next month there would be days spent marching the apples through the peeler and into the pots for applesauce, pears similarly sauced and laced with brown sugar. There was basil to be put down in salt and oil, all the autumn rituals, separating pith from peel. This moment, just past the last stroke of summer, you try to encapsulate, to freeze it, before the frost can touch or blacken. September sunlight slanted in the long, dusty windows where sand dollars collected cobwebs, crane flies staggered amongst jars of seaglass and shells long past their significance. The overwhelming sweetness of the peaches congealed somehow with the light. A few flies droned lazily in the warm air while the marine radio weather, in its uninflected voice, foretold the immediate future.

Brio and I were near the end of daylong undertaking. I always make jam in single batches though I buy the fruit in bulk. It's time-consuming, but better than risking the ruination of whole flats of peaches with a single miscalculation. I have learned this concept the hard way, naturally. Brio's interest in all this had waned and she amused herself putting Baby Herman in school, and being, in general, a joy underfoot.

Soon, when rents drop in the off-season, Sunny and Grant have told me they will get their own place. I'll see them often, of course, but it will be a change for me. I'll be alone. On Labor Day Dorothy returned to Bellevue on the Robbinses' 40-foot Tollycraft powerboat, the old *Strumpet,* renamed *Mom's Victory.* No longer the lonely Maid of Dove, Dorothy is a student at Lake Washington Technical College in hotel and restaurant management. We talk all the time on the phone and I've told her I think she's right, there is a career possible, a cafe, say, that specializes in meat loaf and rice pudding.

I stood at the stove, wooden spoon in hand, like a conductor for the Jam Overture, Peach Rondo, Sure-Jell Gavotte. Peach pulp cooked away on the front burner and on the back, the last of the jars bubbled and chattered in boiling water, and over all this kitchen cacophony, I heard a car pull into the yard and Sass and Squatch going into their usual dither. From the kitchen window I could see Nona's Jeep. Launch, stacking firewood in the back of my truck, saw her too and waved in greeting. He was closely shorn now, past the autumn equinox, and he waved and grinned and greeted Nona, but then—oddly, I thought—his smile faded and he returned to stacking the wood. Then I saw why. Nona had a passenger.

Dark glasses obscured Bethie's eyes, but her mouth still had that bruised pout. Her hair had grown out and grazed along her shoulders. She had tied a sweatshirt around her waist. She was not the athletic Bethie, but neither was she amongst the walking wounded, as when I'd seen her last on her knees between Wade's legs.

She waited till Nona had dealt with the doggies, leashed them in the shade near Sass and Squatch's water dish. Then she followed Nona inside the house, took off her dark glasses and said a sheepish hello to me and Brio.

"I found her at the ferry landing," said Nona, beating herself absently with the dish towel. "She was walking home so I gave her a ride."

I nodded, murmured something, but turned my attention back to the pot of Sure-Jell which had cooked. I took it and poured it over the bowl full of peach pulp and sugar and the smell that dazzled up out of that bowl was overwhelming, concentrating, consecrating all the summer's peaches into one final bouquet too intense to be borne, and so it must disperse. What I felt on seeing Bethie was just that intense; I could not speak till some of my emotion dispersed. I loved her. I was joyed-over to see her again. But dulling all that was, equally, anger, bitterness and recrimination. How could it be otherwise?

"Who are you?" Brio demanded.

Bethie looked hurt. "Don't you remember me? I'm your Aunt Bethie. I'm your mother's sister."

"Is that so?" I asked, pissedly. "The last I heard, you had disavowed Sunny altogether. You said she was not your sister at all." I turned to Brio. "Can you and Baby Herman go to school upstairs or outside?"

"Can she have a cookie?"

"Are you back or just here, Bethie?"

Bethie pondered this, sinking down into a kitchen chair. "I'm back here. I'm not engaged anymore. I broke up with Wade."

"When?" I gave Brio the cookies and she and Baby Herman went outside.

"This morning. I drove his car to the ferry terminal and parked it there and threw the keys in the water."

"And the engagement ring?" asked Nona. "Did that go in the water too?"

"I left it by the kitchen sink. Maybe Jennifer will steal it."

"Where does Wade think you've gone?" I asked.

"Out for cigarettes."

"You hate cigarettes."

"I was going to get them for Jennifer. I had to have a reason to leave. I didn't want it to look too obvious because, well—I just wanted to be casual so I wouldn't be tempted."

"Tempted to what?"

"To explain. To try to talk to Wade. To make him understand why I was leaving. If I tried to talk, I'd just get confused and end up thinking I was wrong. I'd end up wondering how I could have wanted to leave. He'd get me into bed and I never would leave. I knew I just had to get on Route 5 and go north. Catch the ferry and get to Isadora."

"What for?" I didn't ask the question to be flip, but it sounded that way.

"I don't have anywhere else to go." She slid her purse on the floor. "I guess I could have gone to Victoria's, but I knew she'd just take me shopping and get my hair cut. That isn't enough."

Neither Nona nor I said that Victoria's house would not exactly provide a haven for anyone lately. We didn't see Victoria or hear from her. We got our news of Victoria through Dorothy. Eric had told his mother the marriage was breaking up and he was powerless to stop it. Victoria was clearly bent on one of her unremitting courses of action and Eric was no match for her. I didn't say any of this to Bethie and neither did Nona. What would be the point?

Bethie looked up at me plaintively. "Aren't you the least bit happy to see me? Not even a little?"

I picked up the bowl of molten peach jam and poured it, like golden lava, into the waiting jars and freezer containers, scraped out the bowl and capped each container without securing the lids. "I'm afraid of what you might have brought with you. More destruction? More accusations? More pitch and tar and turds you intend to smear on all of us?"

"I didn't bring anything." She stood up, arms out. "Look. Nothing. No clothes. No money. I just left him. It's over."

Of course I was glad to see her. Glad she was Wade-less. Glad that the trembling, sickly girl staked to Wade with no more strength than a sweet pea, that girl was gone. This one was not exactly Bethie The Charmer, but at least she'd gotten tired of being handmaiden to an ersatz god. "How's Jennifer? Your stepdaughter."

"She's not my stepdaughter—and don't tell me she is just because I was living with her father. Nona's already lambasted me with that, all the way from Dog Bay." Bethie took down a cup from a hook and poured cold coffee, zapped it in the microwave. "Jennifer is terrible. You know she's terrible. You saw her. You brought her to my house. She's worse than she was then."

"How could she be any worse? Did her nose rings get infected?"

"Actually they did. Her nose was all red and infected. Ugh. But that was nothing. She's back on drugs. Maybe she was never off. I don't know. I don't care. She's not my stepdaughter and I don't have to live with her anymore."

"So you've left Wade for good?"

"Forever. I told you. I threw his keys in the water."

The phone rang and I moved to pick it up, but Bethie said it was probably Wade. So I left it for the answering machine.

"Why would Wade think you've come here? You were finished with us. He knew that. This is the last place you'd come."

"I've been gone a long time. I left this morning. He would have tried everywhere else."

It was Wade. The three of us listened, Bethie plucking nervously at her lip as his rich voice swelled and seeped into the kitchen, not a note of alarm or indictment in it, just a request: if Elizabeth should come here, please have her call home.

"It's not home. I'm never going back. Never, Celia. It's over and I'm free of him. Really, I'm free. Unfettered," she added expectantly.

I knew what I was supposed to do: take her in my arms and say how wonderful that was. Nona and I were supposed to join in some sort of gospel anthem to Bethie's newfound freedom, but all I said was, Well, that was fine, and I wondered if Bobby Jerome was free too. I turned off the marine radio because they were predicting storms moving in and the barometer was rising.

Bethie looked momentarily confused by the silence. She glanced imploringly at Nona, who kept her Roman general's expression without an ounce of indulgence. Bethie seemed to crumple before us. "I've really hurt everyone badly, haven't I?"

I didn't trust myself to speak. I measured out the sugar for the last batch of jam.

Nona dug through a crate of peaches and found one not overripe, washed it and bit into it. "To call it hurt is like putting a Band-Aid over a bomb site," she said.

At that Bethie began to blather. She always did talk too much when she didn't know what to say, and in this she had not changed. She began to slide out from responsibility for the things she'd said and done, to deconstruct the whole experience, using Wade's own lingo: how truth and lies lived close together, so close you couldn't tell one from the other, what you thought was true turned out to be a fiction and fiction had its roots in truth. On and on.

I couldn't bear it. I picked up my paring knife and used it didactically on a peach. "I'm sure that all that ambiguity suits

Wade Shumley. He thrives in it, like some kind of hothouse fungus, but it doesn't suit me, Bethie. And certainly not in this instance. Say whatever you want about us, about me, about Bobby, about the way all you kids were raised. Say that I was a mediocre parent, or a bad parent, that I was too taken up with my own life, but do not say that Bobby Jerome finger-fucked you and made you perform oral sex on him, that he used your hand to jerk off and that I colluded in this."

Bethie gave little high-pitched gasps.

"Don't you look so shocked at me, Bethie Henry, like it's terrible for me to say these things. *You* said them. That's what you accused Bobby of. A gross breach of trust. You accused me of acquiescing in this, and that together he and I destroyed and blighted your young life. And that is a lie. And that particular lie is not neighbor to the truth, but the enemy of truth, and so is your accusation against Grant and Lee."

"Oh, I know that," she cried. "I wanted to call you and tell you, later, that I knew that never happened. But of course I couldn't talk to you. But really, it was just sort of—well, I didn't even mean, really, to say it. I'm not even sure now that I did actually say it. But Wade thought it and I let him think it." She put her face into her hands and wept. "I loved him," she sobbed. "I loved Wade and I wanted to make him happy."

"And it made him happy to think that your stepbrothers had abused you? That made him happy?"

Bethie didn't answer, just wept on and I looked over at Nona, but neither of us rose to the occasion, to the obligatory *There, there,* not because we didn't know or understand or sympathize with the anguish she felt (and what woman hasn't blurted out those words, *I loved him,* in defense of some foolishness or other) but because I had heard Bethie cry and whimper and drivel on about love—in person or on paper—for almost a year now and I was sick of it.

And then, perhaps because neither Nona nor I rushed up to her with Kleenex and cups of tea and the observation that all men are brutes, she gradually hiccupped her tears down, and got her own Kleenex from the bathroom, blew her nose and asked if we wanted to know what happened.

"I'm curious."

"I'm curious," Nona seconded.

"It was the girl, Jennifer," she admitted. "And it wasn't just because I didn't like her. Though I didn't like her. She came between me and Wade and she made trouble between us. At first she just took all his attention because he didn't know what to do with her. But then it got worse. Then he sort of gave up on her. He left me to deal with her. I was supposed to stay at home and bring her up. He didn't come home till late. Work—it was always work—but I knew, really, that girl just defeated him. I resented it. I didn't want a daughter, especially a teenage daughter. Especially her. She was awful. She was always buzzed up on some drug or another and I could smell marijuana in her clothes like incense. She stole. She brought home the most awful people and they stole. Wade came home one night and the keyboard from the computer had been disconnected and it was gone and so was the VCR. Wade blamed me! Like it was my fault she hung out with thieves and drug addicts. But even through all that, I didn't leave him. I wasn't happy, but I loved him, and I was loyal, and I stayed on for him, not for her. I couldn't stand her. Besides, everything got better when he let me go back to work."

"He let you? That sounds ominous."

"Well, I worked for him," she said with an uncaring shrug. "So he had to tell me when I could go back to work. He was the boss. It was better then. At least I wasn't home with Jennifer all day." Bethie licked her lips and kept her gaze on the kitchen windowsills, all the summers collected there, the single drooping sunflowers Brio had stuck in Coke bottles. "He took more responsibility with Jennifer after that. And it seemed like he was making some progress. She didn't go out as much and the drug addicts quit coming over and she didn't even watch too much TV anymore. She just stayed in her room and cried. Wade kept saying the pain was good for her and soon she would be new and whole."

I remembered Bethie kneeling between his legs, his beckoning to Jennifer, and her going to him, the look on his face. You wouldn't forget that. "I've seen what Wade considers new and whole."

"At first I didn't care that she cried all the time, because I didn't care about her. Anyway Wade can reduce whole audiences to tears. I've watched him with groups. Wade tells them they have to think of those tears like rainwater, rinsing away the old addictions and afflictions and destructive affections and starting all over again. They have to cry so they can be new. But Jennifer was different. It wasn't enough for Jennifer to cry and be new. She had to—" Bethie finished her black coffee in one audible gulp, as if that were the only way she could keep words back down in her throat. "With Jennifer, he was like a wrecking ball. Like he had to pull the old Jennifer-building down, down into dust and rubble. Once she was wrecked, then he could build a whole new Jennifer. And sometimes when I listened to her cry at night, I thought, well, sometimes it seemed so familiar. I was afraid . . ." Bethie took her cup back to the sink and stood there, her back to us.

"What was he using to destroy a girl who was already on drugs?" I asked. "A girl who's been arrested for prostitution, who has spent months in juvie, who's been in rehab before she's six-teen? What could you possibly use to destroy such a girl?"

Pacing the kitchen, reacquainting herself with every homely object in it, Bethie finally said, "Her past. He used her past. I'd listen to her cry and wail like she'd lost everything, like she had been so battered, she'd never heal, like she was in so much pain, she wanted to die, might die if someone couldn't clean up all those addictive and inappropriate behaviors and get them out of her life. She had to get rid of the abuse and the abusers. He was helping her discover so she could recover." Bethie pulled her arms up tight against her body, against the cold, though the kitchen was warm. "I heard him asking her questions that weren't questions, that were, well, suggestions. I heard her crying and coughing up old hurts and it all sounded really familiar. Like my hurts. Like what had happened to me had happened to Jennifer. And then I wondered if it did happen to her. And then"—Bethie's hands knotted—"I wondered if it had happened to me. You know?" she added plaintively. Nona and I were silent. "He was like a wrecking ball. I couldn't stay there and fight him, and I couldn't stay and figure it out. What else could I do? I said I'd get Jennifer some cigarettes."

"And have you figured it out?"

"I only just left this morning."

The phone rang again and we let the machine pick up while the three of us waited. It was Fran. Breathy, excited, worried Fran. This time the message was for me. "Celia, if you know where Elizabeth is, would you please call Wade at home? Or you can call me here and I'll get the message to him." Fran nattered a bunch of phone numbers at us, his, hers, the cell phone, the pager, the ReDiscovery voice mail. "Elizabeth took his car, and no one has seen her since about ten this morning. Wade is sick with worry. We're all very worried about her. I don't mean to alarm you, but Wade is thinking of going to the police."

"He won't call the police." Bethie sagged forward. "I don't care what Fran says. Jennifer was gone once for three days and he didn't call the police."

"What about the car?" I brought the last of the peaches to the table and began peeling them, skinning them swiftly, the juice dripping through my fingers to the bowl.

"He'll say you stole his car," said Nona.

"It'll get towed away. I parked illegally. They'll call him eventually. He'll have to pay. He'll be really disappointed in me."

We heard voices outside, Sass and Squatch putting up their fuss, Sunny's laughter and the sound of her picking up Brio and the little girl shrieking with delight. Sunny and Grant came through the service porch, but suddenly they were silent as oysters.

"I'm back," Bethie said with a nervous laugh. "It's over with Wade. I broke up with him."

Still stunned, Sunny finally managed to ask when.

"About ten. This morning." Then she added, "It's been coming for a long time. Ever since Jennifer. Maybe before. All I know for sure is that I'm through with Wade and I'm not going back there. Ever. Love has its limitations."

"Maybe that's it," said Nona reflectively. "Maybe that's the New Romance. Love being limited. Necessary, but not as central, not the single measure of a woman's success. After all, women's lives are more than compendiums of the men they've slept with. Women are asking more from the world. If the world gives you more, then you need less from men. Women are asking less from love. If you ask for less, you're more easily fulfilled. If you're fulfilled, you can get on with the rest of your life, and all the possibilities in it. Men have to be time-effective for a woman. Romance," she added, beaming, "in the age of efficiency!"

Well, who knew what in the hell she was talking about? But Nona was enormously pleased with herself. You could tell that just to look at her.

"I'm not asking anything more of love," Bethie assured her. "I'd just like my old job back at Duncan Donuts. You think Angie will give me back my old job?"

"A lot has happened in the year since you gave up that job, gave up your apartment, gave up your cats and moved to Seattle to live with Wade." I pulverized the peeled peaches with each of these various observations. I had the sugar all measured. "Angie's hired someone else. And Sunny's working here even if Dorothy isn't."

"Who's Dorothy?"

"Don't you remember! Victoria's mother-in-law?"

"Oh, her." A look of acute peptic distress crossed Bethie's face. "I never should have made Victoria bring them to the party. I never should have made her tell you she got married."

"Well, it looks like she'll be getting divorced pretty soon, if that makes you feel any better." I lined the jam jars up on the counter and took all but one of the bowls to the sink. "So you see, Bethie, life has gone on here on Isadora. Things change."

"Nothing ever changes here. People die. That's the only change possible on this island."

"Russell's moved out. He went back to his ex-wife."

"The one who always used to call here?"

"He only had the one ex-wife. He had a couple of ex-girlfriends."

"Think of Russell without his bald spot," Nona volunteered wistfully.

"Could I work at Henry's House and have my old room back here?"

"The Season's drawing to a close."

"You mean I can't stay here?"

"It's unrealistic of you, Bethie, to come back to Isadora and pick up life just where it was. There are people you have wounded and relationships you have destroyed. Pain inflicted. You know, Bethie, pain like old Wade's favorite pleasure, that kind of pain. And now just because you wish it, everything, everyone can't now miraculously fall in with your plans."

"But all the time I was with Wade, you were always telling me you loved me. All of you," she protested. "You begged me to come back with you, Celia, the day you brought Jennifer. You wanted me home. You said you loved me! You all said you loved me."

"We do love you. We loved you all through that ordeal and we love you now, but there are people you have wronged and somehow you've got to make some of that up. I don't say all at once, but you have to start somewhere."

Bethie began with Sunny, apologized first to Sunny for inflicting pain, for denying they were sisters, for hurting Sunny's father and making Sunny miserable. Bethie told Grant she was sorry. It wasn't true—well, the part about the headless doll and cheating off her homework, the goldfish and the lavender soap, that was true. "But the rest was all just part of a sickness I had."

"You made other people sick too, Bethie." Grant sat down beside Sunny, his hands laced together, and he stared at them.

"Why did you do that, Bethie? Why lash out at all of us like that?"

"It was like—" Bethie started slowly. "Well, when I moved in with Wade, I met all these people, and they were all in such pain. They all had old hurts and old angers and lousy parents, cruel siblings that they had to discover before they could recover. They had to meet the pain and go beyond it and be, well, deepened. It was like, if you weren't in some kind of pain, then you must be a shallow twit. If you were sort of happy and"—she looked around for the word—"energetic, then you couldn't possibly understand anyone else's pain because you didn't know what pain was. And there I was, with Wade, who knew more about pain than anyone. After all his years as a drug addict, Wade—" Bethie squirmed uncomfortably. "I was a prisoner in victimville and it was a dirty little war. I'm sorry to you too, Nona."

"I accept your apology, Bethie. Of course, I wasn't one of the ones indicted."

"I'd do anything to make it all right. With everyone. Even if I can't make it all right, I'd still do anything."

"Then you go back on the afternoon ferry. You can borrow my car if you want," I said, "and you go to Bobby and you see him and you tell him that."

"I'll call."

"No."

"I need time."

"Then take it. Fine. But you can't stay here. If you want to stay here, then you go to Bobby and you ask him to forgive you. You were not the only prisoner in victimville, Bethie. You fell victim to a man who could not bear your strength and high spirits and the fact that your family loved you—weird as we may be, we loved you. So he had to make you weak and tear you away. He wanted to destroy you and hurt us. But Bobby hurt more than anyone because Bobby is not a man with weapons. He doesn't have the instincts of a fighter. These accusations of yours destroyed Bobby and you owe it to him to apologize to his face."

"Janice will eat me alive."

"Janice will. She'll protect him and you'll have to get past her and the Wookie."

"The Wookie too?" Bethie paled slightly. Then she started in how none of this was her fault. She went on and on. Her explanations, like a house of cards, collapsed continually under the weight of her flimsy logic. Then she'd start back up again. I made the whole last batch of jam while she wended her way through excuses and apologies. Bethie had left Wade, but clearly it would take her a while to shake him off. To peel Wade off her brains would be harder than leaving his ring by the sink and his keys in fifty feet of salt water.

She waxed on at length what it was like to be living with Wade the good shepherd, and the rest of his flock. It was like sleeping with Buddha. If you were going to sleep with the Buddha, you had to be Buddhist. "Really," she concluded at last, "the one who ought to apologize to everyone is Wade."

Nona observed coldly, "If love has its limitations, Bethie, so does forgiveness. Don't test the frontiers."

Bethie's shoulders sank. "I didn't mean to hurt everyone. I'm sorry. I've made mistakes. I just want my old life back. I want my own past back. I wish I could have my old name back."

For a minute I didn't know what she meant. Forgot completely that I'd named the girls Harmony and Clarity, that Bethie had christened herself Elizabeth, and her sister, Victoria. I'd forgotten they were ever anything else. But once, a long time ago, I'd named my daughters Harmony and Clarity. Bobby and Linda named their daughter Soleil. Of the three, Sunny alone lived up to, lived into her name. For my girls, their names had brought them neither clarity nor harmony. Quite the opposite. Perhaps I ought to have named them Strife and Obscurity. Clarity was certainly opaque, obscure to me. Through a glass darkly was the erstwhile Clarity. And Harmony? Look at the discord Harmony had wrought. It's hard now to remember that Clarity and Harmony and Soleil all went to school with little girls who answered to Summer and Autumn, Rain and Bluejay, Star and Skye. Their elfin names say more about us, their fey parents and the world we believed in, or maybe just hoped for. Lots of us tried to create such a loving world, but then we got tired, gave up, got jobs, thought of ourselves as Boomers instead of Flower Children. Certainly, were no longer children in any event. We had children— with names like Harmony and Clarity, Sunshine, Yarrow, Dove, Strawberry, Feather. Their world, the world they've inherited, is not at all fey or flowery. To these grown women how awkward their poetic names must feel in an age of efficiency. Isn't that what Nona called it? These years, on either side of the millennium, the turn of the century. The phrase has a nice optimistic savor to it. I guess. It's really more like an epochal equinox. Or maybe the century actually does turn somewhere, deep inside the earth's core, and we'll hear the grind and groan of it, birthing itself, the new century. I will be in it, but not of it. I am of the old century, the greater part of my life lived in the old century. But Clarity, Harmony and Soleil, the greater part of their lives will be lived in the twenty-first century. *Deo Volente.* God willing, Sunny will live well into the next century. *Deo Volente,* let her live well in any event, Grant and Sunny and a life *con brio.*

Bethie agreed at last to go see Bobby. She begged Sunny to go with her. But Sunny said no, and she and Brio left to walk Grant back to the *Pythagoras* tied up at the Useless dock.

I gave Bethie the keys to the Jetta and some money for the ferry.

"What if I weaken?" she asked.

"Then you just dig down a little deeper and find strength you didn't know you had," I replied. "Don't come back unless you've talked to Bobby. Apologized."

"You come see me when you get back, Bethie," said Nona, "you come tell me all about it."

They walked outside and Nona's little dogs went into a frenzy of welcome that sent Sass and Squatch running for cover. Nona, whipping herself with the dish towel, opened the car doors and they all leaped in, the doggies still yapping as they drove downhill. In the old Jetta, Bethie followed.

I went the other direction, over to Henry's House to start

dinner for tonight's guests. Almond pesto is best when the basil, parsley and thyme are picked just before you're going to make it. I started through the orchard on the path Grant had built, some of it already overrun with red clover, waving grasses and creeping weeds. The Season was drawing to a close and in a few weeks I would close up Henry's House and it would be darkened, save for the upstairs lamp. Already the orchard is thick with autumn. The apples still pendulous, blushing and unripe, hang from the branches and late afternoon light trickles through the interstices of the leaves that have already fallen and the fruit that has not.